A Woman Betrayed

A Woman Betrayed

BARBARA DELINSKY

BCA

LONDON · NEW YORK · SYDNEY · TORONTO

This edition published 1992
by BCA by arrangement with
PIATKUS BOOKS Ltd

**The moral right of the author
has been asserted**

*A catalogue record for this book is available
from the British Library*

CN 4689

Printed and bound in Great Britain by
Butler & Tanner Ltd, Frome and London

As always, to Eric, Andrew, Jeremy, and their dad

one

THE SILENCE WAS DEAFENING. LAURA FRYE sat in a corner of the leather sofa in the den, hugged her knees, and listened to it, minute after minute after minute. The wheeze of the heat through the vents couldn't pierce it. Nor could the slap of the rain on the windows, or the rhythmic tick of the small ship's clock on the shelf behind the desk.

It was five in the morning, and her husband still wasn't home. He hadn't called. He hadn't sent a message. His toothbrush was in the bathroom along with his razor, his after-shave, and the sterling comb and brush set Laura had given him for their twentieth anniversary the summer before. The contents of his closet were intact, right down to the small duffel he took with him to the sports club every Monday, Wednesday, and Friday. If he had slept somewhere else, he was totally ill equipped, which wasn't like Jeffrey at all, Laura knew. He was a precise man, a creature of habit. He never traveled, not for so much as a single night, without fresh underwear, a clean shirt, and a bar of deodorant soap.

More than that, he never went anywhere without telling Laura, and that was what frightened her most. She had no idea where he was or what had happened.

Not that she hadn't imagined. Laura wasn't usually prone to

wild wanderings of the mind, but ten hours of waiting had taken its toll. She imagined that he'd had a stroke and lay unconscious across his desk in the deserted offices of Farro and Frye. She imagined that he'd been in an accident on the way home, that the car and everything in it had been burned beyond recognition or, alternately, that he had hit the windshield, climbed out, and begun wandering through the cold December rain not knowing who or where he was. She had gone so far as to imagine that he'd stopped for gas and been taken hostage by a junkie holding up the nearby 7-Eleven.

More rational explanations for his absence had worn thin as night had waned. By no stretch of the imagination could she envision him holed up with a client at five in the morning. Maybe in April, with a new client whose tax records were in chaos. But not the first week in December. And not without telling her. He always called if he was going to be late. Always.

Last night, they had been expected at an opening at the museum. Cherries had catered the affair. Though one of Laura's crews had handled the evening, she had spent the afternoon in Cherries' kitchen stuffing mushrooms, skewering smoked turkey and cherries, and cleaving baby lamb chops apart. She had wanted not only the food but the tables, the trays, and the bar to be perfect, which was why she had followed the truck to the museum to oversee the setting up.

Everything had been flawless. She had come home to change and get Jeff. But Jeff hadn't shown up.

Hugging her knees tighter in an attempt to fill the emptiness inside her, she stared at the phone. It had rung twice during the night. The first call had been from Elise, who was at the museum with her husband and wondered why Laura and Jeff weren't there. The second call had been from Donny for Debra, part of their nightly ritual. Sixteen-year-old sweethearts did that, Laura knew, just as surely as she knew that forty-something husbands who always called their wives if they were going to be late wouldn't *not* call unless something was wrong. So she had made several searching calls herself, but to no avail. The only thing she had learned was that the phone worked fine.

She willed it to ring now, willed Jeff to call and say he had had a late meeting with a client and had nearly fallen asleep at the wheel on the way home, so he'd pulled over to the side of the road to sleep off his fatigue. Of course, that wouldn't explain why the police hadn't spotted his car. Hampshire County wasn't so remote as to be without regular patrols or so seasoned as to take a shiny new Porsche for granted, particularly if that Porsche belonged to one half of a prominent Northampton couple.

The Frye name made the papers often, Jeff's with regard to the tax seminars he gave, Laura's with regard to Cherries. The local press was a tough one, seeming to resist anything upscale, which the restaurant definitely was, but Laura fed enough luminaries on a regular basis to earn frequent mentions. *State Senator DiMento and his entourage were seen debating ways to trim fat from the budget over steamed vegetables and salads at Cherries this week*, wrote Duggan O'Neil of the *Hampshire County Sun*. Duggan O'Neil could cut people to shreds, and he had done his share of cutting where Laura was concerned, but publicity was publicity, Jeff said. Name recognition was important.

Indeed, the police officer with whom Laura had talked earlier on the phone had known just who she was. He even remembered Jeff's car as the one often parked outside the restaurant. But nothing in his records suggested that anyone in the department had seen or heard of the black Porsche that night.

"Tell you what, Miz Frye," he had told her. "Since it's you, I'll make a few calls. Throw in a piece of cherry cheesecake, and I'll even call the state police." But his calls had turned up nothing, and, to her dismay, he had refused to let her file a missing persons report. "Not until he's been gone twenty-four hours."

"But awful things can happen in twenty-four hours!"

"Good things, too, like lost husbands coming home."

Lost husbands coming home. She resented those words with a passion. They suggested she was inept as a wife, inept as a woman, that Jeff had been bored and gone looking for fun and would wander back home when the fun was over. Maybe the cop lived that way, but not Jeff and Laura Frye. They had been together for twenty good years. They loved each other.

So where was he? The question gnawed at her. She imagined him slain by a hitchhiker, accosted by Satanists, sucked up, Porsche and all, by an alien starship. The possibilities were endless, each one more bizarre than the next. Bizarre things did happen, she knew, but to other people. Not to her. And not to Jeff. He was the most steadfast, the most predictable, the most uncorruptible man she'd ever known, which was why his absence made no sense at all.

Unfolding her legs, she rose from the sofa and padded barefoot through the dark living room to the front window. Drawing back the sheers that hung beneath full-length silk swags, she looked out. The wind was up, ruffling the branches of the pines, driving the rain against the flagstone walk and the tall lamp at its head.

At least it wasn't snowing. She remembered times, early in her marriage, when she had been home with the children during storms, waiting for Jeff to return from work. He had been a new CPA then, a struggling one, and they had lived in a rented duplex. Laura used to stand at the window, playing games with the children, drawing pictures on the glass in the fog their breath made. Like clockwork, Jeff had always come through the snow, barely giving her time to worry.

He worked in a new building in the center of town now, and they weren't living in the duplex, or even in that first weathered Victorian, but in a gracious brick Tudor on a tree-lined street, less than a ten-minute drive from his office. It was a fast drive, an easy drive. But for some unknown and frightening reason he hadn't made it.

"Mom?"

Laura whirled around at the sudden sound to find Debra

4

beneath the living room arch. Her eyes were sleepy, her dark hair disheveled. She wore a nightshirt with UMASS COED NA-KED LACROSSE splashed on the front over breasts that had taken a turn for the buxom in the past year.

Aware of her racing heart, Laura tried to smile. "Hi, Deb."

Debra sounded cross. "It's barely five. That's still the middle of the night, Mom. Why are you up?"

Unsure of what to say, just as she'd been unsure the night before when Debra had come home and Jeff hadn't been there, Laura threw back a gentle, "Why are *you*?"

"Because I woke up and remembered last night and started to worry. I mean, Dad's never late like that. I had a dream something awful happened, so I was going to check the garage and make sure the Porsche was—" Her voice stopped short. Her eyes probed Laura's in the dark. "It's there, isn't it?"

Laura shook her head.

"Where is he?"

She shrugged.

"Are you sure he didn't call and tell you something, and then you forgot? You're so busy, sometimes things slip your mind. Or maybe he left a message on the machine, but it got erased. Maybe he spent the night at Nana Lydia's."

Laura had considered that possibility, which was why she had driven past her mother-in-law's house when she had gone out looking for Jeff. In theory, Lydia might have taken ill and called her son, though in all likelihood she would have called Laura first. Laura was her primary caretaker. She was the one who stocked the house with food, took her to the doctor, arranged for the cleaning girl or the exterminator or the plumber.

"He's not there. I checked."

"How about the office?"

"I went there too." To the dismay of the guard, who had looked far more sleepy than Debra, she had insisted on checking the garage for the Porsche, but Jeff's space—the entire garage under his building—had been empty.

"Is he with David?"

"No. I called." David Farro was Jeff's partner, but he hadn't known of any late meetings Jeff might have had. Nor had Jeff's secretary, who had left at five with Jeff still in his office.

"Maybe with a client?"

"Maybe."

"But you were supposed to go to the museum. Wouldn't he have called if he couldn't make it?"

"I would have thought so."

"Maybe something's wrong with the phone."

"No."

"Maybe he had car trouble."

But he would have called, Laura knew. Or had someone call for him. Or the police would have seen him and called.

"So where *is* he?" Debra cried.

Laura was terrified by her own helplessness. "I don't know!"

"He has to be *somewhere*!"

She wrapped her arms around her middle. "Do you have any suggestions?"

"Me?" Debra shot back. "What do I know? You're the adult around here. Besides, you're his wife. You're the one who knows him inside and out. *You're* supposed to know where he is."

Turning back to the window, Laura drew the sheer aside and looked out again.

"Mom?"

"I don't know where he is, babe."

"Great. That's just great."

"No, it's not," Laura acknowledged, nervously scanning the street, "but there isn't an awful lot I can do right now. He'll show up, and I'm sure he'll have a perfectly good explanation for where he's been and why he hasn't called."

"If *I* ever stayed out all night without calling, you'd kill me."

"I may well kill your father," Laura said in a moment's burst of anger. Given what she'd been through, Jeff's explanation was going to have to be inspired if he hoped to be spared her fury.

Then the fury died and fear returned. The possibilities flashed through her mind, one worse than the next. "He'll be home," she insisted, as much for her own sake as for Debra's.

"When?"

"Soon."

"How do you know?"

"I just know."

"What if he's sick, or hurt, or dying somewhere? What if he needs our help, but we're just standing here in a nice warm dry house waiting for him to show up? What if we're losing all this time when we should be out looking for him?"

Debra's questions weren't new. Laura had hit on all of them, more than once. Now she reasoned, "I looked for him last night. I drove around half the city and didn't see the Porsche. I called the police, and they hadn't seen it either. If there was an accident, the police would call me."

"So you're just going to stand here looking out the window? Aren't you *upset*?"

Debra was a sixteen-year-old asking a frightened sixteen-year-old's questions. Laura was a frightened thirty-eight-year-old with no answers, which made her frustration all the greater. Keeping her voice as steady as possible, given the tremulous feeling she had inside, she turned to Debra and said, "Yes, I'm upset. Believe me, I'm upset. I've been upset since seven o'clock last night, when your father was an hour late."

"He never does this, Mom, *never*."

"I know that, Debra. I went to his office. I drove around looking for his car. I called his partner, his secretary, and the police, but they won't do anything until he's been gone a day, and he hasn't been gone half that. What would you have me do? Walk the streets in the rain, calling his name?"

Debra's glare cut through the darkness. "You don't have to be sarcastic."

With a sigh, Laura crossed the floor and caught her daughter's hand. "I'm not being sarcastic. But I'm worried, and your criticism doesn't help."

"I didn't criticize."

"You did." Debra said what was on her mind and always had. Disapproval coming from a little squirt of a child hadn't been so bad. Disapproval coming from someone who was Laura's own five-six and weighed the same one-fifteen, who regularly borrowed Laura's clothes, makeup, and perfume, who drove a car, professed to know how to French-kiss, and was physically capable of having a child of her own was something else. "You think I should be doing more than I am," Laura argued, "but I'm hamstrung, don't you see? I don't know if anything's really wrong. There could be a logical reason for your father's absence. I don't want to blow things out of proportion before I have good cause."

"Twelve hours isn't good cause?" Debra cried and whirled around to leave, only to be held back by Laura's grip.

"Eleven hours," she said with quiet control. "And, yes, it's good cause, babe. But I can't do anything right now but wait. I can't do anything else." The silence that followed was heavy with an unspoken plea for understanding.

Debra lowered her chin. Her hair fell forward, shielding her from Laura's gaze. "What about me? What am I supposed to do?"

Scooping the hair back from Debra's face, Laura tucked it behind an ear. For an instant she caught a glimpse of her daughter's worry, but it was gone by the time Debra raised her head. In its place was defiance. Taking that as part and parcel of the spunk that made Debra special, Laura said, "What you're supposed to do is go back to bed. It's too early to be up."

"Sure. Great idea. Like I'd really be able to sleep." She shot a glance at Laura's sweater and jeans. "Like you really slept yourself." She turned her head a fraction and gave a twitch of her nose. "You've been cooking, haven't you. What's that smell?"

"Borscht."

"Oh, gross."

"It's not so bad." Jeff loved it with sour cream on top. Maybe, deep inside, Laura had been hoping the smell would lure him home.

"I can't believe you were cooking."

"I always cook."

"At work. Not at home. Most of the time you stick us with Chunky Chicken Soup, Frozen French Bread Pizza, or Microwave Meatballs and Spaghetti. You must feel guilty that Dad's missing."

Laura ignored the suggestion, which could have come straight from her own mother's analytical mouth. "He isn't missing, just late."

"So you cooked all night."

"Not all night. Just part of it." In addition to the borscht, she'd done a coq au vin she would probably freeze, since no one planned to be home for dinner for the next two nights. She had also baked a Black Forest cake and two batches of pillow cookies, one of which she would send to Scott.

"Did you sleep at all?" Debra asked.

"A little."

"Aren't you tired?"

"Nah. I'm fine." She was too anxious to sleep, which was why she had cooked. Normally, cooking relaxed her. It hadn't done that last night, but at least it had kept her hands busy.

"Well, I'm fine too," Debra declared. "I'll shower and dress and sit down here with you."

Laura knew what was coming. Debra was social to the core. Rarely did a weekend pass when she wasn't out, if not with Donny, then with Jenna or Kim or Whitney or all three and more. But as drawn as she was to her friends, she was allergic to anything academic. At the slightest excuse, she would stay home for the day. "You'll go to school when it's time," Laura insisted, "just like always."

"I can't go to school. I want to be here."

"There's nothing for you to do here. When your father comes home, he'll want to sleep."

"Assuming he hasn't already slept."

Laura felt a flare of indignance. "Where would he have slept?"

Debra's eyes went wide in innocence. "I don't know. Where do *you* think?"

"I don't know! If I did, we wouldn't be standing here at this hour discussing it!" Hearing the high pitch of her voice, Laura realized just how short-tempered she was—and how uncharacteristic that was. "Look," she said more calmly, "we're going in circles. I know nothing, you know nothing. All we can do for the time being is wait for your father to call. If I haven't heard from him by eight or nine, I can start making calls myself." Framing Debra's face with her hands, she said, "Let's not fight about this. I hate fighting. You know that."

Debra looked to be on the verge of saying something before she caught herself and reconsidered. With a merciful nod, she turned and left the room. Laura listened to her footfall on the stair runner, the occasional creak of a tread, movement along the upstairs hall, then the closing of the bathroom door. Only when she heard the sound of the shower did she turn back toward the den.

"Damn it, Jeff," she whispered, "where *are* you?" It was one thing to put her through hell for a night, another to involve the children. Scott was at school, sleeping in blissful ignorance in his dorm room at Penn. But Debra was home, awake now and aware that her father was missing.

Laura couldn't believe he had willfully stayed out all night. He was a devoted husband and father. *Something was wrong.*

At the door to the den, she stopped. This was Jeff's room, his retreat. Technically it was a library, lined top to bottom with books. The books were still there, but so were a new television and a VCR for fun. He also worked there, which was why the gleaming mahogany desk—which had originally sported a gold-edged blotter, several leather-bound volumes braced by brass bookends, and some scrimshaw—now bore a more functional pad, a computer linked to the one in his office, and a Rolodex filled with the names and addresses of anyone and everyone with whom Jeff had professional dealings.

Should it come down to a search, Laura wouldn't know which names to call first. Jeff didn't discuss clients with her unless they bumped into one at a party. He put a high value on confidentiality, and she respected that. He was a decent person.

Drawn into the room by the musty scent of Jeff's collection of old books, Laura let the atmosphere take the edge off her tension. Gently lit, as it had been all night, by the green clerk's lamp on the desk, the room had a feeling of history, and with good cause. On those shelves were an assortment of books, pictures, and mementos that documented their life together.

Neatly arranged, as was Jeff's style, were books from their college days, Jeff's on such subjects as Financial Reporting, Advanced Federal Taxation, and Auditing, hers on American Literature, Beginning Anthropology, and French. Jeff's shelves progressed to books on advanced accounting issues that he had read for graduate courses, as well as ever-growing collections of the *Journal of Accountancy* and the *Massachusetts CPA Review*. Laura's shelves, reflecting the fact that she had dropped out of college after a year, branched out into photography books, years of *National Geographic*, and diverse fiction. Those books bought used or in paperback early in their marriage were more weathered. The shelves filled more recently held handsomely packaged hardcover books. And, of course, there were the antique volumes, first editions that Laura had given Jeff over the years.

Interspersed with the books were mementos from trips: a Mayan bowl they had bought in the Yucatán the first time they had left the children and flown off for vacation eight years before; a conch shell they had found on a St. Martin beach the year after that; an ironwood sculpture they had bought in Arizona two years later.

The Arizona trip had been special. All four of them had gone. It had been the first time any of them had seen the desert, and Laura, for one, had adored it. She loved the barren beauty of the landscape, the clear sun, the dryness of the air, the hotel, the food. Lifting a photograph taken on that trip, Laura let her finger glide over the glass. Scott had been fourteen, Debra eleven, both healthy, happy, and handsome, both looking markedly like their parents. With their dark hair, lean athletic builds, easy tans, and bright smiles, they were the picture-perfect American family.

Laura's finger lingered on Jeff's face. Where was he? The house was quiet, empty without him. *Where was he?*

Feeling the same itch to do something that she'd felt on and off all night, she returned the picture to the shelf and went out into the kitchen. The sink was clean. So was the counter and the granite island. Other than the pot on the stove, the plastic-wrapped platter of cookies by the refrigerator, and the footed cake dish in the center of the island, there was no evidence that she'd been cooking. She had scrubbed everything clean with the same energy with which she normally worked. She didn't do well with idle time, didn't do well with it at all.

She glanced at her watch. It was five-forty-five. She glanced at the digital readout on the microwave, but it was the same. After letting out a frantic whimper, she dragged in a slow, deep breath and forced herself to relax.

Jeff had to be somewhere. He was alive and well and intact. There was an explanation for what had happened—a misunderstanding, crossed signals. Surely someday they'd laugh over the folly of the night.

Clinging to that thought, Laura headed for the stairs. If Jeff would be coming home soon, she didn't want to look tired and washed out. A bath would help. She felt wound tight.

The master bathroom was her pride and joy. High-ceilinged, skylit, and spacious, it was of variegated marble, deep green and lush. The towels and small area rugs were white, the wallpaper a broad floral sweep of green and white. Though there were several groupings of botanical prints, the main decorative force came from the plants that sprouted in every imaginable spot. They gave the room the feel of a forest glen.

By the time Laura had run the water, undressed, and climbed in, the heat lamp had made the room comfortably warm. She sank down, stretched out, closed her eyes. Had the Jacuzzi not hummed she might have turned it on. But she didn't want to miss a sound. So she took a deep breath and let it out, then repeated the procedure when the jitters in her stomach didn't let up. She concentrated on relaxing her hands, then her thighs, then her knees and feet. Each floated. Each moved with the water as she breathed.

At a creaking from the bedroom, her eyes flew open. "Jeff?" she called excitedly and held her breath.

"It's me, Mom. Are you okay?"

The jitters resumed. Trying not to sound too disappointed, she said, "I'm fine, babe. Just taking a bath."

"Nothing happened while I was in the shower?"

"Nope."

"Want me to listen for the phone?"

Laura knew if the phone rang she'd be out of the tub like a shot. "That'd be great," she said. "I think I'll just soak for a while. Then I'll fix us some breakfast."

"Isn't it a little early for that?"

"I thought I'd do some waffles."

"I'm not hungry."

"And maybe some eggs."

"I'll be downstairs, Mom."

"Okay. I'll be there soon."

Pleased that she'd managed to sound relatively normal, Laura took a hand from the water and studied her nails. She'd done a job on them during the night, destroying the pale polish she wore in ways that her work, for all its manual labor, rarely did. Tonight she and Jeff had a dinner party to go to, tomorrow night a political fund raiser. She'd have to redo them. Before the dinner party. Or the fund raiser.

Where was Jeff?

Feeling panic, she sat up in the tub. She glanced at the door, peered at the watch she'd left on the closed commode. It was five past six. "Come on, Jeff," she cried in an urgent whisper and climbed out. "Come on, come on!"

After slipping into a pair of gabardine slacks and a loose cashmere sweater, she put on a smattering of makeup, pushed a brush through her shoulder-length auburn waves, swallowed two aspirin, and headed down the stairs.

Debra was perched on a stool in the kitchen, wearing her school uniform of lace-edged leggings under a short denim skirt and a high-necked blouse under a large wool sweater. She gave Laura a strange look. "Why are you dressed like that?"

"I have meetings all morning."

"You're going to meetings? Dad's been gone all night, we have no idea where he is, and you're going to *meetings*?"

"He'll show up." Laura looked at her watch. It was nearly six-thirty. "Soon, now. You'll see." She plugged in the waffle iron and pulled a carton of orange juice from the refrigerator. "Want some?"

"How can you think of food at a time like this?"

Laura doubted she'd have anything herself, but she was hoping Debra would, so she poured her a glass of juice. "We have to keep things in perspective. Panicking won't help. We have to stay cool."

"I'm not going to school."

"Yes, you are. And while you're there, if your father hasn't come home, I'll be making calls."

"What if there was an accident, like he skidded off the road into a tree, and the police suddenly see it when the sun comes up?"

"Then they'll come get me."

"Will you come get *me*?"

Seeing the fear in Debra's eyes, Laura reached over and gave her a hug. The contact felt good. "Of course I will. If I hear anything either way, I'll let you know. Fair?"

"Not really. I don't see why I can't stay here. I won't get anything out of school with this on my mind."

She had a point. Not even in the best of times was Debra a student. But Laura wanted her out of the house. No matter how distracted she'd be at school, she would be better off there than waiting at home for the phone to ring. Besides, if Jeff didn't show up, if the morning wore on without any sign of him, if Laura had to call in help, there would be a reality to the situation that didn't quite exist yet. The thought of that made her tremble.

"Do me a favor and get the newspapers?"

Debra's eyes grew wide. "Would there be something in the *Sun*?"

"No, but it's nice to see what's happening in the world." There was an absurd normalcy in headlines of economic recession or strife in the Persian Gulf.

"It's raining."

"It's stopped. Get them, babe? Please?" Without waiting for an answer, Laura opened a deep drawer under the island and pulled out the mixing bowl. By the time Debra returned with the *Wall Street Journal* folded under an arm and the *Hampshire County Sun* open in her hand, Laura was vigorously stirring waffle batter with a wooden spoon. She poured some on the hot iron. Its sizzle overlapped the rustle of newsprint. The waffles were done just as Debra thrust the paper aside.

"Nothing," she announced in disgust. "Where is he?"

Laura forked the waffles onto a plate. "Don't know."

"What happened to him?"

"Should I whip some cream for that?"

"No! Mom, I'm not eating."

"You have to. You love waffles."

"I told you before I wasn't hungry."

"You have to eat."

"I can't!" Pushing away from the island, Debra disappeared into the hall.

Laura felt abruptly deserted. "Where are you going?" One part of her did want to keep Debra home from school, she realized, for the company and the noise if nothing else. The more rational part, the practical part, the protective part would send her on.

"Getting my books," came the distant call.

Blankly Laura looked at the plate of waffles in her hand. She looked at the waffle iron and at the batter remaining in the bowl, and put on a second batch. It was done, and a third was on the way, when Debra returned.

"I really want to stay home."

"I know," Laura said as she whipped cream into a froth, "but you can't."

"What am I supposed to say to my friends?"

"You can say what you want. But there's no need to get them all in a stir. I'm sure everything is fine. There must be a perfectly good explanation for last night. Your father will be home, Debra. I know he will."

"I'm glad one of us is so sure."

Laura wasn't sure at all, and the pretending was growing harder. The longer Jeff was missing, the more ominous the possibilities and the less sure Laura was of anything. But she was a mother, and she was an optimist. She had to be positive for Debra. "I'm sure." She looked at her watch. "It's ten after seven." The bus came at seven-twenty. "Why don't you run on now? Jenna will be there." Jenna was Debra's best friend, and had been since nursery school. The fact that she lived on the very next street from the Fryes had been an added selling point for the house.

"Will you get a message to me if you learn anything?" Debra asked, looking young and frightened as Laura walked her to the door.

"Uh-huh."

"Promise?"

"I promise."

Seemingly satisfied, Debra pulled up the collar of her leather jacket, hitched her backpack to one shoulder, and left. The instant she turned onto the sidewalk and was lost from sight beyond the neighbors' hemlock hedge, Laura made for the phone.

two

dAPHNE PHILLIPS WAS, IN LAURA'S VIEW, one of the classiest women in Hampshire County. Tall and chic, with thick honey-colored hair that she habitually wore sleekly knotted, a fine hand at makeup, and impeccable taste in clothes, she presented a striking figure. Beyond that, she had brains. She had graduated from law school at the top of her class and remained, Laura was sure, better versed in the field of criminal law than any of the ten men in her firm. Beyond *that*, she had tact. She knew when to talk and when not to, when to argue and when to be still. In a town like Northampton, that was important.

Laura and Daphne had been best friends since junior high school. They had studied together, dated together, summered together. Daphne had been the first to know that Laura was dropping out of college to marry Jeff; Laura had been the first to know that Daphne was accepted at Yale. Laura experienced law school through Daphne; Daphne experienced motherhood through Laura. They went to the same hairdresser, the same seamstress, the same gynecologist. They were closer than sisters often were.

Laura needed someone that close to help her now, which was why, when Daphne swept through the door thirty minutes after

Laura called, she felt a wave of relief.

"Tell me again," Daphne ordered. "He didn't come home at all last night?"

"Not once. I've been racking my brain, trying to remember something he may have told me, but there isn't anything, and anyway, if he had plans to go somewhere overnight, he'd have packed a bag. I went through the bathroom, the bedroom, the cedar closet. Nothing's gone." She told Daphne about the calls she had made to David, to Jeff's secretary, to the police.

"Maybe he's with friends," Daphne suggested.

"All night? Jeff wouldn't do that."

"Maybe with an *old* friend?"

Laura shrugged. "Who?" Jeff didn't have many friends from the past. He wasn't the sentimental type.

"Could he have gotten drunk somewhere and passed out?"

"He doesn't drink."

Daphne arched a brow. "He drinks."

"Only one or two," Laura insisted. "He's never even been high. It couldn't be that. And if it were, some bartender would have kicked him out or called the police or called *me*."

"Could he have been with a group from the office?" Daphne asked.

"There is no group. His tennis foursome is the closest he comes to doing things with a group. Jeff doesn't have buddies. His family is his life." She pushed her fingers through her hair in total bewilderment. Her voice fell to a drone. "This isn't like him, Daph. If he says he'll be home by six, he's home by six. If he says he's going to be an hour late, he's an hour late. He is ve-ry organized, ve-ry predictable, ve-ry punctual." With Debra, she'd had to be brave. With Daphne, it wasn't necessary. "It's been light for nearly an hour. Even if the police were blind, if there'd been an accident off to the side of the road some commuter would have seen it by now." Aware that her knees were starting to shake, she drew out a stool and sat down.

"Did you sleep?"

"I couldn't. I feel off balance. This is so unlike Jeff." She looked at Daphne. Daphne was good at solving things. "You know him. You were the maid of honor at my wedding, and you've been in and out of wherever we've lived ever since. Second to me, you probably know him best. Where could he be?"

Daphne drew a stool close so they could sit thigh to thigh, facing each other. "He didn't show up at the museum?"

She shook her head.

"Was he looking forward to going?"

"Uh-huh. He likes things like that. Being seen is an important part of his business."

"Maybe he was feeling overshadowed by the fact that Cherries catered the show."

Laura couldn't believe that. "He's been at other affairs we've catered, and it never bothered him. He's proud of what I do."

"I know, but some men—"

"Not Jeff. He was a CPA long before I was a caterer."

"But the restaurant—"

"He loves the restaurant. It enhances his name. It brings him business. Believe me, Daph, he isn't threatened that way, and even if he were, he wouldn't just disappear." At the sound of the phone, she flew off the stool and snatched it up. "Hello?"

"Hi, Laura, it's David. I'm assuming Jeff finally showed up. Is everything okay?"

Laura's hand shook as she held the receiver to her ear. "He didn't come home, David. He's not here."

"Not there? Didn't go home at all?"

"That's right."

"That's not like Jeff."

Her laugh had an hysterical edge. "Do tell."

"Are you all right?"

"No, I'm not all right. I'm worried sick."

"Have you called the police?"

"For what it was worth." She related the contents of that particular phone call. "The police won't do anything. But he must be out there somewhere. Maybe we should hire a private investigator."

Daphne waved a hand and shook her head.

"No?" Laura asked her.

"Not yet. Not yet."

"I take it someone's with you," David remarked.

"Daphne Phillips."

"Should I come over too?"

Laura wasn't wild about the idea. David was a fine accountant and a good friend, but his company could be cloying. "I'd rather you went to the office and checked out Jeff's desk. Maybe he left a note or jotted something down."

"Good thought. I'll be there in half an hour. I'll call you once I've looked."

Replacing the phone, Laura braced a shoulder against the wall and turned tired eyes on Daphne. "Where could he be?" Her voice was a weak echo of all the other times she'd said the words.

Calm, cool Daphne was looking disconcertingly concerned. "I haven't the foggiest."

"So what should I do? Should I start making calls? I would have last night, except it seemed ridiculous. I was sure Jeff would be home, I was *sure* of it, and I didn't want to start bugging our friends and then have him walk in at eleven or twelve with some perfectly good explanation for where he'd been." Pushing off from the wall, she put the plate of waffles into the microwave. "But it's eight in the morning and he isn't home yet. Am I supposed to sit here or go out looking or call people? What?"

"Have you called Lydia?"

"I can't. Jeff's her pride and joy. I can't tell her he's missing. She's seventy-three and not well."

"What about Jeff's brother?"

Laura took a breath that went down the wrong way. She coughed, and pressed a hand to her heart. "What about him?"

"Maybe he's in some kind of trouble."

"No doubt he's in some kind of trouble." Christian Frye created an uproar wherever he went, often with little more than a look.

"Maybe Jeff took off to help him."

The microwave sounded. Laura removed the plate. "They don't get along."

"But they're brothers."

"They're as different as night and day."

"Still," Daphne argued with quiet persistence, "family is family. It's not inconceivable that if Christian needed help he'd call."

"He might call, but Jeff wouldn't go." Laura opened the refrigerator and took out the whipped cream and the juice that Debra hadn't touched. "You know Christian, Daph. You've seen him at work. He came to our wedding stoned, came to Lydia's sixty-fifth birthday party drunk, has been abrasive at every Thanksgiving he's come to."

"I never thought he was so bad."

"I did—do."

"But you keep inviting him."

"Because he's family!" Laura cried, setting the egg tray and a stick of butter on the counter. "And because I feel bad that he's alone." But every time she saw him, she was on edge, and though she tried not to let it show, Jeff had sensed it. "No, Jeff wouldn't have gone to help Christian."

"Maybe you should call him anyway, just to check."

"I think he's away."

"Try him. It wouldn't hurt."

But it would. Laura knew that, as surely as she knew why Christian had come to her wedding stoned. She couldn't call him. Not about something like this.

She took a spatula from the utensil drawer. "Something awful has happened. Nothing else makes sense."

Daphne came up off the stool. "I have a friend in the police department. I'll give him a call."

"They told me they wouldn't do anything yet."

"He owes me." She was already punching out the number. Into the phone, seconds later, she said, "Detective Melrose, please."

Laura pulled out a skillet.

"Laura, what are you cooking?" Daphne murmured above the receiver.

"Breakfast."

"For you?"

"For you. I have waffles, and I'm making eggs."

Taking her arm, Daphne pushed her down onto a stool. "Stop. Sit. Relax."

"I can't relax," Laura cried. "I don't know what's happening, and I don't give a damn if my mother *does* say I have an unhealthy fixation on control. I want to know where Jeff is, and I want to know now!"

Daphne held up a hand to still the outburst. "Dennis, it's Daphne Phillips." She started to speak, then paused. "Fine, thanks." She started again, paused again. "No, I didn't know he'd been released, but that isn't why I'm calling." Briefly, she outlined the situation. "I know you can't do anything formal until tonight, but given who and what Jeff Frye is, I thought you might do a little snooping." She paused, listened, came back with an indignant, "No, he's not involved in anything dirty. But he's well known in the area, and if it should happen that he's been hurt, it wouldn't look great that the police took their time getting on the stick, *capiche*?"

Unable to sit still, Laura went to the oak table that nestled in the kitchen's windowed bay, opened the large leather purse that sat there, and pulled out her notebook.

"He'll make some calls and look around," Daphne said, joining her a minute later. "And he'll be subtle about it. We don't want the papers thinking there's a story in the air."

The papers. Good God, that would be a nightmare. "Jeffrey Frye, well-known Pioneer Valley CPA, disappears as mysteriously as the cherry crescents at his wife's restaurant," Duggan O'Neil might write.

Loath to deal with that potential twist, Laura looked at her calendar. "I'm supposed to have meetings all morning, but I want to be here when Jeff calls." Her gaze drifted toward the window. Under an overcast sky, the back yard was gray and barren. "*If* Jeff calls. What if he doesn't?"

"He will."

"I sent Debra to school. If Jeff isn't here by the time she gets home, it'll be awful." She sent a frightened glance Daphne's way. "If we don't know anything by then, I'll have to call Scott." Her breath came shorter. "This is unreal."

The silence that followed was proof. Normally, at eight-thirty in the morning, Jeff would be in the kitchen having breakfast. By eight-forty-five, he would leave the house. By nine, he would be at his desk opening the mail.

The phone rang. Laura jumped for it.

"There's nothing here," David announced without preface. "I've gone over his desk, the credenza, the bookshelves. The place is immaculate," which was typical Jeff, Laura knew. He was a neat man. He turned his socks right-side-out before putting them into the hamper, hung his trousers with the creases knife-edge to knife-edge, stacked books on his nightstand three at a time, in the order in which they were to be read. When other women complained that their husbands were slobs, Laura counted her blessings. Jeff was the ideal husband for a woman with kids and a job.

Fighting a numbing disappointment, she forced herself to think clearly. "What's his schedule today? When's his first appointment?"

"Nine-thirty," David said, adding in a more solicitous tone, "I'm sure there's some answer here. Jeff wouldn't just up and leave you."

Leave you. For an instant her blood ran so fast she couldn't hear past its rush. Then she swallowed. "Of course he wouldn't. Something's happened to him. I have to find out what."

"I think I should come over."

"No. Stay there. Maybe you could make a few calls." She raised questioning eyes to Daphne, who held out her hand for the phone. "Hold on, David. Here's Daphne."

"David? Be nonchalant. As your people come in, ask if they've seen him. Say you need him for something." She paused, heard David out, then said, "We don't want to embarrass him if he turns up with a perfectly good explanation for where he's been. Mostly, we don't want one person to smell something wrong and call another and then another. It's important to keep things under control."

Laura agreed with that, though she wished she felt more in control herself. Her mind was skipping back and forth, from the immediate present to the night that had passed, from hope to bewilderment to fear. Her eyes were dry and tired, but her heart didn't seem to sense the fatigue. It was pounding against her ribs without respite.

Leaving Daphne, she wandered into the dining room. Her fingertips skimmed the sculpted top of a Chippendale chair, slid down its side, and came to an unsteady rest on the edge of the table. On Thanksgiving Day, less than two weeks before, the table had been covered with food and the room filled with people. Twenty-six, they'd had in all, from immediate family to extended family to friends and friends' families and even a few employees. Laura loved doing things that way, and everyone present liked it too. Even Maddie was mellow—no doubt on her good behavior, with Gretchen in from Sacramento—and what a coup that had been on Laura's part, getting her mother and younger sister together for a whole weekend. The two were like fire and water, which was why Gretchen had fled the East Coast in the first place. But somewhere in the course of the past few years, Maddie had accepted that if she wanted to see Gretchen she would have to behave. She couldn't constantly badger, constantly scrutinize, constantly analyze. She had to keep her big mouth shut.

Laura, who hadn't broken off with her mother the way

Gretchen had and therefore still felt the brunt of her hounding, shuddered at the thought of what Maddie would have to say about Jeff's disappearance. She prayed he would materialize and the mystery be solved before Maddie knew about it.

"We're set with David," Daphne said from the doorway. "Are you okay?"

Laura gave a shaky smile. "I'm okay." She took an uneven breath. "What do I do now?"

"Want to call a few friends?"

She went to the window. "He'd have come here before going to any friend. I mean, who does he have? There's us, and the people in the office. And his tennis group. They played on Monday. They're due to play again later today," she realized.

"Call one of them," Daphne suggested in a low, gently coaxing voice. "Maybe he canceled. That'd be a start."

"Only if he planned to be gone. Are you thinking he did?"

"No. I'm just trying to get a general fix on him."

Laura barely heard. She was feeling a vast loneliness. "How could he plan to be gone without telling me, without taking his things, without saying goodbye to Debra?"

Coming close to wrap an arm around her, Daphne said, "I shouldn't have mentioned it. There's no need to think about it now."

"It couldn't have been deliberate. We've been happily married for twenty years. He loves me, loves the kids, loves the house."

"You're right. It couldn't have been deliberate."

The phone rang. Laura broke away to get it. "Hello?"

"Thank goodness I caught you," came Madeline McVey's strident voice. "I was worried you'd already left. Do you have a minute?"

Laura's eyes went wild. "Uh, this is a bad time, Mom."

"But I have to leave soon. I won't be free again until after dinner tonight, and we really should settle this now."

The knot in her stomach was familiar. For a split second Laura was eight years old again, being called into the parlor

that was Maddie's home office to explain why she hadn't vol-
unteered to do a project for the Science Fair. Needing to know
what her offense was this time, she asked, "Settle what?"

"There's a problem here regarding the department Christmas
party. We have you booked for the nineteenth at the Dean's
house, but there's been some grumbling from people who want
to hold it off-campus. Not that it matters to me—"

"Can you hold on a second?" Laura interrupted loudly. Without waiting for permission, she put Maddie on hold. Pressing
the receiver to her chest, she looked frantically around at Daphne.
"I can't take this now."

"Tell her you'll call later."

"What if later's worse?"

"Tell her you're waiting for another call."

"She knows I have two lines."

"Tell her you feel ill."

"She'll say it's morning sickness and go off on a diatribe about
women having children at my age."

Daphne paled. "*Are* you pregnant?"

"God, no! I don't have the time or strength to be pregnant!
I'm thirty-eight years old!"

"And scared of your mother."

"No more. No more. Not for a long time."

"Then talk with her now and get it done."

Laura stared hard at Daphne before turning back to the phone
and punching in the call. "Sorry about that, Mom. What were
you saying about the party?"

"There is a contingent in my department," Maddie began
again, injecting faint censure in her tone to chide Laura for the
delay, "who want to hold it off-campus. They say we owe it to
our graduate students to make the party as festive as possible."
She snorted. "As if they'll be better psychologists for it. The
Dean's house is festive, don't you think?"

"Definitely," Laura said.

"Well, you and I are in the minority. I could make an issue

of it, but then they'll say I'm afraid to let go of the past. Now, I ask you, have I ever been afraid to move forward? Not once! I am the most enlightened member of that department!"

Laura didn't doubt it for a minute. Nor did she doubt, given that at sixty-seven her mother was the oldest active member of the department and its chairman, that some of the younger members would like to see her replaced. The rest were thrilled to have her fight their battles. She was a formidable opponent.

Placatingly, Laura said, "I'm sure they appreciate all you do. And they want the best."

"They want the restaurant," Maddie informed her. "Can you handle us?"

Forcing herself to think business when every other instinct protested, Laura pictured the schedule on her office wall, where PARTY QUOTA FILLED was written in bold red print beside DECEMBER. She had been thrilled to write it there for the success it marked, and she should have been thrilled to brag about that success to Maddie. But she didn't have it in her to brag just then, so she simply said, "It's a little late to be making changes."

"Three weeks' notice? We're not canceling, just switching from a catered affair at the school to one at the restaurant." Maddie's voice grew softer, in the dangerous way it had of doing. "Laura, will this present a problem for you?"

The challenge was there, as old and familiar as Laura's earliest memories. Maddie McVey was a woman of singular drive and power. A lifelong academician, she was not only the head of her department but a high-muck-a-muck in professional organizations, all of which made her a hard act to follow. Laura often wondered if that was why she herself had dropped out of college. Maddie had been appalled when she did and only slightly less appalled when Debra had finally gone off to school and Laura had started selling cherry cheesecake out of her home. That had been ten years ago. When that small business evolved into a catering service, Maddie was hardly impressed. As a career, gastronomy wasn't on her acceptable list. Then, two years ago, the restaurant had opened. Its success meant Laura could finally deal with her mother from a position of strength.

Given the mystery of Jeff's absence and the anxiety Laura was feeling, she clung to what little strength she had. "There's no problem. I can shift things around. But I'll have to get back to you on the exact time."

"We booked for cocktails at six and dinner at seven."

"You booked for the Dean's house. If you want to hold the party at the restaurant, you may have to make it a little earlier or a little later. The schedule is full. I'll fit you in, but you'll have to be flexible."

There was a pause at the other end of the line. Laura knew those pauses. They were designed to intimidate. But she was in the right in this case, even powerful, and while she had never aspired to power per se, holding a bit of it over her mother for a change felt good.

Lord knew little else in the last twelve hours had felt good.

"I don't have much choice, I suppose," Maddie finally conceded. Then, as though she simply couldn't resist, she issued another challenge. "I trust the cost won't be greater."

"For you, Mother? Same price."

"Very good," Maddie decided. "Call me as soon as you know the time. We'll talk more then."

Laura hung up the phone. She had barely savored the fact that she'd held her ground when worry about Jeff returned in full. Her eye caught on the answering machine. "Maybe I did miss it somehow."

"What?" Daphne asked.

"A message from Jeff." She pressed the button to rerun the last batch of messages.

The machine beeped. "Laura, it's Sue. We have a problem here. The guys loaded the wrong filet mignon onto our truck. We got the stuffed one, but our client ordered it plain. The plain one must have gone with Dave. I'm calling Dee right now, in case you're at the shop. If you're not, she'll have to handle it." The message beeped off.

"Sue Hirshorn," Laura explained. "She heads one of my crews. She reached me at Cherries."

The machine beeped again. "This is Dr. Larimer's office calling to confirm that Jeffrey Frye has an appointment with the dentist at noon on Wednesday."

Laura's eyes shot to Daphne's as the message beeped off, but before she could tell her about Jeff's toothache, the next message came on.

"Hi, Mom." It was Scott's voice, rising above a background clatter. At its happy-go-lucky sound, Laura pressed her fingertips to her mouth. "Guess I missed you again. I just wanted to tell you that I got a B-plus on that Ec test I thought I fleegled. The art paper's coming along okay. And I'm working out. The whole team is. Uh, what else? Oh. We had a wild party here last weekend." There was raucous laughter, then a muted, "Shut up, you guys." Then, "My friends ate all the food you sent back. They loved it." Hoots and applause supported that. "So thanks. I guess that's all. Talk with you soon. 'Bye."

"What happened to the shy little guy who used to collect seashells with me on the beach at St. Croix?" Daphne asked.

Laura's eyes were glued to the machine. "He's grown up." She stared, waited, finally let out a discouraged breath when the machine said that was her last message.

Daphne touched her arm. "He'll show up. We'll find him."

Laura's thoughts barreled ahead. "What about Christmas? What about the reservations I made for Saba after New Year's? What about the surprise birthday party that invitations are being printed for even as we speak?"

"He'll be here."

"What if he isn't?" The phone rang. Grabbing it, she gasped out a high-pitched "Hello?"

"It's me. You sound strange. Is everything okay?"

"Oh, God, Elise."

"He isn't home?"

"Not yet. Not all night. Something's wrong."

"I'm coming over."

The phone went dead before Laura could argue, not that she would have. Elise Schuler was, besides Daphne, one of her closest friends. They had been roommates at Smith before Laura dropped out; she swore that Elise was the only thing she had liked about the school. They had grown even closer in the years that followed. Indeed, it was at a party at Laura's that Elise had met one of Jeff's clients, the man she had been married to for six years now. The marriage wasn't quite made in heaven. Peter Schuler was older than Elise and conventional in ways that doubled that difference. But Elise had wanted children, and Peter was accommodating. So she had two little girls under the age of five, plus the maid and the au pair that Peter insisted upon, which left her time for Cherries and Laura. Laura thanked heaven for that. Offbeat to the point of being mistaken as daffy, Elise was a bundle of energy with a heart of gold. Daphne might be the one to tell Laura what to do next, but Elise would keep her spirits up.

Given that it was nearly nine, that David hadn't called with news from the office or Daphne's detective with news from the police station, Laura had the awful feeling her spirits would need all the uplifting they could get.

three

JEFFREY FRYE CAME AWAKE TO A FIERCE throbbing in his head. He put up a hand to still it, but it was pervasive, radiating through his scalp in a way that one clammy palm, no matter how large, couldn't possibly touch. Hangovers were like that, he'd been told, and now he knew. Not that he regretted drinking himself into a stupor. It had been the only thing to do. Like a rite of passage long overdue. As if, six weeks before his forty-second birthday, he had finally become a man.

That thought echoed in his head, ricocheting between the pain there and a world of deeper meaning. He tried to open his eyes, to determine whether what he'd done was real or still a dream, but his lids resisted. So, leaving his fingers splayed on the top of his head, he lay still, very still, and let the unfamiliarity of his surroundings tell him what he needed to know.

His bed was narrow, a simple wood frame that accommodated his length with little room to spare. The sheets were stiff and smelled of the plastic packaging he had taken them from the night before. They were askew now in a commentary on his bed-making skills, the upshot of which was that with each shallow breath he felt the scratch of wool blankets against his skin. The blankets had a smell too, a newness that was at odds with the rest of the place.

Lying on that bed with his eyes closed and his head aching, he was aware of mustiness and the odor of age. A fisherman had once lived here, he could smell that, and the fisherman had a dog. If the fisherman had a wife, she hadn't washed her hair with apple shampoo, or scented her drawers with sachets, or sprayed her pulse points with Joy like Jeff's woman did. There was nothing soft or sweet about the odor of the place, or about its sound. A winter rain that should have been snow beat a harsh tattoo on the roof, while beyond the scrub pines and the dried sea grass and the broad stairwell of cliffs and boulders, the sea hurled itself against the rocks, over and over again, in a song of defeat.

He had chosen the shore because he loved the sea. When he was little, when his family had vacationed at the beach, he had sat for hours watching the waves. They hypnotized him. He felt their power.

Now, listening, he heard that power and, in a split second's insight, guessed that the song of defeat was his own. But the second was gone as quickly as it had come, and he let it go. He didn't want to think of defeat. Didn't want to think of what he'd left behind. *Couldn't* think of it. So he pressed a hand more tightly to his head, gingerly eased his legs over the side of the bed, and, with painstaking respect for the nausea snaking around his insides, pushed himself to a sitting position.

Determinedly he held himself in place until the world behind his lids stopped spinning. Very slowly, he opened his eyes. He didn't have to move them to take in the entirety of the cottage, it was that small, but he didn't mind small. Small was cozy. It was also practical. Everything he needed was in sight, albeit myopic sight at that moment. He made out the blur of a kitchen sink and cabinets against one wall, a blur of bookshelves and a desk against a second wall, a blur of living room furniture sprouting from a third. In the center of the room was a wood stove, radiating remnants of warmth from the logs he'd lit there the night before. Between the stove and the kitchen was a small round table and two ladder-back chairs.

Everything was made of wood. Everything was scarred from use. Everything needed work. But Jeff wasn't complaining. He needed a place to hide, and there was none better. No one would find him here. The town was too far north, too remote for anyone from civilization to think to look.

No. No one would find him. He had planned things too well. When he had come in search of the cottage the summer before, he had disguised himself, used a false name, and paid in cash. During the fall he had gathered supplies—not only the sheets and blankets but cooking utensils, dishes, and warm winter clothing. He had been infinitely careful about that too, purchasing things in cash, one or two at a time, in stores as far from Northampton as his client base allowed. Within two weeks he would have a beard, within four weeks his hair would grow out, and during that time he could subsist on the food he had been stashing, along with his other supplies, in the back of the Porsche.

The Porsche, the only luxury he'd taken with him, was safely stowed beneath a dark gray tarp in the old boat shed behind the house. The town had been shrouded in thick fog when he had driven down the deserted main street in the morning's wee hours. No one would ever know it was there.

He hadn't taken anything else, other than the clothes on his back, his briefcase, and fifty thousand dollars in small bills. That would last him awhile. His expenses here would be small. The cottage came with its own generator, but he rather liked the hurricane lamps that were suspended from hooks at random spots around the room. Using those, plus wood for heat and the supplies of food he had brought, he wouldn't have to venture out for days. He had even brought books, which meant he wouldn't die of boredom, but even without the books he doubted that would happen. There was work to do on the cottage. For years, after that fisherman of yore, a writer had lived in the place. An eccentric sort, according to the realtor, he had died two years before, which meant that the dirt on the windows was probably older than that. Jeff had brought cleaning supplies. He had even brought a hammer and nails for emergency repairs. When those were done, when he was suitably hairy and grungy, he might just wander into town and hire on as a carpenter's assistant. That was how Christian had started out—no, Christian had started out building a bridge in a remote West African village, but doing odd jobs in a remote New England one would be just as good. No matter that he didn't know much about carpentry. If Christian had learned, so could he. They had the same genes, didn't they? He could build up calluses if he wanted.

Hard to believe, above the throbbing of his head, but for the very first time in his life he could do whatever he wanted. He was free, totally free. Without a name. Without a past. Without the kind of responsibility that tied a man to a desk for eight hours a day, five days a week, fifty weeks a year. He was free.

But he felt like shit.

It could be the cold, he reasoned. The wood stove worked fine, but the place was drafty—something he hadn't noticed the summer before, when the air had been warm. There was a dampness now that was seeping into his bones, making him shake.

But no, the problem was his hangover. With an effort, he maneuvered himself to his feet and crossed the planked floor to the scarred table and the smooth leather briefcase that looked so out of place on it. He shook two aspirins from a bottle and, in a gesture that was suitably macho for a free-as-a-bird man with a stinking hangover, tossed back his head and swallowed them dry.

The gesture was sadly misconceived. His head exploded in pain at the sharp backward movement. His stomach reacted to all that had soured it the night before. Turning blindly, without a thought of being cold or macho or free, he stumbled to the bathroom and threw up.

With the breaking of dawn on the other side of the world, Christian Frye came awake to a heat that, not even in those first semiconscious seconds, let him forget where he was and why. He had been to Australia before. It wasn't one of his favorite places. But he'd been asked to do a job that appealed to him, the timing was right, and with a stretch of the imagination, Australia was in the same neighborhood as Tahiti, where he was heading later that day. Tahiti would be fun. He had been there before, too, and was looking forward to seeing old friends. He was also looking forward to living in luxury for a while, which was something he hadn't done much of here.

His bungalow was little more than a tropical lean-to, a plank floor raised off the ground, with a center post that shared support of the thatched roof with the single wall that stood on the forest side. The ocean side was open to let in what little breeze might push through the trees, though Christian didn't feel any breeze now. The air was warm, humid, and still, draining him of energy before he'd moved an inch. Just then, he would have traded his Nikon for a ceiling fan without a second thought.

Cairns, with its modern waterfront hotels, hadn't been so bad. Nor, a bit farther north, had Port Douglas, where he had stayed on a yacht that was state-of-the-art in everything from hot tubs to women. North of Port Douglas, though, fancies of the flesh had taken a back seat to the lushness of the land, specifically the dense, wild growth of the Daintree.

Rainforests were like that—dense and wild—and the Daintree was the greatest Christian had ever seen. As tropical vegetation went, the Daintree's was richer, larger, more vibrant. In the sunlight that dappled down through a towering canopy of leaves, his camera had captured vivid flares of reds, oranges, and pinks, deep and fertile greens, darker blues and magentas. He had photographed not only plant life but birds, butterflies, rodents, and reptiles. Many of them were found in no other place on earth but this one. The expression "endangered species" was so overused as to be taken for granted. A person couldn't truly understand its meaning until he saw at first hand the beauty to be lost.

Christian had seen that beauty. It wasn't the beauty of a perfectly set diamond, or a Georgian mansion built on a knoll, or a well-dressed woman. Rather, it was raw, primitive, untouched by humans. It was hot and moist, smelling of new growth, old growth, rotting growth, crowded high overhead and closely packed underfoot, stifling at times but alive, always alive.

The goal was to keep it that way, which was why Christian had been asked to photograph it. He had gone through dozens and dozens of rolls of film, now safely stored in his cooler. If even a small number of those pictures helped the cause, the sweat that had poured from him over the last week would be well worth it.

Even now, at dawn, when day was at its coolest, he was sweating. At least he wasn't dressed. Being dressed was the worst. There had been times in the forest when the heat was so oppressive that every stitch he'd worn had been soaked through with sweat. Other times, rain had done the deed. He had been warned that December wasn't the best time to visit, but December fit into his schedule. He liked being away for the holidays, and if that meant the rainforest in the rainy season, so be it. It didn't matter whether it was sweat or pelting downpours that soaked his clothes so that they had to be peeled off, so that they never quite dried, so that they grew increasingly rank. The clothes would be disposed of when he returned to Cairns, and in Tahiti he wouldn't wear much of anything at all.

At that thought, he smiled and stretched, extending an arm over his head to the top of a mercifully long hammock and a leg to its foot. When he relaxed again, he ran a hand through the hair on his chest and middle to his belly. He'd lost weight, no doubt sweated off seven or eight pounds, which was fine. It wouldn't hurt to have a few to play with. He liked being in shape—not that he usually gave much thought to diet or formal exercise, given what he did for a living—but vacations were something else. Good food, less exercise than usual, a minimum of nervous energy; he could put on weight during vacation.

For that reason he was glad he had left for Australia before Thanksgiving. When Laura made a dinner, there were no holds barred. She went all the way, soup to nuts, with a different kind of soup, a different kind of nuts, a different kind of everything else each year, except for the turkey. That big bird—huge bird, given the number of people she usually invited—was the one constant in the meal. Everything else changed according to her whim. Thanksgiving was a time for showing off all she had and did and was. Christmas was more of the same. And though Christian had to hand it to Laura for building a life out of nothing and building it well, he just couldn't be there to watch. It was too painful, too stark a reminder of all he didn't have himself.

So he kept busy over the holidays. That way he didn't have to see things. He didn't have to remember what it had been like once upon a time. And he didn't have to behave like an asshole, tossing around mockery and innuendo in a show of disdain for what Laura and Jeff had made of their lives.

He was getting too old for that anyway. It was growing tiresome—and the irony of that admission was something else. For years, Gaby had said the same thing.

"Why do you do it, Christian?" she used to ask. "You hurt your family and you hurt yourself. You're too old for that kind of thing. Why do you do it?"

He had never had an answer, at least not one he'd been willing to share, and what he wasn't willing to share with Gaby, he wasn't about to share with anyone else. They had been together, on and off, for nearly sixteen years. Best friends, on and off. Lovers, on and off. She had been the closest he had ever come to having a wife. But she was busy producing talk shows in New York, and he was busy building homes in Vermont. And something was missing, some force that told them to grab it while they had it, some incentive for one or the other of them to compromise. Something was missing.

Then Gaby had gotten sick. He had wanted to marry her, but they both knew the gesture was misplaced, a useless weapon against a disease that wouldn't be stopped. So he had stayed with her, held her hand when she was lucid enough to be frightened, dealt with the doctors, and helped make her last days as comfortable as possible. When there was nothing else to be done, he had buried her.

A slow trickle of sweat inched its way down his face as tears might have done if Christian had been the crying type. He missed Gaby. She had been a good friend, a point of reference in his life. For three years, now, she'd been gone, and though he didn't think about her constantly, there were many times when he would have liked to talk with her, take her out, see her smile.

She wouldn't have smiled in the Daintree, Christian realized with a chuckle. Gaby liked her luxuries. She would have hated the heat, hated the humidity, hated the congestion of the forest. She needed space. And silence. Waking up to the cacophonous chatter of starlings nesting nearby wouldn't have thrilled her. Nor, as the day wore on, would the buzz of the insects or the shrill of the cicadas or the screeches and squawks of the other birds of the rainforest. No, Gaby was one for luxury and privacy. She wouldn't have slept as he had, bare save for a thin pair of boxers, in a hut with one wall. She wouldn't have bathed naked in the stream. And she wouldn't have liked walking through the jungle, where one was always watched by creatures one couldn't see.

Even Christian had found that disconcerting at first, though he'd been warned it was so. Every sound he made was heard, every move he made was seen. No doubt he had spotted only a small number of the creatures that spotted him. But he couldn't really blame them for their watchfulness. After all, the forest was their home. He was the trespasser.

But then, wasn't he always?

Four in the afternoon, Boston time, found Taylor Jones wide awake in bed. The bed wasn't his own, but he knew it well. He knew the feel of fresh white percale, the feel of ruffled pillows, the feel of the thick white quilt. He also knew the feel of the woman whose body, even now, fit his with precision. Her skin was warm and smooth, her curves sweet, her desire everything a man could want.

Unfortunately, she was leaving town. Within one short week, the fresh white percale sheets would be stripped from the bed, packed up, and shipped to San Francisco, where a job as the assistant manager of a four-star hotel was waiting. The job was a plum, an honor for a twenty-seven-year-old, a big step up for a woman who planned one day to run the show. But there were hotels all over the country, and four-star ones at that. She wouldn't have chosen this one if leaving the East Coast would have broken her heart.

They had something good going, she and Taylor did, but it was purely physical. He knew that; so did she. They came from different places, liked different people, wanted different things down the road. But the sex was good, so they kept at it. Her moving clear across the country was probably the only way to stop.

"Tack?"

He moved his face against the back of her head, where the hair lay thick and warm. "Mmmm?"

"What are you thinking?"

Inhaling deeply, he held her scent in his lungs like pot, for the maximum effect, before letting it out. "I'm thinking I'm gonna miss you."

"Don't lie."

"I'm not." He raised his head over her cheek. "What did you expect I'd say?"

"That you had to get back to work. That's what you usually say."

She was right. He wasn't the kind to linger or get hung up with sweet nothings when the loving was done. But today was different. He wasn't such a total heel that he couldn't acknowledge in some small way the end of a relationship. "I thought maybe we could go out for dinner. It'd be appropriate, don't you think?"

"Only if we won't be seeing each other again before I leave."

He smoothed a strand of blond hair off her cheek.

In the absence of a response, she raised questioning eyes to his.

"It might be better if we didn't," he finally said. "It won't get any easier."

"It won't be so hard. We don't love each other."

"No." He ran a hand around her breast, feeling the lure of her warmth, even though she'd drained him less than ten minutes before. "But we share this." It was like an addiction. He needed a fix every few days or he was climbing the walls.

She stilled his hand, holding it there, and returned her cheek to the pillow. "It's not enough. I need more. And you need a sweet little homebody for a wife. But you pick the wrong women, Tack. Over and over again you do it. You go for women who have active and visible careers, but that's not the kind who's going to give you the home and hearth and the five kids. Me, I'd only give you heartache, because I have dreams of my own and I can't give them up."

"If you loved me, you would."

She sent him a challenging look. "You don't love *me*. Or if you do, you have a funny way of showing it. Quick sex three or four times a week with one call to set each date and even then you're late. No gifts, no flowers, no wining and dining—"

"You have all the wining and dining you can take with your friends."

"Friends, I might point out, whom you never made any attempt to get to know." Her annoyance mellowed into the indulgence of a friend who knew some things would never change. "You're a bastard, Taylor Jones. God only knows why I've put up with you this long."

"I know why." He grinned. "Great sex."

She nodded. "Great sex. As long as you have me, you take me, and as long as I want you, I let you. The chemistry is there. It's perfect. I'll want you forever, and that's a fact." She put her fingertip to the groove in his chin. "But I've worked my butt off for this career, and now that it's finally getting off the ground I can't let anything stop it. I may marry and have kids someday, but only after I've nailed down a place for myself. I need that place. Can you understand why?"

He could. God knows she'd explained it enough. Hotels were in her blood. Both her grandfathers had owned them. One still did, and that was the hotel chain she wanted. The stipulation was that she earn it. She was determined to do that.

"I understand," he said, but with indifference. Yes, he admired her determination, but he had contempt for the games she and her family played. He had come from nothing, himself. The only games his family had played were ones of survival.

"So my staying here is pointless. It keeps you from looking for other women." She brushed one of his eyebrows with the pad of her thumb. "One of those women will be right for you. One of them will inspire you to be thoughtful and doting."

"Thoughtful and doting? Me?"

"Why not? You make love that way. But it ends the minute we get out of bed, because I'm the wrong woman. Maybe if we were closer in age——"

He cut her off with a shake of his head. "An eight-year difference isn't a hell of a lot. But that's not the problem. We could have been born on the same day, and still we'd have been wrong for each other. You're gloss, and I'm not." She had furs, jewelry, and a Jaguar. Her insurance bill alone probably equaled what he spent on food for a year. He worked for Uncle Sam. No one got rich working for Uncle Sam. In his next life, he decided, he'd be a mega-mogul, but for now he liked his work, particularly when a meaty case came along. "You're going up and up and up. I'm not, and that's okay, because I wouldn't be caught dead in a tux three times a week."

She smiled. "More's the pity. You look great in a tux."

He smiled back. "So. How about dinner?"

"I'd rather see you again before I leave."

But he shook his head. She was the one who was moving. He had to take the upper hand in this, at least.

She slid a hand up his thigh. "You'll want me."

"Damn right." It had been that way from the start. Seeing her fully dressed was tempting enough. Seeing her naked, he didn't stand a chance. And when her hand left his thigh and did wonders between his legs, he was lost.

Covering her, he settled into the slip of her thighs and entered her. His movements were slow and steady, in time more steady than his heart, but he was determined to watch her, to see one last time the look of pleasure on her face when she came. He brought her close, then slowed, brought her closer still, then slowed again. He prolonged her final release as long as he could, until she cried out with its force, until he did with his own.

When it was over and she dozed off, he slipped from the bed. He dressed, watching her all the while, then watched her a little longer before letting himself out. Leaving the waterfront, he walked up State Street to Tremont, across the Commons and the Public Garden, all the way down Commonwealth to Massachusetts Avenue, and over the river to Cambridge. By the time he climbed the three flights to his Central Square apartment, he was half frozen, but he wasn't numb, and if cold turkey was the way to go, numb was what he wanted. So, ignoring the files on his desk that were waiting to be read, he changed out of his suit and went to the gym, where he punished his body with the kind of workout he hadn't done in months. Then, feeling vaguely back in control, he stopped for a pizza with the works to go, went back home, thumbed open a cold Sam Adams, and turned on the Celtics.

four

"I'M SORRY, MRS. FRYE. I KNOW THIS IS difficult for you, but if I repeat myself, it's only to make sure I know the facts." Dennis Melrose, Daphne's police detective, studied his notes. "Your husband was due home at six o'clock last night, but he never arrived. You haven't seen him or heard from him. He hasn't sent a message through a third party."

"That's right," Laura said. She was feeling dazed, trying her best to focus on everything the man was saying but having trouble. It wasn't the detective's fault. He was pleasant enough, in his mid-fifties, with a slight paunch and a more than slightly receding hairline. But she hadn't slept in a day and a half, and she was wrung dry with worry.

"He hasn't called his mother," the detective continued. "He hasn't called his friends. He hasn't called anyone from the office."

David confirmed the last. Standing close behind Laura in a proprietory way, he said, "Total silence. He's had no contact with anyone there. Or with the clients he was supposed to see."

"Did he have many appointments?"

"A full day's worth. Jeff is a successful accountant. Clients like him because he knows what he's doing, and because he's dependable. If he sets up a meeting, he's on time and prepared."

"That's how he is in everything," Laura put in, "which is why this is so bizarre."

44

"Jeff is a family man," Elise said, coming forward in her chair. Between her rhinestone-studded chartreuse sweat suit and the blond hair that stuck out at odd angles from a ponytail at the top of her head, she would have looked ditsy had it not been for her earnest expression and the somber tone of her voice. "In all the time I've known him, he hasn't once given Laura reason to doubt that he'd be home with her and the kids exactly when he was supposed to."

"Something's happened to him," Laura insisted.

The detective studied her with disconcerting innocence. "Do you think there's been foul play?"

"Clearly."

"It isn't possible that he just needed a break?"

"A break from what?" Laura knew the man was doing his job; still, she resented his suggestion. "We're his family. We love him, and he loves us. And he loves his work. Besides, he's already planning a break. We're going to the Caribbean in January."

"What Detective Melrose is asking," Daphne said in a dry tone as she turned away from the window to approach the group, "is whether Jeff might have cracked."

"No way!" Debra cried. She was sitting close beside Laura and hadn't budged from the house since she'd come home from school at two—after skipping history, she had told Laura, with a defiance that Laura didn't have the strength to fight.

"My husband is totally sane," Laura informed the detective. "He's happy and healthy, at least he was when he left here yesterday morning. If anything was bothering him, I would have known."

The detective made a note in his book. "Okay. Can you give me a description? How tall is he?"

She swallowed. Statistics were so stark. But necessary, she told herself. "Six feet."

"Weight?"

"One-sixty."

"He plays tennis," Debra reminded the detective.

David added, "A mean game. He beat the pants off me when we played last summer."

"Okay, he's athletic. And competitive. Eye color?"

"Not competitive," Laura corrected. "He really isn't."

"Sure he is," Daphne said.

"Not intensely. He doesn't get hung up on being first. He's easygoing that way."

When no one challenged her, the detective said, "Eye color?"

"Brown," she answered.

"Hair?"

She put a hand to her throat. Taking Jeff apart, feature by feature, was gruesome in the same way that some of her imaginings had been.

Daphne came to her aid. "Brown, side-parted, trim cut, neatly combed. And he wears glasses. Wire-rimmed ones."

"Is there a picture I can see?"

Laura sent Debra to get one.

"What was he wearing when last seen?"

"Uh, a suit." She tried to think back thirty-six hours, but she'd been busy getting herself and her thoughts organized for the day, while Jeff had been dressing. "A dark suit." All his suits were dark. Dark and sedate, which was the image he chose. "Blue, I think."

"Three-piece?"

"No. Jacket and trousers. White shirt. Striped tie." It was a fair guess. Most of his shirts were white, most of his ties striped.

Debra returned with the picture and handed it to Laura, who held it for a minute, studying Jeff's face. It was a kind face and a dependable one, two qualities that had drawn her to him from the first and hadn't changed. He was a good-looking man, well-kept, in his prime. She was sure he would have been able to defend himself against a mugger—unless a gun or a knife had been involved. With a shudder, she passed the picture to the detective.

"Can I hang on to this for now?" he asked.

She nodded.

He reached for his topcoat. "I'll go back to the station and type all this up. Once the report is filed, we may be able to come up with something."

Laura stood. "How soon?"

"I'll have men at work on it tonight."

"How soon do you think you'll come up with something?"

He slipped the picture from its frame. "As soon as we can."

But Laura needed specifics. Jeff was her husband. She was terrified for him. "In general, what is your experience in cases like this?"

He shrugged. "If there's been foul play, we should be able to pick up on it pretty quick. If not, it may be awhile."

"If not? What do you mean, if not?"

"If he's split on his own."

"He hasn't," Laura said, looking him straight in the eye. One policeman was as bad as the next. But she needed them. They had access to resources she didn't have and experience in locating missing persons. So she would use them.

She walked him to the door and managed a gracious goodbye, but the instant he was gone she set off for the kitchen. She was putting the coq au vin on to heat when the others joined her.

"There," David said with satisfaction. "Now that that's done, we can expect some results." He threw an arm around her shoulder. He was a bear of a man, dark and bearded, as unlikely-looking an accountant as Jeff was a likely-looking one. "Don't worry, hon. The police know what they're doing. This is their business. They'll find him. And in the meanwhile, we have everything under control at the office. Jeff's accounts won't fall behind."

"Did you cancel for tonight?" Elise asked her.

Sliding out from under David's arm, Laura opened a cabinet and rummaged inside. "Uh-huh. It's okay. There were twelve couples invited. One less won't hurt." She had had a worse time explaining to Georgina Babcock why she and Jeff hadn't shown up at the museum, but she'd done it without falling to pieces. Likewise calling the dentist to cancel Jeff's appointment. Likewise calling Lydia. That had been the hardest, trying to learn if Lydia had heard from Jeff without tipping her off about his disappearance.

No, she decided, the call to Scott had been worse. He had been stunned, then frightened. One part of her wished she had spared him that and waited. Selfishly, though, she wanted him home. He was a comfort to her. "Scott is flying in after his classes tomorrow—assuming we haven't found Jeff by then." She set a box of rice on the counter. "He doesn't have classes on Friday."

"Should you have called him so soon?" David asked.

"I was worried he might hear it from someone else."

"But he and Jeff were so close—"

"Are." Laura put a saucepan under the faucet. "He and Jeff *are* so close."

"Scott's nineteen," Debra told David. "He can be here worrying with us. He doesn't have to be pampered all the time."

Laura looked at her. "He isn't pampered."

"He is," she argued, then mimicked, " 'Scott can't do this, he's at school. Scott can't do that, he's at school. Let Scott sleep late, he works so hard. Give Scott a little money, he's earned a little fun.' " The voice became her own again. "What do you think Scott's doing at Penn?"

"Studying," Laura said.

"He's playing. Didn't you hear the message on the machine? He's having the time of his life with his fraternity brothers." Her voice fell. "What a bunch of geeks!"

Laura set the water on to boil. "Scott's friends aren't geeks."

"Didn't you hear the stupid noises they were making?"

"Look who's talking about making stupid noises." Nudging David out of the way, she removed the cutting board from its slot. "What would happen if I were to record every sound you and your friends make at the Stones' concert next week?"

At mention of the concert, Debra went very still. In a vulnerable voice, she said, "I'll be able to go, won't I?"

Laura felt a twinge in the pit of her stomach. She knew just what Debra was thinking. For so long, Jeff had been by her side. Suddenly he wasn't, and she felt disabled. She didn't know how to picture the future, didn't know what would be the same and what wouldn't.

But the confusion wasn't fair to Debra. She was so young. "Of course you'll be able to go to the concert."

"What if Dad's not back?"

"You'll go anyway."

"How can I do that? How can I go and have a fantastic time while he's out there somewhere, missing?"

Laura removed a collander of washed green beans from the refrigerator. "Debra, life isn't going to stop."

"Not for you. Surely not for you. You don't stop for anything. Look at you now. You're fixing a dinner no one is going to eat."

"I'll eat it," David said.

"Do that, and Beth will never forgive me," Laura told him in a subtle hint she followed up not so subtly. "You should run along. You've been a big help, but there's not much more to do."

"I want to be here for you."

"I need some quiet time, I think." David had always liked her a bit more than he should, which was fine as long as Jeff was around. But Jeff wasn't there now, and she felt uncomfortable. "It's okay. I'll be fine."

"There ought to be a man around here."

"Uh, David," Daphne said, predictably annoyed with the comment but in control, "Laura's right. She needs time and space. It's been a tough day. I'm going to try to get her to sleep as soon as she eats, but I can't do that if she has a house full of guests."

"I'm not guests. I'm family. Or almost."

"Then be a dear and understand." Taking him by the arm, she led him from the kitchen. "We'll give you a call if anything happens. If not, Laura will talk with you tomorrow."

More than happy to leave David to Daphne, Laura pulled a long knife from the butcherboard block and began to cut the green beans into small diagonal slices. She hadn't gone through more than a handful when the phone rang.

Debra jumped for it with an expectant "Hello?" After a pause, she said, "Oh. Sure, Gram. Hold on." With a look that said Laura was getting her due, she held out the receiver.

Laura grimaced. She hadn't given a thought to her mother's party. Frantically, she whispered to Elise, "She wants to switch the department Christmas party to the restaurant. It's on the nineteenth. Can we do it?"

Elise held up a let-me-check finger and headed for her purse.

Laura took the phone. "Can I call you back in five minutes, Mom? I'm in the middle of something."

"What's going on over there, Laura?"

Laura swallowed. "What do you mean?"

"Has something happened to Jeff?"

Closing her eyes, she leaned a shoulder against the wall. She should have figured Maddie would find out. It wasn't that the woman was a busybody. Being in a prominent position at the university in a region dominated by academia, she was well known. She was also an authoritative figure, the proverbial horse's mouth, the first one a person would contact to check out something bizarre.

"Who called you?"

"Amanda DeLong. She gave me an earful about Jeffrey just climbing into that car of his and driving away."

Laura felt a flash of anger. "Amanda DeLong is about as reliable now as she was thirty years ago when she left Janie and me in Boston because she finished lunch with her friend, forgot she was supposed to pick us up after the ballet, and drove two hours back home alone. Jeffrey did *not* just climb into his car and drive away!"

"My goodness, you're overreacting."

"Given the day I've had, I can react any way I please!"

"So where's Jeffrey?"

"I don't know! He didn't come home last night. I'm assuming he was hurt or abducted. The police are working on it right now."

"Well," Maddie said with a flourish, "I'm pleased to find out. It's always nice to know about family crises."

Laura sighed. "I'm sorry, Mother, but I've been hoping all day that Jeff would show up so there wouldn't be anything to call you about. We called people—"

" 'We'?"

"David, Daphne, Elise, and me. We called people we thought might have contact with Jeff. Amanda must have talked with Janie. Janie's husband is one of Jeff's tennis partners. They were supposed to play today. We called to let him know Jeff wouldn't be there."

"Does Scott know?"

"I talked with him a little while ago."

"How did he take it?"

"He's upset."

"How do you feel about that?"

"How do you think I feel? I'm upset too."

"I can hear that, Laura, but I'd be careful about letting the children know. With Jeff gone, they'll be looking to you for strength even more than usual, and you'll have to provide it. A trauma like this can wreak havoc with the adolescent self-image—"

"Please, Mom," Laura cut in. She could feel instant analysis coming on. The thought of it made her sweat. "I'm doing all I can. Debra's here, and Scott will be home tomorrow. Until I know more about Jeff, I don't want to get into discussions of psychological ramifications. When it comes to the kids, I'm trusting my instincts as a mother."

"And your instincts as a wife? What do they tell you?"

"That Jeff is out there somewhere needing help."

"Interesting. That can be taken different ways, you know."

Anything could be taken different ways by Maddie when she started in with double meanings, hidden agendas, and Freudian slips. "I have to run, Mom."

"So do I. I have a dinner meeting at seven that will probably run until ten or so, or I'd drop over. Will you be all right?"

Laura wasn't sure, but she knew she'd be better off without Maddie around. "I'll be fine."

"I'd appreciate your keeping me posted, Laura. I don't like hearing family news from other people."

"I'll call you."

"You said you would do that about my party, and you didn't."

Laura sought out Elise, who arrived at her side with the restaurant's December party schedule in her hand. "It's been an impossible day," she said, following Elise's finger. "We've been trying to leave the phone lines open. But I did check. You can have your party at the restaurant as long as you're willing to move it from six to six-thirty. We'll need the extra time to get a four o'clock cocktail party out."

"I suppose that's all right."

"Good. I'm hanging up now, Mom. Have a nice meeting tonight." Before Maddie could say anything more, Laura broke the connection. With barely a breath, she returned to the beans. Her knife blade flew. Heads and tails were discarded, a new handful grabbed, and the slicing repeated, and all the while Laura felt like her competent self. Then the phone rang again, and the knife clattered from her hand. "Hello?"

"Mrs. Frye, this is Donny. Is Deb around?"

With an involuntary moan, Laura looked at Debra, who took off for the other room. Laura put the call on hold, but before she could get back to work the other line rang. "Yes?"

"Laura Frye, please."

The voice was businesslike, not coarse or disguised like a kidnapper's would be, but her heart beat faster. She sent Daphne a frightened look. "Speaking."

"Duggan O'Neil here, from the *Hampshire County Sun.*"

Duggan O'Neil. She saw him in her mind, a man in his mid-forties, rumpled about everything except the pen and paper in his hand. He was nearly as bad as a kidnapper. That pen and paper had power.

The panic she felt showed in her eyes, but she kept her voice commendably steady. "Yes, Mr. O'Neil. How are you?"

"I'm fine, thank you. Actually, I'm wondering how you are. I heard your husband disappeared."

She moistened her lips. "Who told you that?"

"It's a matter of public record. I believe a missing persons report has been filed. Is it true?"

She made a frantic gesture toward Daphne, who made a bewildered gesture back. "Uh, can you hold a second, Mr. O'Neil? My other line is ringing." She put him on hold and crushed the phone to her chest. "He knows about the report, Daph. So much for police discretion. Now it'll be splashed all over tomorrow's *Sun!*"

Daphne came close and spoke softly. "It was inevitable."

"But broadcast from here to kingdom come? That makes it so *real.*"

"It *is* real, Laura. We don't want it to be, but it is."

"Oh, God." She hugged her stomach. If only Jeff were there! Things were getting out of hand, more so, it seemed, with each hour that passed. She wanted to turn back the clock, to rewind things and make life the way it had been. But she couldn't. If Dennis Melrose didn't make sure of that, Duggan O'Neil would. "What should I tell him?" she asked in a nervous whisper.

"As little as possible. Do you want me to talk?"

One part of Laura wanted that more than anything. The other part sensed that if she didn't give Duggan O'Neil a show of composure, she'd suffer for it. "No." She cleared her throat. "I'll do it." Drawing herself straight, she put the phone to her ear and punched in the call. "I'm sorry. How can I help you?"

O'Neil sounded no worse for the wait. "You can confirm that your husband is missing."

"As you said, a report has been filed with the police."

"Then he has disappeared?"

"Yes."

"Do you have any idea where he might be?"

She answered slowly, as though she were talking to a child. "No. That's why I filed a report with the police."

"When was the last time you saw him?"

"When he left for work yesterday morning."

"Did you talk with him during the day?"

"No. I was working all day myself."

"What time was he due home?"

Laura sighed. Bowing her head, she put a hand to the tense muscles at the back of her neck. "That information is all in the police report, Mr. O'Neil. I don't believe I need repeat it again."

"Then tell me about you. How are you feeling about all this?"

She held the phone away, staring at it as though the man at the other end of the line were insane. "How do you think I'm feeling?" she finally asked in disbelief.

"Upset, maybe. Worried."

"Very perceptive, Mr. O'Neil."

If he was bothered by her sarcasm, he didn't let on. "Do you think your husband may have been kidnapped?"

"Anything is possible."

"Would you pay a ransom if one was demanded?"

"Of course. What kind of question is that?"

"Then there's money in the bank?"

Daphne had told her to say as little as possible, but she couldn't let certain questions and their implications pass. "If you're asking whether my husband and I are so wealthy as to provide grounds for a kidnapping, the answer is no. But if a ransom was asked, I'd do anything I could to raise the money."

"Will this hurt business?"

"Excuse me?"

"Your husband is a successful accountant."

"If he's not here," she snapped, "he can't do any accounting, so yes, business will be hurt."

"Easy, Laura," Daphne warned softly, but Duggan O'Neil was speaking again, capturing Laura's full attention.

"I was thinking of you. Cherries is young and still growing. Part of its appeal is that it's upbeat. Something like this can be a real downer. Are you worried?"

Laura could feel her heart pounding, harder and faster, in equal parts anger and distress. Aware that every word she said was being noted for possible publication, she answered, "Mr. O'Neil, my husband is missing. No one knows where he is. The police have been brought in, but they're not rushing back to me with quick discoveries. Right now, I'm doing whatever I can to find Jeff. But Cherries is operating as usual. I have an excellent support staff to carry on when I can't be there."

"That wasn't what I asked."

"If people choose to boycott the restaurant because they feel my husband's disappearance is a threat to them," Laura declared, "that's their choice. Personally, I have more faith in the residents of Hampshire County. They're smart. They're strong. And they appreciate good food, which is what I give them." She took a fast breath. "Now, if you don't mind, Mr. O'Neil—"

"One last question," he said, and she could sense a subtle change in his tone. It should have warned her, but he spoke again before she could hand the receiver to Daphne. "How about the possibility that your husband skipped town on his own?"

Her hand tightened on the phone. "That's not a possibility."

"A mid-life crisis—"

"Not Jeff."

"Perhaps a secret life—"

"No. I'm sorry, Mr. O'Neil, but your wild speculation is not welcome." With a resounding *thwack*, she hung up the phone. "The gall of that man!" She took a wooden spoon to the chicken and began to stir with a vengeance. "Mid-life crisis! Jeff did not—*would* not—willingly leave here." A chicken leg hit the spoon, sending a spatter of sauce up and out. Swearing, she grabbed a dishtowel and began to blot sauce from her sweater.

In the next instant, Elise took over the stove while Daphne put an arm around Laura's waist. "I think you've had enough of this, Laura. You're ready to drop. Come on upstairs."

"My sweater's a mess."

Taking the towel from her hand, Daphne steered her toward the hall. "The dry cleaner will fix it."

Laura didn't fight her. She didn't have the strength. She was suddenly so tired that the thought of standing on her feet for another minute was torture. Once upstairs in the master bedroom, she sank down on top of the paisley comforter that covered the bed, curled up her legs, and closed her eyes.

"I'm sorry," she whispered.

"For what?"

"Caving in. It was just something about that call. Why did he ask that? Why did the police? Is everyone so cynical they have to look for evil motives behind innocent events?"

"A man's disappearance isn't exactly innocent."

"It is if it's Jeff." Laura paused. In a smaller voice, she asked, "Isn't it?" She opened her eyes to look at Daphne, who had come to sit on the edge of the bed. Daphne was smart. She was worldly and realistic. Laura trusted her. "Jeff wouldn't deliberately leave, would he?"

Daphne looked troubled. "Who knows what another person would do? Do any of us really know each other?"

"Yes," Laura insisted, but weakly. "I know Jeff. I know Debra and Scott and my mother and you and Elise."

"But deep inside another person's mind—can anyone else really be there?"

The words weren't spoken lightly. But then, they never were. Daphne was a serious, straightforward woman and a good friend. Laura could count on her for an honest opinion.

"Do you think he might have done it, Daph?"

"Gone on his own?" She gave the possibility more consideration than Laura liked, before shaking her head. "And it doesn't make any sense to dwell on it. The police will do everything they can."

"In the meantime, what do I do? Debra thinks we ought to sit here waiting for something to happen, but what if nothing does? What if Jeff's gone for days? There's a big void here where he should be. What do I do with it?"

"You work. You said it to O'Neil. Business goes on as usual."

"But I don't have to be there. I'm with the production team, not the cast. With Elise handling bookings and PR, and DeeAnn hostessing and managing the restaurant, and people like Sue and Dave and Jasper running the catering crews, I don't have to *be* there."

A bit dryly, Daphne said, "Would you rather be here waiting by the phone every day?"

"You know I wouldn't. I'd go mad."

"Then keep busy."

"People will think I'm awful."

"Since when do you care what people think?"

"Since I got into a business where it mattered. Since Duggan O'Neil pointed it out."

"Duggan O'Neil is a whore," Daphne said with a look of disdain. "He'd suggest anything, just to get a rise out of you. That's his business, Laura." With barely a pause, she said, "What else would you expect from someone who works for Gary Holmes?"

Laura grunted. Garrison Holmes III was the publisher of the *Sun* and as right-wing as they came. His editorials were notorious. The man himself was notorious. In his late seventies and more handsome than any man that age had a right to be, he was on his fourth wife, was rumored to have illegitimate children scattered around the globe, yet raged on against the poor and oppressed for doing the same. That was only one of his pet peeves. Another was the welfare system, which he considered a handout for lazy good-for-nothings. Another was the criminal court system, which he felt pandered to thugs.

"Duggan needs headlines," Daphne went on, "and when they don't pop up on their own, he helps them along."

Laura thought back wearily to the things she'd said. "I gave him a few, I guess."

"Not too bad. If he quotes you, he'll be indicting himself for putting asinine questions to a woman under stress."

"If he quotes me. But you know he won't. He'll pick and choose words and phrases and put them into whatever context he wants. God," she said, "I wish he hadn't called. We could have used a little more time. Come morning, every one of Jeff's clients will know something's wrong."

"They would have found out anyway."

"What will I tell Lydia?"

"That you're doing everything you can to find Jeff."

"And Debra? Everyone at school will know. She has trouble concentrating on work as it is. Now it'll be a whole lot harder. She won't even be able to pretend nothing's wrong."

"Debra will do fine," Daphne insisted and gave an affectionate smile. "She's a hot sketch."

"Mmmm. Mouthy. She can complain that I'm running around doing things with Jeff missing, but she'll be at that Stones concert. Even if Jeff's not back, she'll go. She'll also go to New York with you. She's been asking if the trip was on this year."

"Of course it's on," Daphne said. "I wouldn't miss spending a few days on the town with my favorite sixteen-year-old."

"She adores you, Daph."

"The feeling's mutual." Her voice grew nostalgic. "I remember when she was born. Seems like yesterday."

Laura's voice, too, was soft, but from exhaustion. "It wasn't. I have the gray hairs to prove it."

"Where?"

"Under the color Julian puts on." She let her eyes drift shut. "Same auburn as when I was little."

"Don't talk. Go to sleep."

"Where do you think Jeff is?"

"I don't know."

"Do you think he's okay?"

There was a pause. "Yes, I think he's okay."

"Will he be back?"

"Uh-huh."

Laura took a breath that would have been a yawn if she'd had the strength to open her mouth wide. "I should take this sweater off," she mumbled.

"Later."

She felt the mattress shift when Daphne stood. Moments later, she was covered by the afghan that normally lay on the end of the chaise lounge. "Thanks, Daph," she whispered.

"My pleasure," Daphne whispered back and gave her shoulder a squeeze. "Get some sleep. I'll be downstairs."

Laura wanted to tell Daphne to go home and sleep. She wanted to remind Daphne that she couldn't miss another day of work. Law practices were serious things. Clients depended on Daphne. So did her partners.

But Laura was too tired to say anything more and too eager to escape into oblivion to risk anything that might delay it. So she simply pulled the afghan up to her chin and let go.

five

OVEMENT ON THE BED WOKE HER. Feeling as though she were forcing her way from a sleep miles deep, she shifted, then drifted.

"Mom? Wake up, Mom. There's something you have to see."

It was Debra's voice. A maternal sixth sense nudged Laura further awake. "Hmm?" she whispered.

"Wake up."

With an effort, Laura opened her eyes. Debra was sitting on the edge of the bed in a pool of early morning light that made Laura squint. "What is it, babe?" she murmured, but the words were no sooner out when reality returned in a rush. She pushed herself up, pushed a handful of hair off her face. Wide-eyed, she looked from Debra's pale face to the newspaper she held. Reluctantly, she reached for it.

LOCAL CPA VANISHES WITHOUT A TRACE, the headline read, jumping out at her from the bottom-left column of page one. Beside it was Jeff's picture, but Laura's eyes went to the words that followed.

Jeffrey Frye, prominent Northampton accountant, was officially identified as a missing person by the North-ampton Police Department last night after his wife,

Laura Frye, filed a report. According to that report, Frye failed to return home after work Tuesday night and hasn't been heard from since. In an interview with the *Sun,* a distraught Mrs. Frye confirmed her husband's disappearance and admitted that she had been busy with her own work on Tuesday and hadn't spoken with him since that morning.

A lifelong resident of Hampshire County, Frye graduated from Northampton High in 1967. In 1971, he received a business degree from the University of Massachusetts, where he was known to be a loner but a hard worker. That image carried over into his work and translated into significant earning potential. In addition to bankrolling his wife's restaurant, Cherries, which opened on Main Street two years ago, Frye owns a brick Tudor in the exclusive Child's Park area of Northampton. He also purchased a condominium in Holyoke last summer and a Porsche, which sources say he had always wanted.

His wife insists that Frye's disappearance will have no impact on her business, which sources say is having a record season. According to those sources, Mrs. Frye is capable of carrying on without her husband.

Detective Dennis Melrose of the Northampton Police Department has announced that a search is already under way. So far, there has been no sign of Frye in the area, but the police intend to broaden their search today. A crew is ready to dredge the lake, and the canine corps will comb the surrounding woods.

Melrose did not rule out the possibility that Frye masterminded his own disappearance. "Men have been known to vanish for personal reasons. If we come up with any in this case, we'll certainly check them out."

Mrs. Frye has vehemently denied any possibility that her husband walked out of his own accord.

Laura dropped the paper on the bed. Her jaw was clenched, her lips thin. Fighting fury, she wrapped her arms around Debra and held on tight.

"He didn't leave on his own," Debra asked, "did he?"

"No."

"And he isn't a money grubber."

"No."

"Why does the article sound that way?"

"Because that's how newspapers work. When there isn't much of a story, they try to spice things up."

"I thought journalists were supposed to be accurate."

"Not Duggan O'Neil. We don't own a condo in Holyoke. I don't know where he got that idea."

"Aren't you upset?"

"About the article? I'm livid."

"You don't sound it."

"Because I'm tired." Despite the night's sleep, she felt emotionally drained, which in itself was discouraging. "And confused. And worried. This article is annoying, but it's just an article. Daddy's still missing."

"All the kids in school will know now."

"It'll be okay."

"Fine for you to say. You're not the one who has to walk by them in the halls after your dad was accused, on the front page of the local rag, of masterminding his own disappearance."

"Duggan O'Neil doesn't know what he's talking about."

"Tell that to the kids at school."

"You tell them. They'll listen."

Debra sighed. "You sound so sure. You're *always* so sure."

Laura drew back. She used her thumb to erase the tiny crease between Debra's eyes. "Is there any other way to be?"

"Yeah. Scared."

"I'm that, too. But I can't let it paralyze me."

"So you're going to work today, huh?"

"First I'll have to go over to Nana Lydia's. If she doesn't

see the paper herself, someone else will call her."

"Poor Nana Lydia."

Laura smiled. Debra had always loved Jeff's mother. She felt the same kind of compassion for her that Laura did, but then, Lydia inspired it. She was a soft, sweet, gentle lady. "I wish I could spare her the torment. But she'll have to know."

"Maybe I could come with you when you tell her?"

"Uh-uh. You're going to school."

Pulling a face, Debra said, "And you'll go to the restaurant?"

Laura hesitated. "Maybe."

"Just like nothing's wrong?"

"No. Something's wrong. I won't forget it for a minute. But the police are out looking for your dad, and there's work to be done. Like I told you last night, life goes on."

Twisting away, Debra stood and scowled. "When you say things like that, you sound like the coldest person on earth."

"But you know better," Laura said, in an attempt to tease the scowl away.

"I don't." She took a fast breath, hesitated, then went on. "Y'know, it's not so hard to believe that Dad deliberately skipped that art opening Tuesday night. He hates art. He only goes to those things because you drag him."

Laura was stung by the accusation. "He goes to cultivate clients. It's important to his career."

"So he can bankroll Cherries and buy the brick Tudor and the Porsche?"

"Which, sources say, he always wanted," Laura put in. If Debra could quote Duggan O'Neil, so could she. "What are you suggesting, Debra?"

"Nothing." She headed for the door.

"Should I remind you that your father also pays for your clothes, which aren't cheap, and your vacations, and your braces, and the tutoring that will hopefully keep your grades high enough to get you into a decent college?"

At the door, Debra turned. "I'm not going to college. I've told you that."

"College costs a whole lot, but your father will pay without blinking an eye."

"I'm not going."

Laura saw the stubbornness on Debra's face, just as she'd seen it over and over again in the course of sixteen years. Debra was willful. Sweet and spunky, but willful. But Laura wasn't in the mood to lock horns with her. "We'll discuss that later."

"Yeah," Debra drawled and turned again to leave.

"What does *that* mean?"

"You'll be at Cherries later."

"If I go. But I'll be home after that."

"You'll be busy with other things," Debra called from the hall.

"Then we'll discuss it another time." Laura left the bed and went to the door. "Debra, you're a junior in high school. It's not like a decision has to be made today."

"That's not the point," Debra said, going into her room.

"Then what is?"

"Never mind."

"Debra?" There was no answer. "Debra!"

"I'm getting dressed. Donny is picking me up soon."

"I thought we agreed you'd take the bus to school."

"Given the shit I'll have to take when I *get* to school today, I think a ride might be nice."

Laura opened her mouth to argue, then closed it again. She didn't trust Donny McKenzie. But she did trust Debra, and Debra had a point. School was going to be tough.

Turning back into her own bedroom, Laura remembered when Debra was little, when she could protect her—and Scott—from the outside world. She wished she could do that now, wished it desperately. But she couldn't.

Raising her eyes, she moved them slowly around the room,

from the bed that had never been pulled back that night, to the closets that hadn't been opened, the alarm clock that hadn't been set, the bench that hadn't been sat on, the books that hadn't been read.

She thought of Jeff, whose absence was growing more ominous by the minute, and though Laura had never wanted protection over the years, she felt strangely in need of it now.

Lydia Frye lived in a modest white-frame house off Elm Street. It was the house her husband, William, had owned, the one in which Christian and Jeff had grown up. For twenty years, the house had been in a state of decline. For the last ten of those twenty, Laura had been urging Lydia to sell it and move.

"A garden apartment would be perfect. You wouldn't have the responsibility of upkeep, and there would be people around. I worry about you sometimes."

But Lydia wouldn't hear of moving. She was attached to the house, she argued back. It was hers; she owned it outright. She had lived there too long to abandon it just because the roof needed reshingling or the water heater had gone. So Laura had hired a roofer to do the reshingling and a plumber to replace the water heater. And an electrician to rewire the kitchen. And a tile layer to retile the bathrooms. And she'd been happy to do it, because Lydia was so pleased with the results, and when Lydia was pleased, so was Laura.

Laura adored her mother-in-law. She had felt drawn to her from the first time they'd met, when she and Jeff had announced their engagement. Laura was still seventeen, Jeff was still in college, and they had been dating for only three weeks. Everyone had been stunned except Lydia. She had looked at Laura with approval, then had turned her sparkling eyes on her son and given him her blessing.

Many times over the years, Laura had wondered about that approval. She liked to think that Lydia saw in her many of the same qualities she possessed herself—a keen nesting instinct, natural curiosity, resourcefulness—and though those qualities had taken different twists in Laura over the years, Lydia had supported her all the way. For that reason and others, Laura felt closer to Lydia than to her own mother. Lydia was approachable. Laura could talk to her. She was quiet and nonjudgmental, and though she had definite opinions on most any subject, she didn't foist those opinions on others. She was a liberal in the broadest sense of the word, which was why, Laura assumed, she could let Christian go his own way. Then again, maybe she could do that because she had Jeff.

That thought filled Laura with dread as she drove her Wagoneer up to the small white house on Thursday morning. Fearing that the paper would do damage before Lydia could be properly prepared, Laura had left the house shortly after Debra and driven directly over. The newspaper was on the walk. Tucking it under an arm along with the wedge of Black Forest cake and half a dozen pillow cookies she'd wrapped in a bag, she rang the doorbell—her usual signal: two short, one long, one short—and unlocked the door with her key.

"Lydia?"

"I'll be right there," Lydia called from the room they had converted into a bedroom five years before, when crippling arthritis had made climbing the stairs an ordeal. The room was on the first floor not far from the kitchen, which facilitated things on those bad days when Lydia used a wheelchair.

"Do you need any help?" Laura called.

"No, Laura, I'm fine. I have water on for tea. Why don't you help yourself?"

Any other woman might have wondered what Laura was doing there so early in the morning, but in this, too, Laura and Lydia saw eye to eye. They were both morning people. Laura often stopped at Lydia's before eight.

Going into the kitchen, she had two cups of tea steeping by the time Lydia appeared at the door, and a heartrending picture she made. A small woman, with snow-white hair and the fine features that age like porcelain, she had a fragile look, so much so that Laura had often marveled that she had given birth to such strapping men as Jeff and, even more so, Christian. She was leaning heavily on a cane as she made her way forward.

Meeting her halfway, Laura gave her a hug, then helped her to a chair. "How are you?" she asked softly.

Lydia gave her a sad smile. "Stiff." After the briefest pause, she added, "Worried."

Laura caught her breath. Her eye flew to the paper, which was still in a roll on the table.

"MaryJean Wolsey called," Lydia explained. Her voice creaked as her swollen joints might have had she been on her feet and moving. "When I put what she said together with your very careful phone call yesterday, I knew I didn't need the paper for verification."

"Lord, Lydia, I'm sorry. I was hoping he'd be back before I had to tell you."

"I figured as much. Is there anything new?"

Laura shook her head.

"How are things at the house?"

"Quiet. Strange. Tense."

"Is my favorite granddaughter giving you trouble?"

"Not really. She's just upset." Laura looked at her mother-in-law, looked at the gentle blue eyes—Christian's eyes—that had seen their share of heartache over the years. Lydia had lost one child in infancy, a girl who had come between Christian and Jeff. She had lived through her husband's stroke and early death. She had seen Christian come and go, come and go, and now Jeff, her baby, was missing. "How are you, Lydia?"

"Oh, I'll be all right."

"They'll find him. We have to believe that."

"I know."

Laura could have sworn she heard resignation, which was

odd. She would have expected fear or doubt instead. Puzzled, she took Lydia's gnarled hand. "The police are doing everything they can."

"I'm sure they are."

"And there hasn't been any sign of violence, so we can be hopeful that Jeff is well."

Lydia nodded. Her eyes grew moist.

"What is it?" Laura asked in a whisper.

Lydia's mouth turned down at the corners. She frowned, then shrugged.

"What?"

"I don't know. Something in his eyes when he stopped over here the other day."

"The other day?" He hadn't told Laura.

"Monday afternoon." She smiled and cocked her head toward the vase at the center of the table. "He brought me tulips."

Laura was stunned. She had assumed the flowers to be from one of the friends who periodically stopped in. But from Jeff? Jeff was great at calling the flower shop and having bouquets sent. He did that often. Laura couldn't remember the last time he'd delivered flowers himself.

Feeling a yawing in the pit of her stomach, she forced herself to ask, "Did he say anything unusual?"

"No. Nothing unusual."

"Did he say *anything*?"

"Just that work was going well. And you and Debra were fine, but I already knew that, because I'd talked with you that morning."

Laura took a sip of tea, but it dribbled down a chip on the rim of the cup. She wiped her chin with her hand, then wiped her hand with a paper napkin. "He didn't—uh, say anything about needing to get away?"

"No."

"But there was something in his eyes?" She looked up at

Lydia. "What was it? I have to know."

Lydia took awhile to gather her thoughts. She was still frowning when she said, "A look. Sadness. Discouragement. I knew that look. I used to see it when he was little, when something disappointed him in school, when he didn't do well in a test, or he wasn't elected to the student council, or he asked a girl to the prom and she turned him down." Her wrinkles shifted around the saddest of smiles. "Boys suffer, too, about things like that. And mothers of boys. Your Scott is more like Christian that way; things come easily. Not for Jeffrey, though. He used to try his best, then come in second." She stopped talking. After a minute, more softly, she said, "That was the way he looked, as though he'd tried his best but failed. I'm worried."

So was Laura, more than ever. "Did you ask him about it?"

"Oh, yes. He assured me nothing was wrong. But when he left he didn't say he'd talk with me soon."

The significance of that wasn't lost on Laura. *Talk with you soon, Mom.* It was Jeff's trademark, the way he ended every visit, every phone call to Lydia. He wouldn't tell her he loved her, he was too reserved for that, and he wouldn't tell her he'd see her soon, because if things were busy, he might not. But if he couldn't visit, he did call.

"Was something bothering him, Laura?"

Laura was asking herself the same question. "I don't know," she said. "I didn't see anything. He didn't say anything."

"Was he more quiet than usual?"

"I don't think so, but things have been so busy lately that he hasn't had much of a chance to *be* more quiet than usual. At least, not with the two of us alone." Horrible thoughts were chasing one another around in her mind, making her feel empty and alone. "He wasn't unhappy. He didn't *look* unhappy. If he'd been unhappy, he would have told me."

"He should have."

"Even if he hadn't, I would have *sensed* it. You don't live with a man for twenty years and not be tuned in to his moods," she said with conviction, then added, less sure, "Do you?"

"Only if you don't care for him. But you do, Laura. You've been good to Jeffrey."

Laura wondered how "good" was defined. If it meant looking pretty and acting poised, raising beautiful children, keeping a perfect house, and having a successful career at the same time that she made sure that there were always clean shirts in his drawer, she had been good to Jeff. If it meant spending hours over dinner or an evening or a weekend with him, she hadn't been so good. But he'd never complained. Hadn't he been the one to urge her expansion of Cherries into a large rented kitchen and then a restaurant?

Clinging to those thoughts, she searched Lydia's eyes. "We'll find him."

"Yes."

"Will you come stay at the house until we do?"

"No. I'm comfortable here. I have everything I need. I can get around. And besides, if Jeffrey were to call . . ." her voice trailed off, but the point was made. If Jeff were to call, she wanted to be there for him.

Laura nodded. She wished she could have said she had been thinking solely of Lydia, but her motives were partly selfish. Lydia had a quiet strength that Laura and Debra could have used. "Lydia?"

"Hmmm?"

Laura frowned. She was thinking of what Daphne had suggested. "Is there any chance that Jeff might have contacted Christian?"

Taking a spoon to her tea, Lydia considered that. After several stirrings, she tapped the spoon on the rim of the cup and set it gently in the saucer. "I honestly don't know. For a short time, when they were small, they were close. But that changed. As you know. Things came between them."

Though the words were offered innocently enough, Laura looked away. Of all the things she and Lydia had discussed over the years, the rift between Christian and Jeff wasn't one.

If Lydia was thinking the same thing, she didn't let on. "Christian came to symbolize everything Jeffrey wasn't, which isn't to say that Jeffrey didn't want to be like him a little. But he couldn't. It wasn't in his nature. The times when he was most upset with himself were times when he tried to compare himself to Christian, so I taught him not to make those comparisons. I taught him that he was a very different person from Christian." She sighed. "I don't know if I succeeded, but no, I doubt if Jeffrey would have taken his failures to Christian."

"Failures?" Laura cried. "What failures? Look at Jeff's life. He's been a total success."

"Success is relative. Each person defines it differently."

"But look what he *has*. Look at Scott and Debra and the house and his firm. How can a life with those things be considered anything *but* a success?"

"Success is relative," Lydia repeated.

Laura let out a breath. She supposed that there, too, Lydia was right, though it boggled her mind to think of the kind of life Jeff wanted if he didn't call this one a success.

She had never sensed he was unhappy. Never sensed he wanted anything more. Or anything different.

Maybe he hadn't. Maybe what Lydia had seen in Jeffrey's eyes on Monday afternoon had been nothing more than fatigue or a mother's imaginings. When a woman had as much time on her hands as Lydia did, she might easily dwell on a look or read into an expression something that wasn't really there. Laura didn't do that. She didn't have the time.

At the reminder, she glanced at her watch. "I have to get back to the house." She looked at Lydia. "Will you be okay?"

Lydia smiled. "I'll be fine."

"You won't reconsider and come home with me?"

Lydia shook her head. "MaryJean will be stopping by, and

Theresa from next door. But I'll be near the phone. If you hear anything, you call."

With a promise that she would, Laura gave her a gentle hug and left.

six

RESTAURANTS WERE A DIME A DOZEN IN New England college towns, particularly upscale restaurants with cute names and clever menus that included Buffalo chicken wings, Cobb salads, stir-fry anything, and Häagen-Dazs. Cherries' menu included all those, but Laura had a hook. Her specialty was the fruit, used equally as garnish and ingredient. On a given day, a diner could start with cold cherry soup, move on to cherried duck, and end with cherries jubilee. Not that Laura recommended that particular menu. Cherries were her stock-in-trade, but variety was the spice of life.

That was what she told her staff, whose exacting preparation, artful presentation, and gracious delivery of an ever-evolving array of dishes was what brought patrons back to the restaurant time and again. As for Laura, surrounded continually by food, she rarely ate. Still, when she walked into the restaurant, when she stood in the front foyer and took it all in or worked her way between the tables, greeting people she knew, she felt a sense of pride.

The decor enhanced that pride. Though the restaurant was located in an old stone building that stood shoulder to shoulder with others of its kind and might well have been dark and confining, she had gutted the inside and opened things up, en-

larged windows, put in recessed lighting, and painted everything
white. Then she had decorated with plants—lush, green, live
ones that required a great deal of care but were worth it. So
were the trellised archways dividing one eating area from the
next, and the natural-oak bar, with its high stools, its suspended
stemmed glasses of every size and shape, and the imported porcelain that stood as art. The tables were of wicker, the same
light oak shade, with glass inserts, but the chairs—the chairs
were Laura's pièce de résistance. Interspersed with traditional
wicker ones, all with seats cushioned in rich green and burgundy,
were graceful chairs with high fan backs.

Laura's idea of luxury was sharing brunch with friends at an
alcove table, each of them perched on a peacock throne, shielded
from the rest of the world by lavish cascades of Swedish ivy.

Tuesday mornings were like that. Those were the times, before
the restaurant opened to the public, when she met with Daphne,
Elise, and DeeAnn to talk business. At least, that was what
they were supposed to talk about, but they usually touched on
things like DeeAnn's French manicure, Elise's daughter's birthday party, and Daphne's assault-and-battery-with-intent-to-
murder case, while they ate. Jonah would come in early to cook
for them, sometimes testing out a new recipe, other times preparing tried-and-true goodies such as Brie-baked eggs, bacon-
and-bran muffins, and Bellinis. Eventually the discussion would
turn to the new linen place mats Laura wanted to order, or the
holiday copy Elise was giving the newspapers, or the parking
lot permit Daphne was trying to prize from the city, or DeeAnn's
approach to drunken patrons, and when the four of them parted
ways, Laura was always left with a warm, secure feeling.

She would have given anything for a little of that warm, secure
feeling when she arrived at Cherries on Thursday morning. She
felt chilled to the bone and shaken. There was still no news
about Jeff.

After returning from Lydia's, she had spent two hours on the
phone, first with the police, then with Daphne, then with David,

then with a reporter for a local cable station, then with all those friends who called to say they'd seen the article in the paper and would do anything to help. But none had seen or heard from Jeff.

By ten-thirty, she'd had it with answering the phone and feeling helpless, so she had put on a mint green sweatshirt and leggings set, brightened her pale cheeks with blusher, run a vigorous brush through her hair, and gone to Cherries. She didn't know whether her mind was functioning well enough to accomplish much, but, if nothing else, her appearance would bolster her staff, which had to be wondering what effect Jeff's disappearance would have both on the business and on Laura herself.

She came through the back door and went directly into the kitchen, where, amid gleaming stainless steel counters and the scent of warm fresh-baked bread, four people plus her chef, Jonah, were working. "Hi, guys," she said brightly, but the face she made—half smile, half grimace—was a dead giveaway that business as usual wouldn't be easy.

She was immediately surrounded by concerned employees.

"Hi, Laura."

"How *are* you?"

"We can't *believe* what's happened!"

"If there's anything we can do—"

She raised a hand to stop the barrage. Offering a more genuine if tired smile, she said softly, "Thanks. I'm doin' okay."

"Has there been any word?"

"Not yet."

"No leads?"

"Not yet."

"They'll find him."

"I'm sure they will."

"Have you eaten?"

When she shook her head, the one who had asked, Annie, the baker of the bunch, reached into a nearby bin and handed her a warm croissant. "On the house," she said, grinning.

Laura took the croissant, bit off an end, and rolled her eyes.

"Not that you feel like eating," Annie said with a knowing look.

Annie was in her mid-twenties, as were most of Laura's kitchen staff. Like the others, she hoped to move on one day to bigger and better kitchens, in Boston, New York, or even Paris. In the meantime, she learned her trade under Jonah, who, at twenty-eight, had not only a degree from the Culinary Institute but three years' experience as a sous-chef in Quebec. He was a tough master, but the results were worth it. Working at Cherries held a certain status. Laura knew that if Annie were to leave, it wouldn't be out of discontent or boredom.

"I'll eat," Laura assured her. Catching sight of Jonah separating himself from the others and moving toward the door that led into the restaurant, she joined him out of earshot of the rest.

"Are you okay?" he asked, in a voice so gentle that if it had been anyone but Jonah she would have leaned into him for a hug. But Jonah wasn't a toucher. He was macho and aloof. Of average height with a tapering body, pale gray eyes, and thick blond hair, he was a low-key operator who, with a minimum of words and motion, did wonders in the kitchen. Laura was glad to have him as her chef.

"I'm fine."

"You look tired."

"I am."

"How's things at home?"

"Tough." She pulled at the croissant. "It's the same, but so different. Scottie's coming in later today. He'll stay for the weekend, then go back if nothing's happened by Monday."

"Is Debra behaving?"

Laura smiled. Debra had a crush on Jonah, which meant that, in an attempt to sound mature and independent, she mouthed off whenever she saw him, usually at Laura's expense. "Debra's being Debra. She's upset. She doesn't understand what's happening any more than I do." She took a small bite of the swatch of croissant she'd torn from the whole.

"That was an interesting article in the paper. O'Neil sure got his little digs in. What'd ya do to annoy him?"

"I didn't like some of his questions, and I let him know it." She glanced toward the seating area of the restaurant, where DeeAnn was checking the table settings—stunning, sexy DeeAnn, whose appreciation of men came second only to her appreciation for the finer things in life, like Chanel scarves and Dom Perignon.

"Did you mean what you said about the business?"

Laura looked right back at him. If maintaining morale was the issue, convincing Jonah that all was well was critical. "I did. Everything goes on as usual. Jeff's absence won't affect things here. He wasn't active in the everyday workings of the restaurant."

"He wasn't active in *any* part of the restaurant," Jonah said with an archness that took Laura aback.

A bit defensively, she said, "He was the money behind it."

"Maybe, but it must be showing a profit by now."

"There's still a mortgage on the building and loans for the renovation. But we're breaking even." She put the swatch of croissant in her mouth.

"Take credit where credit is due," Jonah advised. "You're the brains behind this operation. You built the catering service from nothing and you conceived of the restaurant. You were the one who found the building, chose the furnishings, hired the staff. It's been your baby all the way."

"I couldn't have done it without Jeff."

"Sure you could have. You're one strong lady. You can carry on just fine." He winked and drawled, "That's a vote of confidence, Mama." Then he flashed her a brilliant grin.

"Look out for those grins," DeeAnn shouted from across the restaurant. Seconds later, she was headed their way. "Those are killer grins. They blind you; then, when you can't see the forest through the trees, they zap you dead."

"Zap you dead?" Laura echoed. She looked at Jonah, whose grin grew lazy.

"But it's okay," DeeAnn said, coming up between them. "Anyone with buns like these—" she gave the backside in question a pat, "—can zap me dead any day." When Jonah spared her a bored look and calmly sauntered away, she slipped an arm around Laura. "How're you doin'?"

"Hangin' in there, Dee."

"They'll find him."

"God, I hope so."

"I know so. Jeff is too much of a homebody to be gone for long. He'll miss you. He'll come back. You'll see."

Laura eased back to look at DeeAnn. In a controlled voice, she said, "If he didn't leave of his own free will, he may not be able to return that way. Missing me may have nothing to do with it. I don't know why people assume that he just up and took off."

"I'm not assuming that. But Jeff *is* a homebody. He likes this place because it's familiar. He sits there at the bar, getting pleasure watching you come and go, and when he orders it's always one of the same few favorites. You can be sure he'll fight to get back here." She frowned. "What do you think, Laura? He's been gone a day and a half. Where do you think he is?"

Laura had spent nearly every wakeful minute of that day and a half wondering and worrying. Now, croissant in hand as she walked aimlessly into the restaurant, she wondered and worried some more. "I don't know. I don't think it was a car accident. We'd have known. The police have checked all the roads and the hospitals, and there's nothing."

DeeAnn walked beside her. "Are they still planning to dredge the lake?"

Laura shot her a sidelong glance. "You read Duggan O'Neil too?"

"Everyone reads Duggan O'Neil."

"Well, he was wrong about that. Or misleading. The police

are not planning to dredge the lake. He asked whether they'd do it if there was cause, and they said they would. But there isn't any cause. As of nine-thirty this morning, they've been around every inch of that lake, and there isn't a single tire track remotely like one the Porsche would leave." Reaching one of the alcoves, she mounted the step and slipped into a peacock chair. "There's still a chance that he blacked out, came to with amnesia, and is off driving God only knows where. But at some point he'd stop for gas and get a look at his credit card, or the name and address on his license."

DeeAnn slipped into the adjacent chair. "What if he was robbed? If his ID was taken and he had amnesia, he wouldn't know where to go. He could have been tied up and stuck in the back seat, then driven out of the county, out of the state, and into the Midwest. He could have been dumped on a deserted road between cornfields in Wisconsin."

"In the middle of winter," Laura added dryly. "Thanks a heap, Dee." She tugged off a piece of croissant, then dropped both that piece and what was left of the whole on a dish.

"But winter or not, if he's on a road, he'll be found. He'll be *found*, Laura."

Laura nodded. She had to believe that. Even if he *did* leave on his own, which she refused to consider seriously despite Lydia's comment about the look in his eye, he would be found. Fingering the stem of a spoon, where CHERRIES was engraved in tiny block letters, she said, "In the meanwhile, we operate as usual."

"Will you be here or at home?"

"I don't know." She prodded the croissant with the spoon. "Some of each, I guess." One part of her was itching to go to the lower kitchen and pitch in, preparing food for the day's catered events. The other part was already wondering whether anyone had come to the house or called—and she hadn't been gone half an hour. "Scott's coming home. I want to spend time with him. But I want everyone here to know that the business is fine." Setting the spoon aside, she began shredding the croissant.

"People will talk," DeeAnn said softly.

"I know." She pulled one piece off, then another.

"They'll sit here, have a glass or two of wine, and speculate about Jeff over their salads."

"Uh-huh." She pulled off a third piece, then a fourth.

"If they ask me what I know, what should I say?"

Laura gave a crooked grin and pulled some more. "You could hit 'em with that story about the cornfield."

DeeAnn put her hand over Laura's to stop the shredding. "Seriously."

Taking an unsteady breath, Laura said, "Use your judgment. I trust you." And she did. They had met eight years before, when DeeAnn had answered an ad in the paper and come to work for Laura's catering business. She hadn't known much about food, but early on it had become clear that she was a whiz with people. Shapely, with a stylish mane of sandy waves and skin that looked more twenty-six than thirty-six, she was an eye-catching woman and a natural now as the restaurant's hostess. She was friendly and upbeat, good with names, faces, and favorite drinks—and not only with men. Women liked her too. Besides, she was tactful. She knew not to seat the head of the Amherst History Department anywhere near the head of the Smith History Department in the days immediately following the awarding of a hotly contested grant to one or the other. Politics was alive and well in western Massachusetts, and DeeAnn Kirkham was very much tuned in.

Yes, Laura trusted her. DeeAnn was perfectly capable of managing the restaurant in her absence.

Feeling an abrupt need to move, she said, "I think I'll run downstairs." She studied the mangled croissant. "What a mess."

"Not to worry," DeeAnn said and handed her a burgundy napkin that had been folded into a fan nearby. "Wipe up. It's buttery."

Laura wiped. Then she glanced at her watch. It was eleven-fifteen. The restaurant would open at eleven-thirty. "Are you set for lunch?" Even as they talked, two of her waiters had arrived.

"I'm set. You go on. I'll handle things here."

Laura smiled her thanks. The fact was that, aside from the need to be up and active, she wasn't in the mood to face patrons. She knew too many of them, and DeeAnn was right; they would ask questions. Well, she didn't feel like answering. Not until she had something to say.

So she went back through the kitchen and down the stairs. At the bottom, she was greeted by those of the catering crews whose job it was to prepare food. They too had seen the newspaper article. Each offered words of encouragement before returning to work.

Taking an apron from the shelf, Laura joined them, and for a short time she was able to immerse herself in cutting, slicing, stuffing, and skewering. Soft rock wafted from a radio high on the wall, blending in with occasional conversation to create a pleasant environment. As long as Laura concentrated on that environment, she was fine. Inevitably, though, her thoughts turned to Jeff. When twice running she found herself slicing air rather than mushroom, she dropped the knife and mopped her damp upper lip with the back of her hand. She took a breath, picked up the knife again, and resumed slicing, only to stop again several minutes later when her hand began to tremble.

Leaving the slicing to someone else, she turned to packing plastic containers with prepared hors d'oeuvres. After half an hour of that, with her stomach clenching and unclenching in much the way her hands would have done had they been free, she removed the apron, said her goodbyes, and returned home. Holding her breath, she opened the garage door to put the Wagoneer inside—but the Porsche wasn't there, and, once inside the house, she found it as empty as when she had left.

There were three messages on the answering machine, though.

With a rush of hope, she pushed PLAY. After a beep, the first message came on. "This is Grandy Pest Control. We'll be at your house between eight and ten next Monday morning for your quarterly spraying. If the time is bad, call us back." The man gave the number. Laura made a notation on her calendar, then bit her lip and waited.

The machine beeped again. "Hi, Mrs. Frye," a bright female voice said. "This is Diana from the boutique. The sweater you special-ordered just arrived from Wales. We'll have it here whenever you want to pick it up." Three months it had taken, just as they'd said. Laura jotted down the reminder, then held her breath for the last of the messages to replay. She let it out in a rush of frustration when Maddie's voice came on the line.

"You know how I hate these machines, Laura, but this is important. My phone has been ringing off the hook with calls about the article in the *Sun*. Was it absolutely necessary to speak with that man? The suggestion that you are distraught about your husband but perfectly capable of carrying on at work makes you sound heartless, for God's sake. Jeffrey comes across as being shamelessly materialistic, between the house and the restaurant and the car. And what's this about a condominium in Holyoke? You never told me about any condominium. Are there other things you haven't told me? I would like to know what is happening, so I can answer people in an intelligent manner. I'll be in my office between eleven-thirty and twelve-fifteen. Call me there." The machine beeped off.

Slipping onto a stool by the island, Laura put her head in her hands. Yes, the exterminator could come. Yes, she would pick up the sweater she'd ordered. No, she would not call Maddie back. She was a nervous wreck. She needed comfort. It was a sure bet Maddie wouldn't give it.

Scott arrived at six. He had flown into Bradley Field and been picked up by a girl Laura didn't know, someone named Kelly whom he said he'd dated the summer before. Clearly he had kept in touch with her, and though in other circumstances Laura would have invited her in, she was just as happy to see her little red Chevy drive off. She wanted time alone with Scott, wanted to fill him in on all that had happened, wanted to talk about Jeff.

But if she thought that Scott, by virtue of a closeness with his father, might have some idea of what had happened to him, she was wrong. Scott hadn't a clue.

"All those times you two drove into Boston to go to games at Fenway, what did you talk about?"

"Baseball," Scott answered. He was sprawled on his bed, just as he always was within minutes of arriving home from school. His excuse was that he had to put his duffel in his room, but Laura knew he never felt quite at home until he had reclaimed his turf. Banners covered the walls and trophies lined the shelves, along with other memorabilia of the high school days that had been so happy for him. He was happy in college too, Laura knew, but he wasn't the hero he had been. It didn't matter that he was six-two with broad shoulders and a day's stubble, all of which made him gorgeous in her eyes. In the eyes of the thousands of other students at Penn he was a small fish in a big pond. It had taken him most of freshman year to adjust to that, but by the time he returned home in May with his fraternity pin and a healthy grade point average, his ego had been restored.

Laura had been sure that, with Scott so grown up, Jeff would have had heart-to-heart talks with him. "Didn't your father ever talk about work?"

"No. He wanted to get away from it. That was one of the reasons he liked baseball so much. It was a nine-inning escape. When Dad dreams, I think he sees himself as a professional baseball player."

"Do you really?" Laura asked, surprised.

"Sure."

She remembered what Lydia had said about Jeff always coming in second. Christian hadn't gone into professional baseball, but he'd played varsity in college. Five years later and at a different school, Jeff hadn't made the team. He had married her instead.

"Did he ever say that?" she asked.

"No. But the way he followed the game and shouted tips to the players and criticized the manager, you could tell. But hell, Mom, we're only talkin' dreams. Everyone has dreams."

Laura knew that. Still, she wondered. Sitting sideways in the desk chair, she propped her elbows back on the desk. "Do you think he was unhappy with his work?"

"He liked it just fine."

"Enough to want you to do it?" she teased.

Scott made a face. "He knew not to ask. I was never good at math. I could never do what he does. Besides, he knows I want to be a lawyer."

That had been the plan since the summer, when he'd done an internship with the Legal Aid Society, but before that he had alternately debated being an architect, a psychiatrist, and an investment banker. "You still do?"

He nodded. "A prosecutor. Wouldn't it be wild if I tried a case against Daphne some day?"

"I don't wish that on you. She's tough."

"So they say. Then again, maybe when I'm done working for the prosecution, I'll switch over to the defense side, open my own firm, and take Daphne in when the men in her firm think she's getting too old."

"Daphne too old? Don't hold your breath. She'll outlive her partners."

"But she works too hard. She should be having more fun." When Laura eyed him warily, he said, "You're the one who's always trying to fix her up. If she was willing to look at a younger man, I'd have just the one."

"Who?"

"Alex."

"The friend you had home over Thanksgiving?"

"He thought Daphne was cool."

"Scott, Alex isn't twenty-one yet. Daphne is nearly forty."

"So are you, but the guys think you're a looker. If I were Dad, I'd get back here real quick before someone else makes a move."

Any lightness Laura may have felt in the repartee with her son faded fast. "That was inappropriate, Scott."

"I was just kidding."

"But why would you say it? Or even think it? We believe in fidelity. I don't look at other men; your father doesn't look at other women."

"He looks."

"He does not."

"Mom, I've been *with* him when he's looked. He's not blind. He sees a knockout on the street, and he looks. Do you honestly think I'm the only one waiting for the swimsuit edition every year? He's human. He's a man."

"A *faithful* man."

"But no Don Juan."

"What does *that* mean?"

"It means that he isn't what you'd call romantic."

Laura didn't take the criticism to heart. Scott was stretching, courting adulthood. Putting his father down was one way of boosting himself up. But she couldn't be still. "Sure he is."

Folding his arms behind his head, Scott asked, "What has he done in the last six months that you'd call romantic?"

"He sent me flowers last July, on my birthday."

"He made a phone call and charged it," Scott argued, "which couldn't have taken more than three minutes of his time. I don't call that romantic."

Laura remembered the tulips on Lydia's kitchen table, remembered the surprise she had felt knowing Jeff had brought them. "It's the thought that counts. And what about the ring he gave me for our anniversary?"

"You saw it first, when you and Dad were in Northeast

Harbor, and you fell in love with it. Dad thought it was too expensive."

"Unusual," Laura corrected. "He thought it was too unusual." But it was a beautiful ring, hammered gold crisscrossed by silver bands, with a pear-shaped sapphire mounted off-center. "He's used to more traditional things, but he bought it. He phoned the store after we got home and arranged for it to be sent. If that's not romantic, I don't know what is."

"It's a *thing*, Mom. What about something that involves real time and effort and ingenuity?"

"Like what?" Laura asked. She was curious to know what her nineteen-year-old son had in mind.

"Like surprising you with a trip to Paris. Or putting a single rose in a vase and bringing you breakfast in bed. Or hiring a limo and having the guy drive through the Berkshires while Dad makes love to you on the back seat."

Laura arched a brow. "I'm impressed. Where do you get your ideas, Scott?"

He had the good grace to blush, but he wasn't backing down. "Women like romantic gestures. The girls at school are as modern as they come; still, they like it when you give them a book of poems and write something sweet on the flyleaf."

"You do that?"

"Sure."

"I'm really impressed."

"Sure you are, because you're that kind of person. You were always the one who made a big thing out of Valentine's Day or birthdays or Christmas. Dad just went along."

Laura's fingernail caught on a nubby spot on the back of the chair. "Does that have anything to do with what's happening now?" she asked softly.

Scott shrugged. "No. But you idealize him, Mom, and he wasn't perfect."

"Isn't perfect. Your father isn't gone. He'll be back." She tried to sound sure of it, but the conviction wasn't there the way it had been at first. Jeff had been missing for two days. If he'd been in an accident, or suffered from amnesia, he'd already have been found. He didn't have enemies who would want him hurt, and if he had been abducted by a stranger for reasons unknown, surely the Porsche would have been seen.

So, much as she didn't want to, much as she rejected the idea when other people mentioned it, much as the thought of it hurt badly, she had to consider the very remote possibility that Jeff had knowingly driven himself out of town on Tuesday night.

"Scott?"

"Mmmm?"

"Do you think—" she paused, then forced herself on, to get the words out before she lost her nerve, "do you think that it's at all possible your father did want to leave? Do you think maybe he needed a change?"

"If he did, he was crazy."

Laura's smile was a sad one. "You're sweet."

"I mean it," Scott said earnestly.

"And I appreciate that, but I want to know what you think about your father. You're a man—maybe a young one, but still a man. You can vote. You can, God forbid, go to war. You can make love to a woman." When Scott opened his mouth to say something, she held up her hand and said gently, "It's okay. I'd be worried if you couldn't. You're old enough. If you didn't want me to know you were sexually active, you wouldn't have left that box of condoms in your underwear drawer when you went back to school last fall. You knew I'd be putting the clean things back after they were washed. But that's getting off the subject, which is your father. As a man, looking at another man, I want to know if you think he could have left here on his own."

Scott struggled with the question for a moment. "How can I look at him as just another man? He's my father, and you're my mother. Plenty of my friends' parents got divorced while I was growing up, but I never had to worry about that. You and Dad always got along. Our house was always peaceful. Nobody seemed unhappy. When I was saying those things about Dad before, it was more to make the point that, of the two of you, you're the one who's given more. You worked while Dad finished school, then you went back to work when we were little. Dad never changed diapers. You did that, and you fed us and drove us around, and at the same time you were building a career. All Dad did was go to work and come home."

Laura had never looked at their lives that way. "He was always the head of the family."

"In theory. In practice, you're the mover around here. So if you're asking me whether I think Dad walked out, the answer is no. I don't think he'd toss away this life." He paused. "You want my honest opinion?" He sent her a look of scorn far older than his years. "I don't think he has the guts."

Laura didn't get into another discussion with Scott quite like that one. His scorn had stunned her. She had no idea where it had come from, had never seen evidence of it before. But she couldn't deal with it yet. Finding Jeff was her first priority.

The waiting was abominable. She didn't go to the fund raiser for Tom Connolly, who was a gubernatorial candidate from the home district. Even if it had been appropriate, which it wasn't, she was too shaken to stand around with a drink in her hand and a smile on her face, answering questions. Everyone had seen the paper. The phone hadn't stopped ringing. Though the people who called expressed concern for her, beneath each expression of concern was curiosity. People wanted to know the whole scoop. Laura wished she had it.

Friday morning dawned without Jeff, just as Wednesday and Thursday had. Laura sent Debra to school, left Scott to handle things at home, stopped by to see how Lydia was doing, then went to the restaurant. She had always worked alongside her staff, in part for morale, in part because she liked the people, in part simply because she enjoyed the work. Looking on it as therapy, she went down and up, from one kitchen to the other, until, as had happened on Thursday, she needed to go home.

Nothing had happened there. Scott had fielded calls from Maddie, David, and Elise, a local radio talk-show host, and a handful of friends who were disturbed that the small follow-up article in the newspaper held no news of Jeff. Though Laura would have welcomed news of Jeff from any source, she was relieved that the paper's story had been so bland. Every respite was a blessing, particularly since she was beginning to fear, with each passing day, that Jeff would be gone awhile.

That fear increased as the weekend passed. There was no call from a kidnapper demanding a ransom. There was no call from a neighboring state that Jeff had been found wandering in a daze. There was no call from anywhere that a black Porsche had been abandoned, with or without a body in the trunk.

Left with so little by way of alternatives to cling to, she was beginning, more often, to think that maybe Jeff *had* left on his own. She didn't know why he would do it, or how—just disappearing into thin air that way. But it seemed the one possibility that the police kept coming back to, the one possibility that everyone else kept coming back to. She had begun to feel she was rowing against the tide.

On Monday morning, the current picked up.

seven

tAYLOR JONES LEFT THE NORTHAMPTON
Police Station after spending an hour with Dennis Melrose. The
detective had cooperated fully; in Tack's experience, local police
usually did. When the federal government entered a case, it
meant serious business.

The timing couldn't have been better for Tack. The case had
been handed to him two weeks before, after civil agents suspected
fraud and suspended their own investigation. As soon as the tax
forms and bank records that had been gathered were transferred
to his office, he began to pore through them.

When it came right down to it, the case was pretty small-
time. He had worked on ones like it before and knew just how
it would go. He would conduct his investigation, present his
evidence to a grand jury, and get an indictment. The accused
would stand trial and be found guilty. Run-of-the-mill. Interesting, given the gall of the guy; still, run-of-the-mill.

Until the guy took off.

Tack had gotten the call early Saturday morning, when one
of his men caught an item in the *Globe* and made the connection—
which was one hell of a lousy way to find out, in Tack's book.
He should have known sooner, while the trail was still hot. But
as computerized as the IRS was—it scared him sometimes to

know how much—the agency wasn't hooked into local police computers. So four days had passed since the disappearance. Tack knew if the guy had wanted to clear out his bank account, he would have already done it. He sure couldn't do it on Saturday, any more than Tack could put a freeze on the accounts before Monday. But Tack could work. He could milk his own computers of information over the weekend, so he'd be ready to move on Monday.

The diversion was welcome. He had been feeling upended since he'd walked away from Gwen, kind of empty, without direction. Once or twice he had debated going back on his word and calling her. Or hitting a singles bar. But he hated those places like hell. He hated the crowds and the phoniness. Mostly, he hated the desperation. He wasn't desperate. Just horny. And only because he'd been spoiled.

So he'd have to unspoil himself a little, he had decided, which was the whole purpose of cutting it off with her cold turkey. He would put her behind him, give his glands a breather, get busy with other things.

He considered shooting hoop. The guys were still after him to join the winter league, but he hadn't wanted to be tied down. Better still, he could call Freddy Maroni and get tickets for the real thing at the Garden. Freddy had them, right behind the bench. When Freddy had come under investigation by the IRS the year before, Tack had been assigned to the case. So Freddy had put all the tax money he had evaded paying toward buying the slickest lawyer in town, and he'd beaten the rap. But he knew Tack was watching. All Tack had to do was give him a call and Freddy would sell him—at box office price, nothing more, nothing less, as a show of how straight he was—the same tickets that he sold at a monumental markup to any schnook off the street.

Then again, Tack considered taking a leave from the office, driving north to the Laurentians, and playing ski bum for a while. He'd done it before. The resort there knew him. He had been a popular instructor with the ladies. But he'd been younger then. Thinking of ski bunnies gave him the same hollow feeling that thinking of singles bars did. He wasn't looking for a pickup. He wanted more.

The question was how to find it. In the good old days, he could have put an ad in the paper. *Government agent looking for wife. Wants five kids. Needs a brave woman. Will pay passage.* But those days were gone, and thought of putting an ad in the personals made him sick. The kind of woman he wanted wouldn't read the personals. She wouldn't trust them. And even if trust weren't an issue, she would be too proud. She would rather stay home alone reading Robert Parker, or listening to the Eagles, or stripping an old rolltop desk that she'd picked up at a flea market, than date just anyone. She was a resourceful woman.

But he was resourceful himself, which was why he was where he was. The Criminal Investigation Division was small, as was the number of cases it handled each year, but it had a glamour the other IRS divisions lacked. A position in Criminal Investigation was highly coveted. Tack had it and made the most of it. Agents worked under him and were glad to do it.

So he'd been given the Frye case, and the disappearance of its lead player couldn't have suited his needs better. The investigation would take awhile, with most of that time spent in and around Hampshire County. Coming off the highway, he'd seen a Hilton. That wouldn't be a bad place to stay. Melrose had already offered him an office to use. He could keep in touch with Boston by phone, could go back there one day a week, maybe two, but for the rest of the time he would be out of sight and sound of anything that would remind him of Gwen.

He didn't love her. They had never had much to say to each other of a substantial nature. He was trying to enforce the law while she took advantage of every tax loophole around, and though that was legal, it stuck in his craw. So they couldn't talk about his work, and they couldn't talk about her money, and they didn't like each other's friends or movie preferences or favorite restaurants. But they did have good sex. He acknowledged that, again, as he followed Melrose's unmarked car through the center of Northampton.

When Melrose pulled over, he did the same, then rolled down his window when the detective walked back and hitched his chin toward a nearby building. "Frye's office is in there. His firm takes up the whole second floor." He peered in at Tack. "You say you don't have anything on anyone but Frye?"

"Not yet. But we're looking."

While Melrose returned to his car, Tack studied the building. It was another of the old buff-colored stone ones that lined the main drag. This one stood alone and had arches over the windows. It might have looked like a church if it had had a steeple, but there were just those arches. Tack liked the style.

Driving on, he decided he liked the town. Even in December, when the trees were bare and things should have felt barren, there was a depth to the place. Where there were shops and restaurants, there were posters advertising drama productions or concerts. There was a theater and an art center, then street after street of houses that looked quaint and cozy and academic.

He had a thing for academia. In his next life, he planned to be an economics professor, well published and revered, pursued by presidents at home and abroad. Until then, he was satisfied to live in an apartment halfway between Harvard and MIT, in the no-man's-land that was still vaguely affordable, but he wasn't so far from the Square that he couldn't take advantage of street shows, bookstores, and the ivory tower ambiance that spoke of intellectual superiority.

Northampton, he decided, was a cleaned-up, spread-out version of Cambridge—but with Smithies instead of Cliffies. He'd passed a few cute girls. If any of their professors were in their early thirties, pretty and classy and looking for a tall, suave, handsome kind of guy, he'd be in luck.

He drove on, past side streets that branched less frequently from the main. He saw an elementary school, a modern church, a park that still had a few scattered patches of snow. He saw lots of trees, some stark skeletons of winter, others evergreen. Melrose made a right, and he followed. They drove straight for a while, then Melrose made a left. Before long, they turned onto a street that was more elegant than the rest. When Melrose pulled up in front of a large brick Tudor, Tack did the same, parked the car, and climbed out.

Not bad, he thought, looking at the house. Not bad at all. Actually in good taste, for someone who had probably bilked the government of half a million bucks. He had expected something more showy.

Side by side with the detective, he went up the walk and rang the bell. "Think she'll be home?"

Melrose shrugged. "She goes to the restaurant a lot, but the restaurant's closed on Mondays. She's been staying pretty close to the phone. She should be around."

"You really don't think she knows where he is?"

"I'd put money on it. She's a together lady who's coming apart a little because she's worried sick he's been killed."

"And you don't think she knows of any fraud?"

Melrose shook his head. "Nope."

Rocking back on his heels, Tack blew out a breath, looked at the door, and muttered, "She ain't gonna like what I gotta say."

"Nope," Melrose said.

Then the door opened, and Tack immediately understood why Melrose had been so sure. Assuming that the woman before him was Laura, she was as unnerved, as vulnerable, as innocent-looking as could be—which didn't mean Tack wasn't wary. To the contrary. He was from the big city. He knew looks could deceive, particularly where stolen money was concerned.

"Yes, Detective Melrose?" Sounding frightened and expectant at the same time, she flicked an unsure glance at Tack.

"Uh, Mrs. Frye, this is Taylor Jones. He's an agent with the government. He'd like to talk with you. Can we come in?"

"A government agent?"

Tack held his ID for her to see. "I'm with the IRS, Criminal Investigation Division, out of the Boston District Office. I'd like to ask you some questions about your husband."

"My husband—uh, my husband isn't here. The IRS? *Criminal* Investigation Division?"

"That's right, ma'am."

She looked at Melrose, then back at Tack, either truly bewildered or putting on one hell of an act. Tack had seen that before too. In ten years with the service, he had seen most everything. Bewilderment, confusion, shock—they could come as easily from being caught as from being startled by something new.

"What is this about?" she asked, then turned to Melrose. "Have you learned something about Jeffrey?"

"Not about where he is," Melrose answered. "Just about why he might have gone."

That seemed to frighten Laura more. Her eyes were wider when she looked back at Tack. He could see her mind working, though he could only guess at its direction. "Why did he go?" she asked point-blank.

He glanced beyond her. He wanted to get a look inside the house. "May we come in? It's pretty cold out here."

As though she hadn't realized, she moved quickly aside. "Of course. I'm sorry. Please do."

Tack let Melrose go first, since he'd been there before. Leaving their coats in the foyer, they followed her into the living room. She gestured toward the sofa. "Sit down, please, and tell me what this is about." Rather than sitting, herself, she stood behind an upholstered chair, holding its back hard enough for her fingers to turn white. "Detective Melrose?" she prompted, but Melrose deferred to Tack.

He watched her closely. First reactions could say a lot. "For the past few months, your husband has been the subject of an investigation by the IRS—"

"An investigation?" she cut in. "For what?"

"Tax fraud."

She stared at him, blinked, then moved her head forward, as though she hadn't heard him right. "Excuse me?"

"Tax fraud," he repeated, but he was beginning to think she was legitimately shocked, so he explained. "The investigation started with a random check on a 1040 filed from a post office box here in town. The taxpayer didn't match the profile we have for the income bracket he claimed to be in, so the computer spit out the form for us to take a look. Even though W-2s were submitted to the IRS for that taxpayer, he's been dead for three years."

She frowned. "But what does a tax form from a post office box have to do with my husband?"

"We ran that particular post office box through the computer and found ten other forms listing the same box. Those ten other taxpayers are also dead."

"But what does this have to do with Jeffrey?"

"The post office box was rented in his name."

She flinched. Composing herself, she patted the air with a shaky hand. "Fine. Okay. But that doesn't mean he had anything to do with fraud. Someone else could have rented the box in his name. Or someone else could have fed him information to file. He doesn't run a check on every client who walks into his office. If someone came in claiming to be someone else, he wouldn't have any way of knowing if that someone else was dead."

"Eleven times? Maybe more, if our suspicions pan out. We think he may have used more than one post office box. I have a team working on it now."

"More than one box? What makes you think that?" She sounded more indulgent than disbelieving now, as though she found the whole theory too bizarre to give credence to it.

But Tack wasn't a madman. He had the makings of a solid case. "The refund checks. Running anywhere from eight hundred to twelve hundred, deposited into your account during the months of February, March, April, and May. And that was only for this year. We have no idea what was done in the years before that."

"My account." Not a question but a statement. "You've been examining my account."

"We have that right."

"Without telling me?"

"Without telling you or obtaining a warrant. It's perfectly legal, well within our power. My guess is that the bank notified your husband that we were looking around, and he got real nervous and—" he gestured, "—took off."

Laura stared at him in utter disbelief. Then she looked down and pressed her fingers to her forehead, looked up again, and pressed her fingers to her mouth. Tack noticed she wasn't wearing lipstick, though otherwise she was lightly made up. She had on jeans and a sweater and looked younger than the thirty-eight his file told him she was. She certainly didn't look old enough to have a son in college.

In the next minute, she didn't look old enough to own a restaurant or a catering service or be married to a guy who had committed multiple counts of tax fraud. She looked little more than twenty, totally confused and helpless, and though Tack told himself that could be part of the act too, he was having trouble believing it.

She swallowed. She looked quickly from him to Melrose and back, as if she hoped to see one of them smile and say it was all a gag. Fingers splayed, she rubbed her hands together. "Uh, I think I should call someone," she said in an unsteady voice. Her eyes sought Melrose's. "I can do that, can't I?"

"Sure thing," Melrose said in the kind of gentle voice Tack might have used if he hadn't been in the position he was. Melrose was the good guy, he was the bad guy. That was fine for now.

Tack watched her leave the room, only then realizing that she was barefooted, but even barefooted she had style. So did her home. Pushing up from the sofa, he wandered around. Furniture, art, oriental rugs—nothing was cheap, but nothing was lavish or gaudy either. The government should have decorated *his* office so nicely.

He turned a small crystal swan in his hand. "Think she'll take off through the back door?"

"No," Melrose said from the sofa.

"You're so sure."

"You're so cynical."

Tack sniffed in a breath. "That's my job. Where I work, a person is guilty until proven innocent."

"Not where I work," Melrose shot back without losing a beat. "We get to know people around here. Maybe not all of them, and maybe not well, especially since so many of the academics are just passing through. But people like Laura Frye give this town a good name."

"Her husband sure as hell won't."

"He's an exception. We don't get many like him."

Tack put the swan down. "But you don't think she's involved."

"No."

"Gut instinct?"

"That, and lack of any evidence to the contrary."

"Guilty until proven innocent," Tack reminded him, then caught sight of Laura. She was walking steadily, holding her head up, but she looked pale. "Was that a lawyer you called?" he asked.

"Yes. She's on her way over. She suggested I not say anything more until she arrives." She went to the chair she'd been standing behind and sat this time, folding her legs under her.

Tack returned to the sofa. "Do you think you'll need a lawyer?"

"She's also a friend."

Melrose sat forward, dangling his hands between his knees. "I'm surprised you're alone here now, Mrs. Frye. The driveway was pretty crowded all weekend."

"People dropped in. Friends. Business associates. My mother."

Tack heard the faint pause before the last, but before he could ask its cause, she went on.

"My son was in from college. He went back this morning. My daughter's in school, the restaurant's closed, and everyone else has gone back to work. Jeff's been gone for six days, six long days, without any sign he'll be back. At some point life has to return to normal." She shot a stricken look at the floor before raising her eyes to Tack's. "With or without my lawyer, I want you to know that I find what you're saying really hard to swallow. Jeff worked hard. He built his way up from nothing and earned everything he had. There's no reason why he would do what you suggest."

Tack sent a meaningful glance around the room.

Laura was fast to argue. "We bought this house with money that he earned."

"Did you buy the building your restaurant is in that way?"

"Both this house and that building are mortgaged."

Tack knew all about that. Even before Frye's disappearance, the bank had provided all sorts of nifty information. "So there are mortgage payments, rent for your husband's firm's office and salary to secretaries and associates, loan payments for the restaurant's remodeling, tuition to an Ivy League school, plus living expenses. That's a pretty big nut to crack every month, Mrs. Frye. And that's not counting the Porsche. Or your Wagoneer. Or the operating expenses for your restaurant."

"The restaurant pays for itself."

"With enough profit to help pay for the rest?"

"No. Not yet. In another two or three years, maybe. For now my husband's income pays for the rest."

Tack had dealt with lots of accountants. Those working out of big firms in Boston, with clients who were high-powered people and corporations, could rake it in. Compared to them, Jeffrey Frye was small potatoes. "How much do you think he earns?"

She seemed surprised by the question. "Jeffrey?" She thought about it. "One fifty, maybe two hundred thousand a year. I don't know for sure."

It was Tack's turn to be surprised. "You don't know?"

"Should I?"

"He's your husband."

"But he takes care of everything financial."

"Even to do with your business?"

"No, I do that, but he does the rest. It's always been that way."

Tack knew that many women deferred to their husbands on money matters. But Laura Frye was successful herself, and to be that she had to be bright. Right then, she didn't sound it. "For the record," he drawled, "on your husband's last 1040 he reported an income of ninety thousand dollars."

"Ninety," she echoed. After thinking about that for a minute, she withdrew deeper into her chair. She looked at the floor, frowned, looked at the knotted hands in her lap. She took a breath to speak and changed her mind, then changed it again. "It can't be, this business of tax fraud. It just can't be."

Tack almost felt sorry for her. "The investigation is just starting. We have a whole lot more to wade through before we know the extent of it."

She made a small sound and put a hand to her mouth in a belated attempt to hold it in.

"Are you all right, Mrs. Frye?" Melrose asked.

She held up a hand, but it shook. "Fine. I'm fine, detective. This just doesn't—it can't be—I don't understand." The hand went back to her mouth. In the next instant, the doorbell rang. Before its peal had died, she was on her feet. "That'll be Daphne." She half ran into the hall.

"Who's Daphne?" Tack asked Melrose.

"Daphne Phillips. She's a local lawyer and one tough broad. She's been here a lot since Frye disappeared. She's a close friend."

"Of Frye or his wife?"

"Both."

"But tough?"

"You bet."

"Hell, I hate that type," Tack muttered, but before he could add something choice about ball-busters, Laura returned with her friend in tow. Actually, Daphne Phillips wasn't in tow. She was walking beside Laura, looking like her in so many ways that Tack could imagine they were either related or had been friends forever. The details were different—Daphne was taller, her hair was lighter and pulled into a knot, she wore a silk dress and heels, she had lighter eyes and lighter skin—but they held themselves with the same kind of quiet pride, and they were both looking disturbed.

"Daph, this is—" Laura stopped, drawing a blank on his name.

"Taylor Jones," he filled in, rising, and offered his hand. Her clasp was strong, not strangling but firm. "I'm with the Criminal Investigation Division of the IRS."

"So Laura told me," Daphne said. Retrieving her hand, she turned on Melrose. "How long have you known about this, Dennis?"

"About two hours," he said and sat back on the sofa. Tack had the distinct feeling he wasn't saying another word, which put the burden of explanation smack on his own shoulders. That was fine. He wasn't intimidated by a lady lawyer. He had total faith in who he was and what he was doing.

"I drove out from Boston this morning," he said. "Detective Melrose didn't know I was coming until I showed up at his office. We didn't find out Mr. Frye was missing until Saturday morning."

Daphne looked torn, as though she wanted to say something but couldn't. Disbelief seemed to get the best of her. "Tax fraud?"

"That's what the computer says."

"Computers are machines. What do you say?"

"Tax fraud."

She made a face. "Jeff Frye?"

"That's right."

Laura touched her arm. "There has to be some mistake. Jeff wouldn't do anything like that. He doesn't have a mean bone in his body—or a dishonest one."

"I take it this is still speculation," Daphne said to Tack. "You haven't been to a grand jury yet."

"No. It'll be awhile until I have all the evidence together. Normally I'd have done that from Boston, but Frye's disappearance changes things. If I can speed things up by working here, I can get an indictment, and once I do that I can get the FBI in on the search for him. As far as I'm concerned, though, as of right now he's a fugitive from the law."

Laura began to tremble visibly. Without a word, she moved back to the chair and sat down. Daphne shot her a worried look.

"I'm okay," Laura assured her, but her voice was small.

Daphne turned to Tack. "What is it you want from Mrs. Frye?"

"Information on her husband. Where he might be. What he might be doing. I'm not asking for incriminating evidence, just something to help us find him."

"He's innocent of what you say," Laura put in.

"If we find him, he can tell us that."

Daphne went to Laura, knelt by her chair with her back to

the men and said softly, "You don't have to talk with him. This isn't a deposition. If his questions will be upsetting—"

"This whole *mess* is upsetting," Laura cried. "What's a little more?"

"You could wait for another time."

"But maybe he can help find Jeff."

"I can," Tack said. Seeing the look of helpless desperation on Laura's face, he knew she wasn't covering anything up. She was an innocent victim whose neat little life had been turned upside down. Finding her husband was in her best interest. Tack didn't want her lawyer friend to make things worse by prolonging the ordeal. "If we can locate your husband, we'll be able to straighten things out. But we can't do that as long as he's on the run."

"Maybe he's not on the run," Laura pleaded. "Maybe whoever committed your fraud did something to him so he'd *look* guilty."

"Did something?"

"Had him kidnapped. Or killed."

"Maybe," Tack said. She was desperate for an explanation that would find her husband innocent, and while he didn't think for a minute that Jeff Frye was innocent, if dangling that bit of hope before her would clinch her cooperation, he'd do the dangling. He could be accommodating that way, just as long as he got his conviction in the end.

"Uh, excuse me, could you fellows wait up a minute?"

From halfway down the walk, Tack turned to see Daphne trotting up. Other than one or two wisps of hair that blew in the light breeze, she looked as neat as she had throughout the interview with Laura. That interview had ended several minutes earlier, with Tack nearly as much in the dark about Jeffrey Frye's whereabouts as when he arrived. But Daphne had been okay. Aside from the occasional warning when she felt his questions were coming too fast or too strong, she had kept out of the way. He wondered what she wanted now.

"I have a favor to ask," she said and went on without pause. "When the story of Jeff's disappearance hit the papers last week, it was devastating for Laura. The media are already hounding her. If word of what you've told us leaks out, it'll be worse. Is there any way to keep a lid on things?"

Keeping a lid on things was the last thing Tack wanted. In his experience, breaks in cases came about through tips, anonymous or otherwise. The more publicity there was about Jeffrey Frye, the greater the chance of someone coming forward. But Tack couldn't say that in as many words to Daphne. He didn't want to antagonize her. He might need her help.

So, scratching his head, he said, "I won't be making any public announcements, but I don't really know how things work in this town. Detective Melrose would know more about that."

She caught something in his tone. He could tell by the look she gave him, a look that wasn't exactly dirty but wasn't appreciative, either. Turning to Melrose, she said, "Could you try, Dennis? If Duggan O'Neil gets wind of this, we won't hear the end of it. Jeff will be tried and convicted on page one. You can forget about his getting any kind of a fair trial after that."

"The trial would be in Springfield," Tack couldn't resist pointing out. "That's where the nearest federal courthouse is."

"I know that," Daphne said patiently, and again turned to Melrose. "Word spreads like wildfire. You know how awful it can be."

"Your friend should have thought of that when he was doing the dirty deed," Tack said, then added, "Deeds, plural."

"Alleged deeds," Daphne corrected. "Let's not forget the assumption of innocence here."

Tack shook his head. "Doesn't fly in my department. When it comes to tax fraud, a person's guilty until proven innocent."

"That's unconstitutional," she argued.

He shrugged.

Starting to shake from the cold, she folded her arms under her breasts and said, "Do what you can, Dennis, okay?" Without sparing a glance at Tack, she turned and trotted back to the house.

"Great pair of legs," Tack remarked. Her skirt barely hit her knees, and the legs in question were long and lithe.

"Cool it, bud. She's older than you."

"Really?" He wouldn't have guessed it. "How old?"

"Forty."

That surprised him. He would have given her thirty-four, maybe thirty-five. But forty? That ruled out five kids. Forget Daphne Phillips.

Not that he'd been considering her anyway. With her hair pulled back and her dress just so, she was too cool. Which was a shame. Whispers of her perfume caught in the air, as enticing as they were fleeting. And she really did have a great pair of legs.

Tuesday morning dawned clear and cold, the kind of December day when people take deep, bracing breaths, think about the holiday season, and smile. Laura took a deep, bracing breath when she went out for the paper, but the last thing on her mind when she opened it was the holiday season, and when she saw what was on the front page under Duggan O'Neil's byline, she couldn't possibly have smiled.

MISSING CPA UNDER INVESTIGATION FOR TAX FRAUD, the headline stated. Heart pounding, she read on.

Jeffrey Frye, whose disappearance last week mystified family and friends, has been named as the subject of an intense investigation into tax fraud currently being conducted by the Internal Revenue Service. The investigation is being led by Taylor Jones, Special

Agent with the Criminal Investigation Division of the IRS. Jones arrived in Northampton Monday morning to coordinate his efforts with the Northampton Police Department.

When questioned by the *Sun*, Jones acknowledged that the investigation has been going on for some time but that Frye's disappearance throws a new light on things. "We certainly have to consider the possibility that Mr. Frye left town to escape apprehension by the authorities."

To date, Frye has eluded the police. His wife, Laura Frye, owner of Cherries, claims to have no knowledge of his whereabouts. She was equally mum when questioned about the charges being leveled against her husband by the government. Though Jones refused to elaborate on those charges, the *Sun* has learned that many hundreds of thousands of dollars may be involved, over a period of up to ten years.

A Northampton native, Frye has been living in the exclusive Child's Park area for the last seven years. He is one of the founding partners of Farro and Frye, a local accounting firm. Originally located on Route 9 near the Hadley line, Farro and Frye moved into spacious new quarters on Pleasant Street in 1985. In 1987, Frye bought the old Wentworth Building on Main Street. It was gutted and outfitted to house the kitchen for his wife's catering service, Cherries. Her restaurant opened there after an elaborate renovation in 1988.

According to sources, Frye prided himself on being invited to important social, political, and cultural events in the area. He contributed heavily to Stanton Ferry's unsuccessful bid for a seat in the U.S. House of Representatives last year, and was known to be a supporter of gubernatorial candidate Tom Connolly. Friends report Frye moving into the fast lane in recent years. He reportedly took regular vacations to the Caribbean, was in tight with the yachting crowd out of Newport, and hosted gala parties at his wife's restaurant. He is best known to some for driving around town in his shiny black Porsche.

The Porsche has disappeared, along with Frye. Law enforcement agencies across the country have been put on the alert for both the car and the man. Agent Jones has asked that anyone with information on Frye's whereabouts contact him through the Northampton Police Department.

eight

LAURA WAS AT THE ISLAND, STARING IN horror at the newspaper, when Debra entered the kitchen that morning. She knew she probably looked a sight—pale, after a night with only sporadic sleep, and stricken—but she couldn't help it. She was appalled by the article before her.

"Mom?"

She didn't answer; she didn't know what to say, how to break the news. Debra had gone to the Stones' concert the night before, but Laura knew whatever euphoria remained was about to die an instant death. Within seconds Debra was by her side, looking down at the headline that, even on the fifth reading, cut Laura to the quick. MISSING CPA UNDER INVESTIGATION FOR TAX FRAUD. And there, below the headline, the very first words of the very first paragraph, clear as day and impossible to miss, was Jeff's name.

Debra's jaw dropped. "Tax fraud? *Tax* fraud? What are they talking about?" She leaned closer to Laura.

"The paper says that your father is under investigation for tax fraud."

"Dad?"

Laura nodded.

"That's the most absurd thing I've ever heard. Dad wouldn't

do anything like that." Pulling the paper close, she read past the headline. Laura could feel the anger vibrating from her, growing with each paragraph until she finally exploded. "That's bullshit!" She slapped the paper with her hand. "Total bullshit! They make it sound like Dad is a jet-setter or something, but he isn't at all. We go to the Caribbean once a year, and that's the only vacation we take. He went to *one* yacht race in Newport, and only because he was invited by a client whose cousin was racing. And the gala party at the restaurant was a benefit for AIDS research."

"I couldn't have put it better," Laura remarked.

Debra was too angry to appreciate the compliment. "What they're saying is totally untrue. How can they *do* that, Mom?"

"It's called freedom of speech," Laura said, in a voice that shook with her own anger. "The same words put in different contexts can have different meanings, depending on what the writer wants to convey."

"But that's not fair! Can't you stop him?"

Laura shook her head. "He can print whatever he wants."

"But Dad *didn't* commit tax fraud."

"That was what I told the IRS agent."

"What IRS agent?"

"The one who stopped by yesterday."

"Mom!" Debra cried, and Laura knew that the complaint was aimed at her this time. "Why didn't you tell me?"

"I didn't want to upset you. I keep thinking, expecting, *hoping* that this will all be straightened out. We thought—Daphne and I—that we could keep this latest thing out of the paper. Apparently Duggan O'Neil couldn't resist."

"I'm not a child. You should have told me."

"Maybe," Laura conceded.

The concession seemed to take the wind from Debra's sails. Less angrily, she asked, "What did the IRS agent say when you talked?"

Laura folded the paper to put the offending article out of

sight. It was like a wound, less hurtful when covered. "He said the government has incriminating documents. Until your father is found, he can't defend himself."

"Why isn't he here?" Debra cried, angry now at Jeff. "If he was here, he'd tell them how wrong they are. What's tax fraud, anyway? What do they say he did?"

"They say he filed tax forms in the names of dead people and pocketed the refund checks himself."

"That's impossible."

"No. It can be done."

"I mean, it's impossible to think that Dad did it. He's so straight. Remember the big deal he made about your filing W-2s for me when I worked for Cherries last summer? God forbid someone should think we weren't going to pay taxes on what I earned. So they think he stole tax refunds from dead people? Why on earth would he do that? We have plenty of money."

Laura shot her a dry look. "That's a switch. You're the one who's always saying we don't have enough."

"Because *you* keep saying I can't have a car. Scott got a car when he turned sixteen."

"Scott was on the school newspaper and in the drama club and the debating society. He had something going on at school nearly every night."

"So do I."

"At school?"

Debra didn't answer, but before Laura could wonder about her silence, it ended on a pleading note. "I can't go to school, Mom. Not today. Not after this. Last week was bad enough. The kids were talking behind my back."

"How do you know?"

"I know. Kids always talk behind other kids' backs. When Sara Kaine's parents split, they talked about the man Sara's father found in bed with her mother. When Matt Remson's brother died, they talked about the beer he and his friend drank before they drove off in their car. *This* will keep them talking for weeks. It's all so absurd! My family is the most normal of any of the families I know. None of this makes any sense." As though she had exhausted her supply of indignation, she said, more timidly, "What are we supposed to do?"

Laura pushed a hand through her hair. "First we call Daphne to see what she can do about getting a retraction."

"Do you think she can?"

"She's persuasive. She'll try."

"And if nothing comes of it?"

"We'll have to weather the storm as best we can."

"Are you going to call Scott?"

"Later. He'll be just as angry as you are."

"What about Nana Lydia? She'll be sick."

Laura knew she would be. "I'll go there in a little while." She paused. "Want to come?" She almost smiled at the way Debra's eyes lit up.

"And skip school?"

"Just for today. She loves having you around. If you wouldn't mind going."

"Mind? I *love* Nana Lydia. She's the kindest, gentlest person on earth. She loves it when I call, and listens when I talk, and she remembers every word I say."

"You'd be a comfort to her," Laura said. "If I could leave you with her while I go talk with Gram, that would be one load off my mind."

"Go talk with Gram?" Debra echoed in a pitying way.

"I'd better. If she hasn't seen the paper yet, she will soon, and if she doesn't, someone is sure to call her. She'll be furious."

"Furious at you, Dad, or the paper?"

"Either, both, all three. I'm not sure she'll distinguish between them."

"Gram can be such a pill."

Laura grunted her agreement.

Debra frowned. In a small voice, she said, "How much longer

do you think Dad will be gone?"

Laura tried to sound optimistic. "I don't know."

"What if he's gone awhile? What if this not knowing goes on
for weeks and months and years? We were talking about MIAs
in school last week. Do you know that some families are still
waiting for word twenty years after the fact? Do you know the
agony they must go through day after day after day?"

Laura nodded slowly. "I can begin to imagine it."

But Debra shook her head. "Not me. I can't, and I don't
want to. This is not Vietnam. This is the United States, and
someone out there has to know what happened to Dad. People
don't just vanish. He has to be somewhere."

"I'm sure he is," Laura told herself aloud, "I'm sure he is."

"Tax fraud?" Lydia asked. She was still in bed, which boded
ill. Laura knew it wouldn't be one of Lydia's better days—and
that was before she had broken the news. "Jeffrey?"

Laura sat on the side of the bed, feeling her share of the
heartache. "That's what they say."

Lydia was quiet, frowning at the chenille spread that lay folded
over her feet.

"They haven't proved anything," Laura offered. "It's still not
much more than speculation."

Lydia regarded her sadly. "We have to consider the source
of the speculation. Special agents of the government are usually
pretty accurate."

"Not always," Debra put in from the other side of the bed.
"They can be wrong."

Lydia tried to smile for Debra, but Laura could see that the
smile came hard. She wished she could cheer both grandmother
and granddaughter, but the situation was discouraging. "The
article in the paper wasn't very generous. Duggan O'Neil has
jumped in with both feet, and I'm sure Gary Holmes is loving
it. I think we have to be prepared for more of the same."

Lydia sighed. "Ah, yes. From Gary Holmes, definitely."

"Do you know him?" Debra asked.

"A long time ago I did. He was a hard man then. A leopard doesn't change its spots."

"The key," Laura went on, "is finding Jeff. He can't defend himself until then. They keep asking me where he might be, and I've racked my brain, but I can't come up with one place more than any other for them to look. Can you?"

Lydia lifted a frail shoulder in a helpless little gesture. "I've racked my own brain, but I'm at a loss. If Jeffrey had dreams when he was little, he didn't share them. Did he ever talk to you about retiring somewhere?"

Laura shook her head. "We've been so busy reaching our prime we haven't begun to think of retirement. I told them about the islands. He loved those when we went."

"No, he didn't," Debra said. "He complained about the heat. And the food. And the pace. Everything was so *slow*. He got antsy. Don't you remember?"

"I'm sure it won't do the government any harm to check them out," Lydia said. "Debra, sweetheart, would you be an angel and fix me a cup of tea? You make it just the way I like it."

Debra jumped up. "With a muffin. Mom brought some cherry-raisin ones, and if you don't eat them, she'll force them back on me. She hasn't stopped cooking since Dad left. There's so much food at home!"

"With a muffin," Lydia agreed affectionately. The minute Debra was through the door, though, she sobered and reached for Laura's hand. "Does any of this make sense to you?"

Laura gave way to bewilderment. "None at all."

"Did you have any inkling that he was unhappy?"

"None. Jeff never got philosophical about things. He didn't talk about vague feelings and thoughts. He just wasn't like that."

"No," Lydia mused. "He wasn't with me, either. There was always a part of him he kept to himself, and because he was so good I never pushed him. I figured the proof of the pudding was in the eating, and Jeffrey was a dream to raise. Christian caused havoc, but Jeffrey never gave me a moment's trouble. Still, I never quite knew what he was thinking." She frowned. "Maybe I should have asked more. Maybe I should have been more insistent. Maybe I should have *taught* him to share his thoughts."

Sensing an engulfing grief in the woman, Laura gave her hand a gentle shake. "You're letting yourself believe that he's done something wrong. Don't do that, Lydia."

But Lydia focused her blue eyes on Laura and said, "I have to be realistic. Maybe it's time you were too. You have a wonderfully rosy view of the world, and it's worked perfectly well until now. But you have to take off those rose-colored glasses. The fact is that Jeffrey has disappeared at the very same time that he's under investigation for a crime. Doesn't that seem suspicious to you?"

Laura wanted to argue. For a minute she said nothing. Then, with a frustrated frown, she nodded. "But it doesn't mean he's guilty. It could be that he simply got scared and didn't know what else to do but run. And it could still be that someone else, someone responsible for the crime, is also responsible for his disappearance."

Lydia shivered. "An even more frightening thought. If only we knew more about what went through his mind. Did he like the islands or didn't he? Was he happy with his work or wasn't he? I did ask him those things, and he always said yes, but he never elaborated, so I let it go. I should have pushed."

This time Laura squeezed her hand. "I didn't push either, but how can you push a person Jeff's age? He's not twelve or thirteen or fifteen. Scott's just nineteen, and already there are things I can't push with him any more. You can't force a person to pour out his heart to you."

"No. Jeffrey wasn't the pouring-out kind."

"No."

"And if he didn't pour his heart out to either of *us*, he wouldn't have poured his heart out to anyone else."

"My mother would call his inability to communicate an inborn personality trait."

"Personality traits can be modified. I let him down."

"You didn't," Laura insisted. In the kitchen, the teakettle whistled. Her voice cut through it, steering the conversation in a slightly different direction. "They keep asking me about Christian. They keep suggesting that, as Jeff's only sibling, he might know something."

Lydia looked doubtful.

"When we invited him for Thanksgiving," Laura went on, "he said he was going to be in Australia. The IRS man thought that would be a great place for Jeff to hide."

"Have they found evidence that he flew there?"

"No. But they're still looking."

"Fine," Lydia said. "Let them look. It wouldn't bother me to know he was with Christian. Christian has his faults, but he's strong. Jeffrey could do worse."

Laura wasn't so sure. There were hard feelings between the two men, some of which, she feared, had to do with her. But if Lydia took comfort from the thought, that was fine. Lord knew the poor woman had little else to take comfort from.

An hour later, Laura was at the restaurant nursing a cup of coffee when her mother swept through the door. At sixty-seven, Maddy McVey was still an attractive woman. Taller than Laura by an inch, she was trimly built. Her skirt, blouse, and single strand of pearls were tasteful, if conservative, and her short silver hair was brushed neatly back from her face. She might have caught more eyes if her expression weren't always so stern. It seemed to Laura that a half-scowl had settled permanently over her features.

She was still winding through the tables toward Laura's alcove when, in a booming voice, she said, "I know why you dragged me down here, rather than meeting me at the house, Laura. This is your turf, your pride and joy, and that peacock chair is your fortress. But if you think I'll be intimidated, you think wrong. I'd like some explanations, and I'd like them now."

No matter how conscientiously Laura steeled herself against Maddie, it was never enough. With a sigh, she said, "Actually, I thought the restaurant would be cheerier than the house. Don't you think so?"

Having reached the table, Maddie stood with her purse in her right hand and her left on a chair. "Compared to some of the other restaurants in this town, this one is cheery enough. Those others are old and dark, which isn't to say they don't have charm and a certain ambiance. They remind me of the coffeehouses of my day, where we used to sit talking for hours. But my peer group is gone now, scattered here and abroad, some even dead, and the only thing the darkness does for me is make it harder to read the menu."

"It's plenty light here," Laura coaxed. "You won't have any trouble reading my menu. Would you like something to eat?"

"Do you honestly think I can eat at a time like this?" Maddie demanded. Laura was about tell her that was fine, she didn't have to eat, it would save Jonah some work, when Maddie said, "I will have some of that coffee, though. You have an interesting hazelnut blend."

It was as close to a compliment as she would come, Laura knew. Rather than push for anything else, Laura reached for the silver coffeepot and poured her a cup. By the time she set the pot down again, Maddie had put her coat aside and taken a seat.

"That was a fascinating article in the paper," she declared. She took a sip of the coffee. "Quite an allegation against a man who, according to the people closest to him, is totally honest and uncorruptible."

Laura was quiet. She studied her coffee cup, slowly raised it, took a sip.

"What happened?" Maddie asked.

Without looking up, Laura said, "I don't know."

"Do you believe what the paper is saying?"

"I don't want to."

"But *do* you?"

At Lydia's, optimism was the prime objective. Laura didn't want Lydia's spirits to fall. That wasn't a consideration where Maddie was concerned. Pride was. As disillusioned as Laura might be with Jeff, she wanted to defend him against Maddie's attack. "I don't know."

"You either believe it or you don't, Laura."

"No," Laura said, slowly raising her eyes, "there's a middle ground. I don't believe Jeff did what they say, but I do believe they have some sort of evidence against him."

"Then he's guilty."

"I don't know."

"If they have proof—"

"They need more. Before we condemn him, let's give him the benefit of the doubt."

Maddie's eyes bore into hers, suggesting the indignation that her controlled voice downplayed. "That's a difficult thing to do, given the turmoil he's caused in our lives. You do know the whole town is talking about this."

"Yes. I supposed they would."

"Doesn't that bother you?"

"Of course it does. But I can't control it. If people want to talk, they'll talk."

"If your husband was home where he should be, they wouldn't have anything to talk about—unless what the paper says is true, in which case if he were here he'd be under arrest."

"Mother, there hasn't been any indictment. The only reason all this has come out now is because he disappeared. He hasn't been charged with a thing."

"Yet."

"Do *you* believe it's true?" Laura shot back.

"Frankly, I don't know Jeff well enough to begin to answer that question," Maddie said with an arrogant flourish. "He may have been my son-in-law for twenty years, but we've never been close. We never had a thing in common. We never discussed

anything of significance. He didn't understand my work any more
than I understood his. He was there at your house, he was
cordial, he seemed devoted to you and the children. Beyond
that . . ." Her voice trailed off as she gave an eloquent shrug.
"But you're his wife, Laura. You're the one who's lived with
him all these years. You're the one who's shared a bed with him
and borne his children. If anyone knows what he's done, you
should."

Laura scowled. "Well, I don't."

"Don't you two talk?"

"Of course we talk."

"About substantial things?"

"Yes, about substantial things."

Maddie sat back in her chair and gave Laura a look. "My,
you're defensive. That's just the way you sounded when you told
me you were doing well at Smith. It wasn't until later that I
learned you were doing well indeed—in the one and only class
you bothered to attend. So, fine. You and Jeff didn't deal with
some of the deeper issues you should have. Still, I wouldn't have
taken you for a fool. Didn't you see any of this coming?"

"I saw nothing."

"Where were you? What were you doing?"

"I was working, raising the kids, starting a business."

"In hindsight, was that wise?"

"It was what Jeff and I both wanted."

"Apparently he didn't."

Laura bristled. "Mother, you have no evidence—"

"Did he *never* say anything to suggest that he was into something like this?"

"If he'd done that," Laura cried, able to hold her temper
only so long, "I wouldn't be so mystified!"

"Keep your voice down," Maddie scolded. "Your whole
kitchen staff doesn't have to hear you."

"My whole kitchen staff knows what's going on. I've been
honest with them."

"The question is whether your husband has been honest with you. If he lied about this, God only knows what other things he lied about."

Laura put a hand to her head. "This was a mistake," she said quietly. "It's always a mistake. You have a way of making things worse, not better."

"Did you really expect me to make things better?" Maddie asked with blatant sarcasm. "How could I do that, when your husband is the one who's messed everything up? Good grief, this is being talked about all over campus. It was bad enough when Jeff first disappeared. People could speculate that he experienced a breakdown and had to get away. But now he's been accused of fraud, which throws a sinister light over the whole disappearance. A man who suffers a breakdown is innocent. A man who commits a crime is not. Do you know what that does to me, Laura? I've worked hard to build a reputation—"

Laura interrupted her with a sharp look. "Mother, what my husband has or has not done will in no way affect your professional standing."

"I'm not so sure of that. In the years I've been at the university, politics has come to play an increasingly powerful role. There are people who want me to retire, and if these charges prove true, that may just give the powers-that-be the excuse they need. For the sake of the department, they'll say. For the sake of the *university*, they'll say. I say hogwash, but what I say won't count."

Laura couldn't believe what she was hearing. Dumbfounded, she shook her head. "I can't deal with this, Mother."

"What can't you deal with?"

"This. You. Your position." Her voice started to shake. "Jeff is God-only-knows where, having done or not done God-only-knows what. How it will affect *me*, I don't know, let alone how it will affect my children. You're worried about your job. Well, I'm worried about our *lives*. You're my mother. If you can't give me a little encouragement for a change, maybe you'd best go on back to school."

Maddie looked startled. "I can give you encouragement. What makes you say I can't?"

"Because you never do!" Straightening in the peacock chair, she gave a resigned sigh. "But that's nothing new, is it?"

Maddie stared at her. "Is there something you'd like to say to me?"

"Not now. Now's not the time."

"That's where you're wrong. It *is* the time. If there's something on your mind, by all means get it out. The last thing you should be doing in the middle of all this other turmoil is harboring a deep-seated grudge. Now," she said calmly, "apparently you feel that I haven't been sufficiently encouraging to you over the years. Is that correct?"

"That's correct," Laura said.

"Go on."

"You've criticized most everything I've done."

"Only when I felt criticism was warranted."

"Which is nearly all the time." Laura leaned forward, desperate to make her point. "But don't you see, your standards are impossible to meet! I don't know what you wanted me to do with my life, whether you wanted me to be a miniature version of you or what, but I'm different." She jabbed her chest with a finger. "I'm *me*. I've built the kind of life *I* wanted, and up until a week ago it was a *good* life. A *great* life. I had a husband, two super kids, a house, a successful career. I had everything I wanted, and that should have made you happy, but it didn't, because what I wanted wasn't what you wanted. You're a dictator, Mother. You want things done your way."

"Things *work* when they're done my way," Maddie stated. "Look at my life with your father. He had his doctorate in English literature to match mine in psychology. Then he settled in to writing esoteric books on obscure literary figures, and we nearly starved. It was only when I took over as the breadwinner that we were comfortable again."

"You took over *everything*." Laura remembered the quiet,

almost timid man her father had become in the wake of Maddie's domination. "But why did that have to be? And why does it have to be now? Why must you have the upper hand in everything? Why can't you ever accept that a decision I make, even though it's not necessarily one you'd make, may be the right one for me?"

Maddie pushed her chair from the table and stood. "You're right. This isn't the time to discuss this. You're too upset. Most of what you're saying is nonsense."

"See?" Laura cried. "There you go. You don't like what I say, so you criticize it."

Maddie looked down at her. "You're not making sense, Laura. I am not a dictator. You wanted to drop out of college, so you dropped out of college. You wanted to marry Jeffrey Frye, so you married Jeffrey Frye. You wanted to sell cheesecake, so you sold cheesecake. I have let you go ahead and make your own mistakes."

Laura dropped her chin to her chest in a gesture of defeat. She couldn't win, just couldn't win. When she looked up again, her voice was weary. "And now? What mistake am I making now? Maintaining my husband's innocence until he's proven guilty? Trying to hold my family together? Keeping my business going?"

"The mistake you're making now," Maddie said, "is alienating me. I won't stand around under attack. I don't need that at this stage in my life."

Laura gave a sad smile. "No, I guess you don't. It isn't much fun to be attacked, is it, Mother?"

Maddie gathered her coat. "I'll call you later, Laura. Hopefully you'll be in a more receptive mood." Holding her head high, she left Laura alone in the alcove once more.

nine

tACK WASN'T SURPRISED WHEN DAPHNE
Phillips showed up at the police station midmorning on Tuesday.
He figured if she was any kind of a lawyer she'd be annoyed
by the article in the *Sun*, and if she was tough, like Melrose
said, she'd be more than annoyed. So when he saw her at the
door to the office he was using, he rocked back in his chair,
linked his fingers behind his head, and waited to see what she'd
do.

"I'd like to talk with you, Mr. Jones," she said. She had one
hand on the doorjamb, the other resting with surprising ease
around the straps of the briefcase that hung from her shoulder.

"Sure." He hitched his chin toward a chair. "Come on in."

She moved into the room, but rather than sitting she came
right up to the table he was using as a desk. Regarding him
steadily across it, she said, "We weren't at all pleased with the
article in the *Sun*."

"No. I didn't think you would be."

"It was unfairly damaging to my client."

"Are you representing Mr. Frye?"

"If you folks ever find him, I will. In the meantime I'm representing his wife, whose interests certainly aren't served by
misleading articles like this one."

"Misleading?" Tack shot a glance at the paper, which lay on the side of his desk. "I thought it was pretty accurate, actually."

"Perhaps word for word, but put all together, it has Jeffrey Frye more or less tried and convicted."

Tack shrugged. "I can't be responsible for the way the press presents its material. You'd better take that up with them."

"I have. I just came from Duggan O'Neil's office. He refuses to back off or print any kind of retraction."

"So sue him."

Daphne pursed her lips and shook her head. "He's Gary Holmes's puppet, and Gary Holmes is a powerful man in these parts. One doesn't go up against powerful men without a powerful case. I haven't got a case for libel, and you know it."

Tack did but was surprised that she admitted it. It was a classy thing to do. Actually, that was how she struck him overall: classy. Her suit was that way: wool, with a loose jacket, a short skirt, and a silk blouse, clearly a set, clearly from Saks or Neiman Marcus. Same thing with the perfume she wore, which came to him in sweet bits and snatches. Her behavior was classy, too. Her voice was firm but pleasant. She wasn't the harridan he might have wanted her to be so that he could goad her on. He had a feeling her cool was inbred.

In his next life, he decided, he'd be a classy guy with inbred cool. Back in this life, though, he let his arms drop to his sides. "So what do you want from me?"

"A little restraint. There may be nothing illegal about your saying that Jeffrey left town to avoid being caught, or that hundreds of thousands of dollars, collected over a ten-year period, may be involved, but things like that are incendiary. They spread like wildfire, and I don't care if the federal courthouse is in Springfield, articles like the one that appeared today will make it harder to get an unbiased jury if the case ever comes to trial. Not to mention," she added, and her cool seemed to slip for a minute, "the effect this kind of publicity has on the Frye family. You must know, after talking with her, that Laura Frye is totally in the dark about where her husband is or, if your charges prove true, what he did. This is a woman who up until one week ago thought she had the perfect life. Jeffrey's disappearance alone was enough to turn that life upside down. This latest twist makes the pain and confusion ten times worse. And that's only for Laura. She has a daughter who is sixteen and in school here. Do you know how difficult this is for her? Do you know how cruel other kids can be? Laura let her stay home from school today, but she can't stay home forever. Laura's son, Scott, is out of state, but he'll be back soon for the holidays. Imagine what the holidays are going to be like for these kids."

"Don't tell me they still believe in Santa Claus," Tack said and waited for her to blast him for being a cynical old man. Cynical *young* man. He couldn't forget that she was five years older than he was. She didn't look forty. But forty-year-olds never did, these days. The experts said it had to do with diet and exercise. Tack guessed it had to do with being in his mid-thirties himself. Everything was relative. When he'd been ten, forty had looked old. The closer he got, the less old it looked.

Daphne didn't blast him. Rather, she stayed quiet and calm, but that didn't mean she didn't get her point across. In her calm, quiet way, she was an impassioned speaker. "If they did believe in Santa Claus, they sure as hell won't any more. What's happened is nearly as shocking to them as to Laura. All their lives, they've been the epitome of the average, normal, healthy, happy family. Suddenly that family is torn apart, and no one understands why. They don't know where Jeffrey is or why he left. They can't believe he is guilty of the things you people say, and if he is, that shakes the foundation of their lives even more. Put yourself in their shoes, Mr. Jones. What would *you* be feeling in a situation like that?"

Tack wasn't one for putting himself in other people's shoes. He had a job to do, and compassion only got in the way. Besides, he hadn't been born into any average, normal, healthy, happy family. "You're barking up the wrong tree, counselor. My daddy was a rummy, my mama wiped down tables at the Hayes-Bickford, and my big brother was killed in 'Nam. I can't dig up too much sympathy for people who have it all and then bring disaster on themselves."

"Laura and the kids haven't done a thing. They're good people. So was Jeffrey, we all thought. If any of what you say is true, we were all taken in."

Tack could have sworn he saw a haunting look in those pretty brown eyes. Brown? No, hazel. Pretty, even though haunted. With a sigh, he crossed his arms over his chest. "That surprises me. Being a tough lawyer and all, I would have thought you'd see through him even if the others didn't."

"I didn't see a thing," she said, frowning. "Not a thing."

"And you knew him well?"

She pursed her lips again, thoughtful for a minute. "Very well. But I wasn't looking for evil. Laura can be confronted with evil and not see it, because she doesn't want to. That's the way she is, a starry-eyed optimist. I like to think I'm more realistic. Still, I had no inkling that Jeffrey could or would have done anything like what you say."

"Life does have its little surprises, I guess."

"True." She took a breath that brought her head up a notch, and those pretty hazel eyes had a sudden edge. "But they don't have to be made worse by public crucifixions. If and when Jeff Frye is brought to trial, the public will see and hear all it wants. In the meantime, let's not cater to the lowest of the low curiosity seekers, huh?"

The way she said it made Tack feel like a cad—which he was, only it bothered him coming from her. "Did you tell that to the press too?"

"You bet." Without blinking, she said, "What I want to know from you is exactly what you're doing to find Jeff. I take it the FBI is on the hunt."

He unfolded his arms, took up a pen, and began to doodle. "The FBI can't officially enter a case until a person is declared a fugitive, which won't happen until he's indicted."

"Unofficially?"

"They're in on the hunt. We've been going through airline records, but so far there's nothing. Same with trains and buses."

"Of course there's nothing. He took his car."

"He couldn't very well drive his car across the ocean."

"You think he went abroad?"

"If he wanted to escape the long arm of the law, he'd go as far as he could. He could have stashed the car in an airline lot or stored it somewhere. We're checking out those possibilities."

More softly and with affection, Tack thought, Daphne said, "He really loved that car. It was something he'd always wanted. He took such good care of it. It's hard to believe he would have left it behind."

"He may not have. He may be holed up somewhere not far from here, but we're looking into that too. We're looking into most everything we can. Even the brother."

"Christian?"

"He was in Australia at the time of Frye's disappearance. He's in Tahiti now. If Frye wanted to get away from things here and have a little fun in the process, Tahiti would sound mighty appealing." Tack slanted a grin her way. "There's nothing like a bare-breasted girl to take a man's mind off his problems."

Daphne's mouth turned down. "You've watched *Mutiny on the Bounty* one time too many."

"Right you are, which is why I may just make that trip to Tahiti to check out old Christian myself. Funny, his name being Christian and all. You know, like Fletcher Christian?"

"Yes, I know," she said, sounding annoyed. "But you're barking up the wrong tree if you think you'll find Jeffrey in Tahiti. In the first place he hates hot weather, and in the second place he wouldn't be looking for fun like that."

"Something wrong with him?"

"Of course not, he's just not the type."

"Faithful to his wife all these years?"

"He's not promiscuous. Believe me, he's not promiscuous."

That didn't really answer the question, but he let it go for the time being. "According to you, he's not a thief either, but all the evidence is against him. Why should I believe you about his sex life?"

"Because I've known him for twenty years, and I've known his wife a lot longer." She looked more upset than she'd been since she had arrived. "I know this. Believe me. I *know* this."

Tack was inordinately pleased to get a rise out of her. Rocking back in his chair again, he said, "Okay. I hear you. We'll check it out anyway, of course. That's what Uncle Sam's payin' us to do. If your Jeff has a honey stashed away somewhere, his phone records will be interesting. Bank records, too. Did you know he has a bank card for a little account in his name—not in both their names, like the rest, but in his name alone?"

Daphne shook her head.

"'Course, he won't be able to use it now, any more than he'll be able to take money from any of the other accounts. The whole kit and caboodle's been seized."

For a long minute, she stared dumbly at him. Then her face drained of all color. "Seized?"

"Frozen. Your man is suspected of stealing a whole lot of money from the government, and now he's run from the scene of the crime—"

"But he hasn't been indicted!" she cried.

The look on her face was one of such genuine dismay that the sound of her raised voice didn't give Tack the satisfaction it should have. Putting all four chair legs to the ground, he said, "We don't need an indictment to do what we did. All we need is suspicion that he's contemplating flight. We have more than that. He's already gone. So we have to make sure he can't take any more money with him than he already has."

"He's taken money?"

"Bits and snatches from different accounts for a total of somewhere in the neighborhood of fifty grand. Now, unless that money was taken to pay for legitimate expenses, it looks like that's his spending money."

Daphne closed her eyes for a split second too long to make it a blink. She took a breath. "You didn't tell that to the paper."

"There's a lot I didn't tell the paper."

"Like this business with the bank accounts. You can't do that. You can't freeze things without proving probable cause."

"I sure can. It's called making a 'jeopardy assessment,' and I don't need the say-so of a judge. It's one of the special powers the IRS has."

"Special powers?" She looked appalled. "Those bank accounts are crucial. This isn't a family that plays with the stock market."

"I know. We checked it out. If Frye owned stocks, those would have been seized too. We've frozen every one of his assets."

"But his assets are the family's assets. Laura doesn't have a stash of her own, and the kids certainly don't. What are they supposed to live on?"

"She has a business."

"Right, and she deposits every cent of its take into one of those bank accounts you've frozen. What in the hell is she supposed to do when she goes to do the payroll for the month and finds she can't touch a cent of that money?"

"She should have had her own business account."

"But she doesn't. So what's she supposed to do?"

"Better tell her to open an account of her own and put the take there from here on."

"Okay," Daphne said, eyes flashing. She was back to holding the strap of her briefcase, but so tightly now that her knuckles were white. "I'll tell her that, and maybe, just maybe, her employees will stick with her when she tells them she can only pay half of what she owes them for December and they can forget Christmas bonuses. But what about the money she'll owe the bank for the loan and mortgage on the restaurant building? And the house? And Scott's tuition? First her husband disappears, so she loses his income, then you come along and take control of her savings. That's a double whammy."

Tack did feel sorry for the woman, but there wasn't much he could do. People brought things on themselves. Laura Frye should have paid more attention to what her husband was doing. She shouldn't have been so damn naïve. She should have been tougher, like her lawyer friend here, who was eyeing him like he was the devil himself.

Wanting the advantage of height, he stood. Then, because that advantage felt good, he decided to push it by walking around the table to face Daphne at close range. With a compassion that surprised even himself, he said, "Look. I hear everything you're saying, and it's a shame for your friend and her kids. But I don't make the laws."

"You enforce them. It was your 'assessment' that froze her assets. It could just as easily be your 'assessment' that unfreezes them."

Her face was tipped up to compensate for his height. It was as composed as ever, save for the pleading in her eyes. Standing there, Tack felt a tug. "If I could, I would," he said quietly, "but it's gone too far for that. I've filed records with the agency. A dozen financial institutions have already been notified. It's out of my hands."

Daphne didn't move. Not once did her eyes leave his face, nor did the pleading leave her eyes. Tack sensed this was a woman who cared deeply for her friends. Given the cavalier way he often treated his, he felt vaguely humbled.

"Doesn't it bother you," she asked, seeming almost confused, "to see a woman ruined?"

He tried to come up with a clever answer but found none. In a low, serious voice he said, "If she's innocent, yes, it does."

"Still, you'll put Laura through this?"

"I have no choice. It's the way things work. I'm only doing my job."

"Your job sucks."

He had to smile at her choice of words, but it was a sad smile. "Sometimes. Like now."

For another minute, Daphne continued to look at him. He didn't know what she saw, but he worried that whatever it was didn't overly impress her. That bothered him. He didn't know why, but it did.

"Listen," he said, "we'll do everything we can to find her husband and, after that, to resolve this thing as quickly as possible. That's why I'm working here. To get things done with haste." He drawled the "with haste," since the words weren't exactly his style.

Daphne didn't smile. After another minute, she nodded, tore her eyes from his, and turned to leave.

Tack watched her go, watched those spectacular legs move her body forward. "Counselor?"

She stopped and looked back.

"Like I said, to get things done fast I'm working here instead of operating from Boston. I stayed at the Hilton last night, but I don't think Uncle Sam's going to approve that expense for long. Any suggestions for some clean, cheap digs?" He could have asked Melrose, he knew. He could have asked any one of a dozen others in the Northampton Police Department. But he wanted to asked Daphne. She might know of a cheap place with a little class. And she'd know he was around.

"Try the Valley Inn, on Route Nine heading out of town."

"Thanks," he said and started to raise a hand in a wave, but she had already turned and left.

Laura stood in the front hall, staring at Daphne in utter disbelief. "Come again?"

"Jeff's assets have been frozen," Daphne repeated. Her voice held a chill that spread to Laura, though the words made no sense. "It's something called 'jeopardy assessment.' If a person is under suspicion for something and the agents investigating him have reason to believe he may try to flee, they can make a 'jeopardy assessment' and seize bank accounts, stocks, bonds, homes, cars, whatever."

"They actually come and take these things?"

"No. They just make it so that no one else can."

"You mean Jeff."

"And you."

"But I haven't done anything wrong."

"Your assets are Jeff's. Everything is either held jointly or in his name. The IRS has put a freeze on all of it. You can't touch a thing."

"Daphne, that's absurd," Laura said, but the look on Daphne's face deepened the chill. "Are you saying I can't cash a check?"

"That's right."

"I can't withdraw money from my own bank account?"

"That's right."

"You must be kidding." She gave a scornful laugh that even sounded strange to her own ears. She wasn't normally a scornful person. She wasn't normally sarcastic or bitter. But little in her life had been normal in the last week, and she was still hurting from her meeting with Maddie. "Tell me you're kidding, Daph."

"I can't," Daphne murmured. "Much as I want to, I can't."

"I have no money?"

"You have money. You just can't use it."

Laura couldn't believe what she was hearing. On top of everything else, it was too much. Sagging back against the wall, she ran a shaky hand through her hair. "There has to be some mistake."

Daphne didn't say a word.

"Come on, Daph."

Daphne shrugged.

Laura scrambled to gather her thoughts. It seemed she'd been doing that a lot lately. Too often she found herself feeling overwhelmed by some of the simplest things in life, like deciding what to wear or whether to make dinner. This was far from one of those simple things. "Are you saying," she said very slowly, "that I have no access whatsoever to the money I've put in the bank?"

Daphne sighed.

"What am I supposed to live on?"

"Cherries."

"But my daily take goes right back into overhead—buying supplies, paying staff, mortgage and loan payments. What's left isn't enough for us to live on." With dawning horror, she added, "Jeff's income covered our living expenses, but if Jeff isn't here, there won't be any income, and if I can't touch the money in the bank, I can't pay those bills. My God!" she cried, and felt dizzy. Too many things were happening, none of them fair, none of them under her control. The helplessness was making her sick. Unsteadily, she went to the stairway and lowered herself to the carpet runner. "This is unreal."

Daphne joined her on the step. "I know."

"Things keep getting more and more complicated. Where will it end?"

"I don't know."

Laura fought off her dizziness with a flare of red anger. "They can't *do* this. The government can't *do* this to me."

"They can. It's legal. I just came from checking, and they can do it. The IRS can seize assets without so much as winking at a judge."

"But that's not right!" Laura shouted. She and Daphne were the only ones in the house, the doors and windows were shut, and she didn't care if her voice carried clear to the attic. She was so filled with fury that if she didn't let some of it out—her mother was right—she'd explode. "My husband may be under suspicion, but I'm not, and half of our money is mine. What am I supposed to live on? Tell me that! How am I supposed to survive while Jeff is off twiddling his thumbs somewhere and the IRS diddles around looking for him? I have a business, a house, and two children to support. How does this government, to which I pay huge taxes every year, expect me to live? Those are my own *after-tax dollars* they're preventing me from touching. How am I supposed to make ends meet?"

"For starters," Daphne said in a voice that sounded doubly low in comparison to Laura's, "you'll open an account in your own name. From here on, everything you take in goes there."

Laura could feel panic rising. She tried her best to tamp it down, but it kept coming. "Fine, but that won't cover everything. From the start we knew that with a financial investment like the one we made in the restaurant, we wouldn't see a significant profit for several years. What about the mortgage for this house? Or food for the kids, for God's sake?"

Daphne touched her arm. "Calm. Keep calm."

"I'm trying, but it's getting harder and harder." She hugged her knees. "When Jeff first disappeared, I felt like I'd been dunked in icewater and stretched on a rack. For every day he's been gone, I've been stretched tighter. Now it's like the rack is starting to twist."

She pressed her mouth to her knees, hard enough to feel her teeth through the leggings she wore. She closed her eyes tight, but even that didn't help, so she opened them wide on Daphne.

"How could Jeff *do* this to me? What was he thinking when he left—that if he wasn't here, everything would be fine? He must have known the IRS was on to him, so he just ran away."

"Hold on, Laura. You're starting to talk like he's guilty."

"I don't want to think it, I honestly don't, but after a while, after the questions keep coming with no answers and the coincidences start mounting, I'm beginning to wonder."

"Don't. You're his wife. If you don't believe in his innocence, who will?"

"You're right, I'm his wife, and that means I'm the one left holding the bag," Laura cried. "My name is being smeared in the papers. My daughter doesn't want to go to school. I have no idea how I'm going to manage to pay for basics that I've always taken for granted." Her voice grew beseechful. "Okay. Debra can live without New York. We can live without Saba. But what about sending Scott back to Penn? What about the dentist and the doctor? What about insurance and gas for the car? My God—" she wiped cold beads of sweat from her forehead with the back of her hand, "—the ramifications are mind-boggling. I mean, talk about pulling out the rug!"

Daphne clutched her hands. "Come on, Laura. It's not like you to be pessimistic."

"But my world is falling apart!"

"No, it's not. You have your business, your kids and your health. You also have Maddie—"

"—Who makes everything worse!"

"She's still your mother. She won't let you starve."

Laura shook her head. "I will *not* take money from Maddie. I won't ask her for a red cent."

"Well, that's something to think about another time. The point is that we do have other options."

Laura eyed her warily. "What options?"

"We can appeal this 'jeopardy assessment' through the courts."

"What does that entail?"

"It entails my going through your records and proving that much of what you have in the bank is your money, proceeds from your business."

"But I'm entitled to half of what's in the bank anyway," Laura cried. "If I were divorcing Jeff, that's what I'd get. *At least* that. Or I should. I was the one who supported him while he finished college, and it was money in my own personal account that helped us live when he started working. So now he takes off after stealing hundreds of thousands of dollars. What was going through his mind? Twenty years, we've been married twenty years, yet he could do this to me! And what about Debra and Scott? They're his own flesh and blood. Didn't he wonder what would happen to them when he vanished? What in the world did he *do* with that money?"

She hadn't given that question much thought, since up until then she hadn't allowed herself to think of Jeff being guilty. Now, in her fury, she wondered. Hundreds of thousands of dollars was a lot of money. What had he done with it all?

An awful thought hit her. Several, actually. She looked at Daphne, whose expression was telling, and it was as if the rack she was on took another twist. This one stole her breath. "My God," she whispered. "My God. This house? The Porsche? The restaurant?" It was bad enough to think that her husband was a thief, but to think that she had been enjoying the fruits of the thievery was crushing. She didn't care one way or another about the Porsche, that was Jeff's baby, but she'd been so proud of the house. And the restaurant. If the down payments on those buildings had been made with stolen money, the whole thing was tainted. "So help me," she said in a venomous voice, "if he used that money to make my dreams come true—"

"Don't say it," Daphne interrupted. "Don't say anything you may regret."

Laura looked her in the eye. "You're my best friend. If I can't say it to you, I can't say it to anyone. If these charges against Jeffrey prove true, if he stole money to help build the life I've been so proud of, I'll divorce him."

"You're angry."

"Very, but I mean what I say. I've been in hell for a week now. If that hell goes on much longer, all because Jeffrey wanted to be a big man and buy big things, I'll divorce him."

"You don't know the facts, Laura. If it's true, *if* it's true, there may have been reasons you know nothing about."

"No reason could be that good. Why are you sticking up for him?"

"I'm trying to be reasonable. You're upset. I'm trying to be calm. We don't know the facts."

"Until Jeff gets back, we won't."

"Not true. Jones's investigation will tell us things. Between the bank records and the records at Farro and Frye, he'll be able to piece together how much of Jeff's own income went for what."

Laura could hope that Jeff's income had covered the important things, but she kept remembering what Taylor Jones had said. Jeff had barely earned half of what Laura thought he earned. Either he made up the difference with money obtained through fraud, or he had lied on his income tax form. Neither possibility thrilled her.

But Daphne was right. Until they knew the facts, she had to be calm. That was easier, now that she'd blown off the worst of her steam. She was still livid, but tired. Very tired. "Tell me again about appealing the freeze on our funds. What are our chances of success?"

"They're good. The only problem is time. I'll work as fast as I can. Still, it may be awhile before a judge will hear the case."

"Awhile? Two weeks, four weeks, eight weeks?"

"It could be three to six months. We can make a case for hardship, but you're not exactly on welfare."

Three to six months. Laura thought of the cash flow she would be needing in that time and how she might get it. Jeff would know the answers—but of course she couldn't ask Jeff. "I'll sell the house. I don't need it. The market isn't great, but I could get enough to keep us going."

"You can't sell the house. That's what a freeze on assets is about. You can't sell the house, because the government has taken a lien on it, which means that at this moment it isn't yours to sell."

Irritably, Laura filed that fact. "Then I'll take out a loan. But that would be taking out a loan to make payments on another loan," she argued against herself. "I'd be going round and round in circles."

"In one sense, yes. But a loan would help tide you over until we unfreeze some of those assets."

"Then you think I should do it?"

"I think you should talk to David. Find out what the situation is at the firm. There may be money owed you from there."

"Won't the government take it?"

"Maybe not, if it's put directly into your own private account."

"Won't the government freeze the firm?"

"Not unless there's evidence that David and the others were involved in what Jeff did. Jones will be looking for that."

Laura put her elbows on her knees and her hands on either side of her head. "I'm so confused. So frightened. So tired."

"Still not sleeping?"

"Not well. I wake up and start asking the same questions over and over again, and I never have answers. Jeff's the one with the answers. Wherever he is." Thinking about that, wondering, she was angry all over again. "My God, if he's really done all this to me and the kids, I hope he burns in hell!"

ten

J EFF NORMALLY HATED HOT WEATHER, but he would have gladly burned in hell just then, he was so cold. The wind cut through him sideways as he made his way down the hill into town. Feet, legs, hands, nose, even his eyeballs were cold, and it seemed they'd been that way forever. No matter how valiantly it worked, the wood stove in his cottage couldn't counter the insidious gusts of frigid air that found their way through invisible cracks in the walls.

Going into town was a risk. He had only been in hiding for a week, which was nowhere near long enough for him to look different. The beard on his face itched like hell and looked scruffy enough, but it wasn't yet the mask he wanted, and even though he wore a wool cap on his head, if there had been pictures of him in the papers or on television, he might well be recognized. But he was willing to take that chance. If he didn't go somewhere to warm up for an hour or two, he would go mad.

He would also go mad without human companionship. He had never been without people for so long in his life. His transistor radio offered noise, but it wasn't human. He needed to know that he wasn't at the end of the world. Walking into town would tell him that. It would also give him exercise. He had always climbed stairs in his building, walked around downtown during lunch, shoveled snow or raked leaves or packaged up garbage to take to the dump, and that was aside from his tennis games, which were fierce. In the cottage, there was nothing to do but jog in place and do push-ups and jumping jacks and deep knee bends. He did all those faithfully, morning and night on a regular schedule, and he wandered out on the rocks of his bluff. But he couldn't walk there, couldn't stretch his legs and really *move*.

There was another reason for going into town. He was in desperate need of the diversion. In between reading his books, listening to his radio, and cleaning up the cottage, he inevitably thought about those he had left behind, thought about Laura and David and Daphne and Lydia and how he had let them all down. He wondered how messy things were, whether the IRS had come out in the open, whether they were making life hard for Laura. She would survive, he knew she would, she always had. She would make the most of the situation and carry on. But he wondered about Debra and Scott. They were the toughest part of all this. He worried about them—not about their daily well-being, because Laura would ensure that, but about their feelings for him. He knew they would come to hate him, and he supposed he deserved it; still, the more he dwelt on it, the more pain it caused. With no one to look at, no one to divert his thoughts, no one to ease the isolation he felt, he was becoming an emotional wreck. Living in solitude meant living with a man he didn't particularly like. That was a punishment in and of itself.

So he was risking discovery by taking a walk into town. Not having dealt with any locals except the Bangor realtor from whom he'd bought the cottage, he wasn't sure what brand of humanity he would find. But he wasn't picky. Human contact was human contact. He wasn't any prize himself, after what he'd done.

The town consisted of one main street, down which he had driven the first night, plus several side streets he would have guessed were footpaths if he hadn't seen pickups parked along the way. There were pickups in the main street, too, just a handful drawn up to a string of buildings that housed, in order, a general store with a post office, a laundromat, an auto supply store, and a diner.

He made a mental note about the laundromat, which he figured would be a good place to visit twice a week. Since he hadn't had the foresight to bring clothes this time, he made for the diner. He walked casually, as though he were out for nothing more than a late-afternoon stroll in a place where he'd been living all his life.

The diner was in a low cement building with a flat roof. Between a large Santa face, an arch of flying reindeer, and snowflakes of various shapes and sizes were hand-printed signs advertising breakfast, lunch, and dinner specials. The heat within had steamed up the windows, preventing him from seeing much of what was inside, but the lights were on and the place looked warm and inviting, which was all the temptation he needed.

He pulled open the slatted wood door, setting off some jingle bells that were tacked inside. They were real jingle bells, not the little kind sewn onto a piece of ribbon but big ones attached to a strip of worn leather that had once been a horse's bridle. Seeing that gave Jeff a nice feeling, as did, incredibly, the smell of burgers on the griddle, but the nicest feeling of all came from the immediate warmth he felt. He would have sighed with pleasure had he not been afraid of drawing attention to himself.

His glasses fogged, so he took them off. As had happened more than once in the last week, he was surprised at how much he could see without them. There were two men at the counter, and a man and woman in one of the booths. All four were older than he was and more burly. All four were looking at him by the time he closed the door. Leaving his gloves on lest the smoothness of his hands brand him a foreigner, he nodded and headed for the empty booth at the end of the row. He slid in, keeping his back to the others. Once he felt shielded by the tall wood of the booth, he set his glasses on the table, removed his gloves, and unzipped his parka.

The warmth was heavenly. For a week it seemed he'd been huddled up against the chill. Now, slowly, he opened his hands, relaxed his arms at the elbows, lowered his shoulders, stretched out his legs.

"Hello," a small voice said.

He looked up to see the waitress. She was a young woman, in her late twenties, he guessed. Slim, almost fragile looking with dark hair and pale skin, she wore a white blouse, a loose denim jumper, wool tights, and sneakers. On the collar of her blouse was a plastic Rudolph with a short string hanging from the bottom. It was the kind of pin Debra wouldn't have been caught dead wearing, which went to show how different people were in the sticks. Jeff thought the pin was sweet. And the young woman looked harmless.

"Hi," he murmured.

She gave him a shy smile and said in a careful kind of way, "Do you know what you want?"

He had been so hungry for warmth he hadn't given a thought to food. "Uh, no, I haven't—looked." As he said it, he searched for a menu, but it wasn't between the salt and pepper, and it wasn't on a chalkboard above the counter.

The waitress extended an arm and touched the tabletop with the tip of her pencil, then quickly drew back again. Sure enough, under the sheet of glass that covered the table were signs like those in the window, plus others, each with bits and snatches of a menu.

"Ahhh," he said. Putting his glasses on, he began to read. When he realized that the waitress was still there, he gave her an apologetic look. "Sorry. I'll just be a minute."

"It's okay. There isn't any rush." As though to prove her point, she didn't move.

Fearful that the longer she stood there looking at him the greater the chances would be that something about him would ring a bell, he said, "I'll start with a large bowl of corn chowder and a cup of hot coffee. While you're getting that, I'll decide on the rest." He glanced up to see that she was writing down the order, then looked down again. Though his focus was on the papers under the glass, she was in the corner of his eye. He waited for her to leave, but she didn't. Daring another glance, he saw that she was still writing. She seemed to be concentrating deeply.

For an instant, he wondered if she was making notes on his features to report to the police or, worse, drawing a pencil sketch of him, and he had a momentary urge to up and run. But that would be a dead giveaway that he had something to hide. Besides, she looked so innocent he couldn't imagine her doing either. Seconds after he tempered that fear, she put the tip of the pencil to the paper and said in that same careful voice, as though she were making a deliberate effort to do everything right, "That's one large bowl of corn chowder and one cup of hot coffee. And you'll decide on the rest while I'm getting them."

"That's right."

She shot him another shy smile, then disappeared from his line of sight. He could hear the gentle slap of her sneakers on the cracked linoleum as she moved along the length of the counter toward the kitchen. The men at the counter were talking quietly. The couple in the other booth were eating with a click of forks and knives. From the kitchen came sizzling sounds.

Jeff took a deep breath, flexed more of the chill from his hands, pushed the parka off his shoulders to better enjoy the heat, and sat back in the booth. Within seconds, it seemed, the waitress was back, carrying a white mug in one hand and a coffeepot in the other. She set the mug down near the edge of the table, carefully filled it with coffee, set the coffeepot down, slid the mug closer to him, then picked up the coffeepot.

"The sugar is next to the salt," she said. "Would you like cream?"

He was about to say no—he always drank his coffee black—but there was something rich-sounding about cream, and he felt in need of something rich, so he nodded. "Please."

Again he heard the pit-pat of her sneakers, and before he could do more than empty two sugar packets into the coffee, she was back with a small pitcher of cream, a spoon, and a napkin.

"There are napkins there"—she pointed to the metal container behind the salt and pepper—"but this one's nicer."

"Thank you," Jeff said.

"You're welcome." She lingered for a minute, watching him pour cream into his coffee. Then she moved off again.

He sipped the coffee. The brew was muddy, had probably been sitting for most of the afternoon, but it was good. Since he had neither the pot nor the know-how to brew coffee, he had been making do with instant all week, but he didn't care what the label said, instant just wasn't the same.

"Here you go," the waitress said. Her voice reached him first. He glanced around to see her approaching from behind him, walking slowly, gingerly balancing a large bowl of chowder on an even larger plate. She was working so hard at delivering it without a spill that he almost reached out to help her. But something stopped him. He sensed she wanted to do it herself. There was an element of pride involved. So he waited, his eyes widening a fraction each time the chowder came perilously close to the rim of the bowl, and when the plate finally rested flat on the table, he felt nearly as victorious as she did.

"That looks just fine," he said with enthusiasm, then added an even more enthusiastic, "Delicious, actually," because it did. He had been opening cans all week and either heating the contents in a small pot on the stove, or, as in the case of sardines, tuna, and even hash, eating the food cold. He didn't know how to cook. There had never been any reason to learn. His mother had ruled the kitchen of his childhood, and then he had met Laura. From the beginning she had loved to cook, and she did it so efficiently it wasn't worth his while even to try. In the same amount of time that he would have spent deciding whether to use butter or margerine, she could put a whole meal together. She was so competent it made him sick.

"Is something wrong?" he heard the waitress ask and, looking up, found worried eyes on his face. "You look angry."

He quickly erased his scowl. "No. I'm not. I was just thinking about the soups I usually make for myself, and they look awful, compared to this one." Using the large spoon that lay on the bottom plate, he sampled the chowder. "They taste awful too, compared to this one. This is good." He took another spoonful, then another, enjoying the chowder. It was thick and hot, mildly flavored, faintly sweet. Not only did it taste good, it warmed him all the way down. He gave her a smile and spooned up more.

"Do you always cook for yourself?" she asked.

He swallowed his mouthful. "Um-hmm."

"Don't you have anyone ever to do it for you?"

"No."

"Then you live alone?"

"Yes."

"Where?"

He had been concentrating on the chowder, keeping his eyes downcast, but when one question came after another, albeit slowly, he grew uneasy. So he looked up but, again, saw only innocence on her face, and though he reminded himself how innocent he had looked at home at the same time that he'd been hiding so much, he gave the waitress the benefit of the doubt. After all, he reasoned, he had answers to her questions. He had thought them all out, just for situations like this.

"At the top of the hill," he said with the slight toss of his head in the direction from which he'd come.

Her eyes widened. "Are you the one who's living in the bluff house?"

Jeff wouldn't have called the cottage a house, but there was only one structure at the top of the hill. "I guess so," he said. Then, because he didn't want to make anything big of it, he returned to the soup. The spoon was halfway to his mouth when she disappeared from the corner of his eye. He had taken several more mouthfuls when a different form appeared. This one was larger, far larger, and had on a greasy white apron over an undershirt and jeans. He also had on a mean expression, which Jeff took in at a glance. So he pointed to the bowl with his spoon.

"This is wonderful chowder. Really good."

"You livin' up in the bluff house?" the man asked. His voice was a hoarse smoker's voice, but it was less ominous than his looks.

Jeff figured he had no choice but to answer. "If that's the one up on the hill, I am."

"We heeyad it was bought."

Jeff nodded. He ate another spoonful of chowder.

"Must be cold."

"Um-hmm."

"S'how come ya theya?"

Jeff was prepared for directness. He knew backwoods folk didn't beat around the bush. "I wanted a place of my own, and it was cheap."

"It's fallin' ta pieces."

"Um-hmm. But it's mine."

"Wheya ya from?"

"Pennsylvania."

"Wheya theya?"

"Western part of the state."

"Why'd ya leave?"

"My mother died, so there was no reason to stay."

"Whatcha do theya?"

"Teach."

"Whatcha gonna do heeya?"

"Read and think. Maybe write." Jeff figured that if the previous owner of the cottage had been a writer, he could be too.

"Write what?"

"I don't know. I haven't decided yet."

The man snorted. "Ya ma musta left y'a load a money."

Before Jeff could respond, the waitress was back, eagerly asking, "Can I take his order now, Poppy?"

The large man's face gentled the instant it turned to her. "Do that, Glorie. I gutta cook." He sent Jeff a look that said he'd have more questions another time. Then he sauntered off.

Jeff looked at the waitress, who was waiting expectantly with her pencil poised over her pad. "Poppy? Is that his name?"

She blushed. "That's what I call him. I've been calling him that all my life. He's my daddy. His real name's Gordon."

Jeff had to smile at the way she drawled the name, but aside from the drawl, she had said it well. Given the way her father spoke, her pronunciation was remarkable. She seemed to take the same care with it that she took with her manners. She sounded educated, but not really. It was odd.

Aware that he was staring, Jeff took a quick breath. "Does he own this place?"

She nodded. "And my name isn't really Glorie, it's Gloria, only everyone calls me Glorie. You can too, if you want."

Jeff wasn't in town to make friends; still, he found himself nodding. "Okay." Then, because there was something about her that was very sweet, he said, "You can call me Evan."

"Is that your name?"

He nodded.

"Evan what?"

"Walker. Evan Walker." That was the name he had bought the house under. It was also the name on the birth certificate, the Social Security card, and the driver's license he had in his briefcase. Evan Walker—at least, the one who had been born in South Connellsville, Pennsylvania in 1948—had died two years before, but no one had to know that.

"That's a nice name. And I'm glad you're here. People grow up and move away, but no one moves in very often." She lowered her voice until it was just above a whisper. "It's nice talking with new people. Some of the old ones just keep saying the same things over and over and over—"

"Glorie!" came a call from the kitchen. "Gut that odda?"

Glorie was quickly the waitress again. Looking apologetic, almost fearful, she poised her pencil over the pad. "Have you decided what you'd like to eat?"

Jeff glanced down at the scattered pieces of menu. There was a T-bone steak that sounded good, but it was more expensive than the other things, so he didn't want to get it. Gordon had already decided that he was a do-nothing with lots of money. Loath to foster that image, he looked around for something in the middle price range. "How's your beef stew?"

"Oh, it's delicious. Poppy makes it fresh every morning. It has carrots and potatoes and onions in with the meat, and it comes with cornbread; or if you'd rather have plain rolls, I can bring those instead."

"Cornbread will be fine. How are the portions? Pretty good size?" Her description alone had set his mouth to watering. He felt like he could eat a horse.

"Oh, very good size," she said in an earnest tone. "And if it's not enough, I can bring you seconds. Poppy lets me do that, especially at this time of day. Our biggest rush is at lunch. Poppy doesn't like to throw food away at the end of the day, and he always makes fresh stew the next morning."

"The stew will be wonderful," Jeff decided. He set to finishing the last of his chowder.

By the time it was gone, Glorie delivered the stew, and it was every bit as good as she'd led him to believe. The cornbread was good too, as were seconds on both, and he finished with apple upside-down cake and another cup of coffee. Thinking back to some of the elaborate meals Laura had made, he couldn't remember one he had enjoyed as much as this.

Of course, part of that was because he'd been alone for a week, and because he felt human for the first time in that week, and because Glorie was the most gentle person he'd seen in a long time. He drank the last of his coffee slowly, feeling reluctant to be done and leave. The thought of returning to the cottage on the bluff didn't thrill him.

But it had to be done. That cottage was his hideout until he decided where to go and what to do. So he paid his bill at the diner with some of the wrinkled singles he had stuffed into his pocket, left a healthy tip for Glorie, and said goodbye. Then he walked down the street to the general store.

There were half a dozen people inside. Keeping to himself, he bought a wedge of cheese, a dozen eggs, several cartons of orange juice, and a handful of Hershey bars.

"Pretty cold up theya on the hill," the man at the cash register said. Jeff recognized him as one of the men at the counter in the diner.

"Yup," he said, digging into his pockets. He used tens this time—wrinkled, also by design. "Say, you wouldn't know anyone who wants to sell a truck cheap, would you? I need something to get me around."

"How'd'ya get heeya?"

"A friend dropped me. But I'm stranded now, and I'll be needing some supplies pretty soon." He figured he could venture a little farther in a week or two.

"I can getcha supplies."

"I'll be needing some papers and books and things."

"They's books right theya." He aimed a finger at the single rotating rack of paperback novels. Most of them were dog-eared. Jeff suspected that the fine art of browsing had evolved, here, into the fine art of reading the book in the store.

"Ah," he said and nodded. He didn't want to offend the man. "Good." Walking over to the rack, he found that he had already read some of the books in hardcover. Several others caught his eye, though, and while he probably wouldn't have bought them in Northampton, where Adventure Fiction was tucked way behind Tibetan Culture, Modern Astrological Thinking, and Introspective Therapy, they might just be diverting.

So he picked out a few, nonchalantly took a newspaper from the top of the pile, and went to the cash register to pay for the extra things. "I'd appreciate it if you'd keep an ear out about a truck, though. I'll stop back in a few days."

"Evan Walkah, is it?"

"That's right."

Jeff fastened up his parka, pulled the wool hat lower on his head and the gloves on his hands, lifted the bag holding his purchases, and set out for the bluff.

eleven

IF CHRISTIAN EVER RETIRED, HE WOULD retire to Tahiti. He had decided that long ago, after he had returned to the island for three years running and found it more beautiful each time. He loved the tropical breeze, the towering cliffs, the warmth and honesty of the people. He also loved the glossy black hair of the women. And their deep golden skin. And their grace. And the smiles that sprang so readily to their full Tahitian lips, and the way those lips formed French words to compensate for his primitive grasp of Tahitian.

He stayed on the side of the island far from the dirt, noise, and crowds of Papeete, in a resort owned by an old college friend, a Minnesotan who had come to visit soon after graduation, fallen in love with a Tahitian woman, and stayed. The resort had grown more luxurious over the years to accommodate the cream of the island's visitors.

Whenever he came he took pictures, not only in Papeete and the interior but on other islands in the French Polynesian chain. They were very different from the pictures he had taken in the Daintree, but there was always a travel magazine that would buy them.

Aside from that, he did nothing of an industrious nature. With its lush landscape and its tropical climate, Tahiti was for veg-

150

etating. He either lounged on a cushioned chaise on his own private deck overlooking the lagoon, or sat in his favorite restaurant and watched the people go by, or enjoyed sunsets from the beach. He also visited with friends. Over the years he had come to know not only other transplanted Americans but many of the natives, the *taata Tahiti*. At any given time, if he wanted company, it was his for the asking.

On this particular afternoon he hadn't done any asking, so when a loud knock came at his door that carried out onto the deck, he was puzzled. Setting his drink on the railing, he went back through the bungalow to the front.

The man on the other side was a stranger. He was new to the island, if his pale skin and weary look meant anything. He was also dressed wrong. He had on a white business shirt that was open at the neck and rolled to the elbows, dark suit trousers, and loafers. He was about Christian's height, maybe ten years younger, and not a bad-looking guy, Christian decided, though his hair was too short. But he looked too formal, far too formal, particularly next to Christian, who wore nothing but shorts.

"Just get off the plane?" Christian remarked, propping a hand on the doorjamb.

"After two goddam days in and out of airports, with missed connections at every stop," the man grumbled. More clearly, he said, "Are you Christian Frye?"

"That depends. What do you want?"

"To talk." Pulling a leather folder from the back pocket of his trousers, he flipped it open. "Taylor Jones. Special Agent, Internal Revenue Service."

Christian studied the ID. "You look better in the picture."

With a thanks-a-lot-buddy look, Jones flipped it closed. "Mind if I come in?"

"Yeah, I do. If you're here about those deductions I took for expenses last year, you're wasting your time. My accountant warned me you guys wouldn't like it, but my client lived in Connecticut, four hours from me, and the only way I was going to get my usual crew down there was to put them all up, and the only way I could do that without going broke was to rent a house and a cook. So it cost a bundle, but it was a legitimate business expense." He went suddenly quiet. Something didn't make sense. "The IRS sent you all the way out here just to check on me?"

"Not in that way. Can I come in?"

"Then in what way?"

Jones stared at him hard. "If you let me in, I'll tell you. I'm hot and tired, and I don't give a damn if it's against regulations; I could use a drink. Got anything strong?"

Christian had just the thing, and though he didn't normally fraternize with establishment types like Taylor Jones, if the man was asking to buck regulations, Christian would be the first one to oblige. Gesturing him in with the jerk of a thumb, he closed the door, then went to the bar and fixed one of his specials. He found Jones on the deck looking out over the clear blue lagoon.

"Not bad," the agent remarked.

Christian retrieved his own drink and leaned back against the rail with his legs crossed at the ankles. "It's as close to Eden as I've ever come, which means that I resent anything that threatens to spoil it. So. You're in, and you've got a drink. Now tell me why you're here."

Jones took a healthy swallow of that drink. Once it was down, he flexed his neck. "Better."

"Business, Jones."

The agent lifted a hibiscus blossom from the deck rail, one of the many the hotel staff scattered around fresh each day. "For starters, I wanted to see if you were alone."

Christian took immediate offense. "Hey, the IRS may have a say in how much of my hard-earned money I get to keep, but it doesn't have any say in my love life."

Jones took another drink before he turned to face Christian. "When was the last time you saw your brother?"

"My brother." That didn't make any sense either, but for a

different reason. Most people he knew didn't know he had a brother, much less a sister-in-law, a niece and nephew, and a mother. Family had never been Christian's strong suit. "Jeff?"

"Do you have another?" Jones asked with a look.

"Obviously, you know I don't. You didn't come all the way out here looking for me without trying to nab someone closer. What happened to Jeff?"

"I don't know. No one seems to."

"What's that supposed to mean? Where is he?"

"I thought maybe he'd be here in Eden with you."

"Jeff hates hot weather."

"So why does he go to the Caribbean once a year?"

"Because his wife plans the vacation," Christian said, growing impatient. "Jones, what's going on?"

"When was the last time you saw Jeff?"

"Last June. Laura threw a birthday party for my mother, so I went."

"And you haven't seen him since?"

"No." He waited. "Jones?"

Jones took another drink. Lowering the glass to the railing, he said, "Two weeks ago, your brother failed to come home from work. No one's seen or heard from him since." He looked skeptical. "No one called to tell you?"

"I've been away. Incommunicado. No phones most of the time." But that wasn't the whole story. After taking a drink of his own, Christian said, "We're not close."

"You and Jeff? Or you and the whole family?"

"Him. Them. Same difference." He frowned. "'Failed to come home from work.' Just disappeared?"

"Just disappeared."

That didn't sound like Jeff at all. "Of his own free will?"

"That's what we think."

"But why?"

"Because he's on the verge of being indicted for tax fraud."

Christian laughed. "Tax fraud? Jeff? You're putting me on."

"No," Jones said, "I'm not."

Christian could see that, but it didn't make the allegation any less preposterous. "Jeffrey Frye breaking the law? You obviously don't know my brother."

"Straight as an arrow, huh?"

"Yeah, straight as an arrow, but not dumb or naïve. He'd know exactly how to break the law if he wanted to do it. When we were kids, he used to give me elaborate plans for sneaking out of the house at night without being caught. Or snitching a five from the old man's wallet. Or dialing long distance without having to pay."

"He sounds pretty crafty."

"Yeah, except he wouldn't ever do any of those things himself. He might tell me to do them, but he kept his own hands clean. He didn't have the nerve." Christian swished a finger through his drink. "And you want me to believe Jeff would commit tax fraud? No way, José." He brought the glass to his mouth and took a drink. Then, because the prospect was so intriguing, he asked, "Out of curiosity, how is he supposed to have committed this tax fraud?"

"By filing bogus forms and collecting returns."

"How much?"

"One fifty and counting."

"One hundred and fifty *grand* and counting?" Christian whistled.

"It could total half a million, when all the figures are in."

"Without you guys knowing?" If Jeff had pulled that off, Christian had to hand it to him. The little shit had balls. "How's he supposed to have done it?"

Jones raised a finger from his glass and pointed to the chaise. "Mind if I sit?"

"Be my guest. This is fascinating."

Jones stretched out on the chaise, wiped the sweat from his forehead with an equally sweaty arm, and took a drink. Then he said, "The way we figure it, he chose people from the obituary pages of the paper, waited until they'd been dead a year, submitted W-2s in their names, then 1099s, then 1040s."

"Clever," Christian said. "Sounds like the kind of thinking my brother could have done, but carry it out? Nah. I'm telling you, he wouldn't have the nerve." Even when he was taunted, Jeff had been a coward, and God only knew Christian had taunted him enough. From the time Jeff had been four and Christian nine, they had been arch rivals. Jeff was the angel, Christian the devil, and no amount of goading on Christian's part had led the angel astray. Granted Jeff had never achieved what Christian had on the playing fields or with women—until Laura, which was something else entirely. Still, Jeff was good, with a capital G. "He wouldn't even steal a cookie from the cookie jar, for Christ's sake!"

"Maybe he should have," Jones remarked. "The punishment would have been a helluva lot easier to take than the one he'll get now, if we ever catch him, which brings me back to the reason I'm here, which is fuckin' hard to remember with this drink in my hand." He peered into the glass, where the liquor came barely a third of the way up, with most of that third being ice. "What's in this, anyway?"

"Island stuff."

"Is it the same as you're drinking?"

Christian was drinking iced tea, which was pretty much the same color. "Sure. I live on it."

"Whew, it's potent."

"Throw in jet lag and exhaustion, and you're in a pickle. When was the last time you ate?"

"Real food? Two days ago."

"You'd better eat."

"Yeah, well, I thought of that, but by the time I finally found the damn hotel, the first thing I wanted was a bed, and then the damn room wasn't ready because someone else loves paradise so much he's refusing to leave, so they're trying to find me another place to stay. While they were doing that, I figured I'd check you out."

"Well, you have," Christian said and drained his drink, "and unless you want to check under the bed and in the closet, you can see I'm not harboring any fugitives from justice. But I want to know more about all this, so before you pass out, I suggest we eat. There's a great restaurant next door." He eyed the white shirt and dark trousers with distaste. "Only thing is, you can't go looking like that. Don't you have anything decent?"

With an effort, Jones sat up and put his feet on the floor. "Sure, I do. I didn't come all this way just to talk with you for five minutes. I brought shorts and bathing suits, the works. As far as the agency is concerned, I'll need at least three days here to find you and then interrogate you about anything and everything to do with your brother."

"That won't take any goddamned three days." Christian had a whole lot he could say about his brother as a kid, but he barely knew the man now. They were very different people who had taken very different roads in life.

Jones pushed himself to his feet and regarded Christian with surprising clarity, given what Christian had put in his drink. "Tell you what. If you don't tell on me, I won't tell on you."

"What'd *I* do?"

"Deducted something suspicious."

"It was a legitimate deduction."

Jones shrugged. "Could be. But audits are a pain in the butt. Don't you agree?"

"You're threatening me with an audit?"

"They're done all the time for pettier reasons than this."

"Like what?" Christian had heard stories—none of which surprised him, since he didn't think highly of government workings—but he'd always assumed some exaggeration in the stories. So he was curious about what an authority would say.

"Like tips from an ex-spouse or a business competitor. Like the personal grudge of a legislator, or a friend of the tax agent, or the agent himself."

"That's lousy."

"That's how it is. So. Do we have a deal?"

"Of course we do. I don't give a damn if you stay here three days or five or ten. You can stay here a goddamned month, for all I care. Besides, who in the hell would I sing to? I steer clear of the IRS. Bureaucracies aren't my style."

"So I gather," Jones said and started back into the room.

Christian followed, curious now about Jones's source. "Who's been talking?"

"Frye's wife."

"Ah. Interesting."

"Why's that?"

"Laura and I have our differences."

"She didn't volunteer information. I asked, she answered."

That made more sense. Laura was uncomfortable with any-thing to do with Christian and had been that way for better than twenty years. Yes, she invited him to her home—and the in-vitation always came from her, rather than Jeff, simply because she was the one in the house who did that sort of thing—but she wasn't thrilled when he accepted. Granted, when he came, she was cordial. She gave him the guest room and fed him, but she avoided being alone with him and never allowed him to draw her into a personal discussion. As far as the rest of the world was concerned, she didn't trust him. He suspected she didn't trust herself.

At the door, Jones said, "That restaurant's right next door?"

"Ask in the lobby. They'll direct you."

"Give me fifteen minutes." He paused. "You'll be there, won't you?"

Christian grinned crookedly. "You mean, will I take the time to collect my brother from the shower stall, pack my bags, and skip town?" The glance he shot toward the lagoon took in every bit of opulence along the way. "Would I leave all this for a guy who never once even remembered my goddamned birthday?" Without waiting for an answer, he shut the door.

*　　　　*　　　　*

Twenty minutes later, he and Jones were drinking again, Christian for real this time. But they were also eating, which made things safer. Despite his family's image of him, Christian wasn't a big drinker. The beers with the guys after work didn't count. He drank socially, but that was about it. He liked to be able to control just how drunk he was.

Besides, on Tahiti, he was plenty loose without booze, which was probably why he had said what he had about Jeff back at the bungalow. Normally he kept his gripes to himself—not that a birthday was any big thing, but it was one more little memory of his brother that irked him. He didn't want to get into the big things. They were no one's business, least of all a government agent's. So he stayed fully sober by alternating swallows of Scotch with forkfuls of *poisson cru*.

He wanted to know more about what was happening back in good old Hampshire County. "So Jeff is gone and no one has any idea where he is. Laura must have had some suggestions. She's a wellspring of information." He rather liked those words. They happened to fit.

"No. She didn't have any suggestions."

"Laura, without suggestions?"

"She's pretty much in a state of shock."

"Shock? Laura?" That was nearly as preposterous as the idea of Jeff committing fraud, as far as Christian was concerned. The Laura he had known adapted to whatever situation she was in. When she found herself face to face with adversity, rather than fight it, she would simply turn and go off in another direction. She was like Lydia. So like Lydia.

And there he did feel a twinge. He didn't see eye to eye with his mother, and on some pretty major issues at that. But she was still his mother, the only one he'd ever had. "What about Lydia?" he asked, looking nonchalantly around the restaurant. The vivid clothing rivaled that of the flowers, both totally different from the eminently practical woman back home. "How did she take all this?"

"She's pretty calm. Disturbed about it, but resigned. No help with suggestions about where Jeff could be, though. How about you? Have any ideas?"

Christian wasn't sure he'd hand any over if he had them, but since he didn't, the point was moot. "I can't picture the guy committing a crime, let alone running off. He's led a sheltered life. He's been coddled by controlling women."

"Laura didn't strike me as being controlling."

"No, she doesn't, does she, and that's the kicker. She slides in on the blind side. In her own quiet way, she gets things done just how she wants."

"Is she manipulative?"

"No," Christian said. He scratched his head. "Manipulation implies something negative, and she doesn't have a mean bone in her body. But she has a very specific idea of how things should be done in life, and she knows how to get people to do them in such a way that they think it's their idea."

"Give me an example."

Christian grabbed at the most obvious one. "Marriage. She decided she wanted to drop out of college, get married, and have a family. Jeff was still in school. I doubt he had any intention of getting married until she came along—and made it worth his while," he hastened to add, because it was only fair. "That's the whole point. She does give. She made him a nice home, gave him two nice kids, and then, when he wasn't earning enough money, she started a business of her own to supplement his income."

"Sounds like any guy's dream."

"Not mine," Christian said with feeling. "I don't take to being led around by the nose."

"Were you ever?"

"No."

"Not even by your mother? If she was controlling of Jeff, why wasn't she the same with you?"

"Because the circumstances were different," Christian said.

"And because I'm a different person from my brother."

"That's what they kept saying. You don't look much like his picture. Same coloring, but that's about all. Guess he got the looks in the family."

"Guess so," Christian agreed, because he figured he had it coming after his comment about Jones's mug shot. In point of fact, while he didn't have Jeff's cultured looks, he stood out in a crowd. His height helped—he was six four to Jeff's six even—but there was also a rugged look to him that turned women on, or so they said. He looked exciting, they said. He looked daring and dangerous, they said. He had to take their word for it, because he didn't spend hours looking at himself in the mirror. He wore his hair on the long side because he hated getting it cut. He always had color because so much of his work was outside. And when a man spent his life tossing two-by-fours around, his shoulders were bound to be broad. No, he wasn't at all sensitive about his looks.

"They told me," Jones went on, "that it was a waste of my time to come looking for you, because you would never help Jeff out if he was in trouble."

Christian shouldn't have been sensitive about that either, but he was. "That's not necessarily true."

"You would help him out?"

"If he'd come to me, I might have." He ripped off the tail end of a loaf of French bread. "But the point is he wouldn't have come. Certainly not all the way to Tahiti, all by himself, without Laura to make sure he made his connections, and you know she isn't here." Then Christian thought of something. "I take it you checked out my place in Vermont?"

Jones nodded. "He's not there."

"Are the plants dead?"

"Close to it."

"Jeez, I can't win. I can build a terrific house where nothing was there before, but I can't keep a goddamned plant alive. Did you water them?"

160

"Hell, no. That's not *my* job."

"It's not your job to be breaking and entering either. Did you have a warrant?"

"Didn't need one. I was looking for a fugitive."

Christian figured he wouldn't have much of an argument there. "Did you at least lock up when you left?"

Jones nodded, but he was looking at Christian like he had something else on his mind. "Those were incredible photographs on the walls. Did you do them all?"

"Most of them," Christian said, because there seemed no point in denying it. "I travel a lot. I like visible reminders of where I've been."

"They're impressive. So's your darkroom."

Christian didn't much like the idea of strangers combing through his things. "So you took the Cook's tour."

"Like I said, I was looking for a fugitive. What better place to hide than in a darkroom?"

"I can think of better places. Apparently, so can Jeff." He was pleased to see a moment's discomfort on the agent's face. Jones might be adept at studying tax forms and financial records, at interviewing women and tracking potential witnesses halfway around the world, even at breaking and entering. But he couldn't find Jeffrey Frye.

In all fairness, Christian knew, Jones wasn't as bad as he might have been, particularly when it came to his taste in art. That was probably the reason why, when Jones asked where he learned to take pictures like that, he shared information he usually kept to himself.

"The Peace Corps."

Incredulity. "The Peace Corps? You were in the Peace Corps?"

That was precisely the response Christian usually got, which was why he'd learned not to talk about it. "Something wrong with that?" he asked in annoyance.

"Wrong? No, not wrong. Just surprising."

"If you'd done your homework, you'd have already known it."

"You're not the suspect. Just a potential witness."

"Or accomplice," Christian reminded him, just to keep things interesting. But Jones was more interested in the other.

"The Peace Corps," he said, looking bemused. "I had the impression you were a troublemaker when you were a kid. How did you ever make it into the Peace Corps?"

"People see what they want and believe what they want. I was a wretch at home, but that didn't mean I didn't do anything well. I happen to be smart and athletic."

"And modest."

"Modesty has its place. But you want to know how I got into the Peace Corps, I'll tell you." And he was proud to do it. It wasn't often that he talked about himself, and in his younger days he might as easily have perpetuated a misconception as tell the truth. But his younger days were gone, and at that moment it mattered that the government agent have the facts. "I played four years of varsity sports at Amherst and graduated magna cum laude. I had great recommendations, and I made it through three months of training in Montana, which is more than some of the people who showed up there can say. So I went overseas."

He remembered those days so clearly. They had been good.

"Some people will say I did it to avoid the draft, and given a choice between Africa and Vietnam I'd have chosen Africa any day, but with the lottery number I pulled, I wouldn't have been drafted anyway. Other people said I was a revolutionary with a missionary urge, but I have never in my life been political. The truth of it is that I joined the Peace Corps to get away from home. I wanted to go somewhere where I wouldn't be pre-judged." He smiled at the irony of that. "Little did I know how prejudged I'd be in Africa. I was an American. I was there to upset the natural order of things. I was not a friend."

"So how did you get anything done?" Jones asked.

Therein lay the challenge, and if nothing else, Christian loved a challenge. "First I had to scrounge around and find a job that needed doing—initially, for example, a bridge that needed building. Then I had to scrounge around for materials, then scrounge around for people to help. And all the while I was scrounging, I was getting better at speaking the language and understanding the local customs, so that by the time we got around to actually building the bridge, I was able to convince the people that they would benefit from it."

"That sounds worthwhile. Wasn't your family impressed?"

"If they were, they never told me. We never talked about my experience in Africa."

"Why not?"

Christian knew the answer to that. He had come home from the Peace Corps, after re-upping and serving nearly four years, in March of 1970. He had barely been home for two days, both of which he'd slept through, when he'd gone off in search of women and seen Laura. She had been seventeen, young for a freshman, but intrigued by his beard and his worldliness and his age. In turn, he had been intrigued by her enthusiasm. She seemed to have boundless energy, which she had no intention of expending over books. So he accommodated her. They springskied Tuckerman's Ravine, went to photography exhibits in Cambridge, spent hours listening to Simon and Garfunkel. And they made love. She had boundless energy for that too. They made love for hours and hours in the attic apartment he was borrowing.

He had only planned to stay around for a week but he ended up staying for four, because she could be so persuasive. Then she asked him to marry her. She wanted a home, a husband and kids, and the kind of rosy family life she hadn't grown up with. But he wasn't ready to settle down. He didn't know what he wanted to do with his life, but the last place he wanted to be was Northampton.

So he left. Several weeks later, having no idea where he was, she stopped by his house to find out on the pretense of returning a book of poetry he'd lent her. Jeff was the one who opened the door.

Christian hadn't told his family about the Peace Corps because all the time he had spent in Northampton had been with Laura. Sure, he had told her about his experiences, but afterward she wouldn't have let on to that. The depth and intensity of their relationship was a secret.

And he had no intention of telling Taylor Jones. So he simply said, "We didn't communicate much, my family and me. Once I hit college, I wasn't home a lot. It worked out better that way."

Jones seemed to accept that. "So you started taking pictures in the Peace Corps. Have you ever worked at it professionally?"

"I sell pictures, but that's never been my occupation. I'm a builder."

"But you graduated magna from Amherst. I wouldn't have put the two together."

"Then you're as narrow-minded as the rest. Why in hell can't a smart guy be a builder?"

"He can. It's just unusual. Most smart guys take high-paying jobs where they can call the shots from behind a desk."

Christian raised a cautioning hand. "I went to college—and did well—because I had a point to prove. I wasn't the total misfit they thought, and I didn't get my grades just by charming the teachers. That might have worked in high school, but it didn't in college. I earned those honors so I could thumb my nose at the doubters. But there was no way they were goading me into wearing any three-piece suit for the rest of my life."

"So you wore a dashiki in Africa."

"And oilskins when I was working my way around the Horn on a tramp steamer, then a wet suit when I dove with a salvaging crew off the coast of Florida, and a tool belt when I signed on to frame houses in Nantucket."

"And that's how you got started?"

Christian sat back. "That's how." He crossed his arms over

his chest. "And that's all I have to say. Anyone listening would think you're writing a fucking biography. Have I given you any clues about Jeff?"

"No."

"I didn't think so."

"What about women?"

Christian shook his head. "Forget it. Jeff's a one-woman man."

"Not him, you. Didn't you ever want to get married?"

Wanting to get married wasn't the issue. Wanting a family of his own was. There were times he'd wanted it so badly he could taste the need. But the timing had been wrong with Laura, and Gaby hadn't been the family type.

He shrugged. "It just never happened."

"But there were women."

"Damn right, there were." He caught sight of one approaching and opened an arm to her. "Hey, pretty lady." She was the daughter of the restaurant's owner. Once she was safely in the crook of his elbow, he made the introductions. "Taylor Jones, She'laya Malone."

Looking instantly enthralled by the island's natural beauty, Jones stood and offered a hand. "Tack. Please."

"How are you, Tack?" She'laya asked with a pretty white smile and just a hint of a delicate accent.

"I'm fine," Tack replied.

"Have you just arrived?"

"This afternoon."

"Are you a friend of Christian's?"

"He is," Christian supplied to avoid explanations. "Busy night?"

She'laya sent a look around the crowded room. "As you can see. But if business is good, I cannot complain." She ruffled his hair. "Enjoy your dinner." Nodding to Tack, she left.

Tack slipped back into his seat. "Are they all like that around here?"

"No. She's special." When Tack looked disappointed, he said, "But I know some others who come pretty close. Two sisters, just a little younger than you. They run a dress shop in town. If you want, I'll give them a call."

"Two, as in kinky?"

"No. One as in mine, the other as in yours."

"A double date."

"Only until things get hot, and if they don't, no sweat. Think you can stay awake long enough to give it a try?"

"Sure."

Christian stood. "I'll make the call."

"That's sounds great," Tack warned, "but if you think it's going to stop me from going after your brother, you're wrong."

"You can go after my brother. You can go after him all you want. But that's not why I'm calling the girls."

"Why are you?"

Christian straightened his shoulders. "Because you look like a decent guy. And because you've had a rough day. And because you like my pictures. But mostly," he added with a twist of his lips, "because you can't come to Eden and not taste the fruit."

twelve

MONEY MATTERED. FOR THE FIRST TIME in her life, Laura realized how much. She needed it to buy food for her children. She needed it to keep a roof over their heads. She needed it to pay the people who worked for her, or they would go elsewhere to satisfy their own needs for food and housing. If they left her, she would either have to take on replacements at lower pay or make do with a skeleton staff. In either case, the business would suffer, and if the business suffered there would be less money coming in, which meant she would be even less able to meet the obligations of feeding her children, keeping a roof over their heads, and paying her staff. It was an endless circle, a crisis that would be self-perpetuating unless she did something to stop it.

Jeff had been gone for two weeks. No one knew where he was or what he was doing. He had the Porsche and enough cash to live on for a while—Laura knew that now, but that was the extent of her knowledge. There were times of intense anger when she actually wished they'd find him dead. At least then something would be resolved and she could go on with her life. Not that she was sitting around waiting for the phone to ring the way she had at first. She was determined to be a visible presence at work, so she was busier than ever. Duggan O'Neil was right, she knew. Her personal situation was a downer, and if any of that feeling settled into the restaurant, people wouldn't go there. The atmosphere had to be as upbeat as ever. She had to look and act perfectly normal.

Unfortunately, there was nothing normal about pulling in and out of an empty garage, climbing in and out of an empty bed, or, when Debra was out, cooking for herself. Jeff had always been there. Now he wasn't. And she couldn't forget it for a minute.

The media wouldn't leave her alone. Rarely did a day pass without a call from a reporter. The *Sun* was the worst. Several times a week there were articles to the effect that Jeff was still missing, the FBI was in on the case, the IRS investigation was going ahead full tilt. Wherever she went—grocery store, post office, dry cleaner—people knew what had happened. Some asked outright if there was any word of Jeff, others asked how she was in a you-poor-thing tone, still others carefully avoided her eyes. And just when things began to stabilize, another article would appear. So even if Laura wanted to set aside the whole thing for the sake of sanity, Duggan O'Neil wouldn't let her.

Nor would the IRS. She received near-daily calls from Taylor Jones or one of his cohorts with questions relating to Jeff. Often the calls were follow-ups to calls the agency received. Since Jeff's picture had appeared in the papers, particularly in the *Boston Globe*, dozens of people thought they had seen him. So the IRS wanted to know whether Jeff knew anyone in Andover or Grafton or Barnstable. Each time Laura was asked, her hopes rose, but none of the reported sightings panned out.

And then, in addition to the *Hampshire County Sun* and the IRS, there was the U.S. Mail to contend with. Bills began to arrive. To his credit—if she should credit him with anything, which Laura doubted she should—Jeff had paid the December bills. Come the first of January, though, a new batch was due. Some of the smaller ones, even those for gas, electricity, and the telephone, could be put off for one month without fear of shutoffs, but two months would be chancy. And then there were the big things, like the mortgage payment for the house and Scott's tuition. They had to be paid.

Doing her best to keep a clear head when what she wanted most at times was to burst into tears and crumble, Laura saw that she had two options. The first, which she did the day after she learned of the IRS seizure, was to follow Daphne's suggestion and open a bank account in her own name, into which Cherries' proceeds would be deposited daily. The second, which she hated to do but saw as a necessity, was to take out a loan to cover her expenses until Daphne was able to convince a federal judge that half of what was in the Frye accounts belonged to her.

Going shopping for a loan took preparation. She spent time at Cherries' computer itemizing and totaling the money she would need to keep the business running smoothly, then setting that total against what she estimated the business would make by the week. After she had those figures, she spent time in Jeff's den fumbling her way through his records in an attempt to determine what she would need at home. After those figures were compiled, she spent another several days holding her breath with the hope that maybe, just maybe, Jeff would show up and spare her from begging for money. In the end, she realized that even if he showed up, thanks to the IRS freeze she would come up short. So she swallowed her pride and embarrassment and went.

First she approached the bank where she'd opened her account, but that bank was a small one, the loan officer explained, and simply couldn't offer the loan she wanted.

She could accept that. She didn't like it—it was bad enough asking for money under her present circumstances, which were slightly humiliating—but she could accept it. There were other banks in town. She promptly went to a larger one, but the loan officer there was equally apologetic.

"I'm sorry, Mrs. Frye," he said, studying the application she had filled out, "but a loan would be out of the question. You don't have a credit rating."

"Excuse me?"

"Loans, mortgages, charge cards—your husband has always been the principal signer. Therefore, you don't have a credit rating, and without one I can't grant you a loan."

"But I have my own business," Laura said with what she thought was perfect logic. "You've seen it. You've probably eaten there. Cherries brings in steady money."

"Yes. But you don't have a credit rating."

She felt a surge of frustration. Being denied the money she deperately needed on a technicality seemed almost as wrong as the government freezing her funds to begin with. "I would think that your bank would go out of its way to help a local businesswoman."

"We would if we could. But there are certain rules. The best I can suggest is that you apply for a credit card in your own name. Then, after a time, you can come back and we'll talk."

But "after a time" was no good. Laura needed money by the end of the month. Refusing to be discouraged, she put his obstinacy down to small-town thinking and tried another bank. This one had branches statewide. She hoped its employees would think more broadly.

As fate would have it, the loan officer was a woman. Sure that a woman would better understand what she was going through and the bind she was in, Laura filled out the loan application and presented it along with the figures she had gone to such pains to prepare. But the woman wasn't any more help than the men before her.

"I'm sorry, Mrs. Frye," she said, looking regretfully at Laura's papers, "but given the circumstances I simply cannot justify a loan of this size. You have no collateral. The government has taken a lien on every asset you might have used."

That was a new twist. Being a novice at borrowing, Laura hadn't considered it. Now she did, and it seemed unfair in the same way that the argument about her credit rating was. "But I have a successful business."

"Yes, you do, but there's absolutely nothing behind it. You have a mortgage on the building and loans outstanding on work that was done in it."

"But the business itself is worth something."

"Actually, no," the woman told her, still politely but firmly. "The business is you and your staff. If you were to close up and disappear one day, there would be no way this bank could recoup its loan."

Laura could see her point, but it didn't apply in her case. "That business is the only livelihood I have. It's the only means for me to provide for my children. Believe me, I'm not about to close up and disappear."

But Jeff had done just that, as the woman's awkward look reminded her. Laura was Jeff's wife. Hence, Laura was a risk.

"Guilt by association?" she asked, incredulous. "Is that the problem? I'm a bad risk because of allegations that have been made against my husband? But that's unfair! I'm not my husband, I'm me. I have my own business, and a great reputation in this county. Ask anyone."

"I know that, Mrs. Frye," the woman said. She was about Laura's age, wore a wedding band, and had a photo of two teenagers on the corner of the desk. Laura had thought for sure she'd be on her side, but she wasn't. She was a team player— for the opposing team. "I know your business and your reputation, and you're right, it is a fine one. But you have to understand the precarious position banks have been in lately. What with the downturn in the economy, we've lost large amounts of money on loans. Businesses have folded. Developers have gone bankrupt. We have to be doubly careful."

Laura struggled to stay reasonable and calm. "I'm not asking for a construction loan. I'm asking for a loan to keep my business going until I can free up some of my own money, and I'll pay whatever the going interest rate is. I'm not asking for any favors."

But the woman shook her head. "You're not a good candidate. We simply can't do it at this time. I'm sorry."

Three more banks came up with variations on the same theme. Fighting panic by the end of the day, Laura stopped in at the offices of Farro and Frye to talk with David.

It was a bold move. She hadn't been at the firm since she'd gone looking for Jeff on the night he had disappeared, and given her druthers she wouldn't have come now. The firm was Jeff's minus Jeff. She felt uncomfortable seeing the people he had worked with, people she had entertained at her home many times, people who had respected Jeff once. But that was before Jeff had run off with fifty thousand dollars in cash, before the IRS had begun bandying about criminal charges to the tune of ten times that amount, before the *Sun* had done its thing. She didn't know what they felt about him now—or what they felt about her.

But she was desperate. The thought of returning home without promise of relief was worse than the thought of suffering the censorious stares of the colleagues Jeff had betrayed. Besides, David had been either at the house or calling her on the phone once a day, solicitous to the hilt. *If there's anything I can do, just yell. If you need anything, give a call.* Rather than yelling or calling, she decided to appear in the flesh. She needed a savior, and she needed one fast.

David was poring over a deskful of papers when she appeared at his door, and at first glance he didn't look thrilled to see her. By the time he had jumped up, drawn her into the room, and closed the door, though, the displeasure was gone.

"I didn't expect you here." He put an arm around her shoulder and pulled her close. Bending his dark head over hers, he said, "How are you doing?"

Laura wasn't any happier about the arm around her shoulder than about that fleeting look of displeasure or about having to be there in the first place, but she didn't have much choice. As far as she was concerned, the faster she said her piece and left, the better. "Not great. I've spent the day hitting every bank in Hampshire County, and not one will loan me a cent. I know the firm can't give me a loan per se"—she had asked about that several days before—"and I understand. There are cash-flow problems here, and the IRS watches everything you do. But there has to be money coming in from Jeff's clients. That's money he earned. It'd be a huge help to me if I could have access to it."

"You're discouraged," David said and dropped a kiss on her forehead. "That's normal, hon. Going from bank to bank looking for loans has to be the pits."

She leaned back so she could look up at him without being as close as he wanted. "That's not the point. I'll head into Boston on Thursday to try the banks there, and I'll keep at it until someone gives me a break, but in the meantime I need money."

"What you need," he said, flexing a large hand along her arm, "is to relax. You're tense as a wire."

His touch grated on her skin. She would have shrunk from it if she hadn't been loath to offend him. "I'll relax when I find a way to see us through these next few months. I mean, relatively speaking, I don't need all that much to buy a little time. There's three thousand due on the mortgage for the house, two to pay other bills, eight for Scott's tuition—the tuition payment will carry him through the rest of the year. By the time we have to put down a deposit for next year, I should have my money again." She had to believe that. "So it's really five thousand for the month, plus the tuition. That's not so much, given the amount of money you guys deal with all the time."

David looked pained. "But I don't have access to that money. It's the cash-flow problem I was talking about. There are associates to be paid here, and secretaries and rent."

"The money from Jeff's clients—"

"Goes toward overhead."

"But what about his monthly draw? Isn't it possible for me to get an advance on that?"

"Jeff isn't here. He isn't working."

Studying the benign expression on David's bearded face,

Laura felt a twinge of annoyance. "Jeff's a partner here, and the definition of a partnership is that one covers for another if times are bad. What I'm asking is no different from what I'd be asking if Jeff had a heart attack and couldn't work for a month."

David arched a brow. "But he hasn't had a heart attack. He ran off of his own free will, after committing a crime that is an embarrassment to every person in this firm. Now it's left to us to salvage our reputation. It won't be easy. We'll all have to work our butts off to repair the damage."

Laura was suddenly desperate for breathing room. Along with his look and his tone, David's size had become intimidating. Breaking from his hold, she crossed the office to stand facing the window. "You're telling me that even if you were to go for it, the others wouldn't."

"Some of them are feeling pretty angry."

She turned to confront him. "Do you stick up for Jeff?"

"It's hard to stick up for a guy who's done what he has."

"But he's your friend."

"And because of that, my whole business is suddenly on the line."

"Nothing's been proven. Taylor Jones doesn't have his indictment."

"Only because he's off chasing after Christian in the hope of learning something more. But the indictment will be coming."

"That doesn't mean Jeff is guilty."

David started slowly toward her. In a quiet voice, he asked, "Do you think he's innocent?"

Part of her wanted to. The rest wanted to distance herself from Jeff and what he'd done. Her own reputation had suffered just as much as the firm's, but in different ways. She had wholeheartedly placed her faith and trust in the man. If he was guilty, she'd been a fool. "Someone has to think he's innocent."

"But do you?" David asked again. He stood directly in front of her. When she didn't answer, he touched her cheek. "The worst thing about all this is what he did to you. Sure, he's screwed things up here, but we'll survive. But you—what he did to you is inexcusable."

"He loved me," Laura argued. "We've had a good life."

"But no more. Now you're living through hell."

She tipped up her chin, as much to dislodge his hand from her face as to express the determination she felt. "I'll survive too."

"Let me help." He leaned closer. "Let me make it easier."

She felt the heat of his body and was chilled through and through. "Fine. Lend me money."

If he heard the frost in her voice, he chose to either ignore it or misinterpret it. His own voice was seductively low. "I can't do that. But I can help you. It has to be lonely, all by yourself in that house night after night. And depressing. You need someone to divert your mind."

"I have plenty to divert my mind. What I need is money."

"Come away for the weekend with me, Laura."

"David!" Slipping from him, she went straight to the door. With her hand on the knob, she turned. "You've been saying you'd help me. That's all I've been hearing for the past two weeks. But what you're offering isn't the kind of help I need."

"Sure it is," David replied. He stood straight and tall, without the least bit of remorse. "Every woman needs that kind of comfort."

"What era are you from?"

"Beth needs it. You need it. Every woman I've ever known needs it. Don't look so surprised."

"This isn't surprise," she said, pointing to her face. "This is dismay." She nearly said disgust, which was closer to what she felt, but a germ of wisdom warned her against being so blunt. It was enough that she was rejecting David; men didn't take kindly to rejection, and she might yet need his help. "I can't believe you're suggesting what you are."

He held her gaze. "It's no more than dozens of other men in

this town have been thinking since Jeff disappeared." When she shook her head in denial, he said, "It is. I know. I've heard talk. You're a sexy lady, Laura."

"I'm a *married* lady."

"Whose husband has deserted her."

The word cut deep, eroding what little self-confidence she had left. In an attempt to save it, she argued, "Desertion is the wrong word. We don't know what Jeff was feeling when he left. He may have been torn apart inside but thought he had no other choice. Even as we talk, he may be sitting somewhere thinking about me, and if that's true I wouldn't call what he did desertion."

"He didn't leave you a note."

"Maybe he felt it was better that way."

"If he really cared, he would have left a note."

"He *did* really care. We were married for twenty years."

"That doesn't mean a thing," David mused in a lofty tone. "Believe me."

But Laura refused to do that. In the past two weeks, she'd had her own doubts about the strength of her relationship with Jeff, but she wasn't ready to air those doubts to anyone, least of all someone who was proving to be as traitorous—and lecherous—as David. "Jeff cared. I know he did. But that's not the issue here. The issue is that my husband is missing and you're looking to crawl into my bed. That's *awful*, David. You were supposed to be his friend."

"But you're alone."

"Not quite," she said, drawing an angry breath. "I have Debra and Scott and Lydia and my mother. I have lots of friends and a business to run, and the last thing I want is sexual involvement—and even if I did, you'd be out of the running. You happen to be married too, and your wife is my friend!"

"Not really," David argued. Laura caught defiance in his look. "Beth would have had an affair with Jeff if he'd asked her."

"David!" she cried again. "Why are you saying these things?"

"Because they're true. Beth hasn't been faithful to me. Why should I be faithful to her?"

"Maybe because it's the right thing to do?" Laura asked, though she had the feeling David wouldn't get that message at all. He seemed perfectly comfortable with what he was doing, which apparently already included cheating on Beth. "I have to get home," she murmured and opened the door.

Suddenly he was there, closing it again. With one hand flattened on the wood, serving both to hold the door shut and to curve his body around Laura's, he said in a deep voice by her ear, "I've wanted you for a long time. You know that, don't you?"

She kept her eyes on the door, concentrating more on staying composed than on anything else. Her stomach churned. Her voice shook. "I shouldn't have come here. It was a mistake."

"No. It's good you know how I feel. Okay, maybe this weekend isn't the right one. But another time—"

"Not another time."

"You just tell people you need to get away for a day or two, then I'll manufacture a business trip for me. Or if you don't want to be away overnight, we can go somewhere private for an afternoon. I know some discreet places."

"I'd like to leave now, David."

"Will you think about it?"

Laura had always prided herself on being honest, and the honest thing would have been to tell David to screw himself and leave her the hell alone. But she was still a pragmatist. She knew she might need him for something someday. And while she would never in a million years sleep with him, she was as hesitant to alienate him now as she'd been earlier.

"I don't want sex," she said in a fragmented breath, which was all her revulsion allowed her. "I have to leave."

He didn't move. "I'll call you later."

"If you're calling to ask about this, don't." Bile rose in her throat. She swallowed it down. "I have to leave," she whispered, and something of her frantic feeling must have made it through to David, because he finally stepped back.

"I'll call," he promised.

She fled without looking back.

Laura didn't take David's calls. Under the guise of not being in the mood to talk, she had Debra take messages, and when Debra wasn't home she let the machine do it. Actually, there weren't many calls—not from David or from the others who had been so solicitous when Jeff had first disappeared. People seemed to have lost interest. Either that, or they thought Jeff was guilty.

So Laura reasoned, and she grew more depressed. It didn't help that the search for a loan in Boston proved as futile as the local one had been. But the harshest blow of the week came Saturday morning, when Elise stopped by, clearly worried.

"I think we may have a problem," she said, so meekly that Laura slid closer along the kitchen counter to hear. "We've had a couple of cancellations."

"Everyone has cancellations. We always manage to fill them back up."

"These are for parties."

"For this week?" Laura asked and held her breath. She was desperate for every cent Cherries brought in. That money was the only income she had.

"For after the holidays."

Grateful for small favors, Laura let out a sigh. She found herself holding her breath again, though, when Elise went on.

"For late January and February. Three bookings."

"Which ones?"

"For catering, the Macon Company luncheon and the Kramer anniversary dinner. For the restaurant, the Hickenwright Sweet Sixteen." Elise looked to be in an agony of regret. "I didn't want to say anything, Laura. God knows you have enough on your mind. I was hoping I'd fill in with others before now, but the calls aren't coming in."

They'll come. Just wait. Once the holidays are done, people will start making plans for January and February and March, and they'll call.

Laura thought the words. A month ago, she would have spoken them. She'd been optimistic about the business right from the first, even when small setbacks had hit, and her optimism had always proven out. Now, though, things were different. The cancellations could have been coincidence. Then again, they could be related to the charges against Jeff.

Thinking aloud, Laura said, "Those bookings were made in October and November, if I remember right, which means that we've long since received deposits. Do they know they're forfeiting the deposits?"

Elise nodded. "I asked, and they do. I also asked if there was any particular reason for the cancellation. The Macon Company decided to move its conference from the corporate headquarters to a hotel, and the hotel will do the luncheon. That's logical."

Assuming it was the whole story. "Why did they decide to move the conference?"

"I didn't ask. It didn't seem like my business."

It wasn't, Laura knew; still, she'd have liked to know. If the conference had been moved because there were suddenly more people than could be handled in corporate headquarters, that was fair. If the conference had been moved because Jacob Macon, who knew Laura and Jeff socially and had personally made the initial call to Laura about the luncheon, wanted to dissociate himself from Cherries without causing a stir, that was more disturbing.

"What was Diane Kramer's excuse?"

Elise answered softly. "She said that too many of their guests knew of the connection between Cherries and Jeff, and she didn't want anything to mar the party."

Laura swallowed. "And the Hickenwrights?"

"They were worried we might fold, and they didn't want to

be left in the cold. I told them Cherries wasn't closing. I assured them we were booked solid. I warned them that if they gave up the date and then changed their minds and wanted it back, the slot would be taken." Her voice dropped even more. "They said they'd already made other arrangements for their party."

Laura nodded. "I see." She took a long, loud breath and tried to still the frightened knock of her heart. But the fear was pervasive and real. "Oh, God," she whispered on the exhalation.

Elise immediately had a hand on her arm. "Maybe I shouldn't have said anything yet. We're smack in the middle of the holiday season. People won't be thinking about after the holidays until after the holidays. Bookings will pick up."

Laura gave a wistful thought back to the first of the month. "They were so good for December."

"And they're okay for January and February. Really they are."

"As good as last year?"

"Almost."

"They should be better. We're a year older. We're more established. They should be better."

Elise squeezed her arm and said with greater enthusiasm, "They will be. Just wait, Laura. We'll have ads going in the paper after the first of the year. That'll help."

Hearing near desperation in her enthusiasm, Laura forced a smile. "You're right. I can't help but worry sometimes, but you're right. It's the time of year and the economy. If there'd be any months when things weren't booming, it'd be January, February, and March." She paused, frowned. "Let me know if you get any more calls, though. Either way, cancellations or bookings. I have to know what we're facing."

thirteen

"Peace on earth, goodwill toward men." If you've heard the words once, you've heard them a dozen times. They are being preached from pulpits all around town this week; they appear on greeting cards that fill the mailman's bag; they are written on store windows up and down Main Street.

Another year, another Christmas. The message is the same, yet as much of a dream as ever. War continues to rage in the Middle East, perpetuated by the cowardice of our leaders who, in the name of diplomacy, stand back, shake hands, and smile. Likewise, poison continues to flow from the drug lords of South America into the veins of our children, while government bureaucrats sit at their desks, scratching their heads and mulling over possible courses of action. Infuriated by their impotence, we are driven to action ourselves, only to be arrested in front of abortion clinics where our voices may well save the lives of human beings too tiny to speak for themselves.

How can there be peace on earth when muggers walk the streets, when convicts are parolled long before their sentences have been served, when rapists are freed on technicalities of law? How can there be goodwill toward men without pride and trust, and how can there be pride and trust when intelligent men scheme to steal money that belongs to others?

Before the streets of the world can be cleaned up, the streets of the country must be cleaned up, and before that, the streets of the state, and before that, the city, which brings up the case of Jeffrey Frye. His situation is particularly disheartening because of his local ties. He was born and raised in Northampton, and he established a successful business here. Yet the government claims he willfully defrauded it of hundreds of thousands of dollars, and that is a major blot on our community and on us. He must be apprehended. Until then, we share his guilt.

Bringing Jeffrey Frye to justice will be a beginning. Indeed, it may take many such beginnings before we make serious headway in the quest for peace on earth, but the goal is worth it.

As a child, Laura had hated Christmas. Her parents cared far more for intellectual endeavors than for holidays, which meant that while the rest of the world decorated trees, sang carols, and opened presents, the senior McVeys spent the holiday season reading or writing or comparing notes with colleagues. Santa Claus was someone Laura visited with her little friends, though she knew from the start that he wasn't for real. Her parents told her so. Yes, they bought her gifts so that she wouldn't feel left out, but those gifts were practical, never frivolous, and by the time she and her sister were teenagers, the gift-giving was done.

As early as she could remember, Laura had vowed that when she was an adult in her own home, Christmases would be different. And so they were. Starting the very first year of her marriage, though she and Jeffrey couldn't afford much of anything, she had cooked and decorated and generally dedicated herself to making the holiday a lighthearted and festive affair. It was all the more so after the children were born. For months, Laura would stash small fun gifts in a sack in the back of the closet. She made a ceremony of decorating the tree, with the children inviting friends to join in the fun. She helped them make long strings of popcorn and baked Christmas cookies and lit scented candles. She planned Christmas dinner, much as she did Thanksgiving, with an eye toward brightness, excitement, and pleasure.

Christmas this year was different. Oh, she tried. She bought a tree and had Scott set it up the night he came home from school, then dragged the decorations from the attic and trimmed it well. She had gifts, though nothing that had been bought since Jeff had disappeared, not so much because of the money but because she'd been distracted. But she wanted—needed—a semblance of holiday cheer, so she went through the motions of planning an elegant Christmas dinner.

Then Gary Holmes's editorial appeared in the *Sun* on Monday, Christmas Eve, and it became harder to pretend the holiday was a happy one. Debra was furious at the paper, Scott was furious at Jeff, Maddie was furious at Laura, and Laura didn't know *what* to do.

"You're just as bad as those bureaucrats he mentions," Maddie said across the kitchen island. Classes were out, and though it would have been nice if she'd come over to tell Laura what a success the department party at the restaurant had been, she was far more concerned with the Holmes editorial. "Here you sit on your neat little stool, mulling over your options. Isn't it time to do something, Laura? Don't you think you ought to take the offensive for a change?"

Laura was chopping roasted chestnuts for a turkey stuffing. "What would you have me do?"

"Sue Gary Holmes. He's slandering your family."

"He's only repeating charges the IRS made against Jeff. What he's doing may be irresponsible, but there's nothing illegal about it. I don't have a case." As frustrating as that was, she had already checked with Daphne and knew it was true.

But Maddie was in her bulldog mode. "Sue him anyway. You need a forum to present your side of the case."

"I can't afford the forum, Mother. Lawsuits cost money, and I don't have a whole lot to spare right now." Shoving the chestnuts to the side of the cutting board, she went to work on a bunch of scallions.

"There are times, Laura, when certain things have to be done on principle alone. This is one of those times. We are being scapegoated by that man and his paper for all the ills of the world. I think you ought to fight back."

But Laura wasn't in the mood to fight anyone, so she let her mother talk while she finished the stuffing, then she dashed off to oversee Christmas Eve at the restaurant. In the past, Jeff would have come along with her. Together, they might have returned home for the kids and gone to midnight mass. Laura didn't feel the least bit inspired this year, and she didn't want to force the kids into anything, so she had let them do as they wanted and go out with friends. As a result, the house was grotesquely silent when she returned. She put on a CD of Christmas carols, with the volume turned high to fill the silence, and went back to the kitchen to cook.

Unfortunately, the music couldn't drown out her thoughts, which wouldn't stay put in the harmless spaces she wanted them. They kept darting from Jeff to the kids to the business to the future. Several times her hands began to shake and she had to take a breath and steady herself. Other times she found her eyes filling with tears and had to stop again and wipe them away.

Debra and Scott came home within fifteen minutes of each other, lingering in the kitchen to talk with Laura while she cleaned up. Debra reported on what she claimed was a totally uneventful night watching videos at Jenna's. Scott told of taking Kelly to the local sports bar to watch reruns of the World Series on a five-by-five screen.

He was no sooner done when Debra came out with, "Dad didn't call, did he?"

Laura shook her head.

"Why would he call tonight?" Scott asked Debra.

"Because it's Christmas Eve."

"You think that matters to him, if he's been gone this long?"

"It might," Debra said, scowling. "Don't you think so, Mom?"

Laura would have thought it, if for no other reason than that he knew how much the holiday meant to the kids. But he hadn't called, which she supposed was in keeping with everything else he'd failed to do in the last month. "Maybe we'll hear from him tomorrow."

"Don't hold your breath," Scott said, and Laura felt a pervasive sadness. Scott had always been happy-go-lucky, easy to please and upbeat. Jeff's disappearance had changed him. He'd grown cynical. Innocence had been lost, and she mourned it.

"I know you're angry," she said gently. "So am I, and we have a right to be, in some respects."

"*Some* respects? Try *lots* of respects. He walked out on us. He just took off and left us to deal with a really ugly situation. I saw half a dozen guys in that bar tonight who were in my graduating class, and every one of them saw me, but they weren't coming near. No way. You'da thought I was a leper."

"Maybe it's that shirt," Debra said. "It's puke green."

Scott ignored her. "They read the paper, and if they don't, someone reads it and tells them. They know what he did. The whole town knows what he did, and the stink's rubbing off on us."

"Come on, Scottie," Laura said. "You're the one who wants to be a lawyer, but you're breaking the basic rule. You're making judgments when we don't know the facts."

"We know enough."

"No, we don't," Debra argued. "You two may think he's guilty, but not me. If Dad left here, he had a reason."

"Yeah. He tried to rip off the government and got caught."

"But he may have an explanation for what he did."

"How do you explain grand theft?"

"I don't know," she cried, "but that doesn't mean you can't." She turned to Laura with a trembling voice. "It's Christmas, and I know the restaurant's closed tomorrow and you're planning a big dinner and all, but are we really supposed to celebrate with Dad missing?"

"We have to," Laura insisted softly. Seeing tears in Debra's eyes, she felt her own throat knot. Dropping the dishtowel, she put an arm around her shoulder. Her voice was very low, her head bowed beside Debra's. "It's Christmas, and Christmas is supposed to be a happy time." When Debra opened her mouth to argue, she hurried on. "I know you're not feeling happy. Neither am I. Neither is Scott. But we'll only feel worse if we sit around and mope. We have things to be grateful for. You can think about them tomorrow."

"Name one," Debra muttered.

"Nana Lydia. She'll be here and she loves you, which is more than some of your friends can say about their grandmothers."

Debra relented, but only to the extent that her jaw wasn't thrust out so far. "Won't it be awful for her with Dad not here?"

"It might be. So it's up to us to keep her cheery. Same thing with Gram." Laura looked at Scott. "She's feeling as angry as you are about all this. To her way of thinking, the negative publicity we're getting will drive her career right down the drain."

"Gram McVey's career down the drain?" Scott snorted. "The only way that'll happen is if the American Psychology Association holds its annual conference in the sewer. I mean, she's got it made for life."

Laura tried to see things from her mother's point of view. "She's getting older. For a while now she's been worried that they'll want someone younger to head the department. She thinks this might be the lever they need. So it's a tough holiday for her too. We can't just let her sit alone and brood."

"But to smile and laugh and run around like everything's hunky-dory?" Debra asked. "What if Dad's dead? The police haven't ruled that out."

"If Dad's dead, the laugh's on us," Scott said. "The government can't bring charges against a dead man, so we'll have gone through all this shit for nothing."

"Scott," Laura said in a pleading tone, "don't say things like that. It doesn't do any good."

"Mom's right."

"But it's the truth," Scott insisted.

"It may be," Laura conceded, "but saying it doesn't help. We don't know where Dad is. We don't know what he's doing. I don't accept that he's dead. All we can do for now is to keep on going the way we are, which means having a regular Christmas dinner tomorrow with all the fixings and trying to have a little fun."

"It won't be the same without Dad," was Debra's shaky response. "I want things back the way they were."

Laura hugged her tighter, and not just because Debra sounded young and upset. Laura was frightened herself. The future was full of unknowns. She hadn't been as unsure of what was going to be since she had decided to drop out of Smith, and she'd been young then, without children or a business or employees who depended on her. Now she had a world of responsibility on her shoulders, and Jeff wasn't there to help her. Okay, so he hadn't really done all that much before; still, he'd *been* there. Now he wasn't. And on Christmas Eve, she was frightened and lonely.

Feeling Debra's warmth, knowing that Scott was close by, she drew on remnants of strength to say, "Life doesn't always stay the same. With the passage of time, things change. It's inevitable. But that doesn't mean they have to be worse."

"Do you think life will be better without Dad?" Debra asked.

"It'll be *different*. We have to keep an open mind about things. Like tomorrow. If we sit down to dinner thinking about nothing but the fact that Dad isn't here, it'll be dismal. If we sit down with the idea that the rest of us are together and we're healthy and we have the hope of good things happening in the next few weeks or months—" her voice broke "—we'll be okay." She would have said more, but she didn't trust her voice. She didn't trust her eyes, either. They had filled with tears again. So she closed them to keep the children from seeing the extent of her fear.

Seeming to sense that silence had merit, Debra didn't speak. Neither did Scott, but after a minute, Laura felt his hand on her shoulder. Freeing one of her own, she linked her fingers with his.

Those few silent moments were the highlights of Laura's holiday.

Two days after Christmas, Daphne took Debra to New York. Laura had been hesitant, given the money situation, but Daphne insisted.

"I have money, Laura. I earn plenty, and I have no kids. If I can't spend it on Debra, who can I spend it on?"

"You're already spending it on me," Laura reminded her. Daphne had been dividing her evenings between Jeff's home files and Laura's business records in search of the information she needed to put together a motion to lift the IRS freeze. "You're doing all this work for me, and I can't pay you a cent."

"I don't want a cent. I don't *need* a cent."

"But this is your *time*."

"And you're my friend," Daphne informed her, with a look that brooked no argument. "I don't want to hear another word about it."

Laura didn't say another word. Debra was thrilled to be going off with Daphne, which made Laura happy, and Scott had taken it upon himself to work at Cherries. Laura appreciated his help, enough so that she didn't dwell on the fact that he should be sleeping late and having fun before returning to Penn.

Besides, she had enough else to dwell on. Bills continued to arrive with the mail each day, and no matter how much Laura deposited in her new bank account, no amount of fiddling could get that amount to equal the amount at the bottom of her bills-to-be-paid list.

So she continued to cut back. She spoke to Emmie, who had been coming in twice weekly to do cleaning and laundry, which Laura could do herself, and that included the armloads of clothes she would otherwise have taken to the dry cleaner without thinking twice. Now Laura thought twice. She had already put off the carpet cleaner, put off the painter who was to do the downstairs bathroom, put off buying new linen place mats for the restaurant. She had called Diana at the boutique and asked her to try to sell the Welsh sweater she had special-ordered. She had canceled the trip to Saba, with just enough time to get a refund on her tickets.

But those were all small things in the overall scheme. They barely made a dent in the discrepancy between what she had and what she owed. She had nightmares about having to close Cherries and take a job waiting tables at Timothy's, her chief competitor, and even aside from the nightmares she didn't sleep well. Night after night she woke up in a cold sweat, shaking, afraid she wouldn't be able to hold things together. There were times when she woke up in the morning wanting nothing more than to stay in bed all day and hide from the world. If no one could see her, no one could hurt her, she reasoned. But the reasoning was faulty, she knew. The bills would arrive, whether she opened them or not, and if she didn't pay them, she'd be in worse trouble than ever.

If the government could freeze her assets so that no one could buy or sell her house, could a bank foreclose on it?

Half facetious, half frantic, she put the question to Daphne soon after she returned from New York, and Daphne took it seriously. She asked around in the legal community. She went to the lawbooks for precedents. She learned that Laura could file for a stay of foreclosure if that particular point was reached.

That point was a long way off, Daphne assured her.

But Laura wasn't easily assured. Too much had been knocked out from under her. The rosy world she'd known, where things went her way if she wished it and worked hard enough, didn't exist any more. Her whole future was shaky. There was too much she didn't know.

That was why, rather than arguing with Daphne about stays of foreclosure, she broached another idea. "It's time we hired a private investigator. That's one of the things I think about when I wake up in the middle of the night. I keep asking myself whether we'd have already found Jeff if we'd hired one from the start, and just the wondering is driving me crazy."

It was a minute of silence before Daphne warned, "Sleuths cost."

Laura could see that she wasn't any crazier about the idea of a private investigator than she'd been at the start, but Daphne wasn't the one living with the dregs of Jeff's folly. "True, and I certainly can't walk into someone's office and set down a retainer. But I'd think a private investigator would welcome this case. There's the challenge. And the publicity. And there's the promise of money. Once I get into those bank accounts, I can pay."

Daphne pushed a hand through her hair. She was wearing it loose, in keeping with her weekend outfit of a blazer and jeans, and she looked as classy as ever. She also looked bothered. "Laura, those accounts aren't loaded. There's money in them, but if you're thinking you'll be on Easy Street once you get your half, you're wrong."

"They'd be something. They'd tide me over. They'd give me a *little* to fall back on, at least." She didn't know why Daphne had a problem with private investigators, but she was desperate to make her point. "It'll be four weeks on New Year's Day that he's gone, and I don't know anything more now about where he is than I did then. The police follow up on the phone calls they get, but other than that they're not doing much. Neither is the IRS. And if the FBI is on the case, I know why so many of the Ten Most Wanted are still walking the streets. Jeff has to be somewhere. I want to know where. If I had the time and energy and know-how, I'd go out looking for him myself, but I don't have any of those things, so I'm stuck here waiting for other people to find him. Well, they're not doing it, and I'm tired of waiting. I want to *do* something."

Daphne studied her for a minute. "Let me talk with Taylor Jones."

"Why not a private investigator?"

"Because we shouldn't have to spend our own money to do the government's job."

"But the government isn't doing the job, and I want it done."

"We owe Jones a final shot."

"Do you know any good PIs?"

Daphne nodded. "I've worked with some."

"Call one."

"First, Taylor Jones."

fourteen

TACK HADN'T SEEN DAPHNE SINCE THE morning she had shown up at the police station to blast him for opening his mouth to the press. He had thought about her, though, enough to mystify him. Sure, she had great legs, but he knew lots of women with great legs, so that didn't explain why she kept coming to mind. He figured it had something to do with her style—the way she moved, the way she talked, the way she defended her friends. She intrigued him.

For that reason, he felt distinct pleasure when she appeared at his door.

Actually, there was another reason too. It was after four on the last day of the year. Little more than a skeletal staff remained at the police station, with most everyone else off getting ready for New Year's Eve. But Tack didn't have plans for New Year's Eve—or New Year's Day, for that matter. So he was hanging around the station, shuffling papers on his desk, pretending to be on the verge of a breakthrough in the Frye case, when what he was really doing was feeling sorry for himself.

The smile he gave Daphne was broad and natural and seemed to startle her. She stook stockstill for a long moment. Then, with care, he thought, she ventured a tentative smile of her own. "That's nice," she said, almost curiously. "People in this building usually freeze up when I set foot inside the door."

"Not me. Not today. I need company. Wanna sit?"

The last time she'd come, she had stalked up to his desk and stood the whole time. He half expected her to do the same thing now, especially when she gathered herself in a businesslike way. But then, with a puzzled look, she seemed to pause, and in the next second what he saw in her eyes wasn't businesslike at all.

In the second after that, though, she blinked, and he figured he must have imagined whatever he thought he'd seen. Just when he was beginning to feel sorry for himself again, she came forward and slid into the chair across the desk from him. She lowered her briefcase to the floor. She crossed her legs. And though she deftly smoothed her skirt over her thighs so that little by way of enticement showed, he couldn't help but look. When he finally raised his eyes to hers, her expression was reproachful.

"Sorry," he murmured. He glanced at the side wall to get his bearings, then cleared his throat and looked back at her. "Actually, I'm not sorry. You look great. But then, you always do. You must be used to men staring at you. I'll bet it happens all the time."

She shook her head.

"No?" He couldn't believe that.

"I'm a lawyer. They don't dare."

"Oh." He guessed that said something about the men in Hampshire County and wondered if she meant it as a warning to him. If so, he figured he'd better set her straight. "Well, I dare. You really do look great. Best thing I've seen all day." He grinned and seconds later could have sworn she blushed. When the color remained, he decided it was her makeup, which made more sense, given the image he had of Daphne. He didn't think she was the blushing type. "So how are you doin', counselor?"

"Not bad." Her eyes were still on his face. "That's a nice tan you've got."

"Thanks. There's something about the sun in Tahiti that does it. Hey, you spend all that time running from from one end of the island to the other trying to track down a witness, and you're bound to catch a few rays, right?"

"Did you snorkel?"

"Sure did—when I needed a break from tracking down the witness."

"And wind-surf?"

"When I needed another break. Tracking down witnesses is hard work."

Either her lips were pursed in a prissy way or she was holding back a smile. "I know Christian, Agent Jones. My guess is that once you found him, he did his best to corrupt you."

Tack scratched his head. "I guess you do know him, at that." Remembering the Mahanoa'ee sisters, he had a disconcerting thought. "How *well* do you know him?"

"He's my best friend's brother-in-law. He was at their wedding, and so was I. He was at the kids' christenings, and so was I. He was at Lydia's sixty-fifth birthday bash, and so was I. And that's not to mention the occasional Thanksgiving, Christmas, and Easter dinner."

"That's a lot. He's a lucky guy. It must be real convenient to come visiting and find you waiting."

It was the wrong thing to say. He knew it the instant the words were out of his mouth, when the pleasant look she'd been wearing turned cold as ice and she started to rise.

"Hey," he said, half out of his chair himself, with a hand out to halt her escape. "I'm sorry. That was uncalled-for."

"It was also *wrong*," she informed him. Her eyes flashed, that pretty hazel color he remembered. He wasn't sorry he'd asked after all, particularly when she went on. "There's never been anything between Christian and me. Why you'd think there was is beyond me."

"He's single, you're single—"

"We haven't a blessed thing in common. He's as anti-establishment as I'm establishment, and that's just for starters. I could go on ad infinitum about our differences, but it would be a waste of time for both of us."

"That's okay. I'm in no rush." To prove his point, he sat back in his seat and linked his fingers over his middle.

Daphne didn't quite sit back, but at least her bottom was touching the seat again. "It's New Year's Eve. Everyone's clearing out. Shouldn't you be heading back to Boston or somewhere?"

"There's nothing for me in Boston."

"Uh-huh."

"You don't believe me?"

"Of course, I believe you—" she caught herself "—no, you're right, I don't. You look like the kind of guy who has a girl in every port."

"That sexy, huh?" He rushed on before she could deny it. "Actually, I broke up with someone a few weeks ago, and I've been alone ever since. So there's no one in Boston, and there's no one here, which means I have all the time in the world to sit and talk." He rocked farther back in his chair, folded his hands behind his head, and grinned.

The grin got to her. Again. It seemed to surprise her, make her forget what she was going to say. Then again, Tack mused, maybe that was wishful thinking on his part. But he kept on grinning on the chance it was true, and because he was feeling better than he had for a while.

After staring at him longer than she should have, Daphne shot a glance at the ceiling that reminded him of the one he'd sent toward the wall. When she looked down again, she was in control. "I came here for a reason."

"I figured."

She took a deep breath. "Laura wants to hire a private investigator. Before we go to the expense, I want to know what you've learned. Dennis tells me Christian wasn't any help."

"Not in locating Jeff," Tack confirmed. He had no problem sharing information, particularly if it would win her confidence.

"Christian hasn't seen him or heard from him. We've checked out airlines, bus lines, train lines. We've checked out rental car companies—yes, I know he took the Porsche, but there's always the chance he ditched it somewhere and rented something less conspicuous. We've checked hotels and motels and police in this state and in every contiguous state, then every state contiguous to those contiguous states, and no one's seen hide nor hair of the bastard."

"Has he used any credit cards?"

"No."

"Has he tried to use his bank card?"

"No. He's clever. Hasn't left a single crumb for us to follow."

"So what are you going to do?" Daphne's voice held a challenge that Tack was only too happy to meet.

"We're shifting our focus to his life here. We're talking with friends, clients, business associates." He thought about what he'd found out. "It's interesting."

"How so?"

"No one seems to know him real well. When he was around, they liked him. They even respected him for his know-how or his manner. But when you ask if they thought he was capable of committing a crime like this, they don't immediately say no."

"What do they say?"

"That they didn't know what he was thinking. That there were times when he went through the motions but he just wasn't there." Tack paused again, this time to study her face. She was close to the family. She was close to Jeff. Of all the people he'd spoken with, she was in a position to give him the most. "Did you ever get that feeling?"

"No."

"He seemed attentive?"

"Yes."

"Was he happy?"

She opened her mouth to answer, then closed it again, which surprised Tack. He would have assumed she'd say yes. That had been the family story, that Jeff was happy and content and honest and kind. The guy sounded boring as hell to Tack, which was one of the reasons why he loved it when people paused and thought twice, then gave him answers he didn't expect. The surprises were what made his job interesting, and this case had a few.

"He was as happy as most people," Daphne finally said.

"Is that happy or not?"

"Happy, I guess."

But she seemed to be having trouble with the word, and he wanted to know why. "Either he was happy, or he wasn't. It's a black-and-white issue."

"No, it's not. A person can be wildly happy, meaning that he loves absolutely everything in his life, or he can be relatively happy, meaning that if things were different he would be happier, but since they're not—and can't be—he can live with what he's got."

"Jeff was the relatively happy kind?"

She frowned at her hand, which lay quietly in her lap. "I think so."

"What would have made him happier in life?"

She continued to frown, looking torn now.

Softly, and in earnest, he said, "This is between you and me, Daphne. Totally off the record. I'm trying to get some insight into the man. That's all."

Her eyes rose. A crease came and went between them. In a voice that was as soft as his had been, she said, "I think he'd have been happier if he were married to someone other than Laura."

"But Laura's your best friend."

"I know, and I adore her for her strengths, but those strengths kept Jeff down. I mean, he loved her. But he had to live in her shadow, and that can be hard for a man to do year after year. If he'd married someone not quite so overpowering, he'd have been able to shine more than he did."

Tack scratched his head. "Laura overpowering?" Christian had said something similar, and he'd been doubtful then too. "She didn't strike me that way."

"Of course not. You're seeing her at her worst. She doesn't have any control over what's happening now, and, believe me, it's driving her nuts. But if you look at the way she and Jeff lived, you'll see it. She shaped their lives. When something needed doing, she did it. When something needed arranging, she arranged it. The trip to Saba is a perfect example." She sat back. "You heard about that, didn't you?"

"Just that they were planning to go."

"Let me tell you about those plans. A while back, Laura decided that once every winter the whole family should go some-place warm. In the past, it's been St. Martin or St. John or Nevis. This year it was supposed to be Saba. She rented a villa with seven bedrooms, a maid, and a cook. She booked airline tickets not only for Jeff and the kids and her, but for her mother-in-law, one of Scott's roommates, and me. She arranged for a surrey to meet us at the airport. She arranged for a sloop with a full crew and a scuba instructor to take us island-hopping. She arranged for the cook to do a Caribbean feast on the beach one night. She even found a calypso trio to serenade. And the thing of it is that she arranged all this thinking we'd all be as ecstatic as she was, when in fact Jeff hates hot weather, Scott would rather be with girls, Lydia is terrified of flying, and I can't take the time off from work."

"I'd take time off from work. The trip sounds great."

"The trip is now canceled, but that's not the point. The point is that Laura gets things done. She's a very competent woman. That's tough for a guy who may not be so competent."

"And Jeff wasn't?"

"He could have been, given the chance."

"But he wasn't given the chance. So why didn't he leave her?"

"Because there were lots of things he liked about his life. It gets back to that issue of happiness. He wasn't giving up the good for the unknown."

"Looks like he did," Tack said.

Daphne grew guarded. "We don't know that for sure. Until somebody finds him, we don't know *anything* for sure, which is why we're thinking of hiring a private investigator. If you can't make any headway—"

Tack interrupted her. He heard criticism coming on, and he wasn't in the mood. There was more he wanted to know. "You say Jeff loved his wife."

After a pause, she said, "Yes."

"But her competence frustrated him."

"That was my opinion. Just mine. I don't know whether he identified competence as the problem or not."

"Could he have been physically dissatisfied?"

Daphne was silent. "Physically?"

"Sex. Was it good between them?"

"Since we weren't into a *ménage à trois*, I wouldn't know, Agent Jones."

"The name's Tack, and I realize that," he said. Thought of a *ménage à trois* involving Daphne gave him a jolt somewhere low, but he ignored it. "But did Laura ever hint that things weren't so hot in bed?"

"No. I've told you before. She thought her marriage was great."

"Did *he* ever drop any hints?"

"Why would he do that?"

"Maybe because he had someone on the side and wanted reassurance that what he was doing wasn't so horrible."

Daphne sat still as stone. Her lips—thin lips, Tack saw, but gentle and covered with a stylish buff-colored gloss—were pressed together. Finally they parted. "I've been forthright with you, Agent Jones, more so than I should have been, since the Fryes are my clients. But in the sense that we both want to find Jeff, we're temporarily on the same side. If you know something I don't, why don't you come right out and say it."

Tack took her up on the invitation. "He was having an affair."

Her face drained of color, and though she didn't move an inch, he could see she was shaken. "What?"

"He was having an affair. We have a witness who places him at his condo in Holyoke with a woman who wasn't his wife."

Daphne looked so dismayed that any pleasure he might have gotten from hitting her with a fast one was lost. "You have a witness?" she asked in a low voice.

He nodded. "A neighbor. She didn't know Jeff's name. But I was wandering around out there last week, talking with people, showing his picture. She recognized it right away."

"She was sure it was Jeff?"

"Very."

"Did she know who the woman with him was?"

"No. She mentioned long, loose, sand-colored hair, so we knew it wasn't Laura, and she confirmed it when we showed her Laura's picture."

Daphne stared at him. "Jeff loved Laura. There must be a mistake."

"The witness was certain. She saw him with this other woman more than once."

"How does she know they were lovers? How does she know they weren't just friends or business associates?"

"She saw them kissing in a way that friends wouldn't do."

Daphne compressed her lips. Hesitantly, she asked, "Was there only one woman? Was that all your witness saw?"

"Just one."

"No others brought to the condo at other times?"

"No. She said she rarely saw him there, which was why she always noticed when he came. On the times he was with someone, it was always the woman with the super hair."

Daphne took a slow breath, then swallowed. "Has your witness been down to the station?"

Tack nodded. "This morning."

"Then this is formally entered in your records?" Her voice retained a still quality, as though she were holding her breath.

He nodded.

"Is it common knowledge around here yet?"

"Not unless Melrose talked. He was the only one with me when the witness came in."

"Have you called the *Sun*?"

Tack took offense. The front legs of his chair hit the floor. "Why would I do that? You may find this hard to believe, but my goal in this job is not publicity. It's to find Jeffrey Frye and see that he's brought to trial. I don't get any great kicks out of providing the paper with copy."

She was wary. "You've talked before."

"Because O'Neil called and asked. Mostly I gave yeses and nos in response to his questions. If he tosses out scenarios and I give him yeses and nos, and then he writes his piece like I was the one doing the tossing, it's not *my* fault."

Her wariness faded, but she didn't look away. After a minute, she swallowed again. Then, before Tack's eyes, it was as though the tension left her and she was suddenly, overwhelmingly tired. "Don't tell him about this," she pleaded. "He'll plaster headlines on page one, and it'll be one more humiliation for Laura to endure. This will be the worst. It'll hurt her so much." Her voice caught. She put a shaky finger to her mouth.

Tack remembered the times he'd thought of Daphne Phillips losing her cool and the pleasure he'd found in the thought. She hadn't exactly lost it now. She was still a lady, sitting there with her hair pulled back in a shiny knot, her skirt smooth, and her ankles crossed, but she was clearly upset, and there wasn't any pleasure in it for him.

"Hey," he murmured gently, "I'm not gonna tell." Leaving his chair, he rounded the desk and hunkered down by her side. "I'm not a total bastard, Daphne. I know this isn't easy for Laura, and I won't do anything to make it any worse than it has to be. Obviously I'll be doing my damnedest to identify the woman, but I won't be running to the papers. If I did that, whoever it is will take off, and I'd look like a *real* fool."

Her eyes stayed on his face, searching his eyes, then moving down to his mouth for a second before she dropped her hand to her lap and looked off at the wall. "This case is a nightmare."

"And you're living through it with Laura."

"Oh, I have it easy. I can push it aside to work on other cases, then go home and not notice the silence, because silence is par for the course."

"You live alone?"

"Yeah." She took a fast breath and stood. "And I'd better be going."

He stood too. "Have any hot plans for tonight?"

She threaded the straps of her briefcase over her shoulder and pulled her coat tighter. Then she tipped up her chin. "Actually, I'm planning to read a good book."

"All by yourself?"

"That's the best way to do it."

"What about food?"

"If I get hungry, I'll get something from the freezer."

"I have a better idea," Tack said. He hadn't given it a whole lot of thought, mainly because he hadn't expected Daphne Phillips to fall into his lap this way, but he wasn't blowing what could be a once-in-a-lifetime chance. "Let's get something together."

She blinked. "Uh, I don't think that would be smart."

"Why not? It's New Year's Eve. I'm alone, you're alone, and being alone on New Year's Eve sucks. I'm still new here. I don't know where the hell to go. So you choose. We could eat Italian, Chinese, French. We even could go to Cherries."

She chided him with a look. "Not smart at all. Laura will be there. What do you think she'll think if she sees us together?"

"Let her think you're sweet-talking me into dropping the case against her husband."

"But I'm not doing that," Daphne said with an instructional half smile.

He wanted a full smile. He wanted more of the little curls in his stomach each time he got a whiff of something faint and sweet. He wanted someone to talk with. He wanted a decent meal for a change, not the fast-food stuff he'd been living on. Mostly he didn't want to be alone.

"I won't drop the case against her husband," he told her without a bit of smartness. "I can't. It's not mine to drop. It's the government's. All I am is an agent—"

"Not a good idea," she repeated and started for the door.

"No one has to see us," he argued. "And so what if they do? It's not like there's anything fishy going on. We'd just be discussing business."

At the door, she turned and asked quietly, "Would we?"

"If that was what you wanted."

"What if we got tired of discussing business?"

"Then we could discuss something else."

"Like what?"

"Like whatever book it is you're planning to read, or what kind of job you think the President's doing, or why you ought to plan a trip to Tahiti. Hell, Daphne, we can talk about whatever we want. Isn't that what people do when they go out together?"

He hadn't meant to say it that way, mainly because he knew it would scare her off. God, was she prickly! Prickly, and pretty, and smart, and challenging. Maybe the prickly part came with old age. Maybe prickly was really picky, and she really didn't like him.

He stuck his hands in his slacks pockets. "You're right. I'd probably bore you to tears."

"I didn't say that."

"I'll bet you love that silence of yours."

"Not always."

"Restaurants are awful on New Year's Eve. People drink, and they're loud, and the prices are higher and the service slower. I don't blame you for not wanting to go out."

She tucked her chin to her chest for a long, pensive minute.

Then, reaching a decision, she looked up. "Maybe a drink. It's too early for dinner, but we could go somewhere for a drink. Just one. Just for an hour."

"You're on," he said with a grin. Without waiting to see what effect the grin had, he quickly collected papers from the desk and shoved them into a briefcase, grabbed his topcoat from the hook behind the door, and escorted her out.

Daphne chose a bar on the lower end of Main Street that she claimed was a favorite of the town's legal eagles. Tack didn't see any legal eagles around, but that could have been because of the holiday, or because the place was so dark he wouldn't have been able to see them if they had been there. He was sure that was why she had chosen the place. She wanted privacy for professional reasons. He wanted privacy for other reasons.

She ordered a glass of wine to his Sam Adams, and as soon as the bartender served them up, they slid into a booth near the back of the bar. "So," Tack said, after he'd taken a hefty swallow of his beer, "tell me what a nice girl like you is doing in a small town like this."

Her mouth twitched. "I like small towns. I was born here. I'll probably die here."

"Is that resignation I hear?"

"No. I went to law school in New Haven and could have gone anywhere from there, but I chose to come back. It was what I wanted to do."

"Why?"

She considered that. "My family's here, or was. My parents are dead now, and my brother's long gone. Still, this is where I grew up. I've lived in the same house all my life."

"No kidding," he said. "That's neat."

She smiled. "Yeah. I suppose. I like the place, at any rate, and since the mortgage was paid off a long time ago, it comes dirt cheap."

"How about Hampshire County? Is it a good place to practice law?"

"Yes and no. I have a good practice. It's a criminal one, but the crime here isn't as gruesome as it is in the big city, and that pleases me. I'm not big on blood and guts."

Melrose had called her tough, and on the surface she was. But Tack was beginning to think the toughness ended there. "So things are tamer here. That's the yes. What's the no?"

"People are less liberal." She narrowed it down. "Lawyers are less liberal." And again. "Male lawyers are less liberal."

He understood. "You've had to do the women's lib thing from scratch."

"Uh-huh. When I started practicing, I was the first female lawyer some of these guys had ever met. It's the old story—I had to work twice as hard and be twice as good. It's been an experience."

"But the worst must be over."

"I guess."

"Does that mean the challenge is gone?"

"Not at all. Every case is new and different. Each one is a challenge."

He sat back in the booth and sighed. "In my next life, I think I'll be a lawyer. You guys have exciting lives. Me? I may get an exciting case once a year, but you get 'em all the time, and then there's the glamour of the courtroom, with everyone watching you, and the jurors hanging on your every word, and the press quoting you. By the time my cases end up in court, I'm back in the office with my nose stuck in spread sheets until one in the morning, and by then everyone else has had their fun and is sound asleep, so there isn't a damn thing to do but go home to a cold, empty apartment."

From the dimness across the booth came a quiet reply. "After a long day in court, my house is just as cold and empty. If there's glamour trying a case in front of a jury, it ends on the courthouse steps. Believe me, being a lawyer isn't the answer to a cold, empty house."

It was hard to feel sorry for himself when she sounded sad

like that. "You don't strike me as the type to want glamour."

"I'm not."

"What do you want?"

She finished her wine and set down the glass. "I'm not sure."

"Tell me."

"I would if I could."

He wagged two fingers at the bartender to order seconds for them both. "You want to be a judge someday?"

"Maybe."

"That'd be a nice way to grow old. Lots of adulation."

"But still a big empty house at the end of the day."

"Maybe you'll go into politics. Could you see yourself running for the House of Representatives?"

"No."

"Why not?"

Her mouth twitched again. "I smoked pot in college. Voters around here don't like that."

"I'll smoke pot with you any time you want," Tack said.

"Shhh."

"I mean it."

"I'm sure you do. You'd love to blow my career."

"I'd blow mine too. But then I'd *have* to start over. Don't you ever wonder what you'd do, if you had to do that?" He freed his hands from his empty beer bottle when the bartender took it, then settled in around the new one. "Guys down at the police station wonder about it a lot. I hear them joking, y'know? 'Jeffrey Frye is one lucky sonofabitch,' they say. 'Jeffrey Frye is one *smart* sonafabitch,' they say. 'Wish I could pick up and leave. Wish I had the balls.'" Tack caught her startled gaze and shrugged. "That's what they say."

"They're crude."

"Maybe some of them. But not all. Some of those guys are locked into jobs and debts and obligations they can't stand, and it isn't their fault. They got swept up into it straight from high school, and before they knew it they were in too deep to turn around or bend over or get out. So they think what Frye did was real neat."

"Do you?" Daphne asked.

"Hell, no. He broke the law, and besides that, he deserted his family. There's nothing heroic about that. If I had a family—"

"Why don't you?"

He took a swig of his beer. "Because I go for the wrong women. Gwen told me that, and she's right. I go for smart, sophisticated career types like you, but types like that don't want what I do."

"What do you want?"

"Meat loaf and mashed potatoes waiting, fresh and hot, when I get home from work, a house with a white picket fence, and five kids." He stared at his beer and flexed his jaw. "Pretty backward, huh?"

"Actually," Daphne surprised him by saying, "it's sweet. Impractical, especially if you like smart, sophisticated career types, but sweet."

"Why can't a smart, sophisticated career type want all that?"

"Because she doesn't have the time. She can't be managing a career at the same time that she's cooking meat loaf and mashed potatoes and raising five kids. Much as she might like it."

He fancied he heard wistfulness. "Would you?"

She raised her eyes from her wineglass and gave a quick shake of her head. "I missed the boat. I'm too old."

"No you're not."

"I'm forty." She said it looking him straight in the eye, like she was daring him to be shocked.

"So?" he said calmly.

"So I can't be having five kids at my age."

"You could have one or two."

"If I started right now. But then my career would go down the drain. And, besides, I'm a lousy cook. I've never made meat loaf and mashed potatoes in my life."

"All you have to do is follow a recipe."

She snorted. "That can be easier said than done."

"Hell, it's easy." He suddenly had a brainstorm. "Hey, let's do it now."

"Do what?"

"Make meat loaf and mashed potatoes."

"Are you kidding?"

"I'm dead serious." More so with each passing second, he thought. "You don't want to be seen going out to dinner with me—"

"That's not—"

"But we both have to eat—" he glanced at his watch, "—and if we left here now, we'd have just enough time to pick up stuff at the market before it closed. You must have a cookbook lying around the house."

She looked like she wanted to deny it. Then again, she looked interested. One second to the next, she wavered.

"Come on, Daphne," he said in his most urgent boy scout voice. "It'd be fun. Y'know how long it's been since I've done something just for fun with a woman? I mean, sex is just for fun, but I'm not talking about sex. I'm talking about doing something different and creative and practical. Just dinner. We can make dinner, then eat, then I'll leave so you can read your book. What are we talking about—one more hour, maybe two? I mean, the alternative is going back to that damn motel with a Whopper and fries. Nothing we put together can be as bad as that."

"Don't be so sure," she murmured, but he could see she was leaning in his favor.

"I am sure," he said, and dug in his pocket for bills to pay for their drinks. "Trust me."

On Daphne's recommendation, they walked. Her house wasn't more than fifteen minutes from the center of town, she explained, and there was a market right on the way. Tack was feeling a little high, not from the beer—hell, he could drink a six-pack without feeling a thing—but from the unexpected anticipation of having something to do on New Year's Eve. As he walked, though, he realized that the anticipation wasn't just of doing something, but of doing something with Daphne.

He didn't tell her that, lest she run off into the night and leave him lost on the streets of Northampton. But he was thinking it. He was thinking he couldn't have arranged a nicer date if he'd planned it all out beforehand. Then again, if he'd planned it all out beforehand, he'd never have planned this. He'd have planned something sophisticated to impress her, like a theater date, or something lavish, like dinner and dancing in Boston. He wouldn't have planned something as down-home ordinary as cooking meat loaf and mashed potatoes. But she wasn't complaining, which made him think. He liked her. He really liked her.

The cold air felt good at first, crisp and bracing. Then they cleared the downtown buildings and the wind began to bite. He ducked his head to shield his ears as best he could in the collar of his coat. "Geez, it's cold," he muttered.

"Awful," she agreed, and he thought he heard teeth clicking in the single word.

Shifting the grocery bag to his outside arm, he wrapped his inside one around Daphne and pulled her close. She gave a tiny laugh—a nervous one, he thought—when it took a minute for their strides to coordinate, but she didn't pull away. It felt good having her tucked against him that way. He didn't feel as cold as he had before. Even his ears, which were as exposed as ever, felt warmer. He guessed it had something to do with the rising fire in his blood.

Leaning into the wind, they walked on and on. Daphne directed, pointing with a gloved finger when they had to turn, then putting the hand back in her pocket. When they reached her street, she said, "Almost there," as though that would make him happy. But he could have walked more. Holding Daphne made him feel part of a couple. It was an illusion, he knew; still, he liked it.

The houses on her street were old and set equidistant from

one another on neat little lots. Tack couldn't see much, since the streetlights had long since been swallowed in thick mazes of tree branches that, even bare of leaves, restricted their scope, but he got the impression of vintage New England. Most of the houses had lights by their doors. Some had Christmas lights in front windows.

Daphne's house was dark, making Tack doubly grateful he was with her. Coming home to an empty house on New Year's Eve was bad enough, but coming home to a *dark* empty house was worse. So, though the wind wasn't anywhere near as bad here as before, he kept her anchored to his side as they went up the walk. They took the three steps without faltering. She fished in her bag for her keys, opened the door, and reached in to flip on the outside lights—all without moving from under his arm. If anything, she turned into him more.

He knew he should let her go, but for several seconds longer he waited, giving her a chance to make the move herself. Her head was lowered, like she had something to say but couldn't find the right words. He was beginning to wonder what that something was when she looked up at him, and in the new light the look of silent longing he saw on her face made his heart thud.

Swearing softly, he hurried her into the house and closed the door. Letting the groceries slide unheeded to the floor, he bent his head to hers. He kissed her once, tentatively, and when she didn't protest, a second time. When he felt her respond, he deepened the kiss, and when she responded to that, he was lost.

He hadn't planned it. Christ, he hadn't planned it. But kissing Daphne was the most natural thing in the world. It was also the most exciting, and before he knew it, kissing wasn't enough. His body was heating at an alarming rate, so he shed his coat and let Daphne touch him while his own hands were busy on her ribs, her waist, her breasts. Buttons came undone, flesh met flesh, and breathing grew harder, but there was no stopping the hot and heavy need that flared between them.

He bunched her skirt high on her thighs and reached under-

210

neath. "Okay?" he whispered against her mouth. She gave her tongue in answer, and when he felt her hands on the fastening of his trousers, then his zipper, he didn't ask any more. He was so full, he was ready to burst. With only one goal in mind, he crowded his fingers at the notch of her pantyhouse and pulled, making a hole that his thumb widened, and while that thumb stayed to bask in her heat, he braced his legs between hers, knees against the door, and entered her.

The cry she gave was soft, throaty, and one of such pure female pleasure that he nearly came then and there. But he wanted to wait, wanted Daphne's release to come before his, so he held himself still for a minute, and even that was wild. With her arms high around his neck and her back arched in a way that kept her breasts touching his chest, and her mouth mirroring his, she stirred him up, and that was before he allowed himself to concentrate on how hot and tight she was around him. Realizing he couldn't last long, he began to stroke her inside. Within minutes, she cried out, clutched him even tighter, and held her breath. The rhythmic spasms of her body were his undoing. They hadn't yet begun to abate when he threw his head back, gritted his teeth, and gave her everything he had.

That was the start of what proved to be the most satisfying New Year's Eve Tack had ever spent. As soon as he regained breath and enough strength to move, he discarded the clothes that were hanging half on and half off him and did the same for Daphne. Then, there, just inside the front door in the dark, he learned her body with his hands and tongue until the heat rose again. When it was extinguished, he lifted her like the chivalrous knight he must have been in another life and carried her to the bedroom, where he made love to her again, long and hard.

They did make meat loaf and mashed potatoes. Stark naked, using two candles on the kitchen table for light, they followed the recipe in one of Daphne's mother's cookbooks, and the meat loaf might have been delicious if they hadn't left it in so long. The way Tack figured it, though, a slightly crispy crust was a small price to pay for what they'd been doing that had made it that way, and the potatoes were perfect. Most importantly, once they'd eaten, they had renewed strength, and renewed strength is an important thing to have when two people have the hots for each other. So they went back to bed and made love again, and then again, after they'd slept for a bit.

By the time morning came, even Tack had to admit that he wasn't as young as he used to be. For a guy who worked out all the time, his shoulders and upper arms, even his thighs, were suspiciously sore. But there was working out, and there was working out. What he'd done with Daphne was in a class by itself.

In the light of dawn, she was subdued, and after they'd showered she sent him home. "I need time," she said.

"Can I see you later?"

She shook her head. The movement fascinated him. He drew his fingers through her hair, which, unbound, was wildly light. Putting his nose to her neck, he breathed in the sweet scent that lay there.

"Can I call you later?"

She nodded.

So he got dressed, put on his coat with the collar up, and headed out into the cold. As he walked, he thought about where he had been twenty-four hours before and where he would be right now if he had his way. But life was a compromise. He and Gwen hadn't been able to do it, but things were different with Daphne. He wanted to stay, she wanted him to leave. So he'd left. But he had incredible memories, plus permission to call, plus a small scented sachet he'd pinched from her drawer.

All in all, he figured he'd come out ahead.

fifteen

tHE WAVES HIT THE SHORE WITH STUNNING force, sending a plume of spray high, nearly to the spot where Jeff Frye sat. He didn't budge, though, not when he felt the mist touch his face, not when a new, even larger wave exploded against the rocks below.

It was New Year's Day, and if anything could make him believe that life did go on, it was this. The surf shimmered in, gained speed and strength and size, rolled, crashed, and receded, only to shimmer on the horizon again. So life went through phases, he told himself. Right now he was down. Soon he'd begin to shimmer, then slowly, gradually, eventually gain in speed and strength and size. It would help if he knew where he was headed, but he wasn't any clearer on that than when he left Northampton four weeks before.

Four weeks. It was a long time. He looked different now; his hair was longer, he had the solid beginnings of a beard, and hours sitting here on his rock had given ruddiness to his skin. Thanks to that, and to the laundromat's unforgiving machines, he looked decidedly broken in. The townsfolk no longer stared when he walked down the street, which he did every day. A trip in for the paper and a stop at the diner had become part of his ritual, a necessary part of his life.

Still, he felt empty. He missed home, missed it with a deep, dark ache, so he tried to keep his mind occupied with other things. But it was hard. He read every book he bought, then bought more and read them too; still he had time on his hands. The man at the general store—Horace Stubble was his name— came through with a used pickup, which helped some. Jeff arranged to pay for it in installments, so no one would know how much money he had, and though his first impulse was to clean it and polish it and make it look presentable, he resisted. The last thing he needed was to display the instincts of a Yuppie. Besides, the truck was fully functional without a cleanup, so when he needed supplies, or when he thought he'd go mad if he didn't get out, he drove to one of the local strip malls and wandered around. He never went far and was never gone for long. As lonesome as he was in his cottage on the bluff, he felt a certain security there.

He wondered how Scott was doing at school and whether he understood anything of what Jeff had done. He wondered whether Debra was the butt of school gossip and, if so, how she was taking it. He wondered how badly he'd hurt Lydia, and whether Laura was burying herself in Cherries, and whether Daphne had everything legal under control.

"Ev-an!"

Lost in his thoughts, he didn't hear the voice at first, and then it was a minute more before he identified with the name. But the call came again, closer this time, and he was quickly on his feet, on his guard. The only people who knew that name were from town, but no one from town had ever come to see him before.

"Hi, Ev-an!"

It was Glorie, waving and picking her way through the rocks, nearly unrecognizable with her dark hair hidden under a thick wool hat and her slim body swallowed up in her coat. But her pale skin stood out against the grayness of the day, and her smile stood out against that. Both cried of innocence, identifying her in an instant.

214

Had it been anyone else, Jeff would have been nervous. But in her own sweet, ploddingly slow way, Glorie had become a friend.

Fearful she might slip on the rocks, he hurried to where she was. "What in the world are you doing all the way up here, Glorie?"

She looked suddenly unsure. "I came to see you."

"But it's so cold."

Seeing that he was concerned, not angry, she smiled. "I don't mind."

"Does Poppy know you're here?"

She nodded. "He made me wear this." She tugged at a bright wool scarf that was wound twice around her neck, immobilizing her much as a surgical collar would have done. "And he said not to stay long. But it's a special day, and I knew you were alone, and I wanted to bring you this."

She was wearing a backpack. She tried to grab it, tried to push one of the straps from her shoulder, but between her mittens and the bulk of her coat and scarf, she couldn't grasp a thing. He quickly helped her with it. When it was off, he gave it an experimental heft.

"What's inside?"

"Dinner. I figured you wouldn't cook much up here all by yourself, and we're closed all day. So here's some ham and potatoes and cabbage and rolls that Poppy made. I wrapped it all up in lots of foil. It was hot when I left. Maybe if you take it inside it'll still be warm."

Jeff's mouth was watering. "Let's go see," he said. Holding the backpack in one hand, he took Glorie's hand in the other and led her over the rocks. They were nearly at the cottage when he questioned what he was doing. If his goal was to keep as low a profile as possible, showing Glorie into his home wasn't the wisest thing to do.

But Glorie was Glorie. She was naïve, harmless. He didn't see how she could betray him. With the Porsche under its tarp in the boat shed and his briefcase stashed along with his business clothes far back under the bed, there was nothing of a revealing nature in the shack. Besides, he certainly couldn't turn her away, not after she had made such a kind gesture, not after she had climbed all this way in the cold.

So he pushed the door open and let her inside, and, for the look on her face, Jeff would have thought she was a child in a crystal castle. She was all eyes and an excited smile that turned shy when she looked at him.

"This is nice," she breathed. She tugged her mittens off and stuffed them in her pockets. "It's cozy." She walked around the perimeter of the room, running her hand along the back of the sofa, then along the desk and shelves that Jeff had sanded and polished. She fingered the books. "Have you read *all* these?"

"Most."

"Wow."

Setting the backpack on the table, he began to unload it. Package after package emerged, most warm to the touch. Jeff hadn't eaten since breakfast, which had consisted of two muffins and a dish of cold cereal and milk. Mindful of the New Year's Day dinner Laura had always made and would no doubt be making again, he had opted for nothing. But Poppy's ham smelled incredible, and he was suddenly ravenously hungry.

"Will you share this with me?" he asked.

Glorie was still looking at the books, touching one spine after the next. She shook her head. "I already ate." As though recalling something, she looked around. "If you have some plates, I'll set it out for you." Spotting the cabinets flanking the sink, she headed that way.

Jeff stopped her. "You don't have to wait on me here. It's enough that you brought the food." He steered her toward the table and drew out a chair. "It would make me very happy if you would sit with me while I eat." He realized that he meant it. With Glorie there, he wouldn't be so lonely. "Will you take off your coat?" He had already hung his own on a hook by the door.

She shook her head. "I told Poppy I wouldn't."

He felt a moment's disappointment. The cottage was comfortably warm, now that he'd filled in the cracks in the walls, and with the cleaning and sprucing up he'd done, the place had grown more homelike. He would have liked Glorie to stay awhile. But Poppy was protective. He respected that.

Satisfied that at least she was sitting, he went back to opening foil packages. In an instant, she was on her feet, helping him.

"I don't want you working," he reminded her.

"I'm supposed to work."

"Not here. Here you're my guest."

"I don't think I'd be very good at that. I'd rather help."

She said it in such an earnest way that Jeff gave in. Within minutes, he had a plate of food before him the likes of which he had never expected to see on his bluff. "Whoa," he drawled with a smiling glance around the room, "this is the crowning touch."

"Crowning touch?"

"Pièce de résistance."

"Pee-ess?"

His smile gentled. "It's terrific, Glorie. Thank you."

Pleased, she sat back down in the chair. With the exception of her mittens, she was bundled as tightly as before.

"Are you sure you won't have some?" he asked.

She nodded. Since she seemed perfectly happy—and looked adorable—sitting there enveloped by her coat and hat, Jeff didn't argue. Besides, he was starved. The smells coming from his plate were nearly as incredible as the food looked, and he was familiar enough with Poppy's cooking to know that it would taste every bit as good.

Catching the expectant look on Glorie's face, he took a bite of ham. He followed that up with potatoes, then cabbage. Unable to help himself, he closed his eyes and smiled. "This is so good."

As though she'd been waiting to hear just that, Glorie allowed herself a relieved grin. "Lots of people don't like cabbage. They tell me that at the diner. But Poppy said it goes nice with ham. Nicely."

Jeff could take or leave cabbage, or he could have in the past. But he wasn't leaving any of what Glorie had brought. Everything tasted wonderful.

"Did you have a nice New Year's Eve?" he asked between bites.

She bobbed her head. "Uh-huh."

"What did you do?"

"Poppy took me to visit with the Schmidts. They live a little ways down the coast."

"Are they friends of yours?"

"Uh-huh. They're nice. I really wanted to go to a movie, but Poppy doesn't like the movies. He says they're not good for me."

"Some of them aren't," Jeff said. He thought of Debra, who, at sixteen, could walk into any R-rated movie she liked, which didn't thrill him. But Laura was convinced she was mature enough to handle what she saw, so Jeff had never made an issue of it. He guessed Poppy had more power in his home than Jeff had had.

For a minute he wondered about that home. "Where's your mom?"

"Dead," Glorie said lightly.

"I'm sorry."

"It's okay. I have Poppy." She seemed perfectly happy with that.

Jeff ate more, while Glorie watched. Whenever he looked up, she smiled, but she didn't initiate conversation—which was a new experience for Jeff. Laura had never been at a loss for things to say, and Debra, not to be outdone, had always come in a close second.

The irony of it was that Glorie was being quiet at a time when he really did want to hear the sound of another person's voice. So he asked, "Have you always helped him at the diner?"

She nodded. "When I was going to school I couldn't be there until the end of the day, but I don't have to go to school any more now, so I'm there all the time."

"You must have done well at school. You speak well."

Her eyes lit up and she smiled, then took a breath and looked off toward the books. "It was a special school."

"What kind?"

"For people who need extra help, Poppy says. I wouldn't do well in the school here. I did when I was little, but then there was the accident, and now I have trouble reading, and I can't do math. So Poppy sent me to Longfellow." She got up from the chair and went to the bookshelf. "You've read all these books. You must be very smart."

"No. But I like to read."

"So do I. But it's hard."

Jeff wished he knew something about learning disabilities. In the next instant, he wished he knew more about Glorie, because if she had had an accident, the problem possibly went beyond that of a learning disability.

"Reading is like most anything else," he said. "It takes practice."

"That's what Poppy says. And I do practice, but it's hard."

"What do you read?"

"*National Geographic*," she told him. "Poppy got it for me for my last birthday, and it comes every month. The pictures are so, so pretty." Her voice fell. "Sometimes I just look at the pictures. Poppy would be upset if he knew, but the stories have so many words I don't know that it's easier just to look at the pictures." As though realizing what she'd said, she looked suddenly stricken. "I'm not dumb. I just have . . . trouble sometimes."

Jeff's heart went out to her. "Of course you're not dumb. You're smart and hard-working. You also happen to be the nicest person I've ever had in my home. So I want you to come and sit down and talk with me some more."

She looked relieved, even pleased, but shy. Stuffing her hands in her pockets on top of her mittens, she said softly, "I should be getting back home. Poppy will worry. He wanted to come with me, but he wasn't feeling well, so I told him I'd go alone and come right back. I have to leave."

Jeff stood. He looked down at the meal she'd brought and was touched all over again. He would have liked her to stay. But he understood her father's concern. Reluctantly, he gathered up the empty backpack. He was just about to pass it to her when a jarring thud came at the door. The sound was so loud and unexpected that he jumped. He looked quickly at Glorie, who was looking horrified, and for a heart-stopping instant he wondered if she'd betrayed him after all.

Then she said, "That's Poppy, I know it's Poppy," and while he stood in a state of near paralysis, she went to the door and opened it. "I'm *fine*, Poppy. I *told* you I'd be fine. I brought Evan his food and was just sitting with him for a minute, but I was already getting ready to leave, so there wasn't any need for you to come after me. I thought you said you wanted to stay inside in the warm all day."

Gordon regarded her carefully, then looked past her to Jeff. "I gut worried," he said in a hoarse voice.

"She's fine," Jeff assured him.

"I gut worried," he repeated, looking steadily at Jeff. "She's special, Glorie is. Ya bettuh know it."

"I certainly do."

"Poppy—"

"She isn't like othuh girls," Gordon warned. "She's good an' sweet, an' she may be thirty, but she was sleepin' fuh three a those yee-ahs, an' when she woke up she was younguh than bufoah." He broke into a thick cough.

"Poppy—"

"So ya best know I look out fuh Glorie. She's simple. I won't have ya hurtin' huh."

"I wouldn't hurt her for the world," Jeff said.

"I'll hold ya ta that." Pulling his coat more tightly around him, Gordon held out an arm to Glorie and said in a gentler way, "I'm ready ta lie down some more. Ya bettuh let me take ya home."

Glorie turned to Jeff with a look that was apologetic and, in that, surprisingly astute. "I'm sorry. Poppy worries too much. Will you come to the diner tomorrow?"

"Yes, and please, don't apologize." He glanced back at the table. "You brought me a wonderful New Year's Day dinner. I thank you. Both of you."

With a final shy smile, she and Gordon left. Jeff watched their pickup head down the dirt road. When it disappeared from sight, he closed the door and returned to the table to finish the dinner she'd brought.

All the time he was eating, he thought of Glorie, then of Gordon and the others whose faces he was coming to recognize. He couldn't say he knew them in the way Laura defined "knew," which involved sharing thoughts and backgrounds and interests. But he didn't think that was necessary. He didn't see why friends had to bare their souls to each other, or, for that matter, why they had to share anything more than the simplest of thoughts. Who he was deep inside, what he was thinking—it wasn't anyone's business but his own, and it didn't matter, in the everyday run of things.

That, he decided, was one of the differences between where he'd come from and where he was. Back in Northampton, life was complex. Competition was a big part of it, and when people weren't obsessed with job advancement or social climbing, they turned to reasons and feelings and analyses. Here, life was simpler. The name of the game was living, and that meant earning enough money to buy food and clothes, braving the elements, and maybe—just maybe—going visiting on New Year's Eve.

Part of him believed he could live the simpler life just fine, once he settled into a rhythm. He had started to do that. But he needed more. He needed something to get him up and out in the morning and back home at night. He needed structure in his life.

He couldn't be an accountant. He couldn't be anything noticeable. And while he was proud of the job he'd done fixing up the cottage, he didn't think he had a future as a handyman. His hands were a mess of blisters and cuts, one or two of which probably should have been stitched. But he had survived without getting lockjaw or whatever the hell else people always got shots to avoid, and he supposed the scars added character.

Any help in *that* department was welcome. He was still feeling like a snake when he thought of the way he'd left Northampton. Granted, he hadn't had any choice. Granted, they were better off without him. Still, he felt lousy—all the more so, he supposed, because it was New Year's Day, which had traditionally been for family. So, long after Glorie and Gordon had left, long after he had finished eating their food, long after the time when he should have been reading or doing push-ups or wrestling with the pipes he had bought that, when properly assembled, would provide him with a shower, he thought of Northampton.

By late in the afternoon, he'd had his fill of thinking, so he climbed into the truck and coasted down the hill into town. A phone booth stood at the far side of the gas station. He idled beside it for a minute or two, jiggling the change in his pocket while he tried to decide whether his call could be traced. If he kept it short, it wouldn't be, he figured, but he didn't want to take any chances.

So he drove on. He passed the first strip mall, where he usually did his shopping, passed the second one, where he ventured when he was feeling either brave or bored. Driving farther than he had in four weeks, he finally pulled up at a restaurant that stood closed and lonely at the side of the road. The phone booth looked to be in better repair than the restaurant, which wasn't saying much. The door was off its lower hinge, and the phone book was torn in half. But he didn't need the book, and since there was no one around, he didn't need the door for privacy. He didn't even need it for warmth, since he was bundled up. If his hands shook slightly as he pumped change into the machine, it wasn't from the cold.

The phone rang once, then a second time, and his heart beat louder with each one. Then, just before the third, it was picked up and he heard her.

"Hello?"

"Hi," he said in a quiet, tentative voice.

There was a long pause, then, "Jeff?" His failure to correct her was confirmation enough. "Jeff! My God, we've been so worried! How *are* you? *Where* are you? Are you all right?"

"I'm all right."

"Are you sure? We imagined all kinds of things—that you were hurt or sick or kidnapped. How could you leave without a word that way?"

"I had to. I couldn't tell anyone."

"Not even me?"

"Not even you."

"Not after everything?"

"Especially not then. Think about it."

"That's all I've been doing." Her voice trembled. "I feel so guilty."

"Think how you'd have felt if you'd known I was leaving and no one else did. I couldn't do that to you."

Her voice grew harder, though he wasn't sure whether it was from anger or hurt. "Apparently there were lots of things you couldn't do. Tax fraud, Jeff? You never breathed a word of that to me. I thought we were best friends. I thought we shared secrets. What else couldn't you tell me about?"

"Nothing."

"Were there other women?"

"No," he said in an angry tone that quickly grew tentative again. "Is everyone okay?"

It was a minute before she said, begrudgingly, "As okay as

they can be in the circumstances."

"Hurt? Angry? Disillusioned?"

"All those things. The IRS came out pretty fast with its charges, and the *Sun* loves it." She paused for the briefest minute before crying, "Why, Jeff? Why did you *do* it?"

Jeff didn't want to go into explanations. That wasn't why he had called. "How's my mother doing?"

"You didn't *need* the money. You were doing so *well*."

"How's my mother?"

There was another long pause, then a sigh. "She's a trouper."

"Has Christian been around?"

"Christian's in Tahiti."

"Does Scott hate me?"

"Scott is angry. He feels you let everyone down. Debra misses you, and Laura's trying to carry on. Things are a mess for her, Jeff. She didn't deserve this."

But Jeff didn't want to go into that either. "Has David taken my name off the door?"

"Not yet. When are you coming back?"

"I'm not."

"You have to."

"I can't."

"You have to. Until you do, nothing will be settled, and that would be the cruelest, *cruelest* thing to do to Laura and the kids."

"I'm not coming back."

"Then why did you call?"

He didn't answer.

"Where are you, Jeff? At least tell me that. I won't tell a soul, God knows I won't."

He trusted her. The problem was he didn't trust himself. If he told her where he was and she came looking, he wasn't sure he wouldn't give in if she begged him to return. He had never been strong when it came to women, which was part of the problem. If he'd been able to stand up to Laura once in a while, he might have felt more like a man.

Well, he was a man now. He'd done his thing, and he was determined to stick with it. Let them call him a coward for leaving Northampton when the fire got hot. They were wrong. Leaving Northampton was the bravest thing he had ever done in his life.

"Jeff? Talk to me, Jeff. Are you still there? Jeff!"

Quietly, he replaced the receiver, returned to the truck, and headed back to the bluff.

sixteen

LAURA CONTINUED TO STRIKE OUT ON THE loan scene. The banks in Hartford were as reluctant to give her money as those in Boston had been. David, who was still holding out for an affair, suggested she speak with her life insurance agent about borrowing against Jeff's policy, but the government had reached him first and frozen those funds too. Privately—humbly—she talked with friends who had the resources to loan her money, but none came through. One claimed he'd had a bad year, another mentioned the big wedding his daughter was planning, still another vowed that what money he might have lent her was tied up in investments. A fourth suggested a business arrangement whereby he would buy into Cherries, but Laura wasn't ready for that. She was sure that if her take remained stable, and if the court ruled in her favor, she could survive as an independent restaurateur, which was what she wanted. The business was all she had. Even aside from the pride involved, she couldn't afford to siphon profits off to a silent partner.

On the second of January, Daphne petitioned the court to release to Laura that portion of Jeffrey's assets which by rights were hers. The petition was accompanied by voluminous documents supporting the claim. Daphne had spent long hours compiling them, and Laura was impressed. She was also optimistic.

For the first time since she'd learned of the freeze, something concrete and positive was in the works. Hope was in sight.

When Daphne reminded her not to expect a response to the motion for up to six months, which, she said, was typical of the backlog in the court system, Laura's optimism wavered. "But this isn't a typical case," she argued.

"Not to you," Daphne explained. "To the court it is. Everyone filing petitions feels his case is unique. I've argued for expedience, but I'm sure those others have too. How long it takes will depend on the judge, and I have no control over who's given the case. What I'm saying is that you shouldn't count on immediate relief."

But the bills were still due. Having no other recourse, Laura finally took Daphne and Elise up on their offers, borrowing money from them to pay the most pressing of those bills. She felt bad doing it, but Lydia had no money to spare and Laura refused to ask Maddie, so she was over a barrel.

Her one best hope, she realized over the course of many long middle-of-the-night hours, was to maximize the profit she took from the business. To that extent, once the holidays were past, she pared down the restaurant's staff to the exact number she and Jonah figured they could get by with. They had already lost one waitress, a part-time student who was transferring out of state to study full-time, and they didn't replace her. Likewise, on the catering end, two of her staff were leaving to make a stab at their own service in upstate New York. Rather than having three separate catering crews on the payroll, Laura regrouped into two. Even with Scott and Debra pitching in at odd hours, that meant each of her employees had to work a little harder. She talked with them individually, making a personal plea. That, along with the loyalty she had already accrued, paid off.

So she dared be optimistic again. The business was more efficiently run than ever. Service was remaining at the high level she wanted. She felt she just might be able to make it.

She would have, had business been good in those early January days. But the cancellations Elise had received in December went unfilled, and fewer than normal new bookings came in. Time and again, Laura reminded everyone around her that January was the slowest month of the year. In the wee hours of the night, though, she worried.

Her worry increased when, one week into the new year, a grand jury returned indictments against Jeff. The media started in again with phone calls and visits. Duggan O'Neil carried the story as though it were the most important thing to happen in Hampshire County since Noah Webster published his dictionary in 1828. Gary Holmes wrote not one but two editorials in as many days, decrying modern morality, middle-class greed, and the challenge to law enforcement officials that the Frye case presented.

Laura was beside herself with frustration. The *Sun*'s attention did nothing to improve business, which seemed, to her terrified eye, to be slackening by the day. Both Elise and DeeAnn assured her that this wasn't happening to any significant degree, but she suspected they were just trying to make her feel better. In her darkest, most private moments, she doubted anything could help. Her life had gone from perfect to perfectly horrid with terrifying speed. All its discouraging threads seemed to be spinning around on themselves, growing more tangled by the minute.

When Taylor Jones stopped in at the restaurant the day after the indictments came down, she wasn't alarmed. Things were already so bad she was sure nothing he said or did could make them worse. And she was right, at first. He updated her on the leads the government was following in its search for Jeff and questioned her on whether she'd seen him, heard from him, or had the slightest contact with him, no matter how indirect. He told her he'd learned that the fraud went back eight years, that Jeff had apparently worked alone, and that Farro and Frye had been uninvolved in the scheme.

Then he told her what else he'd learned.

They were sitting in her office, with the door closed, when

he announced that he had a witness placing Jeff on more than one occasion with a woman at the condo in Holyoke. Actually, "announced" was the wrong word, since he sounded almost apologetic, but the message hit Laura as though he had screamed it at the top of his lungs.

She instantly denied it. "That can't be. Jeff wouldn't have had an affair." Of all the indignities she'd suffered in the last month, that one would be the worst. She couldn't conceive of its being true.

But Tack was confident. "The witness consistently identified Jeff's picture. She picked it out of a large group we gave her and then gave us his height and build, neither of which was apparent from the photo."

Laura's head began to buzz. Like pieces of an ugly puzzle, one element of Jeff's treachery fit into another. Still, publicly, she had to maintain his innocence. There was loyalty involved, and self-defense.

"It couldn't have been Jeff," she insisted.

"The witness is certain."

"She's wrong. Jeff couldn't have had an affair."

"How do you know?"

"I'm his wife. I know."

"The wife is usually the last to know when it comes to affairs."

Her heart was pounding. "Jeff wouldn't betray me that way."

Taylor Jones's voice dropped. "You didn't believe he would willingly vanish, or commit tax fraud, but the evidence says he did both those things."

"You haven't proven either."

"No, but the evidence is strong."

A sharp rap came at the door, followed immediately by Daphne, who regarded Laura with concern. "DeeAnn let me know he was here." Her gaze sharpened when it flipped to the agent. "As the Fryes' attorney, I'd like to be notified before meetings like this."

Though he had risen at her entrance, he appeared otherwise

undaunted. "Mrs. Frye isn't being charged with anything."

"She has the right to representation." To Laura, Daphne said, "Is everything all right?"

Laura fought hysteria. "Not really. He says Jeff was having an affair."

Daphne froze for an instant; then, in the next instant, boiled. Her anger was a visible thing. Knowing that she had an impassioned defender in Daphne was vague solace for the devastation Laura was feeling.

Swinging the door shut with more force than was necessary, Daphne said slowly and with barely contained fury, "I thought you were going to hold off telling her about this."

It was a minute before the implication registered, and then Laura was appalled. "You knew?"

"I knew," Daphne admitted. "He told me last week."

"But you didn't say anything to me!" Laura cried, feeling betrayed. She knew it was irrational, given all Daphne was doing for her, and it was probable that the betrayal she felt was really related to Jeff. But Daphne was the one who was there.

Daphne defended her inaction. "It was right after the holidays, which had been hard enough on you. I didn't see the point in making things worse."

"But this *affects* me."

"It's an unsubstantiated claim."

"He has a *witness*, Daphne."

"But no warm body. If Jeff was having an affair, he had to have it *with* someone. Agent Jones doesn't have any idea who that was."

"Yes, I do," Tack said. Both pairs of eyes flew his way.

"Who?" Laura asked, but the agent was looking at Daphne.

"When I first told you about this, I had no leads on the woman, and as long as that was so, I agreed with you that there was no need to further upset Mrs. Frye."

"What's a little more?" Laura cried, but Tack didn't take his eyes off Daphne.

"My witness is certain that the woman in question is the hostess here at the restaurant." At Laura's gasp, he turned to her. "We had to identify the woman in case your husband was in contact with her. We figured she may have been someone local, so we took our witness around to the places your husband frequented. One look at DeeAnn Kirkham, and she made a positive identification."

"DeeAnn," Laura breathed and clutched at the pain cutting through her chest. "DeeAnn." Tears came to her eyes. She *adored* DeeAnn. She *depended* on DeeAnn. It was bad enough to think Jeff had had an affair; it was much worse to think he'd had one with DeeAnn. "It can't be."

Still standing, Tack said, "We didn't leave it there. We took the witness all over town, but she kept coming back to your hostess. She said that the hair was the thing, that sandy color, the thickness, and the length. The woman she saw with your husband had great hair. She said that over and over again: great hair."

"Lots of woman in this town have great hair," Laura argued. She was desperate to discredit the witness's claim. *Jeff couldn't have had an affair.* "Lots of woman in this town have sandy hair. Look at Daphne. Hers is that color, but I wouldn't accuse her of having an affair with Jeff. DeeAnn isn't only my hostess, she's my *friend*."

"She's very attractive," Tack remarked.

Daphne bristled. "What does that have to do with anything?"

"Attractive women attract men," he answered, then asked Laura, "What do you know about her personal life?"

Laura could barely think. The accusation—even the idea—that Jeff had gone looking for sex was devastating. Putting her fingers to her temples, she tried to slow the wild whirl inside. "I—uh, I know she dates."

"Lots of men, or is there someone special?"

She wanted to say there was someone special with whom DeeAnn was head over heels in love, but there wasn't. Dee dated a lot. Her taste ran toward men who were mature enough to appreciate the fine points of feminine allure and wealthy enough to reward those points accordingly. Laura wouldn't have put Jeff into either of those categories.

"Laura?" Daphne prompted. "Was there anyone special?"

"Uh, no. No one special."

"Does she pick up men here?" Tack asked.

"No!" Laura cried, because the implication of that turned her stomach. "This isn't a singles bar."

He reworded the question. "Does she meet men here?"

Laura wanted to answer as definitively as before, but she couldn't. "I suppose she might. Men are in and out all the time." And DeeAnn was an inveterate flirt, which, irony of ironies, was one of the things Laura had always loved about her. She did things Laura might have wanted to do but couldn't. Watching her was great fun. Or had been. The idea was fast turning sour. Laura took a shallow breath. "What do I do, Daph?"

Daphne deferred to Tack. "What do you suggest?"

"Let me talk with her," he said. "I don't think she had anything to do with the tax fraud scheme, but if she's heard from him and hasn't come forward, she'll be considered an accessory after the fact. She ought to know that."

"What do *I* do, Daph?" Laura asked. She was feeling battered again, as though she'd taken another hit and was on her knees, needing help to get up but not sure what to do once she got there. "Do I assume it's true and confront her? Do I scream and yell? Do I fire her on the spot?"

Daphne pulled up a chair and sat close. "What do you want to do?"

"I want to beg her to tell me it isn't true. I like DeeAnn. I've always liked DeeAnn. If it turns out she was having an affair with Jeff, I'll be crushed."

"I doubt she'll confess to it. Unless she does, you won't know for sure."

There was so much lately that Laura didn't know for sure

that she wanted to scream. But screaming wouldn't accomplish a thing. Nor, she realized, would shooting questions at Daphne. In the end, the decision was hers. She had to regain control. "Let's call her in. I need to hear what she has to say." Clinging to the idea of control, she left Daphne with Taylor Jones while she went into the heart of the restaurant.

DeeAnn's eye was easily caught. The smallest movement of Laura's head brought her over. As she approached, Laura watched her face for signs of a guilty conscience. All she saw was concern.

"You're not upset that I called Daphne, are you? That guy may be big and gorgeous, but he's trouble with a capital T. Is everything okay?"

"I'm not sure," Laura said. She was quivering inside, trying not to let it show. "Do me a favor? Get Kammie to cover and come talk with us for a minute."

"Sure, hon," DeeAnn said and set off to find the waitress.

Laura had always known DeeAnn was a knockout, but that fact took on added significance as she watched her walk off. The features were right—the casually styled hair, the bright clothing, the slender legs, slightly flared hips, full breasts. But there was something else, something sensual in her walk, in the way she cocked her head, the set of her eyes, her smile. Laura had never before had cause to compare herself to DeeAnn. Now she did. And she came up short. Next to DeeAnn, she was efficient and bland. If, somewhere beneath that placid exterior of his in a place Laura hadn't known existed, Jeff had wanted a temptress, Laura wouldn't have been it. DeeAnn might have.

Shrinking back into the shadows of the hall, Laura waited with her arms crossed hard over her breasts until DeeAnn appeared. Without a word, she led the way back to her office.

Inside, DeeAnn looked from one face to the next. "Uh-oh," she said in a singsong voice that in other circumstances might have been amusing. "Something's up."

Laura stood back against the wall and focused expectantly

on Tack, who took her cue and, in a straightforward, no-nonsense way, filled DeeAnn in on what they'd been discussing. By the time he was done, Laura was feeling more raw than ever and DeeAnn was looking stunned. Her eyes flew to Daphne and, after a minute, to Laura, but she didn't say a word.

"Is it true?" Laura forced herself to ask.

DeeAnn gave a quick, jerky shake of her head—too quick and too jerky for Laura, who had had optimism thrown in her face once too often. This time she was being smart. She was believing the worst.

Tack seemed skeptical of DeeAnn's denial too, because he said, "As far as the law goes, whether you were his mistress or not doesn't matter. All I want to know is whether you've been in contact with him since he disappeared."

Eyes wide, DeeAnn shook her head.

Turning sideways to the wall, Laura huddled into herself. Behind her, the conversation went on. She was aware of its hum, but none of the words registered over the clamor of her thoughts. *Jeff had had an affair. He'd slept with another woman.* She tried to grasp the idea, but it was too repulsive to hold. In the next breath there were other ideas to repulse her. *Where were you? Why didn't you see? How could you not have known?*

The disillusionment that had come before was nothing compared to this. Fidelity had been a given in her relationship with Jeff, or so she'd thought. Apparently Jeff hadn't thought so. While she'd been raising the kids, keeping the house, and building a business to supplement Jeff's income, he had been having affairs in a condo he'd bought on the sly.

Feeling suddenly nauseated, she pressed a hand to her mouth, but instantly knew that wouldn't be enough. Wordlessly, she ran down the hall to the bathroom, where she was violently sick.

A soft knock came at the door, then Daphne's gentle plea. "Let me in, Laura."

Still hanging over the toilet bowl, she took a deep breath. Helplessly, she retched once, then again. She was taking another breath when the doorknob jiggled.

"I want to help, Laura. Open up."

Laura flushed the toilet and straightened, holding the edge of the sink for support. She ran the cold water and rinsed out her mouth.

"Please, Laura."

Reaching back, Laura turned the doorknob enough to unlock the door, then sank down on the toilet seat and put her head in her hands.

Daphne went right to the sink. "It'll be okay," she soothed. "Everything's going to be okay." She moved Laura's hands out of the way and pressed a cool cloth to her forehead. Moving her hair aside, she pressed a second one to the back of her neck. "He's a bastard. He never should have broken it to you like that."

Laura assumed the bastard to be Jeff. It was a minute before she realized Daphne was referring to Taylor Jones. "He was just doing his job," she reasoned in a paper-thin voice.

"If he wanted to do *that*, he could find Jeff, for God's sake. I don't know why they're having so much trouble finding one man."

Laura knew. "Jeff is clever. Apparently, much more so than any of us ever thought." Her voice broke as the reality of what she'd been told slammed into her again.

Daphne rubbed her back. "You're a survivor, Laura. You'll do fine."

"How could he *do* that to me?" she cried. "How could he be off sleeping with other women—how could he be digging up the names of dead people—how could he be plotting his disappearance—and still get up in the morning and look me in the eye like everything was fine and dandy? I had no idea, Daph, no idea at all. Was I so preoccupied with my own life that I didn't see? Or am I just stupid?"

Daphne kept on rubbing. "You're being too hard on yourself."

"I *should* be hard on myself. I was married to that man for twenty years, but I didn't know him. I thought I did. I honestly thought I did. But I guess I thought wrong, which doesn't say a whole lot for my insight or intelligence or sensitivity. Or sex appeal," she added morosely.

"You have sex appeal."

"Yeah. That's why my husband felt the need to sneak off with other women."

The hand on her back grew gruffer. "You don't know that there were other women. You don't even know that there was *one* other woman."

"It was Dee."

"She said no."

"What else could she say?" Laura squeezed her eyes shut for a minute. "Dee. Of all people. Right under my nose!" She made an anguished sound, then slowly straightened. Taking the cloth from her forehead, she pressed it against first one cheek, then the other. "Oh, God," she breathed, feeling weak and discouraged, "what do I do? I could fire her, but that'd be like cutting off my nose to spite my face. She's a real plus here. If she left, I'd have to look for someone else, and I'm not sure I have the strength for that."

"Then keep her. It might be better to have her nearby where you can watch what she's doing. If she understands that you're giving her the benefit of the doubt and trusting her, she may tell us if Jeff gets in touch with her."

Laura's mind drifted. Her life used to be so simple—busy, but simple. All that had changed. "What a nightmare," she whispered.

"You'll come out all right."

"But when? How long will this go on?"

"Until they find Jeff, I guess."

"No. Longer than that. Because if they find Jeff, he'll be arrested and charged and booked, and then we'll be stuck with the horror of a trial." Her mind drifted again. She found herself wondering whether she'd be able to stand behind Jeff through a trial, after what he'd done to her. If everything Taylor Jones said was true, Jeff didn't deserve her support. When she looked past the hurt of his betrayal, there was anger enough to choke a horse.

"I need some air," she muttered and pushed herself to her feet. Tossing the cloths into the sink, she left the bathroom. DeeAnn was still with Taylor Jones, waiting for Laura's verdict. But Laura avoided her eyes, grabbed her coat, and left. She was too wrapped up in her own unhappiness to care that DeeAnn was in limbo. If the woman had been with Jeff, she deserved the worst. Letting her stay on the job was about as compassionate as Laura could be.

The January cold hit her face with welcome force. She breathed it in and fought a wave of dizziness as she walked quickly down the street. She pulled up the collar of her coat against the wind, then pulled it higher for privacy. She didn't want to be seen. She didn't want to be recognized. She didn't want to be talked about or laughed at or pitied.

Doing an abrupt about-face, she headed for the parking lot behind Cherries, climbed into the Wagoneer, and drove off. There was better protection from knowing eyes in the car, particularly once she left the streets of Northampton behind. She headed south simply because that was one way to go. She wondered if Jeff had gone that way too. But she wasn't Jeff; she'd be back. She would be home by the end of the day, because she had Debra and Scott to care for, and Lydia, and the house, and the business. She wouldn't shirk her responsibility like Jeff had. She wasn't a coward, or a cheat.

But that didn't mean one part of her didn't want to keep driving and driving until she reached a place where no one knew her, and no one knew what a fool she'd been. She had trusted Jeff. She had built her life around him. She had worried when he disappeared, had even defended him when the first charges came up.

These new charges were something else. *Jeff . . . DeeAnn . . .*

an affair. People had affairs all the time. Men wandered, marriages fell apart. But not Laura's. She didn't understand how things had gone awry.

With the blare of a horn on her immediate right, she slammed on her brakes, then, heart pounding, glided through the intersection that she had distractedly entered too soon. Driving on, she gradually stopped shaking, but her distraction persisted. She kept wondering what she'd done wrong, but the only thing she could come up with was that she had wanted everything to be right. Was that her crime? If so, it seemed totally unfair. She hadn't hurt a soul in her life. The people around her were happy.

Or were they? Had she chosen to think that, just as she'd chosen to think Jeff was honest, hard-working, and faithful? Had she been wrong about *all* those things?

Not sure what to think and what not to, she turned the Wagoneer around and headed home to cook dinner. With a recipe card telling her exactly how much of what ingredients to use, she was safe. She supposed it was only fair that if her children had to be stuck with a mother who couldn't keep their father happy and in his own bed, at least they should be well fed.

Patiently Tack stood by while Daphne told DeeAnn that Laura wanted her to stay on as Cherries' hostess. Personally, he didn't understand why Laura would want that. He would have thought Laura would kick her out in two seconds flat. Apparently she was more forgiving than most women—either that, or more practical, which was probably the case. She had a business to run, and DeeAnn did her part well.

Daphne must have agreed with the decision, because, if anything, when she talked to DeeAnn, she sounded solicitous. Her voice was quiet, even gentle, making him wonder exactly where Daphne's loyalties lay. As soon as DeeAnn left the office, he asked her about it.

"Considering that she's been fingered as the mistress of your best friend's husband, you were very kind."

Daphne closed the door and turned on him with startling speed. Her voice was hushed but harsh. "She denied it. For God's sake, Tack, did you have to tell Laura?"

He should have known she'd still be ticked off. She wasn't one to let things go, though he thought he'd explained himself perfectly well. "Yes, I did," he said, coming to his feet. "It was time."

"Did you see how upset she was?"

He had. He wasn't *that* unfeeling, and he didn't like Daphne thinking he was. So he gentled his voice. "Do you think she'd be any less upset if she found out a month or two from now?"

"Yes. She's barely gotten over the shock of Jeff's leaving. A month or two from now, it wouldn't have been so raw."

"It'd be raw. A woman like Laura would be hurt whenever she learned something like that." He scratched his head. "It absolutely amazes me that she didn't see any of this coming."

"She wanted to see a perfect life, so that was what she saw."

"But she isn't dumb. She isn't blind. How could all this have been happening without her sensing *anything*?"

"You tell me," Daphne said, daring him with a straight-in-the-eye look. "You're a man. You tell me whether it's possible for a man to tell his wife one thing and do something else. You tell me if it's possible for a man to let his closest friends believe one thing and do something else. You tell me if it's possible for a man to lead a double life."

Tack came close. His voice was only as loud as it had to be to cross the few inches between them. "It's possible. I feel like I'm doing it now. I'm on your side at night and on the opposite side during the day." He looked at her mouth, at the mutinous set of those thin, strangely delicate lips, and the sides blurred. "Don't look at me like I'm the enemy, Daph."

"You are," Daphne complained and flattened herself against the door. "You upset my friend and sent her running off."

"Me? I wasn't the one who lied to her. I wasn't the one who

deserted her. I wasn't the one who two-timed her. Hell, I've got more than enough to keep me busy with you." Unable to resist her closeness, he ducked his head for a kiss. She evaded his mouth.

"Not here, Tack. Someone could come in."

"Not with you standing against the door," he said. Taking her chin in his hand, he forced her face around and held it still while he covered her mouth.

She protested the kiss by keeping her mouth closed, and though she pushed against his chest, he had no intention of budging. When she discovered that, she tried to say his name in complaint. He took advantage of the opening to deepen the kiss.

He guessed she'd take thirty seconds to give in. She actually did it in fifteen. Not that it took great brains to figure out why. They had been together five nights of the last eight, crafting a history that positively smoked. When he had been with Gwen, he thought no one could drive him hotter or higher, but Daphne had proved him wrong. She was dynamite undressed. She was also dynamite dressed, and he meant that in terms of her mind. Gwen hadn't held great appeal for him that way, but Daphne and he had interests in common. Law enforcement was one of them. The fact that they came at it from different sides was appealing. They challenged each other. Being adversaries in the Frye case and being lovers at the same time was naughty and very exciting.

Could a man live a double life? Damn straight.

"Tack," she murmured against his mouth when he allowed her a breath. "Oh, Tack."

"What, sweetheart?"

She looped her arms around his neck. "I'm worried. This is all such a mess."

"Give Laura time, and she'll do okay. Cream always rises to the top."

She smiled against his jaw. "That's a nice thing to say."

"She's a nice woman."

"Does that mean you'll forget about this business with DeeAnn?"

"I can't do that."

"Sure you can. It has nothing to do with the charges you brought against Jeff."

Tack liked Daphne a lot, but he wasn't about to compromise himself or his job. "Come on," he chided, "you know as well as I do that when it comes to a trial, there are issues of motive to consider. And character. The government will try to show that Jeff Frye was devious. What better way than to come up with a mistress? And that's totally aside from the fact that, in terms of finding the man, DeeAnn may be our strongest link."

"She isn't in touch with him."

"How do you know?"

"She said so."

"And you believe her?"

"Yes."

The conviction in her voice reminded him of the gentle way she'd dealt with DeeAnn earlier and the questions he'd had about that. Drawing back his head, he looked at her. "How close are you to DeeAnn?"

"Not as close as Laura. I only know her through Cherries. We have brunch every Tuesday—Laura, Elise, DeeAnn, and me. I like the woman."

"Did she have an affair with Jeff?"

"I didn't see her do it."

"Do you think she did?"

Daphne considered that for a minute, then shrugged.

"My witness is solid," he warned. "You can plead on DeeAnn's behalf all you want, but you're not changing my mind." He had a thought and smiled. "Go ahead. Plead."

Some of the thought must have come out in the smile, because Daphne smiled back at him. "Not here."

"Then where? Can we go for a quickie in the men's room?"

"I can't go into the men's room."

"Then the ladies' room."

"You can't go into the ladies' room."

"Then my motel room. It's not far."

But she shook her head.

"Tell you what," he said. "I'll meet you after work and take you to dinner. That's a damn good offer, coming from me." She should only know. Gwen would be green with envy. "You pick the place. If you'll be more comfortable, we'll drive a distance."

At his final words, she sobered. Slowly, she drew her hands down from his neck. "I want to make sure Laura's okay, first. Call me later?"

Though disappointed, he respected the compassion Daphne felt for her friend. With a last sweet, sucking kiss, he let her go.

seventeen

JEFF'S BETRAYAL CUT TO THE QUICK. IT was a nagging ache in the back of Laura's mind, held in abeyance if she kept busy, but hovering, always hovering. Of all the injustices Jeff had done her, this was the most personal and the most humiliating. For that reason, she didn't say anything to Lydia or, God forbid, to Maddie. For other reasons as well, she didn't say anything to Debra or Scott.

Debra, who missed Jeff badly, still held out the hope that he would return. She staunchly maintained his innocence to her friends at school and was quick to defend him at home when she felt either Laura or Scott said something of a derogatory nature. Laura had been increasingly careful not to do that as the weeks had worn on, and she was particularly careful now. After all, she reasoned, Jeff was still Debra's father. It was natural that he hold a special place in her heart.

He held a special place in Scott's heart, too, though that place was far less positive. Scott was angry. He was angry for Laura, in a protective way that touched her deeply, and angry for himself. Even without Maddie's analysis, Laura could understand that. Being male, Scott identified with Jeff. He took Jeff's behavior more personally than Debra would, almost as a reflection of his own, and he was affronted. Laura knew that telling him about Jeff's infidelity would only add fuel to his anger.

So she was quiet. She knew that if the *Sun* got wind of this twist in the case, the whole world would quickly know, and that prospect was so humiliating as to be nearly unthinkable. But if she spent her days worrying about the *Sun*, she wouldn't be able to function, and if she couldn't function, what little that still worked in her life would unravel. She couldn't have that. She had to carry on. She had to hold things together.

To that end, she left the house early the next morning. After visiting with Lydia, she went on to Cherries to work. She was in the kitchen alongside her staff, chopping and listening to their chatter, almost forgetting that her world was so crazy, when DeeAnn came in. "Can I have a minute out front?" she asked softly.

Laura kept her composure. She nodded. She set down the knife she was using, wiped her hands on a nearby towel, hooked her apron at the back of the door, and followed DeeAnn into the restaurant.

As soon as they'd come far enough to allow for privacy, DeeAnn stopped. Looking worlds away from her usual confident self, she faced Laura and, in a nervous voice, said, "You don't believe me, do you?"

Furious at DeeAnn and Jeff and the entire situation, Laura said tightly, "I don't know what to believe any more." She had been wrong about so many things.

"I didn't have an affair with Jeff."

"Why did that witness identify you?"

"I don't know." She waited for Laura to say something, but Laura had nothing to say. "Are you sure you want me to stay?"

"I'm sure."

"If my being here will upset you, it may not be the wisest thing."

Of course, your being here will upset me, Laura wanted to scream. *Every time I look at you, I think of what Jeff did. I feel ugly and unappealing. I feel betrayed.* But she refused to say any of that. She wasn't giving DeeAnn the satisfaction. So she pressed her fingertips to her mouth and, after a minute, took a calming breath. "Since the beginning of December, it's been one upset after another. If I let each one get to me, I'd be an absolute wreck. I want you to stay because, quite frankly, I don't have the time or strength to find and train someone new. You're very good at what you do."

Still DeeAnn persisted. "Another person would have fired me on the spot. I can understand if that's what you want."

"What do *you* want?" Laura asked in frustration.

"To stay. To help keep the restaurant going. To help see you through this mess."

"Then stay. I've already said you should." Maddie would have called her a masochist for that, but what did Maddie know about business? "But let's pray that the papers don't pick up this part of the story, because if that happens and you're named, I'll have no choice but to let you go. Business is shaky enough, and you're the first thing people see when they walk in here. It would be suicide."

That talk with DeeAnn was on Wednesday. When there was no article in the *Sun* that day or the next, Laura began to think that Taylor Jones might be keeping his promise to Daphne, and when Friday came and went without a word, she let herself relax just a bit. She didn't know where Jeff was, what he was doing, when he'd be back, or what would happen then, but she was holding her own. Each day she did that was a victory.

Then Saturday morning's paper arrived with a front-page article about the "mystery woman" with whom Jeffrey Frye had been seen in the months before his disappearance.

"Why are they doing this to us?" Debra cried the instant she saw the paper. "Why do they make up stories like this?"

Laura was more upset than Debra. Just when she had begun to believe that the downhill spiral was ending, that things were leveling off, that life might actually go uphill from there, she'd been knocked down again.

"They didn't make up the story," she said defeatedly. "The police have a witness who claims to have seen your father with a woman."

Scott, who had been brooding over the article before Debra had come down, felt called upon to add, "At his condo. More than once."

"I know that, Scottie," Laura said. She didn't need the reminder. The mechanics of Jeff's infidelity haunted her.

"It's a lie, isn't it?" Debra asked.

Laura wanted to deny it, but how could she? "We won't know until we ask your father."

"Or find the woman," Scott put in, then hit the counter with the full force of his rower's fist. "Damn it, what's *with* him? A man is supposed to love his family. He's supposed to want to be with them. He's supposed to want to take *care* of them. So why didn't he feel all that? What's so awful about us? We're not good enough for him? This house isn't good enough for him? *You're* not good enough for him? What the fuck did he want?"

Laura put shaky fingers to her forehead. "Maybe he didn't know. Maybe it was a mid-life crisis. I don't know, Scottie. I just don't know."

"I do," Debra said, looking straight at Laura. "He wanted someone to be with and talk with and do things with. You weren't ever around, so he went looking for someone else."

"Shut up, Debra," Scott warned, but Laura clutched his arm hard to keep him from saying more. She didn't want them going at each other. She couldn't bear the thought of internal warfare, when it seemed the rest of the world was against them.

"You may be right," she told Debra. "But, if so, he never told me he wanted something I wasn't giving. He never complained. He never nagged. He never commented. He never hinted. So how was I to know?"

"You should have seen he was unhappy."

"Did *you*?" Laura asked. "Did he look unhappy to you?" When Debra didn't answer, she said, "People are supposed to speak up if things are bothering them. I'm not a mind reader. I don't stand around here monitoring tiny little changes in facial expression. I don't have time for that. If you want to criticize me for being too busy with my business, go ahead. That's your right. I've tried to do my best juggling family and career. Obviously, you don't think I've done a very good job. Fine. Learn from my mistakes and do better when you're grown and have a family of your own." The phone rang. Rolling on a wave of anger, she snatched it up. "Hello!"

"Did you know about this, Laura?"

Laura sank back against the wall, only then realizing that she was trembling. And Maddie's call wouldn't help, that was for sure. "Oh, hi, Mom," she said in a breezy voice. "Yeah, I'm okay. How are you?"

"Did you know he was having an affair?"

"Sure." The voice stayed breezy. "That was why I was so puzzled when he left. That was why I was terrified he'd been in an accident. That was why I told the IRS agent he couldn't possibly have committed tax fraud. My husband *never* does anything I don't know about."

Maddie was silent for a time before coaxing softly, "Go on."

Laura sighed. "I'm done."

"Do you feel better now?"

"I'll feel better when you stop asking insulting questions. If I'd known Jeff was having an affair, do you honestly think I would have stuck up for him all this time? Give me credit for *something*, Mother."

"You're upset."

"That's a brilliant deduction."

"Sarcasm doesn't become you, Laura."

The anger Laura felt spilled out. "If you're going to complain that my husband's having an affair with a mystery woman may hurt your career, don't. I only have a certain amount of sympathy, and right now I'm saving it for Debra and Scott. And myself. I'm saving it for myself. God only knows I've earned it." There were tears in her eyes. She handed the phone to Scott. "Talk with Gram," she whispered brokenly. "I can't do it now."

Too upset to care what Scott said to his grandmother, she turned away and went to the semicircle of windows overlooking the yard. She stared out, hugging herself against the emptiness she felt, so lost in her private unhappiness that she jumped when Debra slipped an arm around her waist.

"Don't cry, Mom. If you do, I will, and if I do, my eyes will be puffy for the rest of the day, and I'm going out with Jace."

Laura blotted an eye with the heel of her hand. "Jace?"

"You know Jace."

For the life of her, she couldn't remember the name, let alone put a face to it, and though it was the least appropriate time to be discussing Debra's love life, there was a lightness to it that Laura grabbed at. "Have I met him?"

"No, but I've mentioned him lots of times. He's this swell guy from school."

"What's his last name?"

"Holzworth."

Still nothing clicked, but that didn't mean anything. If Laura had been half as inattentive as Debra seemed to think, she might have heard the name dozens of times without taking it in. "What about Donny?"

"Donny's going out with Julie."

"But you were with Donny on New Year's Eve."

"I went to the party with him, but he spent more time with Julie than with me. But that's okay. Jace was there, and we've been wanting to go out for a while. Mom, do you think this thing in the paper will turn him off?"

"Did the other stuff turn him off?"

"No. He doesn't blame me for what my father is accused of doing. Some of the kids do, but not Jace. He's mature that way."

"Mmm," Laura said. "It *is* a mature thing to do, not to blame one person for another person's misdeeds." She gave Debra a pointed look.

Debra got the message, but she wasn't entirely ceding the point. "I'm not saying you *made* Dad go out and do all those things. I'm just saying that maybe if you had paid more attention to him, either he wouldn't have done them or you would have known."

"He always encouraged me in my career."

"Because it was what you wanted. He knew you loved to cook. You've always loved to cook." She smiled in a young, innocent way that instantly lifted Laura's heart. "Remember the chocolate-covered heart-shaped waffles you used to make for Valentine's Day?"

"I remember," Laura said with a smile of her own, but hers was sad. Those days seemed so simple, and so far off. "You always loved them."

"So did my friends. They loved coming here for Valentine's Day—and St. Patrick's Day, and Patriot's Day, and the Fourth of July. You always made holidays fun."

"Then I did something right?" Laura asked, needing all the encouragement she could get.

"Sure you did. You were more of a supermom than any of my friends' moms, but it wasn't just for us, it was for you too. You liked being that way. You liked having the kids ooh and aah and race over here thinking you were terrific, even though all you were doing was what you liked doing best. You liked doing stuff in the kitchen. We knew that, and Dad knew that, so when you started Cherries, *of course* he was behind you. But that didn't mean he liked it when you were out all the time."

"Did he tell you that?"

"No, but he was thinking it."

"Was he, or were you?"

Debra looked for a minute like she was caught. Then she gave Laura a disgruntled look. "You're as bad as Gram, with the questions that always have a message. Yes, I was thinking it.

You were always busy, always doing something."

"I was home."

"*Doing* something. If you weren't cooking, you were doing business on the phone or making lists for yourself or sorting through the mail. You never do one thing at a time. It's always two or three. There were times when I wanted to be the *only* thing you were doing."

You're a selfish twerp," Scott announced, coming up from behind. "Y'know, Debra, you've had a hell of a lot more than most kids, and you never complained."

Debra separated herself from Laura. "I was too young to appreciate it."

"Sounds like you still are."

She tipped up her chin. "I can appreciate money. And you're a fine one to talk. *You're* the one whose school costs a bundle. *You're* the one who had to join a fraternity. *You're* the one who had to get a whole new wardrobe this year because you said your clothes weren't right. *You're* the one with the car."

"Don't mention clothes to me. You spend ten times as much on clothes as me any day."

"Only because I'm still growing."

"Yeah, *out*. Get any bigger and you'll need hoists to hold 'em up."

Debra made a face. "You're dis-gus-ting."

"She's right, Scottie," Laura put in. Her head had started to pound. "That was unnecessary."

"Well, so's her criticism of me. At least I *worked* in high school. All she does is sashay down the halls, waving her butt at the guys."

"Scott!"

"So I'm normal," Debra shot back. "When you were in high school, the most important thing in your life was the football team. You *loved* those guys. If that isn't perverted—"

"Debra!"

Scott was livid. "Let her talk. She's just proving how stupid she is. Mention male bonding to her, and she'll think it's a service offered by the post office. Stupid and juvenile."

"Better that than gay, dork."

"Debra!"

Scott barked with laughter. "Gay? Uh-huh. Why don't you ask Christina Lakeley about that. Or Megan Tucker. Or Jenny Spitz. Gay?" He leaned close. "Don't let Kelly hear you say that, or she'll *know* how dumb you are. Remember, Kelly's a senior."

"So what?"

"So she knows the guy you have your eyes on—"

"Debra doesn't date seniors," Laura tried to tell him, but he went right on.

"—and she won't hesitate to tip him off about you."

"Let her," Debra challenged. "She might also be interested in hearing about Christina Lakeley, Megan Tucker, and Jenny Spitz."

"Enough," Laura cried, holding up her hands, which she promptly put on either side of her head. "I can't take this. Not on top of everything else."

"You twerp," Scott said to Debra, who wasn't giving an inch.

"I'll talk if you do."

Laura kicked the leg of the chair. "Enough! *Stop it!*"

"I can't stand being in the same room as him," Debra announced and ran from the kitchen.

"If she opens her big mouth to Kelly, I'll kill her," were Scott's parting words before he, too, was gone.

Laura was left in the sudden silence with a foot that hurt, a heart that ached, and the terrifying vision of things falling apart.

The vision kept coming back to her. Repeatedly over the weekend she had panic attacks, times when she broke into a cold sweat, when her heart throbbed and her hands shook. No amount of positive thinking helped. Not even Cherries was the escape it had once been, since DeeAnn was there to remind her of all that was wrong.

Things were falling apart. The cohesive family unit she had worked so hard for had been shattered by Jeff's disappearance. Scott and Debra weren't talking to each other. Lydia was weak. Maddie was carping. Money was scarce. Business stunk.

And Monday was Jeff's birthday. There was a bittersweetness to that which occupied Laura's mind as she lay in bed in the day's predawn hours. Jeff had cheated on her. He had lied and stolen and bought her dreams with dirty money—and all the while she'd been planning a surprise birthday party for him.

The day should have been a happy one. They should have just returned from Saba, all rested and brown, anticipating the party that night. Instead, Laura dragged herself from bed feeling numb, taking comfort from the knowledge that with all that had gone wrong nothing else could faze her.

Debra didn't want to go to school. She was tired of being the butt of school gossip and was sure things would be even worse after the weekend's article in the *Sun*. It took ten minutes of arguing before Laura finally got her off to the bus.

Scott, who was organizing himself to return to school that Wednesday, ended a flurry of phone calls with the decision to move out of the dorm and into the fraternity house. Laura was hesitant. She wanted him to have fun, but not so much fun that his grades fell, which she was afraid might happen if he lived in the house. His enthusiasm was so welcome, though, after the bleakness of the vacation, that she gave in with little more than token argument.

Then Lydia decided she was too stiff to go to the doctor and wanted to postpone her morning appointment. Laura was worried about her pallor and didn't want to wait another week to check it out, so she insisted they go. The doctor detected a slight heart murmur that he wanted to watch, which meant twice-weekly appointments and more worry.

Returning home shortly before noon, Laura found Scott staring at a widening pool of moisture on the ceiling of the front hall. "I don't know what happened," he said. "I showered an hour ago, and when I came downstairs, this was here." His bathroom was directly over the hall, and the spot was spreading smack in the middle like a drawn-on chandelier.

"I don't believe it," Laura cried in dismay, and went to call the plumber. Repairing the ceiling would have to wait until she had more money, but the leak itself had to be stopped.

She was hanging up the phone when she saw that there were two messages on the machine. They had come fifteen minutes apart—which said something about the length of time Scott had dallied in the shower. Both were hang-ups.

She listened, saved them, listened again. They were from the same person, she knew. The static was the same.

Convinced that it was Jeff, she sat by the phone for the next two hours waiting for him to call back, and all the while she thought of what she would say. She imagined her way, line by line, through one dialogue after another, and though each one played up a different emotion, anger was always a factor. Whether blistering, scornful, or leashed, it was there, all the more so as the hours passed. More than anything, she realized, she wanted to yell at him. She wanted to tell him what he'd done to her life. She wanted to tell him he was a snake. But he didn't call, and by the time she acknowledged that he wasn't going to, she was suffering acute frustration.

That was when the doorbell rang. Dennis Melrose stood there, looking somber. Beside him were two uniformed officers. Laura didn't like the way they looked either.

"May we come in, Mrs. Frye?" the detective asked.

She stepped back, then closed the door when the three were inside. Warily she looked from one face to the next before settling on Melrose as the spokesperson. "Is something wrong?" She would have laughed at her own words if the detective hadn't looked so grim.

"Is your son here?"

"Scott?" Her heart beat a little faster. "Uh, no. He's out visiting a friend."

"Do you expect him home soon?"

"In an hour, maybe. Why?"

Melrose pulled a piece of paper from his pocket. "I have a warrant for his arrest."

She stared at the paper. Her heart beat much faster. "Scott? For what?"

"Rape."

"Rape? Are you crazy?"

"I wish I were," he said. "Charges were filed by a young woman named Megan Tucker."

Laura recognized the name. "Megan? Scott *dated* Megan Tucker. He wouldn't rape her." The idea of it was absurd. "This is a joke, isn't it, detective? On top of everything else, this really is a joke." But the piece of paper was still in his hand, the look of regret still in his eye.

"I'm sorry, Mrs. Frye. We spent a good part of yesterday with the young woman and a good part of today investigating her story. I may not like it, but there was probable cause to go for an arrest warrant. It's signed by the court."

With an effort, Laura remained calm. She tucked her hands in her jeans to keep them from shaking. "When was this supposed to have happened?"

"Last August the twenty-sixth."

Scott had dated Megan in August but had broken off with her to go back to school. He had left for Penn on the twenty-eighth. Laura remembered that well. Scott's leaving was always hard for her.

"Why did it take her so long to come forward?"

"Rape is an emotional crime. Victims are often silent for years."

"And the timing of this doesn't strike you as strange?" Laura asked. Her voice was higher than normal, but she couldn't help it. Trying to stay calm was just fine, except that her son, her first-born, the absolute apple of her eye, was being accused of rape. "It seems pretty obvious to me, detective, that Megan Tucker has been following the Frye case in the papers, and either she or her family decided to cash in on a good thing. Is she pregnant?" If the girl needed money, that would explain it.

"She lost the baby last fall. It was a spontaneous abortion."

"I'll bet," Laura said. "I'll also bet that if she was ever carrying a baby, it wasn't Scott's. He uses condoms. My son is responsible that way." She had a sudden intense need to have Melrose and his men gone. "Whatever the girl said isn't true. You'd best take that piece of paper back to the station and rip it up."

"I can't do that," Melrose told her. "It's a warrant for Scott's arrest. I'm bound to serve it and take him in."

Take him in. Oh, God. Her heart skipped a beat this time. "What do you mean?"

"He'll have to be booked."

She knew what that entailed and couldn't imagine her son going through it. "But he hasn't done anything wrong!"

"He's been accused," Melrose explained patiently. "At the arraignment, he can plead not guilty. But I do have to bring him in. Do you know where he is?"

"No." Laura wouldn't tell him even if she did. Scott couldn't be *booked*. He was an innocent kid!

"Then do you mind if we wait here until he gets back?"

She did mind it. She didn't want them anywhere near her house, and she didn't want them touching her son. "You can't wait here. You can't arrest Scott. He hasn't done anything."

With a glance at his sidekicks, Melrose turned and started for the door. "We'll be outside in the car." He was about to open the door when Laura heard the muted sound of the garage door rising. Melrose heard it too and paused. "Is that him?"

Since Jeff was gone, Scott had been parking in his space. "No, it's my daughter coming home from school," Laura lied. Knowing that Debra was going downtown with her friends after school, she ran back through the kitchen. She didn't know what to say to Scott, but she couldn't let the police get him. She had no faith in the legal system, not after the last month, when she'd lost so much without committing a single crime. Scott was her son. She wasn't having him booked and fingerprinted and photographed. She wasn't having him dirtied in any stinking jail while the arbitrators of justice played their games. She didn't care *what* Megan Tucker said. Scott hadn't raped her.

But it wasn't Scott who came through the kitchen door. It was Christian, wearing corduroy jeans, a sweater, and a shearling jacket. He looked large and tanned, stunning in a rugged way. But the sight of him was one trauma too many, shattering Laura's fragile composure.

eighteen

"**N**O," LAURA SAID AND BACKED UP TO the wall. "No! No-ooo!" Screaming the last, she flattened her hands over her ears, then moved them up until her arms covered her head. She slid down the wall on her spine and hit the floor, where she curled into a ball.

Christian's voice was suddenly inches away. "Laura? Jesus, what's wrong?"

She spoke in muffled bursts. "Not you. Not on top of everything else. Go, Christian. Leave. I can't handle you too."

"What's *wrong* with you?"

"Everything! My life is in pieces!"

He paused. "Is this pessimism I hear coming from Mary Sunshine?"

"Leave, Christian!" she screamed. "*Get out of here!*"

"I'm not leaving until I know what's going on."

In a high-pitched voice, she reeled off the problems. "Jeff left, then they froze my money so I can't pay my bills, then the IRS indicted him for tax fraud. The *Sun* is tearing us to shreds, and Cherries' business is off. They say Jeff was having an affair with my friend, and now"—she raised her head, uncaring that Christian saw her tears—"now they want to arrest Scott for rape." The tears welled. "Scott. My Scott!"

Christian shot a glance toward the door. "What the hell is she talking about?"

Laura realized that Melrose and his men were there. Not wanting to see them, she returned her face to her knees.

Close by her ear, and with a hand on her neck, Christian murmured, "I'll be right back."

Then the hand was gone, and Laura had her wish. Christian disappeared into the hall with Melrose, leaving her alone in the kitchen. She couldn't deal with Christian, simply couldn't deal with him. For twenty years he had tormented her. She had only to look at him to feel his pull, and he knew it. So he had taunted her with a goading look, a suggestive word, a scornful smile. Ever fearful that Jeff would learn the truth, she was nervous and uneasy when Christian was near—and that was when she felt strong. She didn't feel strong now. Christian would have to turn around his RV or pickup truck or jeep, or whatever he was driving this time, and go away. She had too much else to handle.

Christian! Of all times to show up! Jeff had been gone for six weeks, and Christian hadn't so much as called his mother to see how she was. He hadn't called Laura to see if she'd heard from Jeff. He hadn't even sent a postcard telling them how great it was in Tahiti. No doubt he'd been too busy having fun, which, she knew, was vintage Christian. Put kindly, he was a free spirit. Put less kindly, he was a self-centered hedonist.

Christian was more likely to commit tax fraud than Jeff. Christian was more likely to commit rape than Scott.

Scott. Innocent Scott. Booked, fingerprinted, photographed in that hideous way the police photographed the dregs of society. She couldn't let that happen.

"Laura?"

She jumped when Christian's voice came at her again. "Please leave," she begged.

"These men want to arrest Scott," he said in a gentle but firm voice. "Whether the charge is justified or not, they have a warrant, and there's nothing we can do about it. I don't want Scott talking to the police unless he has an attorney with him. Can your friend Daphne handle this, or should I call someone else?"

She wanted to tell him that he had to get out of her house, that he would only make things worse, that she didn't need his help. But there was an assuredness in his voice that reached out to the part of her that felt sheer panic. If she was selling her soul to the devil, so be it. She'd do that to help her son.

"Daphne," she whispered.

"I'll call her now. Where's Scott and when will he be home?"

"He was with Kelly before. By now he's probably working out at the health club. He said he'd be home by five."

"That gives us an hour and a half. The detective and his men will wait."

Her head came up fast. "Don't tell them where Scott is!" She had nightmarish visions of the police storming the health club and leading a handcuffed Scott off in front of everyone he knew.

"I won't. They're in the other room. Let me get Daphne over here. What's her number?"

Laura said it wrong the first time, confusing Daphne's work number with Jeff's. When she finally got it right, she turned her head away with her cheek on her knee, wound her arms tightly around her legs, and listened while Christian made the call. His voice was low, level, commanding. He seemed to be in control of the situation.

She was glad someone was, since she sure as hell wasn't.

Seconds later, he had hunkered down on her blind side. "Daphne's in court. She's supposed to finish up at four and go back to the office. I told her secretary to get a message to her at the courthouse. I said it was urgent."

Laura hugged her knees tighter. "It is. It's Scott they're waiting for. They want to take him away. For rape!" She felt a hand on her hair. It was soothing, like his voice.

"The cop says Scott knows the girl."

"They dated last summer."

"Do you know her?"

"I met her once. She's a senior. She's pretty, like all the girls Scott dates. He's such a good-looking guy." She cried out at the injustice of it. "He doesn't deserve this. Not Scott. If Megan Tucker had a thing for him and was angry that he ended it to go back to school, that's *her* problem."

"She charged him with rape, so it's Scott's problem too."

Laura raised her face to his. "Whose side are you on? I meant what I said a little while ago, Christian. I can't cope with you along with everything else. Since Jeff left, nothing's gone right. I'm trying to hang on, but it isn't easy, and if you think you can come along and start taunting me, you can think again. I don't want you here. Not like that." His face blurred before her eyes. She swiveled sideways, away from him, and put her cheek to the wall.

After a silence, he said, "I'd like to help."

"I'm not sure anyone can. Things are so awful."

After another silence, he said, "They must be, or you wouldn't be down this way. You were always the most optimistic person I knew."

"It's hard to be optimistic when you get whipped at every turn. I've had six weeks of traumas, one after another." She covered her face with a hand. "This thing with Scott is the worst. The police are waiting out there to arrest my son the minute he steps foot in this house." Her fingers went rigid, and her voice slowed. "I don't know why this is happening to me."

Christian smoothed strands of hair, one by one, back from her face. "We'll get it straightened out, Laura. We will."

Dropping her hand to her knee, she closed her eyes and went limp against the wall. "I feel so tired. At the beginning, I could bounce back. I could find excuses for why things were happening, and even when those excuses fell apart I could count my blessings. But it's like they keep taking those blessings away from me one by one, and now I'm so drained I don't know what to do. I could handle Jeff's disappearance. I could deal with the bank accounts being frozen. I could survive the articles in the paper, and business slowing down, and even Jeff having an affair."

"Did they really say that?"

"Would I make it up? It's devastating." So much so that pride was forgotten. "It makes me feel like a worthless, empty shell parading as a woman, and that's okay, because you're right, it's not the end of the world. But if they do anything to Scott, I'll die."

"They won't do anything to Scott."

She gave a bitter bark of a laugh. "Two months ago, I would have agreed. I mean, he's not guilty, right? Some girl's gone a little nuts, right? Justice will prevail, right?" She sighed. "After a while, when one unfair thing after another happens, you lose faith."

"Don't do that, Laura. It's no way to live."

"And this is? I don't sleep because my mind keeps churning things around. I don't eat because my stomach keeps churning things around. I can't walk down the street without someone turning to stare, because the *newspaper* keeps churning things around." She squeezed her eyes shut. "The paper will crucify Scott."

"Not if I can help it," Christian vowed. He took her by the arms. "Come on, Laura. I want you up at the table. You can have some tea while I make my calls."

"Who are you calling?"

"For starters, Tack Jones. I want to find out what's going on."

Laura let herself be settled into a chair. "He's the enemy. He won't help."

"He'll help." Christian spoke with such conviction that she simply watched while he put on a teakettle, then pulled out his wallet and took a business card from it. Within minutes, he was talking with Tack.

Laura didn't move. She wasn't sure whether she was so exhausted that she didn't have the energy, or whether she was saving up what little energy she did have for the moment when

Scott would be home, or whether it was Christian's presence that kept her still. Years ago, she had gone weak in the knees every time she'd set eyes on him.

He still looked good.

More than that, he sounded strong. She didn't have to follow his conversation to know he was asking pointed questions. And he'd get his answers. Christian was that way. When he dedicated himself to something—be it taking photographs, disrupting a family gathering, or making a seventeen-year-old girl fall in love—he succeeded.

The teakettle whistled. Pure reflex had Laura on her feet, but a motion from Christian sent her back to her seat. She watched him take out the mugs, then the tea bags, then the sugar. Seven months had passed since he'd been in her house; still, he remembered where things were. But that was Christian too. He had an incredible memory. He was one of the few people she knew who, like her, could do two things at once—which he proceeded to demonstrate by fixing her tea with two sugars, like she always drank it, without missing a beat in his talk with Tack.

He stretched the phone cord to bring her the tea. Laura wrapped her hands around the warm mug. She was so tired. Every time she thought of the ordeal that was sure to come before the day was done, she started to shake. But the shaking was more distant now than it had been, as though she didn't have enough energy for that either, another frightening thought. She had to be there for Scott. She had to be strong for him. She was his mother. With Jeff gone, she was all he had.

She sipped her tea, then took another sip when the sweetness went down the right way. Her gaze drifted to the window. She wished it were summer, with the crabapple trees full, the grass a rich green, and birds swooping about. If she could have had warmth and sunshine just then, she wouldn't have begrudged the squirrels her birdseed, she was that desperate for something cheery and light.

Christian slid into a chair with his own mug of tea. Looking at it, Laura realized she didn't know many male tea drinkers. She imagined men were drawn to coffee because it had a more macho image. Jeff was a coffee drinker. But not Christian. Twenty-one years ago he'd been drinking tea, and he still was.

Her eyes rose to his face, but he was looking at his mug and seemed lost in thought. She wondered whether he was considering putting his coat back on and leaving, now that he knew how bad things were. He had left her once before, when things weren't bad at all. She wouldn't put it past him to do it again.

Still he sat brooding. She was starting to wonder if he would wait until after his tea to leave, when he raised his head and met her eyes. "Why didn't you tell me?"

"About what?" She thought she had blurted out most everything when she'd been crouched on the floor.

"The money. Tack says you're strapped."

"How does Tack know?"

"He knows. Is it true?"

There didn't seem any point in denying it. Christian knew so much already, he might as well know it all. She was too tired to play games. "When you find yourself one day suddenly cut off from every cent you have to your name so that you're basically starting from scratch, you're strapped."

"You should have told me."

"How? You were in Tahiti."

"Tack knew where I was. You knew he had seen me. You could have gotten a phone number from him."

Laura looked off toward the yard. She supposed she had known that. But she hadn't wanted to call Christian. She hadn't wanted him to know how badly she'd failed.

He tapped the side of his mug. "Tack said Daphne and Elise are helping you out."

She frowned. "How does *he* know?"

The tapping stopped. "I'll help too. I've got money sitting in the bank doing nothing. I'll get a draft tomorrow and deposit it in your account."

She took a deep breath. "That's not necessary. I think I have things under control. I borrowed enough from Daphne and Elise to get me through the worst of this month, and if business is good—"

"It isn't. You said that before."

She let out the rest of the breath and turned back to the window, only to freeze moments later when the garage door went up. "Oh, God," she whispered. The pounding in her chest started again. "Oh, God, Christian, they'll take him to jail."

Christian looked at the door to the hall, where the detective had materialized, then swung around in time to see Debra breeze in from the garage. She began talking the instant she saw Laura.

"What is that *police* car doing outside? And the Miata. Whose is that?" She caught sight of Christian and her eyes went wide. In a hushed voice that reflected the mix of awe and amusement that Debra and Scott both held for their uncle, she said, "Oh, wow, we knew you'd get in trouble one day. What did you do, Christian?"

"Nothing yet," Laura said.

"The police cars aren't for him?" The wide eyes went from Laura to the detective. "Why are they here?"

Laura tried to say it, but the words wouldn't come. With wide eyes of her own, she stared at Debra for a minute before looking frantically at Christian.

"They want to ask your brother a few questions," Christian explained.

"Questions about what?"

"A girl he used to date."

"Which one?"

"Megan Tucker," Dennis Melrose said from the door.

"What's she done now?" Debra asked, in a way that suggested she fully expected Megan to be in trouble.

Laura pulled out of her silence to grab onto that. "Do you know her?"

"I know who she is. Most everyone does."

"Why?" Christian asked.

"She's popular. She's pretty."

"Does she go out a lot?"

"Sure. She gives boys what they want. What'd she do?" Debra asked the detective, who promptly looked at Laura, but she couldn't get the words past her throat any more than before. Again she sought Christian's help.

"She filed criminal charges against Scott," he said.

"For what?"

The room was silent. Debra's eyes went from one face to the next. "What's going *on*?"

"Rape," Laura blurted out. "She says Scott raped her."

Debra's jaw dropped. "Are you kidding?"

The disbelief on her face was so genuine Laura wanted to hug her. For the time being, though, she only shook her head.

Debra stared at the detective. "Megan's lying. If she says Scott raped her, she's lying. I know my brother, and he may be obnoxious—"

"Debra—"

"Babe—"

"—but that's to me, because I'm his sister," Debra finished in defiance of Christian and Laura's simultaneous attempts to warn her into silence. "Scott's a nice guy. He treats his dates well. He gives them little gifts and does these romantic things that any girl would be crazy not to like. If he wanted sex, he wouldn't have to rape a girl to get it." She deposited her backpack on the island with a thud. "He sure wouldn't have to rape Megan. She practically gives it out on the street corner, and I'm not the only one who'd say that. Ask anyone. She's known for it."

Christian grinned at her. He winked at Laura, then turned his grin on the detective. "There you have it, Detective Melrose. Your first character witness. She won't help your case."

"Neither will I," Daphne said from the hall, having let herself in through the front door. She looked livid. "I'll fight you tooth and nail, and if either of you guys—" her eyes touched briefly on the uniformed officers, "—think that's a typically feminine response, you'd better believe it. It's feminine and hard and can be very unpleasant if you're on the other end. I've known Scott Frye since he was born, and if there's one kid who is incapable of rape, he's it. Dennis, what *gives?* You know as well as I do that girl's lying. I won't know why until I look into the case, but my guess is she's jumping on the bandwagon. She sees what the paper is doing to this family, she hears the scuttlebutt around town, and hell, date rape is a hot topic, so why not? She figures she'll get a little sympathy, a little attention, maybe even some money. Is she suing for damages?"

"I don't know," Melrose said. "The only thing that concerns me is the criminal complaint."

"Well, it *should* concern you. It's a trumped-up charge."

The detective looked uncomfortable. "You know how the system works, Daphne. If the girl comes in, swears she's been raped, and wants to file charges, we have to investigate. You may be able to get the charges dismissed at the probable-cause hearing, but in the meantime I have to book the boy."

A small, involuntary sound came from Laura's throat. Resting her elbow on the table, she put her forehead in her palm. Daphne continued to spar with the detective, though it was an exercise in futility, Laura knew. After a minute, Christian touched her arm.

"Hangin' in there?" he asked.

She nodded.

A minute later, the detective retreated from the kitchen. Fishing in her bag for a notebook, Daphne turned to Debra. She spoke quietly but with purpose. "While we're waiting for Scott, I want you to tell me everything you know about Megan Tucker—who her friends are, who she dates, whether she belongs to any clubs or has any school extracurricular activities."

Debra told her what she knew. When Laura didn't hear anything to significantly change her impression of the girl's motive, she tuned out of the discussion and turned her thoughts to Scott.

"He'll be okay," Christian leaned close again to say.

Laura's sigh came out as a moan against her wrist. "He has to be. He's such a good kid. *Such* a good kid. He works hard, he does well, and he has promise. His whole future is ahead of him. The thought of it being spoiled by some spiteful little bitch makes me sick." She curled her fingers into a fist. "Damn Jeff. Damn his greed and his cowardice." Lowering her hand, she looked at Christian. "I keep wondering if he knows what's going on. For all we know, he's hiding out somewhere ten miles away, following the stories in the paper."

"If that were so, they'd have found the Porsche. Boy, I'll bet he loved that car. It had the flash he never did. When did he get it? He didn't have it when I was here in June."

"He bought it in July."

"Did he pay in cash?"

Laura pressed her lips together for a minute. She'd asked herself that question over and over, and each time she felt greater self-reproach. "I don't know. I didn't ask. Pretty dumb of me, huh? An expensive car like that, and I didn't ask if we could afford it. But if I'd done that," she defended herself as she'd done so many times in her mind, "it would have been like I doubted him, and that would have been an insult. It was my job to build him up, not knock him down. Or so I thought." In a dry murmur, she added, "Looks like I thought wrong on a whole lot of things. I thought he cared for me. I thought he cared for the kids. Let's see if he comes forward when he learns about *this*."

Christian shook his head. "He's probably long gone. He's probably somewhere where he couldn't possibly get either the *Globe* or the *Sun* without tipping his hand. Jeff's crafty. More than any of us thought. He pulled off that scam for eight years before anyone caught on, and now he's eluding the FBI. He's being careful. I doubt he'd go looking for news, and that's even if he wanted it, which I doubt he does. If he made the decision to cut loose, he won't want to know about the mess he left behind."

"Which is something I'll never understand as long as I live," Laura said in defeat. "I'll never understand *any* of this." Elbows on the table, she linked her fingers and pressed them to her mouth, which was propitious. They were able to stifle her cry when the garage door opened for the third time.

nineteen

IT TOOK SCOTT LONGER TO ENTER THE kitchen. He had to pull into the garage and turn off the car. Pressing those fingers harder to her mouth, Laura listened to the car door opening, then slamming shut. She heard his footsteps on the landing. His entrance was on a burst of energy, much the way Debra's had been, but he came to an abrupt halt when he saw the faces turned his way—including those of Melrose and his men.

"Yo, Christian! You throwing a party?" he asked curiously. He was wearing an open parka over sweatpants and a sweatshirt, and his hair fell in spikes on his forehead.

Laura went to him and slipped an arm through his. Her voice shook. "We have a problem here."

Scott looked suddenly frightened. "They found Dad?"

"No."

"But it has to do with Dad."

"No."

He looked at Christian. "Are you in trouble?"

Christian shook his head. "Not me. You."

"Me?"

Daphne came up. "Megan Tucker is accusing you of rape."

"She's what?"

"Accusing you of rape."

Scott looked dumbfounded. *"Megan Tucker?"*

"That's right." Daphne glanced at the detective. "Back off, Dennis. We'd like a few minutes alone."

"We'll be waiting outside," Melrose told her.

Scott stared after him until he was gone, then turned back to Daphne. "Rape?"

Laura held his arm tightly. She could feel the tension there, even through the layers of his clothes. "She says it happened last August."

His eyes flashed. "She lies."

"That's what *I* said," Debra put in.

"Why would I rape her?" Scott cried. "She gives it out like there's no tomorrow."

Debra bobbed her head. "That's what *I* said."

"It doesn't matter what either of you says right now," Daphne explained. "What matters, Scott, is what the girl said and the fact that those men out there hold a warrant for your arrest."

Laura saw his color drain, felt the tremor that shot through his arm, and it nearly tore her apart. She opened her mouth to reassure him, but her throat was thick and tight and no words came out.

"My arrest? For what? I didn't rape Megan Tucker. I didn't do anything but date her for a few weeks."

"Did you sleep with her?" Daphne asked.

Scott looked at Debra, then at Laura. "Yeah, I slept with her. I'd have been a fool not to. She's pretty and she's sexy and she's willing. *More* than willing. I did not rape her."

"I know," Laura managed through the knot in her throat. Her knees had started to shake, and she felt perilously close to tears, but she ignored both. "She's a sick girl."

"So where does that leave me?"

"You'll have to go down to the station—" Daphne began.

"The *police* station? I'm not going to the police station! I haven't done anything wrong!"

"You'll tell them that," Laura urged, but that was as much as she got out before her lower lip began to tremble.

Daphne took over. "I'll be with you. We'll go down to the station. They'll go through the formalities of charging you. We'll get bail set, then you'll be home. Tomorrow morning you'll be arraigned—ten minutes in court—and then you'll go back to school like you planned."

"With a rape charge hanging over my head."

"Yes," Daphne conceded. "But while you're gone, I'll be working to get the charges dismissed."

Laura had bleak visions of the agony lasting for months, even years. "Can't you get them dismissed now?"

"Not now. Maybe soon. I have to learn more about the case. Once Scott's back here, we can talk about his relationship with Megan Tucker. By then we'll have a copy of the statement she gave the police." To Scott, she said, "Let's go on down now and get this over with. The sooner we're back here, the better."

Laura released Scott's arm and looked frantically around the floor. "I just—uh, I need some shoes."

Christian materialized beside her. "Stay here, Laura. I'll go with Daphne. It'll be better that way." He went for his jacket.

Laura swallowed back her tears. "Oh, God, no. I wouldn't think of not being there. I *have* to be there."

"Christian's right," Daphne said. "It's a routine thing. No one's making any kind of statement. Stay here."

"But I want to be with Scott." She looked up at him. "I've always been there for you. I couldn't not be there now."

"Stay here, Mom," he said in a voice that was tense but very grown up. "Stay here with Debra. It'll be awful enough for me there. It'll be worse if you have to see it all."

"I don't mind," she argued. She felt more frightened than she had ever been in her life. "I never minded when you were a little boy and threw up, or bashed your lip playing and bled all over the place."

"I'm not a little boy anymore, and this isn't play."

Her breath caught. Of all the things he might have said, that stopped her cold. Because he was right. On both counts. And she didn't want either to be true. "But what'll I do here?"

"Fix dinner," Christian said. Taking Scott by the shoulder, he moved him toward the garage. "We'll all be hungry when we get back. I haven't had a decent home-cooked meal since I was here last June. Do something special, Laura. And you help her, Debra," he called over his shoulder. "Stay here with her and help."

"I'm not leaving," Debra said in a frightened voice, but the only one who heard her was Laura, since the other three were gone.

The garage door rolled open, then rolled shut. Debra moved close to Laura, who was hugging herself against the pain.

"Whose car are they taking?" she whispered.

"Daphne's," Laura whispered back. She thought to run to the front window and watch, but her legs wouldn't work.

"Will Scott have to go with the police?"

"Maybe."

"They won't handcuff him, will they?"

Laura was asking herself the same thing. "I don't think so. He's going in with his lawyer. They know he's not running away."

The whispering went on. "Will they fingerprint him and stuff?"

"I think so."

"That's *awful*."

Laura turned to find Debra looking so distraught she immediately took her in her arms. What she wanted to say was, Don't worry, babe, it'll be all right, Scott will be right back, this whole thing's a mistake, but she had no faith in the words. Words were empty. Reason didn't always prevail. The only thing with meaning was the warmth of another human being, the closeness and the comfort. Debra must have agreed, because they stood there holding each other, silent in a silent house, for a long time.

"You're shaking," Debra whispered at one point.

"It's getting better," Laura whispered back, and held her a bit longer. Finally, knowing that Christian's suggestion was good in ways that went well beyond food, she took a deep breath and said, "Okay. What should I make?"

Mercifully, Debra didn't ask how she could possibly cook. Instead, she said, "What do you have?"

Laura studied the refrigerator, then the freezer. She took a flank steak from the latter and put it in the microwave to defrost, then began piling fresh vegetables onto the counter. "I don't know how long they'll be. I can slice everything now, then put it in the wok when they get home." It made sense, she thought, and was pleased that *something* did. So she took out the cutting board and a knife and went to work.

She sliced scallions, celery, and spinach.

"Don't you usually leave the spinach leaves whole?" Debra asked. She stood at the counter watching.

"I need to cut," Laura told her, but she dropped the knife with a clatter when the phone rang.

Debra reached it before she could. "Hello?" After a silence, during which time Laura felt her life was on hold, she repeated the greeting. "Hello?"

"What do you hear?" Laura whispered.

"Nothing," Debra whispered back. "*Hello.*" After another second, she hung up the phone. "Must have been a wrong number."

Laura wanted to ask if there had been static, but then Debra would wonder why she'd asked, and to tell her would be like putting her on the alert that her father might be calling any time, which wasn't the truth.

So Laura said nothing and went back to her chopping. Between thoughts of Scott and thoughts of Jeff, she was nowhere near as efficient as usual. Her hands weren't steady. Her concentration was off.

"What do you think they're doing to Scott?" Debra asked nervously.

"Booking him."

"Do you think he's scared?"

"Uh-huh."

"Will Daphne be with him the whole time?"

"I hope so."

"And Christian. Funny his showing up today. I mean, on Dad's birthday and all."

Laura dropped the knife and wiped shaky hands on her jeans. Going back to the refrigerator, she took out several sweet potatoes and began to pare them.

"Can I do something?" Debra asked.

Laura shook her head. "I need to keep busy."

"Christian told me to help."

"You can set the table."

While Debra did that, Laura set about cutting the potatoes down to shoestring size, but she had barely cut the first potato into quarters when the knife went too far and cut into the heel of her hand. Swearing, she grabbed the nearby dishtowel and pressed it to the cut.

Debra looked over her shoulder. "Is it bad?"

"Nah."

"Let me see."

"It's fine. Do me a favor and get a Band-Aid."

While Debra went to the bathroom, Laura took off the towel and put her hand under the faucet. The cut wasn't fine. It was deep. But it wouldn't kill her. Neither would the sight of the blood flowing from it, though it made her weak in ways the sight of blood never had before.

Debra brought the tin of Band-Aids. Laura put one on as tightly as she could, but she'd barely thrown away the tabs when blood began seeping through the pad.

"That's disgusting," Debra said. "It's really bleeding. Maybe it needs to be stitched."

Laura felt vaguely light-headed. "All it needs is to be wrapped tighter. Were there any gauze pads with the Band-Aids?" When

Debra went to check, she stumbled to a chair, and while she put pressure on her hand, she hung her head between her knees. She hadn't fainted many times in her life, but she knew the signs.

"Mom? Are you okay?"

She raised her head and took a breath. "I'm fine, babe. Just a little woozy there for a minute."

"Maybe you should lie down."

"I'm okay." She opened two gauze pads, removed the blood-ied Band-Aid, and pressed the pads in place, then taped them there with a new Band-Aid. "There." Tossing the papers in the basket, she pushed herself up, took some ice water from the refrigerator, and sipped it. It helped.

"You look pale," Debra told her. "Are you sure you're not going to pass out?"

"No. I'm okay now." To prove it, she went back to work. Before long, the potatoes were arranged in tiny slices beside the other vegetables on a plate. She gathered the ingredients for the sauce, then put white rice on to boil.

Then she looked at Debra. "What should I do for dessert?"

"There are a million things already in the refrigerator."

"Humor me, babe. I have to work. How about a hot fruit compote?" Scott loved that. She took out the ingredients, most of which were canned, and began to arrange them in a large baking dish. All too soon the dish was in the oven, and she was looking at Debra again. She pressed the heel of her hand, which was beginning to throb. She glanced worriedly at the clock.

"They've been gone an hour," Debra said. "Is that good or bad?"

"I don't know."

"Does your hand hurt?"

"A little. It'll be okay."

"Shouldn't they be back soon?"

Laura nodded.

"Y'know, Megan Tucker really is awful. She goes through a guy a month. No judge will take her word over Scott's."

"I hope it never comes to that," Laura said. "With any luck, we can get the charges dismissed." Needing to do something—and remembering the brief comfort she'd found earlier—she said, "Want some tea?"

"I hate tea. Tea is for when you're sick and your stomach is upset. When we were little, you used to make us drink it. I don't think I'll ever be able to look at it without thinking of dry toast and Kaopectate. No, thanks."

Laura put the light on under the kettle.

"Mom?"

"Mmm?"

"You've known for a while that Scott was sleeping with girls, haven't you?"

Unsure where the conversation was leading and, therefore, how much she should say, Laura shrugged. "Why do you ask?"

"Did you know when he first did it?"

"He didn't run right home and tell me, if that's what you're asking."

"Did you talk about it beforehand with him—I mean, about birth control and stuff?"

Laura nodded. "Like I talked with you."

"Did Dad give him condoms?"

Laura doubted that. She doubted if Jeff had even discussed the matter with Scott. He had been uncomfortable talking about intimate things. "I assume Scott went into a drugstore and bought them himself." She glanced at the clock and wondered what was happening and when they'd be home. She wished she'd gone with them. The waiting was awful.

"Boys are lucky. They can do that so easily. If a girl wants to go on the pill, she has to go to a doctor, and then her parents know beforehand what she's going to do."

"Maybe it's better that way," Laura said. "Girls are more vulnerable. They *should* think seriously about what they do." She wandered into the dining room.

Debra followed her. "That's a sexist thing to say."

276

"Maybe." She pulled back the sheer and looked out into the night, but the red Miata parked in the driveway was the only car in sight.

"What if I wanted to go on the pill? Would you let me?"

"You're only sixteen."

"Maybe Scott was sixteen when he did it."

"Scott wasn't sixteen. He was eighteen."

"He was not. He was dating Jenny Spitz when he was seventeen, and Jenny's hot stuff."

"Scott was over eighteen when he was first with a girl."

"Okay. But the girls were sixteen and seventeen. That's the way things work. Girls who are my age date guys who are seventeen and eighteen."

"Donny's your age."

"Jace isn't."

Laura looked at her, but the darkness hid her expression. "How old is Jace?"

"He's a senior."

"How old is he?"

"Eighteen."

"I didn't know that."

"I'm sure I said it at some point. You just didn't hear. But it's no big thing. He's the nicest guy in the world."

So was Scott, Laura mused, looking back at the window, and now he was being taken for a ride by a girl he had made love to and shouldn't have. Unless the Frye luck changed, the mistake could prove to be disastrous.

Headlights came from down the street. Laura held her breath, half expecting the car to go on by. When it turned into the driveway, she whispered, "Thank God." Whirling around, she ran back through the kitchen to the garage. She opened the door and, barefooted, waited at the edge of the cement for Scott to get out of the car.

Daphne got out, then Christian. Something about the way they looked at her, even before their doors slammed shut in the night, made Laura cold all over.

"Where is he?"

"They're keeping him overnight," Daphne said.

Christian put an arm around her shoulder and turned her back toward the kitchen. "Come on inside. It's cold."

Laura shrugged off his arm. "Why isn't he home?"

"There was a problem with bail," Daphne said.

Christian's arm returned to propel her forward, but she didn't take her eyes off Daphne. "What kind of problem?"

"Since it was after four, there wasn't a judge around, so they had to call a bail commissioner. He didn't want to set bail."

"Why not?" Debra asked from the door, then stepped aside as they came through.

"He felt that, given the seriousness of the charge, it was better to wait until morning."

Laura began to shiver. "Scott's spending the night in jail?"

Christian's arm tightened around her. "The arraignment will be first thing tomorrow morning. The judge will set bail then."

Laura looked up at him and swallowed hard. "He's in jail?"

"He'll be okay, Laura. Trust me. He will."

The words seemed to come from farther and farther away. She felt light-headed again, and this time there was a buzzing in her ears. "I want . . . I think . . . I have to . . ." The world turned stark white. The next thing she knew, she was on the living room sofa, with no idea how she'd gotten there. Debra and Daphne were hovering in her periphery, but Christian was the one pressing a damp cloth to her forehead. "I must have . . ."

"You did," he said. "Very elegantly." He tugged at the Band-Aid on her hand, then whistled through his teeth when he got a look at what was beneath.

Laura glanced down, but the bloody gauze made her close her eyes and moan.

"I'm taking her to the hospital," Christian told the other two. Laura didn't have the strength to argue. "Debra, can you find me something warm for her feet, socks and sneakers or some-thing?" When she went off, he looked back at the hand. "How did you do this?"

"I was holding the potato. I should have put it on the cutting board."

"That's great. Just great." To Daphne he said, "Think Julia Child cuts potatoes in her hand?"

Laura turned her face away. "What kind of jail is it? Is it filthy? Crowded?"

"Not in this town," Daphne leaned over to assure her. "He'll be in his own cell. They'll give him dinner. He'll have a cot to sleep on, and he'll be as warm as he wants."

"How early can he get out?"

"Court is at nine."

"Nine!"

"He'll be okay, Laura. Christian and I talked with him for a while before we left. He's a strong kid. He'll do just fine."

All that might be true, but he was still Laura's son, and each time she thought of where he was, she felt chilled to the bone. Shivering, she pushed herself up.

"Dizzy?" Christian asked.

She opened the cloth and pressed it over her face for a minute before setting it aside. "I'm okay."

Debra returned with sneakers and socks, which Christian promptly went to work putting on. When Laura bent over to do it herself, he pushed her hand away. "Any fresh gauze for that cut, Deb?" Debra ran off.

"I can do this," Laura insisted.

Christian shot her an annoyed look. "I'm sure you can, but why should you have to if I'm willing to do it for you?"

"Because I'm not helpless."

"No, but you're upset and dizzy, and that hand probably hurts like hell. So do me a favor?" He reached out and took the fresh gauze from a slightly breathless Debra. "Hold your hand higher than your heart, press this gauze to it, and let me do the rest, okay?"

Laura couldn't remember the last time someone had helped her dress. She wanted to protest, but it wasn't worth the effort. She wanted to feel embarrassed, but she didn't have the strength. So she concentrated on doing what Christian had said, holding her hand in the vicinity of her neck, pressing the gauze to the cut. When he finished tying her sneakers, he drew her to her feet and guided her into the hall. With his help, she put on her coat, and when he tucked her into the passenger's seat of the Miata, she sank down and closed her eyes.

The hospital was ten minutes away. Laura was silent during the drive. She felt Christian look her way from time to time. Twice he asked how she was, but all she did was nod. She kept thinking of Scott and wanting to cry.

Determinedly, she held it in. Christian did most of the talking at the hospital, and, having decided not to fight, it was a relief to let him. It was also a relief to have him by her side the whole time, where she could lean against him for comfort. She wasn't normally a coward, and she didn't shy from physical pain, but she wasn't herself. She was weak, battered, stripped down, and frightened, so frightened. So she took what he offered.

In no more than half an hour, the cut was sewn up and they were back in the car heading home. Again she was silent. Her throat kept tightening up, and if it wasn't her throat, it was the sting of tears in her eyes.

"Feeling okay?" Christian asked, sounding concerned in spite of the lightness he forced into his voice.

That concern made her throat even tighter, but she managed to push out an "Uh-huh."

Several minutes later, he asked, "Does it hurt much?"

"It's still numb," she answered, wishing she were as numb as the hand. But her mind seemed to be working with remarkable clarity, producing pictures she didn't want to see.

"Are you hungry?" he asked several minutes after that.

She shook her head. When, soon after, they pulled up at the house, went through the garage and into the kitchen, and the smell of sukiyaki hit her, she knew she couldn't eat a thing.

After assuring a frightened Debra that she was fine, she excused herself and went upstairs to her bedroom. Without so much as kicking off her sneakers, she pulled back a corner of the bedspread, climbed under it, pulled it to her ears, and gave in to the tears that had been wanting to come for such a long, long time.

That was how Christian found her. He had seen those tears threatening time and again at the hospital, and he knew they had to do not with her hand but with everything else happening in her life. He also knew she wouldn't let them fall in front of other people. She was too proud and independent for that.

Christian understood pride and independence. They were mainstays of his own personality. But so was determination. When he had first driven into Northampton that afternoon, he hadn't expected half of what he'd found. Seeing Laura vulnerable had shaken him. He wasn't sure he knew what had happened to her, but he wasn't leaving until he found out. And while he was there, he planned to help. That was in his nature too. He helped his friends. He would have helped his family if he hadn't been shut out from the time he'd been nine. And he had let them do that. He had played into their hands, given them reason to think the worst of him, given himself reason to walk away from the hurt. But he wasn't doing that now. Now he could do some good.

That was why, when Laura cried between sobs, "Leave me alone—please, Christian—just leave me alone!" he kicked off his shoes and climbed right into bed with her. Propping himself against the headboard, he took her in his arms and held her tightly until her resistance faded. Then he rubbed her back, smoothed her hair from her face, and held her gently until she cried herself to sleep.

twenty

SCOTT WAS ARRAIGNED THE NEXT MORN-
ing. After entering a plea of not guilty, he was released on his
own recognizance—though not without a fight from the assistant
district attorney, who argued that the family history suggested
Scott might flee before his trial. Daphne argued that given Scott's
age, the total absence of a criminal record, his enrollment at
Penn, and his mother's position in the community, the concept
of flight was absurd, and the judge agreed.

That was the first time Laura felt that anything legal had gone
her way, and it gave her an iota of encouragement. With Christian at the wheel of the Wagoneer, they drove Scott home. While
Scott showered, Christian took the *Sun* out of the wastebasket,
where Laura had thrown it that morning.

"This is quite an article," he commented dryly.

She stood against the counter with her arms crossed in distaste.
"It's nothing more than Duggan O'Neil has been doing regularly
since Jeff disappeared. He puts in every detail he can dig up,
then speculates about others. Wait a day or two. Gary Holmes
is sure to write an editorial about this."

"What's his problem? Did you put rotten cherries in his pie?"

"I don't serve rotten cherries, so I have no idea what his
problem is. My mother thinks I should yell and scream and

threaten lawsuits, but that would be a waste of time. The *Sun* isn't doing anything illegal, just cruel. Every time there's an article, we feel the fallout, and I'm not only talking about business. People stare. They talk. I'm getting used to it, I suppose, but it isn't so easy for Debra. Some of her friends—supposed friends—are ignoring her. She's being excluded from parties. Parties wouldn't matter to me, but they do to her. She's a social kid."

"She's a knockout."

Laura couldn't resist a small smile. "Yeah."

"She looks like you."

Her eyes met his. For a minute she thought she saw admiration, then she decided she was wrong. Christian had lost interest in her years ago. Apparently, so had Jeff, which didn't make her worthy of much admiration, at least not of the appealing-woman type.

"About last night." She lowered her eyes to her hand. It was neatly bandaged, and though it was sore, there was no blood in sight. "Thanks are due. I kind of fell apart. I'm glad you were here."

"I'm happy I was," Christian said quietly.

His tone brought her head right back up. The Christian who had visited over the last twenty years would have been more apt to throw out a smug "Yeah, I saved the day, you really were a mess." This one reminded her of the younger, gentler, totally mesmerizing man she had known before Jeff.

"Why are you here?" she asked. She kept wondering about that. Christian wasn't one to pop in. As far as she could recall, he had never come without an invitation before. "What made you come yesterday? What made you come at all?"

He folded the paper, then folded it again and returned it to the trash. Pensive, he straightened. "It had been awhile. I hadn't heard anything from Jones, and I wondered what was happening." He paused. "I was just in from Tahiti and didn't have much else to do." He paused again, looking hesitant. With an uncertain frown, he said, "Yesterday was Jeff's birthday. When he was a baby, it was always a fun day. He loved the party and the presents, and I loved seeing that."

Laura was instantly skeptical. "You resented Jeff from the day he was born."

"Not true," Christian insisted. "I loved him when he was little. He was so cute and so good and so serious. I worked as hard as everyone else to make him happy, and he was happy on his birthday." He thumbed the edge of the footed cake plate that held, under a glass dome, two thirds of an apple torte. "I guess I thought maybe he'd show up yesterday, or write, or call."

Laura heard the shower cut off. She figured she'd give Scott a few minutes to get dressed before she went up. "He may have called. There were some hang-ups."

"No sound?"

Laura shook her head. "Two on the machine had a little static. Debra answered a third, so I don't know."

"Is there a tap on the phone?"

"You mean, is the FBI monitoring my calls?" She listened for little beeps, and though she didn't hear any, she was conscious of everything she said on the phone. "I assume so. They don't trust me to tell them if he called. Isn't that a laugh? The man has torn apart everything I've wanted and worked for, and they think I'd protect him."

"You are his wife," Christian pointed out.

"Which is why I'm so angry." She had promised herself that she wouldn't ask the question again, still it slipped out. "How could he do this to me, Christian? How could a rational man who supposedly loved his family turn on them this way?"

"He didn't turn on you. He ran away."

"Same difference. I was his wife. If something was bothering him, he should have told me. I keep going over the last few years in my mind." She raised her good hand to her head, as though that might help her. "I keep trying to remember if he was unusually quiet, or sullen, or moody, or impatient. But he wasn't any of those things, or if he was I didn't see it. Maybe Debra's right. Maybe I was too busy to see it. But I've had hours to look back now, and I don't see a thing." Her hand fell. She looked at the injured one, ran her fingertips over the gauze. "Did he ever say anything to you?"

"He wouldn't have."

"You were his brother."

"Yeah. And he met *you* when you went to return *my* poetry book." He lowered his voice. "How much did he know about us, Laura?"

She felt a moment's pain that had nothing to do with her hand. "Not much. He knew we knew each other. That's all."

"Did he know we were together?"

"I don't know."

"He must have sensed something."

She shrugged.

"He must have known you weren't a virgin."

"He never said anything."

"Do you think he suspected it was me?"

"He never said anything," she repeated. She didn't want to talk about that. She didn't see the relevance. What had happened between Christian and her had been over for years. "He couldn't have been holding a grudge all that time. He loved me."

"But he left."

She let out a breath. "Yes." She shot a glance at the ceiling. "I want to talk with Scott." Without another look at Christian, she left the kitchen.

Scott was in his bedroom, scrubbed clean and looking forlorn as he sat on the edge of the bed with his elbows on his knees. Slipping down beside him, Laura touched his back. "I'm glad you're home."

"Me too."

"Was it awful?"

He nodded.

"Want to talk about it?"

He shook his head.

She extended her arm to rub his shoulder, and as she did, her mind drifted back to when he was little, when he used to come to her for comfort if something hurt. She had held him on her lap then, rocking him gently, cooing the way mothers do when the message is more love and closeness than anything else. In time, when he grew too big for her lap, she used to sit beside him and press him close. Now he was too big even for that. He was man-sized, just like the charges Megan Tucker had brought.

"Why do you think she did it?" Laura asked softly.

He shrugged. His eyes were glued to the shag carpet that had hidden a multitude of sins over the years. The sins were bigger now, Laura mused. There was no hiding them.

"She didn't want to break up," he said. "She wanted to visit me at school. I told her I didn't want that. She got angry."

"This was at the pizza house?" Laura had learned some of the details from Daphne. They were in the report the police had prepared.

Scott nodded. "I didn't want to argue with her, especially not there, with all her friends watching. And I didn't want to just end it like that, so I grabbed her hand and pulled her to the car." He looked back at Laura. "I wasn't rough. I didn't do anything more than I'd have done if I was annoyed with Debra."

"That isn't saying a whole lot, Scott. You and Debra can really go at it."

"I didn't hurt Megan. I got her to the car and drove her back to her house, and the bitch of it is that we didn't even make love. Not that night. I went inside for a while, and we rehashed the whole thing about my going back to school. I don't think she would have minded if it had been her idea to break up. She likes to call the shots. But it was me who did it, and that got her pissed."

"Where were her parents?"

"They're divorced. She lives with her mother."

"So where was she?"

"Out with her boyfriend."

Laura moaned. "Setting a good example."

"The thing is, Mrs. Tucker's a nice lady. The few times I met her, she was really nice. Maybe it was the boyfriend's idea to go for the money—" they had learned that Megan was suing for damages, "—and in order to do that they had to charge me with rape."

"Maybe." Laura wasn't even thinking about the civil suit. The criminal one was the more frightening of the two by far. "Did you know she was pregnant and miscarried?"

He paled, but an instant later there was anger in his eyes. "No, but if so, it wasn't mine. I never made love with her, ever, without using something."

Laura had told the police as much the day before, though she'd been walking on thin ice with the declaration. Just because she'd found a half-filled box of condoms in his drawer didn't mean he hadn't slipped up once or twice.

"Are you sure, Scott? Maybe in the heat of the moment—"

"Never. Hey, I may have been dumb to date her in the first place, but I wasn't so dumb as to be careless. And I'm not talkin' about a baby. I'm talking about *disease*. Megan's been around more than most girls. The guys joke about it. Nobody's lookin' to pick up anything from her." With a snort, he stared off at the wall. "So instead of VD, I pick up a rape charge. That's gonna do great things for my future."

"We'll get it dropped."

"And if we don't?" When he looked back at her, the fear on his face was clear as day, making him look young and vulnerable. "What if Daphne can't get me off? I mean, if Megan has friends who say they saw us argue, and I have friends who say she sleeps around, it'll boil down to her word against mine."

"Daphne says there aren't any medical records to support her claim."

"But there's still her word, and she can lie like a pro. I know three guys who were dating her at the same time, and she conned each into thinking he was the only one. It was her idea of a joke. She wanted to see if she could pull it off."

"Do you know the guys?"

"You bet."

"Think they'd testify?"

The frightened look eased a little. "Probably."

"Well, that's something." Laura took comfort from it herself, but the comfort was short-lived.

"What if it doesn't work? What if nothing works?"

"Don't think about that."

"What if I'm convicted and have to spend time in prison? *Prison*, Mom. Prison's different from jail. Last night was scary enough. I don't think I could *survive* prison."

"You are not going to prison."

"If I'm convicted, I will. And even if Daphne manages to make a deal so I don't have to, if I'm convicted I can forget about being a lawyer."

"That won't happen."

"A convicted felon would have one hell of a time getting into law school, and if he did make it, he'd have one hell of a time getting admitted to the bar." He kicked out at the leg of the desk. "I can't believe this is happening to me. *Shit*." He kicked again, harder.

Laura flinched with each kick. She knew how upset he was, and his upset magnified her own. Only an act of will kept her voice low and steady. "Daphne's going to get the charges dismissed."

"And if she doesn't?"

"She will."

"Come on, Mom. Daphne isn't the only one involved here. There's a prosecutor and a judge, and if we go to trial there's a jury. And there's Megan."

"But you're not guilty."

"I know that, and you know that, but do you think other people will believe it? I saw that piece in the paper today. The cop brought it along with my breakfast. He thought I'd get a kick out of seeing my name in type. Hell, maybe some kids would, but not me. I feel branded"—he stamped his forehead with a fist—"like I've got an R for rapist stuck right here. I mean, forget a relationship with Kelly. She won't want to be seen with me. And if word gets back to Penn—"

"Stop it, Scott!" Laura cut in. She couldn't bear to hear the things he was saying. More than that, she couldn't bear to see the glitter of tears in his eyes. "If Kelly can't handle this, she isn't the girl for you. Same with your fraternity. You've been hit with false charges. If the people you call friends—people who supposedly know you and know you wouldn't commit rape—don't stand by you, then that says something about *them*."

"But where does it leave *me*?" he cried. "My whole life will be screwed up, and I haven't done anything wrong!"

Laura didn't know what to say, so she just worked at relaxing the tense muscles in his back. After a bit, when his eyes weren't looking as wild or as moist, she slipped her arm around his waist. "We'll make it, Scott. We will make it."

He sighed. "I don't know. Things keep getting worse."

"But this is the turning point."

"How do you know?"

"Because nothing worse can *happen*," she said on a note of mild hysteria. "Look at it that way. Can you come up with anything worse than what we've already suffered?"

"Yeah. My being convicted."

"No. That can't happen. Try again."

"Dad being found and tried and convicted."

Laura thought about that. "Okay. That would be pretty bad. But would it be worse than this not knowing that we're living with now?"

Scott didn't answer at first. After a minute, he dug his heel into the rug. "Do you miss him?"

"I haven't had time to miss him. I've been too busy trying to hold things together."

"If they found him and brought him back, then put him on trial, would you stand by him?"

Laura had asked herself the same thing more than once. Anger was never far from the surface when she thought of Jeff, but that anger couldn't erase certain facts. "He was my husband for twenty years, and he's your father. That's worth something."

"Do you love him?"

She chose her words with care. Scott was Jeff's son and would continue to be, regardless of what happened between his parents. "I did."

"Do you now?"

"I don't know the man he is now. Obviously," she admitted dryly, "I didn't know the man he was then."

"Would you take him back?"

"He's not coming back."

"But if he did? If he came back and was arraigned and let out on bail like me, would you take him back?"

You ask tough questions, Laura wanted to say. Instead, she sighed. "I think that would depend on what he had to say for himself. Assuming he's guilty of what they say, he was wrong. He's hurt us dreadfully. I don't know if I can just pick up where we left off. I don't know if that's possible. Too much has happened." She focused on Scott. "What would you want to do? You feel a whole lot of anger toward your father. Would you want him back?"

"I suppose if he explained why he did what he did, if he could make it make sense, if he *wanted* to live with us." He frowned. "Assuming I'm here. I might be in jail."

"Don't say that."

"Anyway, I'm not the one who'd have to live with him. You are."

Tucking her hands in her lap, Laura leaned against his arm. Somewhere in the course of the discussion, she had ceased to be the comforter, which was incredible, given the mess of Megan Tucker's claim. But Scott was growing up fast. Talking with him was like talking with a friend.

"Well," she said, "I don't have to make a decision now. The best I can do is to take each day as it comes."

"I'm glad Christian's here for you."

"For me?"

"Sure. If Dad isn't, it's nice that Christian is. Boy, he really came through last night. He kept talking to me, and what he said made sense. He calmed me down a lot."

He had calmed Laura down a lot too, if she wanted to count holding her while she cried her heart out. "Funny," she confessed, "when he showed up here, I thought that was the end. I mean, *really* the end. I thought he was one more awful thing in a line of perfectly awful things, and I just couldn't take another one. But he was okay."

"Will he be sticking around?"

All Laura knew was that he had put his duffel bag in the guest room and his shaving kit in Scott's bathroom and made himself right at home in the kitchen, but that was no more than he'd done any other time he had come for a visit. "You know Christian. He's a free spirit. He comes and goes as he pleases."

"Is he gay?"

Laura sputtered out a startled laugh. "God, no! What makes you ask that?"

"He never got married. It's strange. He was with that pretty lady—Gaby—for a while, but he never married her. I wondered if she was a front."

Laura gave a vigorous shake of her head. "Gaby was for real. And I'm sure there were—are—plenty of other women in his life. Christian is as virile as they come."

"So why didn't he ever get married?"

"I guess he didn't want to. He likes his freedom."

Scott mulled over that possibility. "I think he misses having a family."

"Christian?" Laura shook her head. "If he wanted one, he'd have had one."

"Maybe." Scott looked at the rug again, then straightened and dropped his head back. "Shit, what am I gonna do?"

Laura didn't have to be told that his mind was back on the rape charge. She was surprised he'd been able to talk around it for so long, though she was glad he had. They both needed the break.

"You'll get packed," she told him, "and tomorrow you'll go back to school just like you planned."

"How am I supposed to concentrate on classes?"

"You will, somehow. What's the alternative, Scott? Are you going to sit for three weeks worrying about the hearing?"

"Maybe I should get drunk and stay drunk for three weeks."

"Don't you dare," she shot back, teasing, then realized it wasn't a teasing matter. Scott was a good kid. She had never had to lecture him before. But he had never been charged with a felony before. "It's important that you behave. I mean, really behave. It's not like anyone's watching every move you make, but if something happens at Penn—like a wild party with lots of drinking or, God forbid, some girl screaming that she was abused, or even hazing that gets out of hand—word could get back here. The prosecution would love it. You know that, don't you?"

"I know it," Scott said.

"So think twice about everything you do. And remember—" her voice softened, "—if you want to talk, I'm just a phone call away."

"You sound like an ad."

"I'm serious. Call me whenever you want. If you get the urge to come home, get on a plane and come home."

"That's not the kind of expense we need right now." He rolled his eyes. "This whole thing will cost a fortune."

"It's money well spent."

"It's money we don't have."

"We will. Business will pick up. The charges against you will be dropped. Daphne's petition will dazzle the judge, so he'll release my money. Things will get better. You'll see."

Scott gave her a look that said he thought she was either incredibly wonderful or totally insane. "It blows my mind that you can still be positive, with all that's happened."

Laura decided it blew her own mind a little. Granted, the positive feeling was coming and going in waves, but that was an improvement over the evening before. Those hours, first when she'd waited with Debra for Scott to come home, then when she'd learned he was being held in jail, had been the lowest of her life. She felt as though she'd hit rock bottom and had nowhere to go but up.

"You really think things will get better?" Scott asked.

"Yes."

"How can you be sure?"

"I can't. I just feel it."

"You were sure they'd find Dad, then you were sure he couldn't have committed a crime, but it looks like you were wrong on both counts."

"This is different."

"Why?"

"Why?" Laura didn't know why. All she knew was that she didn't feel as low as she had. "Maybe because Christian's here now," she said, and stood up. "Come down to the restaurant with me?"

He sat back, with his weight on his hands. "I don't want to be seen. I think I'll stay here."

"You have to be seen sometime. What better time and place than Cherries?"

"I'll hurt business."

"You couldn't do that. Come on, Scott. I could use your help."

"I have to pack."

"You'll pack later. I'll help. So will Debra."

"I ought to call Kelly."

"Do that, then come with me. Please? It'd make me very happy."

"That's blackmail."

"What's one more crime? Really."

Scott scowled at her, then looked away. By the time he looked back the corners of his mouth were turning up, and though the upturn was reluctant, Laura knew she'd won.

twenty-one

CHRISTIAN SINGLED OUT THE KEY FROM
the others on his ring. He wasn't sure why he'd kept it there all
these years; it only added to the bulk of the ring and wasn't
worth the weight when he considered how seldom he used it.
But over the years when he had changed key rings, this one had
gone right along with the rest.

It was the first key he had ever owned. William Frye had
given it to him on the morning Lydia went to the hospital to give
birth to Jeff. Christian had been five at the time, and for the
first few days, wearing that key on a string around his neck, he
had felt very grown up. Then the novelty of coming home to an
empty house and being alone for hours wore off. After a while
it was scary. He remembered sitting on a wooden bench in the
tiny breakfast nook, wondering what was happening to his
mother, wondering what was happening to the baby coming out
of her stomach, wondering what was happening to his father that
he had to be gone from the house for so long.

After a week, his mother was home and the wondering ended,
but by then life had changed. He was the big brother, which
meant he went off to school with his key and had to be content
to come home and watch his parents dote on the baby. He tried
to understand when they explained that his little sister had died

in her crib when she was just Jeff's age, so they had to watch Jeff all the time. But he didn't like it.

In his child's mind, the key was the culprit. He tried losing it, but his teacher found it in the wastebasket before the janitor could take it away. He tried flattening it under the tire of his father's Ford, but it wouldn't flatten. He tried flushing it down the toilet, but it stayed in the bowl like a dead weight until his mother fished it out.

The key had been all over the world with him, a good luck charm perhaps, since he had emerged from more than his share of adventures unscathed, but for years it was also the embodiment of his anger. It opened the door to the house from which he had been locked out for so long.

In time, the anger had faded. He built his own life, found his own pleasures. Still, there was something about that key.

He turned it in his hand once, then turned it back and slipped it into the lock. With an easy twist, the door opened. He pushed it wider, stepped inside, closed it behind him, and all the while he fought the scent of memory. Small things had changed, Laura's doing, he knew—the attractive wooden coat tree just inside the door, a throw rug on the floor, a pale floral print on the walls—but the shape of it all was the same as it had been in his mind for forty-seven years.

"Hello?" he called. His mother knew he was in town—Laura's doing also—though he hadn't spoken with her yet. He might have postponed this visit longer, if it hadn't been for two things. The first was that Laura wanted to be alone with Scott before he went back to school, which left Christian with time on his hands. The second was that someone had to tell Lydia about the arraignment, and though a tiny voice inside Christian said it wouldn't kill Lydia to brood over the morning paper for a while, a louder voice said that would be cruel.

When there was no response to his call, he called again, then stood listening in the tiny front hall, feeling very much a stranger. He didn't know his mother well and wasn't sure what to do next, which was the strangest thing of all. He wasn't an indecisive person. Nor was he bashful. Here, in his mother's house, he felt both.

Not hearing any sound at all, he started down the hall toward Lydia's room. "Mom?" he called tentatively. The name came uneasily, rusty from disuse, but he didn't want to frighten her, or embarrass her if she was getting dressed. Still getting no answer, he cautiously peered into her room. She was propped against two pillows in bed. Her eyes were closed, her head sagged on her shoulder, and for a minute he had the awful thought that she was dead. Then she jerked, and her hand came up to her ear before dropping gently back to the bed.

Christian was surprised by the tightening in his chest. He had never seen his mother this way. She was seventy-three. He had helped celebrate her birthday in June. But she hadn't looked old then, with her snow-white hair and pale, almost translucent skin. She had looked pretty, in a delicate way, which was how he always remembered her. Now she looked old, too old for seventy-three.

As though sensing his presence, she straightened her head and slowly opened her eyes. They focused on him for a minute before she seemed to realize who he was.

"Christian," she said softly. He imagined there was a thread of pleasure in the sound.

"Hi." He gave her a self-conscious smile. "I—uh, let myself in. If you want to sleep more, I can come back another time."

"No. Don't go. I can sleep later." She looked fully awake, though she had continued to speak slowly and softly.

He shifted against the doorjamb. "So. How've you been?"

She gave a sad smile. "Stiff and weak. Getting old isn't all it's cracked up to be. There are things I want to do, but I just don't have the strength. It's frustrating."

He nodded. She was watching him closely, taking in each of his features, one by one, in a ritual he knew well. Whenever he came home, she did the same thing, just looked at him for a long time with an unfathomable expression on her face. He always had the feeling that she was cataloging who he was for comparison with who she would like him to be.

"You're looking good, Christian. They tell me you were in Tahiti."

"I have friends there. They make me feel right at home." It sounded like a dig, though he hadn't meant it as one. He was glad when Lydia didn't seem to take offense.

"You've been missing out on all the excitement."

"So I hear. I got back right in time for this biggie. Laura wanted me to tell you that Scott's okay. He was arraigned this morning and released on his own recognizance. There'll be a probable-cause hearing in a few weeks. With a little luck, Daphne will get the charges dismissed then."

Lydia lay quietly for a minute. Though she continued to look at Christian, her concentration wasn't as intense. She seemed to drift. He could imagine where.

Finally, in a voice that was slow and thin, she said, "My heart is breaking over everything that's happened. On the one hand, I don't understand any of it. On the other, it's all crystal clear. I lie here asking myself what I did wrong."

"You didn't—"

"I did. I did lots of things wrong. You know that more than anyone else, Christian."

He hadn't expected a confession, and though years ago he might have welcomed one, it made him uncomfortable now. Lydia was a small, sad figure, sufficiently depleted without chipping away at the past. "We all make mistakes."

"True, but some are more far-ranging than others. A mother's mistakes, in particular, can be that way."

"More so than a father's?" he asked in a spurt of bitterness. "Seems to me my father made some pretty far-reaching mistakes. So did Jeff, as a father. Look at the havoc he's caused for his kids. Scott would never be facing this charge if Jeff's actions hadn't set the scene."

Lydia considered that. "Maybe not. But Jeffrey wouldn't have done what he did if it weren't for me. I took something valuable from him when I pampered him all those years." Her eyes clouded. "I thought I was doing the right thing. We were so afraid we'd lose him as a baby and then so grateful when we didn't, and he was such a good boy. Things didn't come easily for him.

"It starts when you're young, don't you see?" she went on. "People are who they are because of how they were raised. Lessons learned then are hard to shake. Look at you. I couldn't give you what you needed. I made you feel like a left shoe. So here you are in middle age without a wife and children of your own."

"That wasn't your doing. I chose not to have a wife."

"Man wasn't put on earth to be a solitary figure. He was put here to enrich his life by sharing it with a wife and having children."

"How do you know I haven't had children?" he asked. "How do you know there aren't a bunch of little Christian Fryes running around?" The bitterness was back. "Lots of men make women pregnant, then leave them." Pivoting from the door, he went into the kitchen. He was standing at the sink several minutes later, looking angrily out the window, when he heard the sound of Lydia's cane. The shuffle of her feet seemed almost an afterthought. "You didn't have to get up," he said without turning. "I'm not staying long."

Her voice came with surprising strength. "You can stay as long as you want. It's good to see you, Christian."

He wasn't sure whether to believe her or not. With one son gone, it would be natural for a mother to turn to the only other one she had, even if that son had been an unwelcome adjunct to the family for a good many years.

Very softly, she said, "I know what you're thinking. You're thinking the only reason I'm happy to see you is that Jeff's gone, but that isn't true. I love you, Christian. I've always loved you."

"Could've fooled me."

She was quiet for so long that he dared a look at her. The look was surprisingly downward. Lydia had always been a petite woman, but she seemed to have shrunk inches since he'd seen her last. That shook him a little.

The look on her face shook him too. He saw deep sorrow there, and unless it was wishful thinking on his part, the sorrow was genuine. "We all have to make decisions in life. Some are more crucial than others. The crucial ones are the ones we have to live with, and it isn't always easy, especially when there are other people involved. William Frye was good to me. He provided me with a stable home and security, and I needed those things. And he did love me. Whatever quarrel you had with him, you have to admit that. He did love me."

Begrudgingly, Christian agreed. The kind of love he had seen between Bill and Lydia wasn't the kind of love he had dreamed about for himself. It was too sedate, too studied, too deliberate and controlled. Apparently that was what his mother had wanted.

"I apologize to you," Lydia went on.

Christian was instantly unsettled. "Don't."

"I have to. It's been something I've been thinking about for a long time, only I never had the chance. Every time you were home there were either lots of people around or you were unapproachable."

"Diplomatically put."

She acknowledged that with a bob of her head. "You didn't have to act out in that way, you know. I was aware you were home. Everyone was. You're not the kind of man who could ever fade into the woodwork."

"I didn't do it for attention."

"Then why?"

He ran a hand along the lip of the porcelain sink. There was a crack in the lower left corner that had been there forever. He rubbed it with his thumb like he used to do when he was a child.

"I was angry. Everything was so perfect around here. I wanted to spoil things a little."

"You certainly succeeded."

"Yeah," he said without pride.

"Are you planning to do it this time?"

Annoyed at the suggestion, he shot her a sharp glance, but she seemed truly worried, which made him think twice about saying something smart. She had reason to worry. He had been difficult for years.

"No, I'm not planning to do it this time," he said quietly. "Things are bad enough. No one needs me to make them worse."

"Then what are you planning to do?"

He shrugged. "Laura's in pretty bad shape. I thought I'd loan her some money."

"She wouldn't take any from me or from her mother."

"That's because neither of you have much to spare. I do."

"Will she take it?"

"She'd better."

"That's generous of you."

"Maybe it's selfish," he said. Leaving the sink, he went to the breakfast nook. Though sanded and freshly painted, the table was as small as he remembered, the bench seats as narrow. He had outgrown them when he was fourteen, which, in hindsight, was perfectly understandable given the size he'd grown to be. At the time it seemed one more way in which he didn't fit in. "Maybe I'm trying to buy forgiveness for years of giving her a hard time."

He heard Lydia moving behind him. The refrigerator door opened, then shut. He heard the rattle of plates, the clink of knives. When he looked back, he saw her arranging muffins.

"Don't put anything out on my behalf," he said.

"They're wonderful muffins. Laura made them."

He didn't have to be told that. Laura took good enough care of his mother to put Jeff and him to shame. "Yeah, and she made me a big breakfast. When she's nervous, she cooks."

Lydia smiled fondly at that, looking for a minute like the woman he remembered. The smile faded as she carried the plate of muffins to the table. "Will you have tea with it?"

"Only if you want some." When she turned back toward the stove, he said, "Why don't you sit and let me do it."

"No. *You* sit." She paused with her hand on the kettle. "I've been doing a lot of reminiscing since Jeffrey's been gone. Do you remember that his favorite meal growing up was meat pie with peas mixed in with the hamburger and mashed potatoes piled on top?"

"I remember." It would have been impossible for him not to. They had eaten it once every week or two, and a big deal was made about it each time.

Lydia turned to him with a stricken look on her face. "I don't know what yours was. I've been trying to remember, but I can't. Did you have one?"

He certainly did. "Lamb chops. With mint jelly. And those little rolls you used to make."

"Why didn't I know that?"

"Because you never asked and I never said. No one else was wild about lamb chops. You didn't make them often."

Silently, she turned back to the stove, and while she waited for the water to boil he looked around the kitchen. It was old, like the rest of the house, but clean and well kept, which was no more than he'd have expected of Lydia. He knew she had help. Still, he suspected she did more herself than either Laura or the cleaning girl imagined.

When the tea was done, he carried it to the table, then squeezed onto one of the benches. He had to sit sideways, half sprawling along the bench. It was a minute before Lydia was seated across from him and several minutes after that before either of them spoke, and then it was Lydia, sounding oddly shy.

"This is the first time we've been alone in a long, long time. I've missed you, Christian."

He couldn't believe that. "You didn't miss me. You had Jeff."

"Jeff wasn't you."

"But he was special to you. He was the one who didn't die."

"You didn't die."

"It wasn't the same." He studied his tea. Lydia was right. It had been a long time since they'd been alone. They had never had the kind of relationship Laura had with Scott. If they had, he might have asked certain things sooner—one of which refused to be repressed any longer. "If you hadn't been pregnant with me, would you have married Bill?"

Lydia let out a breath. It was another little while before she answered. "I'm not sure. I might have waited longer. I might have waited to see who else would come along."

He tried to imagine growing up under the wing of another man, but only one came to mind. Over the years, Christian had fashioned him into a more stately replica of himself. "Did you love him?"

Lydia began a subtle rocking. "Your father? Yes, I loved him."

"But you wouldn't marry him."

"No. I couldn't have been happy with him. He was—" she frowned, struggling to find the right words, which then came in a rush—"too flashy, too opinionated, too controversial, too public. He wanted to rock the boat. He frightened me."

"But you loved him." It was a puzzle Christian had been trying to figure out for years. "If you loved him, how could you turn away from him?"

"It was a decision of the mind, not the heart. Haven't you ever made decisions like that?"

He could remember one, though he hadn't identified it as such at the time. "Did you ever regret it?"

"Often," she said. She tipped her chin up just enough to give him another glimpse of the purposeful woman she had been in her prime. "I knew passion with him. Sons don't like to think of their mothers as being sexual creatures, but with him I was. With him, I forgot about everything else. With him, I was someone totally different from myself. Yes, there have been many times over the years when I regretted my decision, many times when I'd have given most anything for a few more minutes of what I had with him. But those times always passed, and not once did I think my decision was a mistake. I may have made mistakes in the way I treated you and Jeff, but in the choice I made regarding him, I know I was right."

Restless, Christian extricated himself from the bench and began to prowl the kitchen. "Is he still alive?"

"Yes."

"Do you ever see him?"

"No."

"Does he still live around here?"

"I never said he lived around here. You won't catch me that way."

He faced her with his hands low on his hips. "I can't catch you any way, but that's not fair. I'm forty-seven years old, for Christ's sake. I have a right to know who my father is."

Lydia gave him a pained look. "I made a vow that's even older than that. I promised him, Christian. When I found out I was pregnant, he wanted to marry me, but I knew the marriage wouldn't last—he was already involved with someone else—and I knew it would kill me when it didn't. So I refused him. He was furious. He gave me a choice. Either he could expose me for being a tramp—and in those days the ramifications of that were harsh—or I could go my way and find someone else, but if I did that, I was never to tell you who he was. He kept his part of the bargain. He never talked about me. So I have to keep mine and never talk about him."

Christian had heard the story before. If anything, it grew harder to take the older he was. "Did he plan to tell me himself?"

"Has he yet?"

"Will he?"

"Only he knows that."

Christian felt a little like a sitting duck, knowing that someone

304

out in the world had information about him that he didn't have. "Do you think he watches me?"

"I doubt that. You move around a lot."

"But I'm headquartered in Vermont. I'm never gone from there for more than a month, maybe two at the most, without checking in, and during the building season I'm around much more. Do you think I know him?" It wasn't a thought he lived with every day, just one that came at times when a man of the right age took an interest in him.

"I don't know that."

"The bastard," Christian muttered, feeling an old, familiar frustration. "Isn't he *curious* about me? Doesn't he want to see who I am or what I've done with my life? What kind of man can turn off feelings that way?"

"Some can," Lydia whispered. "I thought you had. You've been so difficult all these years."

"I told you. I was angry."

"Maybe he is too."

"Angry because you wouldn't marry him? After all these years?" He tried again. "Has he married?"

She nodded. "More than once. Never happily."

"Is he successful?"

She bobbed a thin shoulder. "Success is relative."

"Is he rich?"

"He lives well."

"Then you've kept tabs on him?"

"I loved him once. The sound of his voice made my heart pound, the sight of him made me quiver. Of course I've kept tabs on him. What woman wouldn't?"

She was trying to be light about it; still, Christian saw sadness in her eyes, and he felt the frisson of a different anger. "Is it painful?"

The sadness spread to her smile. "It's growing old that's painful. That's when reality hits. You find yourself with special memories that have nowhere to go and dreams that will never be fulfilled, and it doesn't matter how whimsical or impossible those dreams were. While they were yours, they were lovely." She sighed. "At my age, there isn't much point left in dreaming. That's the painful part."

"Do you want to see him?"

Still smiling that sad smile, she tipped her head. "I already do. In you. You're a lot like him, Christian. Same size, same coloring, same build. Same dominant personality. Are you happy in life?"

"You've never asked me that before."

"Well, I'm asking you now. Are you happy?"

"If I weren't, I'd do something different."

"But are you happy?"

Something about the way she said it again made him stop to consider the question. Something about the way she was looking at him, as though she really *cared* if he was happy, made him answer honestly.

"I have a rewarding life. I do things I like, when I like, with people I like. If you're asking whether there are things I want that I don't have, the answer is yes."

"What is it you want?"

He looked straight into the same blue eyes he'd been seeing in the mirror for forty-seven years. "The name of my father."

"I can't tell you that. What else?"

"My own private island in the South Seas."

"I can't give you that. What else?"

"Laura."

Lydia sucked in a breath. "Be careful, Christian. That's a dangerous one. Laura is Jeffrey's wife."

"Jeffrey is gone."

"She's been his for twenty years."

"And she was mine before that."

"I know."

He had thought to shock her with his announcement, but he was the one to be shocked. "You do?"

She nodded. "That time you came home from the Peace Corps, when you took over your friend's attic apartment—did you think I imagined you were alone? You're your father's son, Christian. I knew you were with a woman. It wasn't until Laura came to return your book that I knew who she was."

"But you didn't tell Jeff?"

"Why should I? You were long gone, and anyway I figured you weren't ready to settle down. You were your father's son in that respect too. But you'd picked a fine woman. I liked Laura from the start. She had strength and spirit. I knew she'd take care of Jeffrey. Left to his own devices, he could have done worse."

"But she was with me before she was with him. Doesn't that bother you?"

"Should it? She was faithful to him. She was a good wife. What more could a mother ask for her son?" She glanced away and her eyes glazed. "Of course," she said in a distant voice, "maybe it wasn't the best thing for him after all. Maybe if he'd picked his own wife he would have been better off. Maybe he'd have been happier with someone less strong, someone who needed him more. Maybe I made a mistake in that too." Her eyes returned to Christian. "But be careful, Christian. She is still his wife, and he could well come back."

"And if he doesn't? If we never see hide nor hair of him again? You love Laura like a daughter. Would you be satisfied to see her with me," he goaded, "knowing that I'm my father's son?"

Lydia didn't bat an eyelash. "You're also your mother's son, and though children inherit some things, they learn about others by example. One of the reasons I married William Frye was because he was dedicated to me. I wanted to raise you in a stable home, just the kind your father couldn't give me. If nothing else, I like to think that from Bill and me you learned the sanctity of commitment." Her breath wavered like a feeble hand in the air. "If Jeffrey is truly gone, and if you are truly committed to

Laura, I think I could go in peace."

She lowered her head. Wrapping both thin hands around her teacup, she raised it to her lips and slowly sipped from it. Watching her, Christian felt more warmth for his mother than he had felt in years.

twenty-two

dAPHNE SPENT HOURS INTERROGATING Scott. She wanted to know every detail of his relationship with Megan Tucker: when they met, who their mutual friends were, when they started dating, what they did together, when they first made love, and how often after that. Scott squirmed at some of the questions, Laura squirmed at some of the answers, but both could appreciate their importance. Brutal honesty was the only thing that could help Daphne plan her case.

He left for school on Wednesday morning. Laura and Christian drove him to the airport, and though in other circumstances Laura might have wanted to be alone with him before he left, she was grateful for Christian's company. Sending Scott off was always difficult for her, now even more so. By the time they left the terminal to return to the car, she was teary-eyed. She was glad not to have to drive.

Christian handed her a tissue and let her collect herself. Finally, when the car was cruising north on Route 91, he said, "So. Are we going to work?"

"I am," Laura replied. Keeping busy was both therapeutic and practical. "But you don't have to hang around again today. Why don't you just drop me off? You must have other things to do."

"What other things?"

She shrugged. "People to visit."

"There aren't any people."

"Old flames."

"You're the only one."

"Oh, come on," she said. She turned to the window. "That was a long time ago. I was so young it frightens me sometimes."

"I thought you were twenty when I first met you."

She shot him a disbelieving look.

"I did," he insisted. "I thought you were a junior. I had no idea you were a freshman, let alone such a young one. You looked older. You acted older."

Laura didn't know whether that was a compliment or not. "My mother had me skip the third grade. She managed to convince the teachers that I was so brilliant my psyche would suffer if they didn't push me ahead."

"Did you mind?"

"Then? No. I minded in seventh and eighth grades when all the other girls were getting bras and I wasn't."

"You caught up," Christian said.

His words reminded her of the intimacy they had once shared. Christian had been her first lover. He had known her body in ways not even Jeff had. The memories were exciting, poignant, sweet. But she couldn't pursue them.

Looking at him, she said in a quiet voice, "I mean it, Christian. You don't have to hang around. You posted bail for Scott, then you insisted on putting money in my account. On top of that, you spent yesterday packing food and hauling crates. You even tended bar." She was still amazed at that. "Where'd you learn to mix drinks so well?"

"Charleston, South Carolina," he drawled, "during my thumb-around-the-country phase." Laura didn't know about that phase, which meant it had come after the Peace Corps. She knew about most of the adventures that had come before. Intrigued by them, she had questioned him mercilessly during the

month they were together. There had been times when she suspected he made love to her simply to get her to stop talking. "I
was passing through and ran out of money," he went on. "When
you need money, you can learn things real fast."

"We didn't get any complaints from the customers."

"Of course not."

"But if you wanted to work, you'd be back in Vermont."

He shook his head. "Bad season. Can't do a thing till the
ground thaws."

"So what would you normally be doing?"

"I don't know. Working in my darkroom. Drawing up house
plans. Drinking beer with the guys. But none of those things is
urgent. I can do them just as well in a couple of weeks."

"Is that how long you're staying?"

He took his eyes from the highway for a second. "That
depends."

She wasn't sure what to make of his look. At this stage in
her life, Christian was an enigma. "On what?"

"On how much there is to do here. Yesterday there was a
lot."

"That's because my hand was sore, so I couldn't do anything
for myself."

"You're understaffed."

"Just barely, but I can't hire anyone else until business picks
up. My hand feels better today, and it'll feel better tomorrow,
so I'll be able to do more."

She returned her attention to the window. They passed a
semitrailer with license plates from five different states, a four-
by-four from Alabama, a sedan from Delaware, a VW from
Utah. Glimpsing their drivers, Laura wondered where they were
headed and why. She let her eyes wander out over the landscape
beyond the highway, and her mind wandered even farther, trans-
porting her somewhere warm and carefree. The place didn't have
a name. It didn't need one. It could have been any one of dozens
of spots. In the impulse of the moment, she didn't care which.

"Ah, for a week away from it all," she whispered.

Christian's easy "You could do it" brought her back to reality.

"Uh-uh. Even aside from work, there's Debra. I couldn't leave her alone. And what would Scott think if I just up and took off?" She sighed. "But, boy, it's tempting. Maybe this is what Jeff was feeling. I haven't committed a crime and I'm not living with the threat of discovery, but there's a tiny part of me that would love to turn this car around and keep driving and driving. I mean, I wouldn't do it. I couldn't. But one part of me would love to."

"You'll get back on your feet."

"I know." She lapsed into silence, thinking about the day when things might return to normal, which wasn't to say they'd ever be the way they were before. That could never happen. Her life was irrevocably changed. "There's still Jeff. Where he's concerned, I'm in limbo. What if he never shows up? What if the FBI doesn't find him?"

Christian straightened his fingers before relaxing them around the steering wheel again. "You won't be in limbo long, Laura. Limbo isn't your style. You're a doer. Whether they find Jeff or not, you'll go on with your life."

He sounded so confident she believed him, but then, that was a weakness of hers. She always believed Christian. When he had first approached her so many years ago, after watching her cross the campus with her friends, and told her she had a captivating laugh, she believed him. When, later, over French bread and cheese and wine in his tiny attic room, he told her she had a captivating mind, she believed him. And when, later still, they lay on his rumpled sheets after making the newest, gentlest, sweetest kind of love, he told her she had a captivating body, she believed him. She had even believed him when, days later, in the sleepy afterglow of yet another coupling, he told her he would love her forever.

Clearly he hadn't, and that alone should have been reason enough to make her distrustful. But it didn't. Nor did it tarnish her view of him. For the first time in nearly twenty-one years, allowing herself to remember the fit of their bodies in bed, she felt a warm current spread through her. Even when she pulled herself back to the present, the warmth remained as long as she continued to look at him. She couldn't deny it. She found him as appealing as ever.

That thought unsettled her, but it wasn't so disturbing that she asked him to leave. He went along with her to Cherries that day, and the next and the next, and he made himself useful. When she dared suggest, only half in jest, that she put him on the payroll, he gave her such a dirty look she didn't mention it again.

Given the heartache he'd caused during her marriage to Jeff, he was a surprising comfort to her now. She kept waiting for him to do something to mock her—to get drunk while tending bar, or deliberately botch up drinks, or seduce DeeAnn—but he didn't.

And Laura watched, particularly on the matter of DeeAnn. With his broad shoulders and tapering body, the rangy way he had of walking, and an irresistible pair of blue eyes, Christian was far more appealing than Jeff, Laura thought. She wanted to see whether DeeAnn would make a play for him or vice versa.

Neither happened. They chatted every so often, but Laura couldn't detect serious interest in either of them. Besides, by his own choice, Christian was with Laura nearly all the time. They went to Lydia's together. They went to the supermarket together. They went to Cherries together, and when they were done there they came home. With Debra either at a friend's house or in her room on the phone, they took to retreating to the den to unwind with tea or hot chocolate or wine, whatever took their fancy on a given night. And they talked.

"How do you feel?" Christian asked one night, nearly a week after Scott had left.

"Right now, tired," she answered. Slipping off her shoes, she curled her legs under her and settled more comfortably at one end of the sofa. Christian was at the other end, with his feet up, not far from hers. "It was a long day."

"I mean, in general. You're looking better. Not as pinched."

She couldn't take offense. Christian had seen her at her absolute worst. "I'm only waking up one or two times a night. For a while there, it was three or four."

"What wakes you?"

"Thoughts. Fears. Nightmares."

"You're worried about the hearing."

It was two weeks off, and, yes, she was worried. Daphne had connected with some of Megan's friends but was hitting a wall of silence where helpful information was concerned. Still, she claimed to be undaunted. Laura couldn't make that claim. But there was more. "Other things, too. I start thinking about me, and about everything that's happened since December, and it scares me."

"In what sense?"

She dropped her eyes to the mug in her hand. They were drinking hot chocolate that night. Christian had made it, and though he had blobbed far more whipped cream on top than she would have, she didn't complain. It was a treat to have someone fix it for her, especially in her own home, especially when she was tired.

Absently brushing the foam at the top, she said, "I really messed up. I didn't see things I should have. I didn't see what Jeff was doing or what he was feeling. I didn't see that anything was wrong with my marriage, and that makes me wonder what other things I didn't see over the years. So I wake up and I think back, and I imagine everything else I missed."

"Like what?"

She didn't look at him. "Like vacations I planned that Jeff really didn't want to take, or presents I bought him that he didn't really want." She pointed around the mug. "See those books up there? The first editions? I thought they were the most incredible gifts. I used to drive all over the state looking for them and spend hours and hours picking each one out. One or two were falling apart, so I had them rebound; then I wrapped each one up in paper that matched either the subject or the binding. And you know what? After a while, Jeff knew the shape. I mean, you can't disguise the shape of a book very well. We'd joke about it—what could *this* be?—and he'd so-o-o carefully take off the wrapping and fold it up and put it aside, then open the book and nod and smile and say all the right things, then very carefully put it on the shelf next to the others. And that was that. I doubt if he ever gave any of them a second look. But I did. If I had a free minute, I'd come in here and read a few pages, or look at the faded script on the flyleaf, or just touch the binding. There's such a luxurious feel to old leather." She raised the cup to her lips, then lowered it without a sip and raised her eyes to Christian's. "So who wanted a collection of ancient books in the first place? Did he or did I?"

"Does it matter?" Christian asked. "You put time and thought into each purchase. That should have been present enough for Jeff."

Laura wasn't letting herself off the hook so easily. "But was I putting in the time for him or for me? I loved shopping for those things. Suppose he said he wanted to collect tin soldiers. Would I have loved shopping for those?"

"Probably, knowing you. Even if you didn't like tin soldiers, you would have made a game of it. Besides, if Jeff didn't like the books, he should have said something."

"And hurt my feelings? Do you honestly think he could have done that? This is a man who stole money from the government to underwrite the restaurant his wife wanted so badly."

Christian gave her a gentle nudge with his foot to soften his words. "But was that to please him or you? Take your argument and turn it around. Did he underwrite the restaurant to please you or to make himself feel good? Cherries was an asset for him. It was good for his business. It painted him as a successful businessman."

Laura knew all that was true, but she wasn't caught up in Jeff's faults. She was caught up in her own. Tucking her foot against Christian's for the warmth of it, she pointed to the shelf with the photograph. "He didn't want that picture taken. We were playing tennis when the photographer came around, and he didn't want to stop. He was worse than the kids. But he did stop. And he went on the jeep tour of the desert. And he went into every ticky-tacky cowboy store I dragged him to. And he ate everything Southwestern and Tex-Mex and *straight* Mex, but it's only now, looking back, that I realize he wasn't the one who was raving about the trip when we got home. He wasn't the one who wanted to go back. It was me and the kids." She sent Christian a beseechful look. "Why didn't I see that? Everyone's right. He hates hot weather. But I ignored that. All those years, I planned what I thought would be terrific trips and just assumed Jeff would agree, and all those years he just went along. It's no wonder he finally cracked."

Christian reached for her foot and drew it up under his thigh. "So you're gonna take full blame for what he did?"

"No. But some. I have to take some." She looked down again, frowning, and before she knew it, the words spilled out. "I messed up. I failed him. Husbands don't wander if they're satisfied at home."

"Sure they do. They can have perfectly wonderful wives but still have bizarre needs driving them on. Jeff's might have been as simple as needing to know he's still attractive to women. He saw himself moving into his forties and had a little mid-life crisis."

"Did you?" Laura asked, catching his gaze.

"I didn't need to. I'm a bachelor. It wasn't like I'd been with one woman for twenty years. Even with Gaby it was on and off, and during the off times there were others. They did for me what DeeAnn might have done for Jeff." For a minute, he looked puzzled. "She's a nice woman. Seems honest. I'd never have pegged her for an affair with a married man."

"Me neither," Laura murmured, "but that's my problem too."

He stroked her leg. "You're too hard on yourself."

"Maybe it's about time," she said with a sigh. Closing her eyes, she laid her head back on the sofa, but her thoughts drifed to gentler places. Sitting with Christian, hearing his voice, feeling his hand on her leg was so relaxing that she couldn't sustain anger against herself, Jeff, or anyone else for long. She couldn't even move when Debra burst in to ask if she could use the Wagoneer on the weekend. "You can use my car if I can use Christian's," she said and looked at him.

"Your mom can use mine," Christian told Debra, who vanished as quickly as she'd come, leaving Laura with her eyes closed again, thinking it was nice having Christian around.

She thought the same thing the next night, and the next. She kept bracing herself for the day when he would announce he was restless and had to move on, but that day didn't come. On the weekend, in and around work, he dragged her to a theater production in Springfield that she enjoyed, and on Monday, when the restaurant was closed, he took her to Boston.

"I shouldn't be doing this," she grumbled in the car on the way.

"Why not? You work six days out of seven. You need a break."

"I should be cleaning the house or doing the books at the restaurant or cooking. We need new recipes."

"Jonah has all the new recipes you need, the restaurant books will wait, and the house is spotless. You clean every morning, then you go to work, and you refuse to accept any of the invitations to dinners or parties that you get, so you have to do *something* for fun."

Laura thought of Scott's hearing, which was little more than a week off. "I'll have fun when this is over. I'll relax then."

Christian didn't argue, but he proceeded to take her to a show at the museum, lunch at Biba's, then shopping on Newbury Street. To her horror she spent money, but by that time she was feeling slightly reckless and very much removed from reality anyway, and when Christian insisted on traipsing across town to the North End for cannoli he claimed he'd been hankering for for twenty-one years, she went happily along.

They headed home with the intention of taking Debra out for dinner, only to find her in a panic about a chemistry test she was having the next day. She was mollified by the sweater Laura had bought her, but seconds after admiring it she was out the door, gone to Jenna's to study.

That left Laura and Christian alone. They considered taking Lydia out, until they realized she would have already eaten. They considered taking Daphne out, but they didn't want to talk law, and seeing Daphne would necessitate that. They didn't begin to consider taking Maddie out, since neither one of them wanted the aggravation, so they debated going out at all, since they'd been out all day.

In the end, they brought in Chinese and ate it with chopsticks straight from the carton. Laura couldn't remember the last time she'd done that—yes, she could. It was with Christian years ago. She and Jeff had brought in Chinese many times, but by then it had become a matter of pride that she make the table look pretty regardless of what they were eating. So she emptied each carton into a serving dish and set the table with forks and knives, since Jeff wasn't wild about chopsticks. She had probably even put a rose in a vase in the center. That was the kind of thing she used to do, not because it was romantic but because it was part of her image of the good wife.

With Christian, she would have done it because it was romantic, which was precisely why she didn't do it now. She was fully aware of him as a man without any help from a rose.

She did have roses in the house, though, fresh ones brought by David Farro that morning. It was the first time she'd seen or heard from him in weeks. The roses were white and could have been either a peace offering or a bribe. Either way, she wasn't interested. Though she invited him into the house, she made sure Christian was with them, standing beside her every minute. If David jumped to conclusions, so be it. She wanted him to know she had a protector, and if he chose to assume that the protection extended to long, lonely nights, fine. After the humiliation she had suffered, having a ruggedly handsome man by her side wouldn't hurt.

Loath to think of David, she left the white roses in the living room while she and Christian ate perched on stools at the granite island in the kitchen. Their talk was light and relaxed, moving from chopstick technique to travel in China to travel anywhere to Christian's recent trip. Having never seen a rainforest, Laura wanted to hear all about the Daintree. Having never been to Tahiti, she wanted to hear all about that too. Not only was Christian an adventurer, he was an eloquent speaker. Both had been true years before. Neither had changed.

When she had had enough Chow Gai Kew, Shrimp Mona Mona, and fried rice to keep her for weeks, Christian decided he wanted a piece of the coconut torte she'd made the day before. While he went for it, she cleared the cartons away, emptying what little remained of the food into the disposal. When she tried to turn it on, the water promptly backed up in the sink. She flipped the switch several times, rolled up her sleeve, stuck her hand down the disposal, and swished the food around. Then she tried the switch again. There was a noise and a funneling of the water, but nothing went down.

"Something's caught," Christian decided.

"Looks it." She worked a tool around inside the disposal to no avail.

"What'd ya put down here?" he asked. He whipped his sweater over his head and rolled up his sleeves.

"Food."

He hunkered down to study the underparts of the sink. "Food you're not supposed to put down?"

"Food I *always* put down," she said, squatting right beside him. "This is my field. I know what a disposal takes and what it doesn't."

He reached underneath to check the pipes. "Think Debra put something down here?"

"I don't know when. She was at school all day, and if she had dinner before we got home we would have seen the remains. She's not real good about cleaning up after herself."

Christian stood, turned the switch to watch the funneling action again, then headed for the garage. He returned with the large red toolbox Laura had bought Jeff—not for this house but for the Victorian before it, which had been old and in need of repairs. He may have opened the box five times over the years. It looked nearly as new now as when she'd bought it.

Wrench in hand, Christian returned to the floor, angled himself under the sink—no mean feat, given his size—and set about removing the elbow. "Got a pot to catch the water in?"

She pulled one from a cabinet and passed it in, then sat on her heels and watched him work. He was perfectly at ease with the wrench in his hand and knew just what he was doing. "God, it's amazing," she breathed.

"What?" he asked.

"How different you two are. I doubt if Jeff ever held that wrench in his hand. He probably wouldn't know what it's called, let alone how to use it."

"He never had to learn, that's all."

"No, it's more than that. You could show him what to do with it, and he'd still do it wrong. Some people, all they need is to be shown and an innate ability takes over. I mean, I can look at what you're doing and understand that the elbow is clogged and has to be removed and cleaned. Jeff wouldn't necessarily make the connection, but you do. And that's only the first of your differences. The list is endless: personality, manner, tastes. How can two brothers be so unlike?"

In a voice that reflected the strain of something he was trying to turn, Christian said, "Haven't figured that one out yet?"

Laura tried to see his face but couldn't. Figured what out? A bizarre thought came to mind, but she ruled it out. "Explain, Christian."

He pushed harder at whatever he was doing. The muscles of his forearm strained with the effort. His voice held that same distant, distracted quality when he said, "Bill Frye wasn't my father. Lydia had a lover before she married him."

"That's impossible," Laura said with calm confidence.

He chuckled. "Oh, it's possible. The little lady had a very passionate love affair that produced yours truly."

"How do you know that?"

"She told me."

Laura's calm confidence slipped a bit. "Told you? I can't even picture her saying it, let alone doing it."

"I'm the living proof," was all Christian said before his hand moved suddenly. "Here we go." There was the clatter of the wrench being set aside, then a rush of water into the pot. Seconds later, he emerged holding a curved piece of pipe. "Let's take a look." Standing at the sink, which had quickly drained, he worked his finger into the curve and began tugging out fibrous strands. "What's this?"

"Bear grass," Laura said. She should have known. Nothing David ever did came without strings. "It's the tall green stuff that was packed with David's roses. I cut it to go in the vase and threw the ends down the drain."

Christian looked vaguely amused. "This is your field, huh?"

"Food is. Flowers aren't." She put her hand on his arm. "Christian, are you serious about Bill Frye?"

He went back to pulling shreds of bear grass from the pipe. "Dead serious."

"If he wasn't your father, who was?"

"I don't know. She won't tell me."

"If she won't tell you that, why did she tell you anything?"

"Because I went through a hard time when Bill died. I was nineteen and into the self-analysis college kids used to do. I stood there at his funeral, and the only thing I felt was the same anger I'd been feeling for years. There was no grief. None at all. I thought there was something wrong with me. I guess she was afraid I'd be permanently damaged if she didn't clue me in."

"Did it help?"

"Oh, yeah. It explained lots of things." He shook the last of the bear grass from the pipe. "Might have been nice if she'd told me a little sooner, while all the other damage was being done."

"What other damage?"

"The pain."

He disappeared under the sink again, giving Laura time to digest what he'd said. It made sense, so much sense—Christian being so different, Christian being the renegade, Christian being the family outcast. He and Jeff shared a mother, which explained a certain familial resemblance, but Christian's size clearly came from his father. Whether his daring came from his father too or was simply a reaction to the passivity in his home was something else.

Sliding down against the cabinet to the floor, Laura said, "Tell me about the pain."

Christian didn't, at first. He finished what he was doing under the sink, took out the wrench and the pot, and closed the cabinet door before sitting back against it. Laura handed him a cloth to wipe his hands, then the piece of coconut torte he'd cut. He took a bite. "Good torte."

"Christian."

He spread his legs, knees bent, and set the plate on the floor between them. After taking another bite, he put his head back against the cabinet. "I adored Jeff when he was little. My life had changed drastically with his coming, but I just assumed that was what happened to all families with babies, and even though I hated that part, I didn't take it out on Jeff. I couldn't. He was so cute. He was so innocent, so totally dependent. I used to play with him for hours, and he'd smile for me more than he'd smile for anyone else. When I came home from school, he'd grin and kick his little arms and legs"—he smiled at the memory—"and then, when he could walk, he used to be waiting at the window for me. You know how good that made me feel? My parents were totally focused on this kid, but the kid was totally focused on me." His grin faded. "Then, right around the time Jeff turned four, the old man decided I wasn't such a good influence on him. It started with his birthday, I guess."

"What happened on his birthday?"

Christian picked at the torte for a minute. "They planned this birthday party for him, you know? They could barely afford it—they sure wouldn't have done anything like that for me—but they brought in a magician to entertain the neighborhood kids. I thought the magician was great, but the kids were pretty antsy by the time he was done, and there was still another hour before they were supposed to go home. So everyone bundled up and went outside to try out the sled Jeff got for his birthday. It was a Flexible Flyer, a real beauty, runners all waxed and ready to go. We went to the hill down the street, and the old man thought that since it was Jeff's birthday and his gift, he should be the first one on the sled. But Jeff didn't know how to use the damn thing. So I got on behind him and steered with my feet and we went down the hill like a whip—right into a tree. Jeff started bleeding all over the place, and I caught hell for being irresponsible."

His eyes were pleading. "I didn't want him hurt. I adored the kid. I've never felt so helpless in my life as when he was crying and bleeding." The plea seemed suspended in air for a minute, before he ended it by looking away.

"Anyway, from that day on, the old man had me pegged. I was the enemy. I was the one who would hurt Jeff if given the chance. If Jeff did anything wrong—I mean, we're not talking real trouble here, but stuff like writing his name backwards or calling someone a jerk or refusing to eat his dinner—it was my fault. And the worst of it was he turned Jeff against me. The kid who adored me grew to blame me for everything too."

Laura was appalled. "But where was Lydia through all this? I can't believe she'd just stand there and let him bully you."

He sighed. "Lydia had made a bargain. Bill Frye would marry her, give her his name and support, and provide a name for her bastard son, in exchange for her giving him the home and family he wanted. If she was bothered by the things he said and did to me, she never let on. She was determined to stick to her part of the bargain. Frankly. I think she bought into the business about my being a 'bad' kid. That way she could condone his attitude toward me."

Laura shook her head. "Lydia's too smart for that. If you acted out, she would have understood why."

"*Your* mother would understand why," Christian argued. "That's her profession. And you'd understand why too, because you're Maddie's daughter. But Lydia wasn't into that. For all practical purposes, she wore blinkers. She'd made a deal with Bill, and she wouldn't allow herself to see or think evil of him."

"Was he evil?" Laura asked. She couldn't begin to imagine what Christian had suffered, living all those years with a man who must have resented his presence.

"No. He loved my mother, and he loved Jeff. It was just me he had trouble with." He took a bite of the cake, chewed, swallowed. "So I gave him cause. God knows I gave him cause. He thought I was bad, so I *was* bad. He thought I was fresh, so I *was* fresh. He thought I was stupid, so I *was* stupid—until it occurred to me that my brains were my only revenge, so I started to study. He's probably responsible for my getting into a school like Amherst. I swear, I did it to spite him."

"You did not."

"I did," he insisted.

"Do you regret it?"

"I regret the anger I felt. No one should have to live with anger like that. Because of it, I probably missed out on a lot of what was happening around me."

"But you've done well."

"In some ways. I have a good business. I lead a comfortable life." He smiled. "Think old Bill's turning over in his grave?

Think he's dying ten times over, seeing I'm not the total waste he thought I'd be? Shit, if he were alive now, he'd be blaming me for getting Jeff into trouble. He'd be telling the police I was the one behind it. Bill needed a scapegoat for anything that went wrong, and I was it." He rolled to his feet. "So that's why Jeff and I are so different. And that's why I was a hell of a kid to raise." He stuffed the remains of his torte down the disposal and muttered, "Let's test this fuckin' thing."

The disposal worked perfectly.

Aching for the little boy who'd been hurt, for the bigger one who'd been angry, and for the grown man who tried but couldn't hide the bitterness he felt, Laura slipped an arm around his waist. "I'm sorry."

"For what?" He stared at the sink. "It wasn't your fault."

"I'm sorry you had to go through that. I never knew."

"It's not the kind of thing you tell people. You're the only one who knows, besides Lydia."

"Jeff doesn't know?"

He shook his head.

She moved her hand on his back, over muscles that were hard and well toned. Nearly twenty-one years had passed since she'd touched him there, but little of his strength had been lost. Likewise, the years had been kind to his face. Crow's-feet at the corners of his eyes added character, tiny grooves on either side of his mouth added dash. His dark hair, now sprinkled with gray, was thick and vibrant and rakishly long.

Twenty-one years ago she had thought him compelling. He was even more so now.

"I wish Jeff had known," she said softly.

He looked down at her. "Why?"

"He might have been kinder."

"He was kind enough," Christian said with an odd smile on his mouth and his eyes on her lips. "He let me see you."

Laura's heart tripped. She was trying to decide whether he meant what she thought he meant when the back door opened and Debra burst in. She came to an abrupt halt when she saw them.

"Hi, babe," Laura said. She dropped her arm from Christian's back and turned to greet Debra, but before she could say another word, Debra was on her way to the hall. "Everything okay?" Laura called after her. When she didn't get an answer, she gave Christian a worried look. "I think I'd better check."

He touched her cheek lightly with the back of his hand and sent her off.

The instant she reached Debra's door, Debra turned on her. "What are you doing?" she asked furiously, sounding so incredibly like Maddie that Laura had to blink.

"Excuse me?"

"What are you doing with him?"

Laura drew back. "With Christian?"

"Is there any other man you've been with twenty-four hours a day for the last two weeks? Anyone walking in here without knowing would think *he* was your husband. Really, Mom, it's disgusting. Dad is somewhere out there in trouble, and you're here fooling around with his brother."

Laura was stunned. "I'm not fooling around with Christian."

"Sure looked that way to me. I'm not just talking about tonight. Most other nights the two of you are in the den playing footsie. It makes me wonder what's going on all the time I'm not here."

"Nothing's going on," Laura said defensively, then couldn't believe she'd said it. Debra was her daughter, not her mother. Laura wouldn't even have taken this kind of criticism from Maddie. Flaring with anger of her own, she said, "And if it were, it wouldn't be any of your business."

"It is so. You're married to *my father*."

"And *your father* deserted me. He left me with no money, no resources, no inkling of what was going on. All he left was dirty laundry piled up from the life he was leading behind my back."

The argument didn't dent Debra's fury. "He's still your husband—" she jutted her chin toward the door, "—and *he's* your brother-in-law."

"That's right. My brother-in-law. He's family, and that's why he's here in this house. He's here out of concern for his brother and concern for his brother's family, and, whether you like it or not, that includes me."

"Oh, he's concerned all right. He's concerned about whether he's going to be able to pull it off."

"Pull what off?"

"Stealing his brother's wife." Her eyes sparked. "Are you having an affair with him?"

Laura was outraged. "Of course not."

"But you could. I can see it. You spend more time with him that you ever spent with Dad."

"That's because Christian is *here*. He isn't in an office with his head buried in piles of papers, he isn't having conferences with clients, and he isn't working at the computer in the den."

"Ah, so now you're saying Dad was wrong for working so hard?"

"I'm simply saying that Christian *isn't* working so hard, which is why he has time to hang around."

"You could tell him to go home."

"I don't want him to go home. He's the first relief I've had in almost two months of nonstop trauma. He'll stay here as long as he wants."

For the first time, Debra's fury seemed to waver. Her eyes grew larger and more frightened. "Do you honestly think Dad will come home while he's here? Dad hated it when Christian came to visit. If you keep Christian here, Dad will never come back."

Suddenly seeing the source of her fear, Laura felt her own anger break. "Oh, babe," she said softly and went to put her arms around Debra, but Debra stepped away and grew sullen.

"I don't like having him around."

"I'm sorry you feel that way," Laura said quietly.

"You're not. You're just thinking about yourself."

"I'm thinking about you and Scott, too. Christian is helping me through this, and when things are better for me, they're better for all of us. Whether you like it or not, your father has opted out of our lives. For all practical purposes, I'm the head of the house."

"You always were."

"Your father was."

"He wasn't. Can't you see that yet? Can't you *admit* it yet?"

Laura studied her fingernails, running the pad of her thumb over the polish. She had done a lot of thinking in the weeks past, with her eyes wide open in ways they had never been before. Debra was right. Laura hadn't wanted to admit it aloud, because she hadn't wanted to further belittle Jeff in his children's eyes. But Jeff was gone and Laura was here, and now her credibility was at stake.

Raising her eyes, she said, "Okay. I suppose I did run things. I gave your father credit where credit was due and then some, but in the final analysis he didn't take the lead."

If she had been hoping that the confession would calm Debra into a workable truce, she was wrong. Debra wasted no time in turning that confession against her. "He *couldn't* take the lead. You always did things your way. You wouldn't give him a chance."

"I gave him plenty of chances. He just wouldn't take them."

"Because he knew you'd be angry if things didn't go your way. Face it, Mom. You're a dictator."

"Careful, Debra—"

"That's what drove Dad away. He couldn't stand not being able to express himself, so he did it in a way that told you what he thought of you, then he took off."

"You've been talking to Gram." It was the only explanation Laura could find for Debra's attack.

"I didn't need to. Between you and her, I've heard enough about self-expression and repression and resentment and rebellion to get me college credits in psychology—if I wanted them, which I don't, because I'm not going to college; I'm not getting into that rat race. And don't say that you didn't finish college and you're still in the rat race, because that's just *you*. You're as ambitious as Gram is. It's no wonder Dad ran off!"

Laura was feeling a combination of hurt and indignance that threatened a short-circuit in her system. Stiffening, she said, "This discussion is going nowhere. You're angry—"

"I'm right!"

"—and because you're angry, you're saying things that are better left unsaid at this point. I'm going downstairs. We'll discuss this another time." She left the room.

"My feelings won't change," Debra yelled after her.

Laura kept walking down the stairs. She knew that Debra missed her father and feared he would never come back. She was blaming the one person who was the most accessible. But Laura was also the most vulnerable. For that reason, she would wait until Debra calmed down before tackling the discussion again.

tACK CAME OUT OF A LIGHT DOZE TO BRING Daphne closer. It wasn't easy, given the tangle of sheets, and he had to do a little pulling and tugging—both of the sheets and of Daphne—to manage it, but when he finally had himself propped against the pillows with Daphne tucked against him, he knew the effort was worth it. With gentle fingers he combed her hair back from her face. Just as gently, he slipped a hand down her back to the warm curve of her hip.

"Mmmmm," she purred.

"You up?"

"When you touch me?" she murmured sleepily. "Always."

He smiled. Daphne was good for his ego. She didn't always say a whole lot, but the words were right when she did, and when she didn't, she knew all the right moves. She made him feel tall and handsome and important and smart. Mostly, she made him feel wanted.

"I thought we were supposed to work," he teased. The light was on, casting a dim glow over the papers on the floor by the side of the bed.

"So did I. But this happens every time. Why I listen to you when you suggest we work in bed is beyond me."

"You listen to me because you know exactly what's going to

happen. Face it, Daph. You're insatiable."

"Pot calling the kettle black?" she asked and drew in a deep breath. On the way out it stirred the hair on his chest. "It's chemistry," she murmured and snuggled closer.

Chemistry was part of it, Tack knew, but there was more. Daphne intrigued him. She had from the first, and she still did, and it wasn't simply the slope of her back or the thrust of her breasts or the shapeliness of the lovely, long legs that could wind around his waist and make him explode. If it had only been those things, he would love her and leave her, like he'd done with Gwen. But he stayed with Daphne. They made love, and he spent the night. He kept his room at the Inn more for show than anything else, since he was rarely there, and he returned to Boston only when absolutely necessary.

"It's your mind," he told her. "I've always been intrigued by legal minds."

"That's because you've always wanted to be a lawyer. Why wait for your next life? Why not go to law school now?"

"Because it costs money. And it takes time. And it means studying. I'd hate that, at my age."

"Old man." She ran a thumb over his nipple.

He tightened up and gave her a squeeze, but he didn't want to make love again. Not yet. First he wanted to talk. "Does my age bother you?"

"Should it?"

"Traditionally the man is older."

She flipped her head so that she could see him. "Traditionally the woman is younger. Does my age bother you?"

"Only the idea that at your age you don't want five kids."

She frowned. "Five. You always say five. Why five?"

"Because five means that one or two can be strange but the other three still have one another. Three's a good number."

"Try one. Maybe two."

"Are you considering it?" he asked.

"Of course not. But overpopulation is a problem. When you

leave me behind and go on to that twenty-five-year-old who wants all the babies you do, you should remember that."

He took a handful of hair from her shoulder and brought it to his face. His voice was muffled behind it. "I'm not going on. You're my last stop. Mmmm, do I love the smell of this." She used apple shampoo. The faint tang of it, mingling with the scent of woman and sex, gave him a hard-on every time. He doubted he'd ever be able to walk through an apple orchard again without wearing an overcoat.

Ignoring his erection, she crawled up his body so that her face was inches from his. "Why do you say things like that, Tack?"

"Because I *do* love the smell."

"About us." The look on her face fell somewhere between frustration and longing. "You say things about us that are crazy."

"They're not. We're wild about each other. We can talk work or music or sports and never get bored. We both like pizza, we both sleep late on Sundays, and we're both slobs. Baby, it doesn't get much better than that. Trust me. In my infinite experience, I know."

"Your infinite experience," she echoed, and her expression eased.

"That's right."

After grinning that dry grin of hers, she ducked her head and put a wet kiss on his neck. "You're outrageous."

"Not gorgeous?"

"That too. And sexy." Somewhere between outrageous and gorgeous, she had extended a hand to his groin, and what that hand was doing to him would have made him hard even without the smells he loved. If there was more to talk about, he couldn't remember what. By the time she straddled him and took him inside, the only thing he was thinking about was coming so hard and high and long in her that she would be his slave forever.

This time when they were done, they showered. While Daphne went to fix a snack, Tack neatened the bed. It wasn't that he didn't like love wrinkles, but Daphne had to work, and unless the bed looked less bawdy, he'd never let her.

She returned with a plate of what she called lover's hors d'oeuvres, so named, she claimed, because no amount of love-making could overdo or underdo them. They consisted of cucumber slices on Ritz crackers, topped with a dollop of peanut butter.

Tack smacked his lips, as the peanut butter dissolved in his mouth, and came out with a slightly gummy "These're good."

She climbed into bed beside him. "You're easy to please." She punched at the pillow behind her and then, when it was arranged to her satisfaction, pulled the sheet to her waist.

"Are all your men this easy?"

"All my men," she drawled. "Sure."

He studied her expression, but it told nothing of her deeper thoughts or needs. He would have given anything to be inside her head. "You always make light of that."

"They don't matter. Not when I'm with you." She helped herself to a cracker.

"When you're not with me, do you think about them?"

He saw the same tiny would-have-missed-it-if-he-didn't-know-her-so-well look come and go from her eyes. "No. They're in the past." The cracker went into her mouth whole.

"Did one of them hurt you?"

Chewing, she eyed him curiously. When she had swallowed, she said, "Why do you ask that?"

"You have a look sometimes. It worries me."

She took his hand. "You're imagining things."

"I hope so. I keep wondering why none of them snatched you up."

"None of them snatched me up because I wasn't up for the snatching. I was too busy with my life. None of them barged into it like you have."

"Is it so awful, what I've done?"

"Would I be sitting here naked beside you if it were?" She

held a hand across him and wiggled her fingers. "Hand me my stuff."

"I fit into your life."

"Uh-huh." She wiggled her fingers again.

"It's not like I'm screwing up your career."

"You will be, if you don't let me work."

"But I want to talk about us."

She sighed and dropped her head. When she brought it back up, the longing was there, all alone, on her face. "I know you do, but it frightens me. I've spent my whole life building a career, and no man's threatened that until you."

"I'm not threatening it."

"You're offering things that one part of me wants so badly I could choke on the wanting."

"Then *take*."

"I can't! Not so fast, at least. I have to get over the next few months with Laura before I can think of where to go from there."

"Laura means so much?"

"She's my oldest friend. I have a history with her, and with Jeff. I have to see her problems resolved."

There was something about the way she mentioned Jeff that always annoyed him. He was jealous of her loyalty. "You're worried we'll have a falling out when it comes to a disposition of the case, but let me tell you, a disposition's way off there in dreamland. We're no closer to finding Jeff than we were six weeks ago."

"No response from the dentists?"

On the premise that Jeff might have needed dental care, since he had had a toothache that was to have been tended the day he disappeared, Tack had put notices in dental publications all over the country. He had thought it a clever tactic at the time, but it hadn't produced. "No response. Zip from acquaintances and clients, and Zip from family. You'd think the guy would call *someone*."

Lips pursed, Daphne sank back against the headboard. After

a minute, she said, "Laura gets hang-ups."

"I know. The tap picked up a couple and we checked them out, but they were wrong numbers—probably people expecting someone to pick up and say 'Pizza House' or 'Gas Company' or something." When Daphne's lips went back to being pursed, he said, "He may never show up."

"Where does that leave Laura?"

"Where does that leave *us*?"

She drew in a breath and closed her eyes, neither of which was the response Tack wanted. He wanted her to throw her arms around him, look him in the eye, and say she'd go off with him whether Jeff showed up or not. But she was cool, the old Daphne he'd first met, the one with walls around herself.

"Don't do that," he whispered and rolled to face her.

She opened her eyes. "What?"

"Shut me out. When we're making love, you don't. You're hot and open and almost as greedy as me, and that's the way you are with lots of the other things we do. But there are times, like just then, when you close your eyes and go off into another world. I don't like being left behind."

"I'm just tired. I'm worried about this hearing. I've known Scott since he was a baby. I have to get those charges dismissed."

He knew she had closed her eyes against the discussion of "us," not Scott. He let her get away with the change of subject because Scott did mean a lot to her. "If you can't do it, Daphne, no one can."

"I wonder. Maybe I shouldn't be representing him. Maybe I'm too close."

"But you're the best," he said with conviction. Several times he had stolen into the courtroom while Daphne was in action. She was forceful, in a low-key way, and quick. Nothing slipped past her. "Besides, Scott's case will be stronger with a woman presenting it—a woman claiming that the woman who cried rape is a fraud."

"She is. Megan Tucker got a whiff of anti-Frye sentiment and jumped into the fray."

He had enough of a feel for court proceedings to know that that wouldn't be the crux of Daphne's argument. "Are you going with lack of evidence?"

She nodded. "There's nothing of a physical nature, absolutely nothing. Sure, the doctors said Megan was a little hyper when they saw her at the time of the miscarriage, but she didn't say anything about rape then, or about not wanting the baby, or about who the father was. The timing is even iffy. She miscarried at the end of November, which doctors guessed was the end of her first trimester, but they only guessed. She could as easily have conceived in September as in August, and Scott was back at school then."

"What about her claims of severe emotional strain?"

"They weren't severe enough to send her to a psychiatrist," Daphne said dryly. "So she was difficult at home; her friends tell me she's always difficult at home. So she's failing math and French; she nearly failed them last spring. If anything happened to that girl in August, it didn't affect her social life. She was active all fall, right up until the miscarriage. Her mother was furious with her after that. There were harsh words at the hospital; one of the doctors made a notation to that effect on her record. Then Jeff disappeared."

"It couldn't have been that alone that got her going."

"No. When he first disappeared and we thought he might have been sick or hurt, sympathy was in his favor. Then you guys showed up."

"Daph—"

"I know." She curled a hand against his chest. "You did what you had to do. But then the paper took over and went above and beyond that, and Megan must have got to thinking. When the mystery woman business hit the stands, that was all she needed. The world reads that Jeff cheated on his wife, so the world will believe that Jeff's son raped his date. Megan has her answer. She becomes the good girl who was wronged." She sighed. "It's Megan's word against Scott's, but in the current political atmosphere that may give Megan the edge."

For a minute she was lost in thought.

"I wish my case were stronger. The Rape Shield Law prevents me from talking about Megan's past sexual history, so the fact that she's loose does no good. I may be able to undermine her word if I catch inconsistencies in her testimony, but my guess is the prosecutor will have her well prepared. I was hoping to pick up something from her friends, and there's still one of them who looks like she has something to say. She was a friend of Scott's too, and I think she still likes him. But she's keeping quiet. I've given her my card twice, with both phone numbers on it, but I haven't heard a word."

"Scott must be terrified."

"Uh-huh. I talked with him yesterday. He's having trouble doing his schoolwork, and this is a kid who usually gets great grades, at an Ivy League college, no less."

"Is Laura nervous?"

"Very. I'm glad Christian's there. He's a help."

"Nice guy, Christian."

Daphne studied him for a suspicious moment. "What did you two do in Tahiti?"

"Me and Christian?"

"Do you know anyone else there?"

Tack put on his choirboy look. "He showed me around. That's all."

"Are you sure? There are times when I wonder. Tahitian women are supposed to be spectacular-looking."

"They are."

"Tack."

"Well, if I said they weren't, you'd know I was lying. Tahitian women are gorgeous." He kissed the tip of her nose and lowered his voice. "But that doesn't mean I prefer them to American women. Not one of those women can hold a candle to you."

Daphne rolled her eyes.

"I'm serious." To prove it, he took her mouth in a sucking

kiss that threatened to go on and on and might have, if she hadn't pulled sharply on his chest hair.

"I have to work," she said. Drawing back, she wiggled her fingers in the direction of the papers he'd taken from her earlier.

Reaching to the floor, he handed her the papers, along with the glasses she used for reading. The frames were large and round and made her look delightfully bookish from the neck up. From the neck down, with the sheet barely brushing her navel, she looked wanton.

"Come on, Tack. If you don't stop leering, I'll have to put on a nightgown."

"I'll stop leering," he said and looked quickly away.

He gave her half an hour, which he thought was generous indeed, given the size of his need. By then, she was willing to be distracted.

That willingness decreased the closer they came to the time of the hearing. She was preoccupied with the case, mentally running through every contingency, determined to push the parameters of a probable-cause hearing to its limits. It wasn't a trial to determine guilt or innocence, simply a hearing to determine whether there was cause to believe that a crime had been committed. If that determination was made, the case would be bound over to the grand jury for indictment.

Night after night, Tack watched her with those owl-eyed glasses on her nose, poring through her papers, making notes to herself, even mouthing responses. "The problem is twofold," she complained. "Not only do I have to convince the judge that there isn't probable cause to bring Scott to trial, I have to convince the prosecutor that there isn't even enough to take to a grand jury. If he wants to be stubborn, he could go ahead and do that anyway."

Tack knew about stubborn prosecutors. He'd seen plenty in his day. Usually they were on his side, though. It was odd rooting for the defense, but root for the defense he did. He wanted Daphne to get her dismissal so badly that if there were anything he could have done to help, even if it verged on the unethical, he'd have done it. She had lost cases before, she told him, and she was philosophical about it. She knew she couldn't win all the time. She also knew that a loss sometimes had to do with things totally unrelated to the lawyer's skill or performance. But she wanted this win so badly.

The day before the hearing, she got a break in the case. The girl Daphne had been pursuing with gentle insistence, the one who was Megan's friend but liked Scott, called her. Accompanied by her parents, she met with Daphne in her office. Several hours later, when Daphne arrived home, she was ebullient.

"This is it," she told Tack. "It's the first viable weapon I've found." But by the time she had spent hours plotting out exactly how she was going to use it, she was sober again.

The next morning she was so far away from him mentally that he was frightened. "You'll do fine, Daph," he said, as she put on her pantyhose.

"Mmmm."

She was buttoning up her silk blouse when he said, "Hearing's at eleven?"

"Mm-hm."

He waited until she had the blouse tucked into a matching skirt before asking, "How long do you think it'll last?"

She shrugged and reached for the blazer that went with the set.

He really wanted to know so he'd know when to call her. "Thirty minutes? An hour? Six hours?"

She adjusted her collar. "I don't know."

"Can you give me some idea?"

"I don't know," she repeated in a tone that was too harsh for his liking.

"Are you always a crab before trials?"

She shot him a look. "No one's asking you to stay here."

He knew that only too well. Not once had Daphne said "Come

spend the night with me" or "Don't leave till next week" or "What would I do without you?" He stayed at her place because he wanted to, and because she didn't tell him to leave. In poetic moments, he imagined that Daphne said all those things to him with her body. But he wasn't, first and foremost, a poetic guy. He was a pragmatist who happened to be in love with her.

"I'm not complaining," he said, while she checked the knot of her hair for any loose strands. "I'm just trying to figure out whether it's me or the trial."

"It's the trial," she said and grabbed her purse.

He followed her from the bedroom downstairs to the kitchen, where the pot of coffee he'd made was waiting. While she poured a glass of juice, he fixed her a mug of the dark brew.

"Then it'll be better when it's over?"

"Depends on the outcome," she warned. "If I lose, I'll be in a blue funk for a week."

"That's lovely."

She shrugged. "It's always been that way."

"Charming."

"Maybe you'd like to avoid me for a while."

"I wouldn't like that at all," Tack said. Slipping his hands inside her blazer, he brought her against him. All he wore was a short terry robe, and though he was barefoot to her heels, he still had the height advantage. "Are you trying to get rid of me?"

"Of course not. I'm just warning you about my moods."

"Warning taken. Now, if you can give me some idea how long the fuckin' hearing will last, I can call you when it's done. I'll be sitting on pins and needles. You know that."

She had been leaning back to hold her juice glass between them. Now she rested it in the vee of his robe. "I know," she said more gently.

He tipped up her chin. "How long?"

"Two hours. Maybe three. I can't be more specific."

Tack could accept that. "I'll be thinking of you the whole

time. You know that too, don't you?"

Almost shyly, she raised her eyes to his and whispered, "I know."

That shy look, her nearness, the sweet scent of her perfume—Joy, appropriately enough—all had an effect. Determinedly, Tack stepped back. "Here." He handed her the mug of coffee. "Drink up."

twenty-four

IF DAPHNE WAS TENSE ON THE MORNING of the hearing, Laura was nearly beside herself with worry. Scott had come home from Penn the day before, looking pale and far older than his years. He wouldn't talk much and spent most of his time in his room, where all that was old and familiar gave him comfort. Laura went regularly to his door, but either he feigned sleep or told her he was fine or refused whatever food she brought. Debra, too, tried to get him to talk, but he wouldn't.

Christian was the only one who made it over the threshold for any length of time, which made Laura infinitely grateful—again—that he was there. He was the male figure Scott needed. She didn't know what they talked about; she didn't feel she should ask. All she needed was the reassurance that Scott was all right, and Christian gave her that.

More than once it occurred to her that if Jeff had been around and Scott had been in the same mess, Jeff wouldn't have been the comfort Christian was. If the thought was disloyal, she didn't care. It was the truth. Christian was, always had been, the stronger of the two. She was grateful he was there for her son.

She was also grateful, in a roundabout way, that Scott opened only to him. It was good for Christian. He hadn't ever had children of his own; he had hardly had family of his own. But he was genuinely fond of Scott, and clearly the feeling was returned. Each time he came down from Scott's room, his expression told Laura how much that meant to him.

Conversely, Debra treated him like a nonentity. One look at him when she entered the house, and her expression soured. She spoke to him only when he spoke to her and walked right past him whenever she could. When Laura would have scolded, though, Christian stopped her.

"She has a right to resent me. I'm here, and her father isn't."

"But she's being ugly."

"I can take it," Christian assured her.

So Laura let it go. She didn't have the heart for a confrontation with Debra. Not until the hearing was done.

The arrangement, by order of Daphne, who had been over for hours the afternoon before, was for the whole family to be in the courtroom for the judge and prosecutor to see. With Lydia too weak to attend, that meant Laura, Scott and Debra, Christian, and Maddie. Debra was thrilled to take a day off from school. Maddie wasn't.

"I don't see why my face is needed," she argued when Laura asked her to come.

"Daphne says it would help Scott's case if we presented a cohesive, supportive unit," Laura explained. Willing to do most anything for Scott, she poured it on thickly. "You're the matriarch of the family. Of all of us, you have the most highly regarded position. Just by being there, you'll add credibility both to Scott's character and to Daphne's arguments."

"This is not the kind of publicity I need."

"I know that, Mother, but I'm asking you—begging you— to be there for Scott. Do it if for no other reason than that he sends you Mother's Day cards every year."

"You send those for him."

"Only when he was little. He does it now." Granted, Laura had to remind him, and she did it more so Lydia would receive a card than Maddie, but Maddie didn't have to know that.

"He's thinking of you at times when he doesn't have to. Can't you think of him now?"

"I've never bought into emotional blackmail, Laura."

"Will you come?"

Maddie paused, then sighed. "How long will it take?"

"Maybe an hour." Daphne had said it would probably go longer, but Laura hoped that, once there, Maddie would understand the importance of staying. "I don't ask you for much, Mom, but I'm asking for this. One hour of your time, for Scott."

Maddie finally agreed and showed up at the house at ten-thirty that morning. They all got into the Wagoneer, which was also part of the image of the wholesome American family that Daphne wanted to project—and wisely so. A group of photographers was waiting on the courthouse steps. Christian promptly went to talk with them, buying time for Laura, the kids, and Maddie to slip into the courthouse.

"They'll be there on the way out," Laura said worriedly when he joined them inside.

He grinned. "Yeah, but by then the charges will be dropped, so they can take all the pictures they want. It'll be the best publicity you've had."

Laura liked the sound of that. She also liked his grin, which was so bold and confident that she would have savored it like a charm, had not Daphne been waiting just inside the door to guide them to a small office to wait until the case was called.

They were a quiet group. Scott sat at the table with his legs sprawled, his head bowed, and his hands fisted in his lap. He looked pale, but so handsome in his shirt and tie, blazer, and slacks that Laura wanted to cry. Tears actually came to her eyes at one point, but before they could drop, Christian put a hand on her shoulder to give her strength.

On the surface, she was remarkably calm. Her suit looked good, her hair looked good, her makeup looked good. Inside, she was a mass of raw nerve ends. *What if the charges aren't dropped? What if he's put on trial and found guilty? What if he goes to jail?* The minutes ticked by too slowly, then again too quickly. She wasn't ready when a court officer appeared at the door and led them to the courtroom down the hall.

Scott sat within the bar at the defense table with Daphne. Laura sat between Debra and Christian in the first row of benches directly behind them. Since this wasn't a trial, there were no jurors. There were plenty of spectators, though. The courtroom was packed. There were even people standing at the back of the room, so Debra said.

Laura didn't look back. Nor did she look to the side, where Megan Tucker sat with her mother. Rather, she sat with her hands folded tightly in her lap and her face forward. She rose with the others when the judge entered, then sat down again and listened in a mother's silent agony while the charges against Scott were read into the record.

The Assistant District Attorney immediately called Megan Tucker to the stand and, question by question, led her in recounting her version of the events leading up to and through the night of August twenty-sixth. She told of being picked up by Scott, of going to the pizza place and arguing over their future. She claimed she wanted to end the relationship but Scott didn't; and when she demanded he drive her home, he argued; and when they reached her house, he pushed her inside and raped her.

"He did not," Debra whispered. Megan was the enemy, temporarily relieving Laura of that onus.

Laura squeezed her hand. She felt the same blazing fury she had heard in Debra's whisper. That Megan should sit there, looking demure in her high-necked sweater and skirt and her pitifully innocent expression while she was lying through her teeth, was a travesty of justice.

"Now, Miss Tucker," the prosecutor went on. "Would you tell the judge what you did when Mr. Frye left the house?"

"I stayed in my bedroom. I was afraid he'd come back."

"Did you call the police?"

"No."

"Did you call your mother?"

"No."

"Did you go to the hospital?"

"No."

"Why didn't you do any of those things?"

"I was scared. I thought no one would believe me. I had been dating Scott. We had already . . . done things together."

"You mean, you'd had sex?" the prosecutor asked.

"Yes," Megan admitted, looking embarrassed.

Debra choked out a disparaging sound.

Laura squeezed her hand again.

"Tell me, Miss Tucker," the prosecutor continued, "how did you feel in the weeks following this night?"

"Upset." She paused. "Used. Dirty."

"Still, you didn't seek help. Can you tell us why?"

"The same reasons as before. Also because I was afraid my mother would be angry. She hadn't wanted me to date Scott."

"Why not?"

"She thought he was arrogant."

Debra made another whispered sound.

"But you did date him," the prosecutor said. "You dated him for five weeks. When you decided you didn't want to see him any more, he raped you. And it's taken you five months to come forward. Why now, Miss Tucker?"

Laura was asking herself the same question.

Megan looked down at her lap. "I finally told my mother. I just couldn't keep it in any longer. It was messing up my whole life." She raised her eyes. "My mother understood. We talked it all out. I finally realized the only way I could get over what had happened was to go to the police."

"Thank you, Miss Tucker," the prosecutor said and turned to Daphne. "Your witness."

"He didn't ask her about the miscarriage," Debra whispered to Laura.

346

Laura whispered back, "Daphne said he wouldn't. It's not appropriate here."

"But her mother was angry about it. That's why Megan tried to pin something on Scott."

Daphne was conferring quietly with Scott.

"What's she saying?" Debra whispered again, but Laura could only shake her head. Debra added, "The IRS agent is here. He's standing in the back by the door."

Laura shot a worried look around. Then she leaned close to Christian and whispered, "Why is Taylor Jones here? He doesn't think Jeff will show up, does he?" The thought of that made Laura very nervous. Jeff was the last person she wanted to see just then.

"No. He likes Daphne."

Laura smiled feebly at the joke, but the smile vanished the instant Daphne rose to approach the witness stand. She took her time, moving smoothly and with confidence. Laura couldn't see her face but guessed she was looking straight at Megan.

"Before I begin, Miss Tucker, I'd like to remind you that a few minutes ago you swore to tell the whole truth and nothing but the truth. You understand what that means, don't you?"

"Yes."

"Do you understand that if you tell anything other than the truth you will have committed perjury?"

"Yes."

"Good." She straightened her shoulders and took a breath. "You have stated that you began dating Scott Frye on the twenty-third of July. Is that correct?"

"Yes."

"You have also stated that during the five weeks you dated Mr. Frye, you had sexual relations with him. Is that correct?"

In a quieter voice, Megan said, "Yes."

"Would you please tell the court when you first had sex with Mr. Frye?"

The prosecutor rose. "Objection. This is irrelevant to the issue of rape. Miss Tucker has already admitted that she had sex with the defendant. That should suffice."

But the judge looked curious. "I'd like to see where defense counsel is headed." He nodded to Daphne to proceed.

She rephrased the question for Megan. "How soon after you began dating Mr. Frye did you have sex with him?"

"I don't know. I didn't keep track."

"Eighteen years old, and you take something like this for granted?"

"Objection."

"Sustained."

Daphne put a hand on the dark wood bordering the witness stand. "Did you have sex with Mr. Frye the first time you went out with him? The truth, Miss Tucker, so help you God."

Megan hesitated for a minute before murmuring, "Yes."

"Was there any coercion involved on that occasion?"

"No."

"You dated Mr. Frye for five weeks. During those five weeks, how often did you see him?"

"Nearly every night."

"Did you have sex with him on each of those nights?"

"No," Megan said with mild indignance.

"Did you have sex with him, perhaps, every other night?"

"No."

"How about three times a week? Is that a fair guess?"

"Objection," the prosecutor said.

But the judge overruled the objection and instructed the witness to answer. Daphne repeated her question. "Three times a week?"

"Maybe."

"Is that a yes or a no?"

After another pause, Megan said, "Yes."

"And was that by mutual choice?"

"Yes."

"You had sex with Mr. Frye of your own volition?"

"Yes."

"If I understand correctly, then," Daphne summed up, "you had sex with my client somewhere in the vicinity of fifteen times without any show of force on my client's part. Is that right?"

"Yes," Megan said. Tossing her hair back from her shoulders, she tried to look composed.

Daphne nodded. She turned away from Megan, took several steps, turned back. "Just a few minutes ago, you testified, under oath, that the incident of which you accuse my client was—I believe your exact words were—'messing up my whole life.' Is that true?"

"Yes."

"Could you tell the court in what way?"

The prosecutor stood. "Objection, your honor. Defense counsel must know that the issue of Miss Tucker's emotional health is not relevant to this hearing. We are here simply to determine whether there is probable cause to find that a rape occurred, not to discuss the aftereffects."

Daphne approached the bench. "Your honor, given that the prosecution has no physical evidence whatsoever to show probable cause, the only thing left is the emotional. And if I may remind the Assistant District Attorney—" she looked at him, "he was the one to introduce this matter in direct examination, —which gives me the right to raise it now."

"I'll allow it," the judge stated.

Laura was grateful for every small victory. She took a deep breath, only then realizing how tense she was.

"Daphne's good," Christian whispered.

"Yes," Laura whispered back.

"So's the judge. We lucked out."

"God, I hope so."

Daphne returned to Megan. "Miss Tucker, would you please tell the court in what ways your whole life was messed up after the alleged incident with Mr. Frye?"

Megan shot an unsure glance at the prosecutor. The unsureness remained when she told Daphne, "I couldn't concentrate. My grades went down. I started flunking French and math."

Daphne nodded. "Would you tell the court what marks you received in those two subjects on your final report card last June?"

Megan swallowed. In a small voice, she said, "D."

In a loud voice, Daphne said, "D? In both courses?"

"Yes."

Laura heard several murmurs and a snicker or two from behind her, but she didn't turn. She wasn't amused. Nor did she feel a stitch of compassion for Megan Tucker.

Apparently Daphne didn't either, because she said, "Tell me something, Miss Tucker. You didn't start dating Mr. Frye until July. What happened last spring to mess you up then?"

"Objection!"

"Sustained. Counselor Phillips, you know that's not relevant to this case. Please limit yourself to questions that are."

Daphne nodded. Walking over to the jury box, she rested an arm on its mahogany rail. "You say that your whole life was messed up, Miss Tucker. Did that extend to your social life?"

Megan made a tiny movement with her head. "I don't know what you mean."

"Have you dated since the alleged incident with Mr. Frye?"

"Yes."

"One fellow? Two? Three?"

"Objection." The prosecutor rose. "Miss Tucker is protected by law from this line of questioning."

"I'm not talking about sex, your honor," Daphne argued, approaching the bench. "I'm talking about simple dating. I believe this is relevant to the issue of the messed-up life that Miss Tucker claims resulted from the alleged rape."

The judge nodded. "You may proceed."

Daphne faced Megan. "Yes or no—and I remind you that you are under oath—is it fair to say that you dated on a regular basis last fall?"

Megan tipped up her chin. "Yes, but it wasn't—"

Daphne cut her off. "Yes or no. Just answer the question, please."

"Yes," Megan said, looking bothered.

"Ah. Then you weren't so messed up that you couldn't date. Tell me," she asked, sounding genuinely curious, "how soon after the alleged rape occurred did you start dating again?" When Megan didn't answer, Daphne simplified the question. "Another yes or no, please. Is it true that you started dating a sophomore at U Mass named Jim Krupp on August the thirty-first, five days after the alleged incident with Mr. Frye?"

Megan pouted. "I don't remember the date."

"Do you remember the boy?" Daphne asked.

"Yes."

"Do you remember that you went to a fraternity party to kick off the Labor Day weekend?"

"Yes."

"Do you remember the party being on Friday night?"

"Yes."

"Do you remember leaving the fraternity house after the party with Jim Krupp?"

"I may have."

"Yes or no, please."

Reluctantly, Megan said, "Yes."

"Do you remember going out with the same young man on Saturday night and then again on Sunday night?"

"Yes," she snapped.

"So within five days of allegedly being raped, you were back to dating on a regular basis. Did you have sex with Jim Krupp on the first date too?"

"Objection!"

"Sustained. Please, counselor, you know the rules."

"Sorry, your honor," Daphne said and returned to the defense table to confer with Scott again.

The prosecutor ran a hand through his hair.

"He's getting nervous," Christian whispered.

"That's good," Laura whispered back. Clutching her hands tightly in her lap, she kept her eyes on Daphne, who was back before Megan.

"I just want to go over one or two things again, Miss Tucker. A bit earlier, you testified that you wanted to break up with Scott Frye, but that he wanted to keep dating you. Is that correct?"

"Yes."

"Did you hear from him after the night of the alleged rape?"

"No."

"You must have been pleased."

"I was relieved. I was afraid he'd try to see me again."

"And you didn't want that?"

"No, I did not."

Daphne nodded. "I wonder if you can tell me who Bethany Ludden is."

"Objection," the prosecutor said. "I don't see the relevance of this line of questioning."

"Please, your honor, the relevance will be obvious in just a moment."

"Go ahead," the judge said.

"Who is Bethany Ludden?" Daphne asked Megan.

Megan looked wary. "She's my friend."

"A good friend?"

"My best friend."

"Have you known each other long?"

"Since first grade."

"Is it the kind of relationship where you confide in each other?"

"Yes."

"You tell her things you don't tell anyone else?"

"Sometimes," Megan said. Her wariness remained, but Daphne looked unconcerned. Returning to the defense table, she removed a small piece of paper from among those by her brief-case, brought it back to the witness stand and handed it to Megan.

For the benefit of the judge, she said, "This is a note that was passed back and forth between two young women during class one day last January. Miss Tucker, I wonder if you could identify the handwriting on this note for the court?"

Megan had gone white. She didn't say a word.

"May I remind you that, if necessary, I can bring in a handwriting expert to make the identification. You can save us time and money, which is the least you can do under the circumstances. Whose handwriting do you see?"

Megan pressed her lips together. She didn't look up, not in the direction of the prosecutor, not toward her mother. "Mine," she said in a thin voice.

"Your handwriting. This is your handwriting. Is that correct?"

"Yes."

"And who else's?"

"Bethany's." She took a quick breath. "But I don't know how you got this, because Bethany would never—"

"This is a note," Daphne interrupted firmly, "passed back and forth between Bethany and yourself. If I may—" she swept the note from Megan's limp fingers, "—I'd like to read this for the record, your honor. It starts in Bethany's handwriting, with the question *What is going on?* Each word is underlined. Megan has written back, *Didn't you read the paper?* To which Bethany replied, *But it's absurd. He didn't rape you. Scott's the nicest guy you ever dated.*"

"She was jealous!" Megan cried.

But Daphne went on. "Megan wrote back, *He dumped me. He's been home for two vacations since the summer, and the rat hasn't called me once. He deserves this.* Bethany argued, *Not rape. That'll screw up his life.* Megan replied, *That's his problem.*"

A wave of low murmurs swept through the courtroom. With the same smooth, confident movements that had characterized her presentation, Daphne laid the note before the judge.

Debra clutched Laura's hand. Laura held her breath.

"Miss Tucker," Daphne said, pressing her advantage, "I would like you to tell us, under oath, that what you wrote in that letter is the truth."

Megan's eyes brimmed with tears. "The letter was supposed to be destroyed. She said she burned it."

"Was what you wrote in that letter the truth?"

The tears overflowed. "This wasn't my idea. I wouldn't have done anything, except everyone kept telling me—"

"The truth, Miss Tucker," Daphne prodded, emphasizing each word. "Is what you wrote in that letter the truth?"

"Yes!" she shouted, then put her head in her hands as the courtroom erupted.

With a dignity that held threads of triumph, Daphne returned to sit beside Scott. The Assistant District Attorney looked disgusted. Laura pressed her cheek to Christian's shoulder for a minute before taking Debra's hand.

The judge rapped his gavel. When the crowd quieted, he directed a solemn gaze at the prosecutor. "I find this case appalling. In a day and age where women are finally receiving protection against the perpetrators of legitimate brutality, this is an embarrassment. It is an embarrassment to the women's movement, which has worked long and hard for women's rights, and an embarrassment to the government, which should have known better. It is also an embarrassment to the taxpayers of this commonwealth, whose money has been wasted on a case that had no business seeing the light of day." He turned to Megan, who was crying silently on the stand. "Miss Tucker, I would suggest that you learn a lesson from this. Pettiness and a young woman's vanity have no place in a court of law." He hit the gavel hard against the desk. "The charges against the defendant are hereby dismissed." Rising, he left the bench for his chambers.

Scott hugged Daphne, then vaulted over the railing to give Laura a bone-crushing hug. Grinning through her tears, Laura hugged Daphne next, then Debra, then even her mother. Then she threw her arms around Christian and clung to him as the courtroom slowly emptied. Her eyes were still damp when she finally drew back.

Thank you, she mouthed, hugged him again, then turned to

the others. "This calls for a celebration." She rubbed her hands together. "There's a table waiting for us at the restaurant. Jonah's been cooking, just in case we're hungry. Are we?"

They were, of course. It took awhile to get there, since the press wanted statements. Christian was right. After all that had come before, positive publicity was welcome. Not even Maddie seemed to mind.

The height of the lunch hour had passed by the time they arrived at Cherries, which was just as well. Half of the staff celebrated along with them. Uncorking a bottle of the restaurant's best champagne, they toasted Daphne, then Scott, then the judge, then Daphne again. Laura smiled and laughed more than she had in two full months. For the first time since Jeff had vanished and life as she'd known it had fallen apart, she was optimistic not because she was trying to convince one of the kids or herself that things would be all right but because she truly believed it.

After a stop to celebrate the victory with Lydia, they arrived home shortly before four. Daphne left to check in at the office. Maddie left to check in at school. Debra left to check in with Jenna.

Scott, who hadn't stopped smiling, was sprawled in the kitchen chair, talking with Laura and Christian. Actually, his talk consisted of one effusive expression of relief after another. "Man, am I relieved," he said with one grand sigh. "Wow, do I feel better!" he said with another. With a third, he said, "I feel like a million bucks!"

"You aren't the only one," Laura told him. She also felt tired, incredibly tired. The strain of the past weeks was finally hitting her, she knew, but she had no intention of sleeping until Scott was headed back to school. Just a few hours; then he'd be gone and she could sleep to her heart's content.

So they sat in the kitchen talking about the trial, about Scott's school, about his fraternity. Much as she wanted to hear everything, Laura couldn't keep her head up. When Christian suggested he take Scott to say goodbye to Lydia, Laura wanted to protest but couldn't. She put her head down on her pillow, fell instantly asleep, and remained so until, much later, Scott shook her shoulder.

"Time to go," he whispered. It was nearly seven. His flight was at eight.

Fighting grogginess, Laura pulled herself up, put on jeans and a sweater, and went downstairs. Debra had been home but was back at Jenna's. Christian was waiting to drive them to the airport.

The parting was easier. Scott was happy, which made all the difference in the world. Laura made it to the terminal and back to the car without crying, but once there, the same pervasive fatigue hit her again. When Christian opened his arm, she curled up against him and quickly fell back to sleep.

This time when she woke up, she was many miles from Northampton.

twenty-five

WAKEFULNESS CAME SLOWLY. CHRISTIAN was such an accommodating cushion that Laura was tempted to stay snuggled against him and go back to sleep. She might have done it if she hadn't caught a glimpse of the dashboard clock. It was nine-thirty. They should have been home long ago.

"Where are we?" She pushed herself up and peered out the window, but other than sparsely scattered headlights and tail-lights that reflected off snow on each side of the road, she saw nothing.

"About halfway between Brattleboro and St. Johnsbury."

She was groggy and hence slow on the uptake. It was a minute before she realized. "That's in Vermont."

"Right."

"What are we doing in Vermont?"

"I'm taking you home. I thought it was time you met my houseplants."

They were light words, offered in a tone that wasn't quite so light. Laura tried to make out his expression in the dark. "Are you serious?"

"Actually, most of the houseplants are dead, but I *am* taking you home."

She moved a little away from him. "To your place."

"That's right."

She moved a little farther away. "Uh, Christian, I hate to tell you this, but I have to be in Northampton for an early meeting tomorrow morning."

"No, you don't," Christian said. "Elise is going for you. She loves the linen people. She's also handling the meeting with the organic gardeners tomorrow afternoon, and the one Friday morning with the graphic designer. DeeAnn and Jonah are running the restaurant, and Maddie is staying with Debra. You're cleared through Monday. It's vacation time."

Backed against the passenger door, Laura stared at him. "I don't believe this."

"Believe it. Everything's arranged."

"But when did you do it?"

"Before, when you were sleeping. You're exhausted, Laura. You've been driving hard since Jeff disappeared. You need a rest."

It had been years since anyone had made a decision like that for her. "Don't I get any say in the matter?"

"No."

"Christian, that's not right!"

"Of course it is. You would have said you couldn't go. You would have said you had too much to do."

"I *do*."

He shook his head. "You have great friends and a great staff. You picked them and trained them, and everyone I spoke with was thrilled to take over so you could get away."

Laura was feeling confused, trying to take in what he'd done, while at the same time figure out how she felt about it. She wasn't really angry. The more she thought about it, she wasn't angry at all. She was actually feeling . . . well cared for. "My *mother* is staying with Debra?"

He nodded.

"She wouldn't do that out of the goodness of her heart. You must have had to promise her something."

"Not much."

"What?"

"A new roof."

"Christian, that's crazy! She won't forget. She'll hold you to it."

"I expect her to, but it's no sweat, Laura. I do roofs with my eyes closed. They're part of building houses, and building houses is my livelihood." He paused. "Aren't you curious to see the house I built for myself?"

She was, more and more so as the reality of her unplanned escape hit her. Not only was she curious to see his house, but where he worked and who he worked with. She knew nothing but the bare bones of Christian's life.

"Cleared till Monday?" she asked.

"*Through* Monday. I said we'd be back that night."

Five days of relaxation. Five days of doing nothing. Five days of sleeping. Five days of letting someone else run the show.

The idea was growing on her. She hadn't had five days off in over a year, and that had been a family vacation, and on family vacations she was nearly as busy making arrangements as she was at home. She liked things that way. Except that she'd never been as tired before.

Five days of rest. The idea was growing on her fast.

Relaxing against the door, she studied Christian. His profile was faintly outlined by the dashboard lights—*her* dashboard lights—which got her to thinking. "Did Debra agree to this?" Debra thought something was going on between Laura and Christian, and she was furious about it. Laura couldn't see her conceding anything to Christian unless there had been a bribe involved.

"Debra agreed. I left her the Miata."

"I had a feeling you were going to say that."

"She was thrilled."

"The car may never be the same."

He shrugged. "It's only a car."

Granted, there was a big difference between a Miata and a Porsche; still, Laura couldn't help but think of Jeff and his car. She hadn't ever seen him as excited as he was on the day he had driven it home. He used to wash it every weekend, more often if it got at all dirty. He spent hours polishing it, had it waxed before winter, even bought a car vacuum and regularly did the seats and the floor mats. Laura hadn't wanted to drive it. The kids did, but he never let them.

And here was Christian saying, It's only a car. He was incredible.

But that wasn't the only way he was incredible. He had materialized just when she needed him most and had helped her out immeasurably. He had loaned her the money she desperately needed, had guided Scott through a tough time, had stood beside them. And now he was surprising her with a vacation.

"No one's ever done anything like this for me before," she said, feeling deeply touched that Christian had.

"That's because you're too competent. You do everything for yourself. You beat other people to the punch. I succeeded because I caught you in a rare moment of weakness. If you hadn't been dead to the world back at the house, you would have heard me making phone calls, and if you'd done that, you would have nixed the idea. Am I right?"

"Probably." Her mind went back again, not to Jeff this time but farther, to the glory days she had spent with Christian twenty-one years before. She had been young and eager to do whatever he suggested, and he had been full of suggestions. More than once, he had picked her up after class and spirited her off toward an unknown destination.

"Just like old times?" he asked, darting her a quick look.

"That depends. Do I have a change of clothes?" Often, back then, she hadn't.

"Sure do. I packed for you while you were sleeping."

So it wasn't quite like old times. She had clean clothes of her own. She also had the body of a thirty-eight-year-old woman who had given birth to two children. And she had a wedding band on her left hand.

Just then, she wished the ring were gone. She wished she were eighteen again, with all the freedom in the world to run with her senses and all the freedom in the world to love Christian.

She did love him. She supposed, deep down, she always had. She had fallen in love with him twenty-one years before and had spent the intervening years wishing it weren't so. Now he was back, the same spontaneous and compelling man, but grown up, with new strengths and interests, plus a history to give him even greater depth.

Her pulse raced. Taking a measured breath to slow it, she looked out at the night. "How much longer?"

"Forty-five minutes."

She took another breath, put her temple to the glass, and closed her eyes.

"Want to put your head on my shoulder again?" he asked.

"No." She didn't dare. "This is fine."

They rode on in silence for a time. Once, when she opened her eyes, the headlights bounced off a highway sign that confirmed they were heading north through Vermont. She could make out trees rising from a thin layer of snow on either side of the highway, but beyond the beam of the headlights all was dark. "Are there towns out there?"

"Sure, but they're back from the highway. We'll be taking the next exit, and then you'll see. The center of town is fifteen minutes down the road."

He was as good as his word. Fifteen minutes after they left the highway, they encountered a patch of civilization. The post office was at one end, a white-spired church at the other. In between were an assortment of clothing, crafts, home supply, and food shops.

"Are they cute?" she asked. She couldn't quite tell.

"You can decide for yourself. We'll come in tomorrow. I have to warn you—the refrigerator's empty. I haven't been up here for more than a night since before Thanksgiving."

"Aren't you curious to see if it's still standing?"

"Oh, it's standing, all right. Friends check on it for me. If something happened, they'd call."

Laura wanted to ask what kind of house it was. She wanted to ask when he built it, how large it was, whether he designed it himself—but they were such basic questions she was embarrassed to ask them. He was her brother-in-law and, before that, her lover. She should have known the answers already. But she had never asked. In all the years Christian had been coming to visit, she had never asked a single personal question.

You were afraid of the answers, Maddie would have said if she had known anything of what had gone on years before. You were afraid of finding him more interesting than Jeff. And she would have been right.

Now Laura sat with her hands in the pockets of her wool topcoat, watching the road to see where Christian would turn off. They passed a pair of mailboxes, though she didn't see any houses nearby. They rounded a curve, swung straight, rounded a curve that was the reverse of the first. The headlights reflected off a low fence, beyond which the landscape fell off to what Laura assumed was a brook or a gully. She searched the road ahead.

"What do you look for?"

"We go down a short incline—this is it now—then up again." The car crested the rise and leveled. "There's a mailbox coming up on the right—there." He turned onto a narrow plowed lane.

Laura kept her eyes peeled for a house and was still looking when Christian suddenly turned left, stopped the Wagoneer, and climbed out. They were a scant five feet from a garage. She leaned forward to see what the garage was attached to, but the darkness hid the details. All she could do was to wait for Christian to open the garage door and return to the car.

"There's a circular drive that curves around to the front of the house," he explained, driving into the garage. "If it were daylight, I would have shown you the view from there—both of the house and of the valley. That'll have to wait until morning."

Laura nodded. She didn't know whether she was more excited or nervous. There was an intimacy in being here that she wasn't quite sure how to handle.

After closing the garage, Christian unlocked a door that led into the lower level of the house. "It'll be cold. I'll have the heat up in a minute." He strode ahead to see to that, leaving her to follow more slowly.

The house was multilevel, presumably designed to fit into the hillside. The style was clearly modern. Everything she saw was sleek and clean, from structure to decor. The main living area was open, with a sweeping cathedral ceiling, a broad expanse of windows, and an integration of function that had sectional sofas and low coffee tables flowing into a dining area, which in turn flowed into a sleek kitchen, which flowed into a den.

What caught her breath were the photographs, huge black-and-white prints simply framed, that hung on the walls at intervals broad enough to give each one the attention it deserved. Laura moved closer. One photograph was of a lone sandpiper running at the edge of the surf. Another was of a cornstalk, its full husks set in relief against a bold autumn sky. Yet another was of a tall, textured Douglas fir, so intricate in detail she could almost feel its needles. In the lower right corner of each picture, in small penciled script, was the artist's signature.

She darted a glance back to where Christian stood in what would have been the hall had there been walls. "I had no idea," she said, and felt the same kind of embarrassment she had felt earlier in the car. Christian was a gifted photographer. She should have known.

Years before he had been interested in photography. In the month they had been together, he had taken her to half a dozen exhibits, and she had become hooked herself. In the years since then, she had seen every major photography exhibit in the area and gathered a sizable collection of books. Maddie would have said she had been making a subconscious effort to remember Christian. Maybe so.

He was good. She should have known.

Coming back to where he stood, she looked more humbly out over the room. The photographs got to her, but so did the flow of the room, the cream, tan, and brown colorings, and the surprisingly soft look of the modern furnishings. Aside from the occasional wilted fern, the overall effect was peaceful.

"Come on," he said with a toss of his head back toward the hall. "I'll show you around."

A spacious side wing held two sprawling upper levels, each with two bedrooms, and a lower level housed Christian's darkroom. More of his photographs were hung in the halls and the bedrooms. Laura stopped before one, a head-on shot of a stunning dark-skinned woman. The fact that the woman was barebreasted was incidental to the arresting expression on her face. "Tahitian?"

"Very much so."

"Lover?"

"Not mine."

"She's beautiful."

They walked back through the house to the living area. Though the heat had begun to come up, taking the nip from the air, Laura hugged her coat around her. "Make yourself at home," Christian said. "I'll get the things from the car. I'm putting you in the top bedroom. Is that okay?"

"It's fine," she said and went off toward the kitchen in an attempt to look casual. She had wondered where she would sleep. Christian's bedroom was on the lower of the bedroom levels, which meant that there would be two spare bedrooms plus a handful of stairs between them. The arrangement was respectable enough.

She wished her thoughts were. She had been living in the same house as Christian for the past three weeks, but it wasn't the same. This was his house. There were no children around,

364

no neighbors, no friends, no mothers. There was no work to do by way of sublimation. She couldn't even cook, since there was no food in the fridge.

Telling herself that the restlessness she felt was an aftershock from all she'd been through with Scott, she crossed through the kitchen to the den. One full wall was covered by a built-in unit in natural ash. A large television sat at its center, with a stereo system above it. Other than those and strategically placed speakers, the only things showing were two shelves of photography books. Other books, cassettes, and compact discs were stored behind cabinet doors.

Make yourself at home, Christian had said, so she put on a Boston Symphony Orchestra recording of Tchaikovsky's piano concertos. Still wearing her coat, she settled into a large Eames chair, kicked off her shoes, and tucked up her legs. She closed her eyes, took a slow deep breath and let it out in a *whoosh*, then repeated the procedure, and all the while she directed relaxing thoughts from one part of her body to the next.

She didn't hear Christian until he materialized with two glasses of wine. Taking one, she sipped it slowly.

"When you're done with that," he suggested from the sofa, "you may want to use the Jacuzzi. There's one in the bathroom by your room."

There was also one in the bathroom connected to *his* bedroom. She had spotted it during the tour. Resting her head against the leather, she smiled. "You live a cushy life, Christian."

"No more so than you."

"But I never claimed to be antiestablishment. Jacuzzis are as establishment as you get."

"In my line of work, they're a necessity. I'm damned sore when I get home some days."

She thought of his work and the questions she wanted to ask, then she thought of him in his Jacuzzi. The image lingered. Not quite ready to shake it off, she closed her eyes and let the music take her where it would. By the time the tape was done, she had finished her wine and was feeling mellow enough to be able to say, "I think I'll have that soak now," without feeling self-conscious. Softly, because she felt it was needed, she added, "Thanks, Christian. I'm glad you brought me here."

"My pleasure." His eyes followed her until she reached the stairs, warming her all the way.

The Jacuzzi took over from there. She lay in it until she was nearly asleep. Feeling clean, soft, and drained of all but the last bit of energy, she climbed out, dried off, and put on a nightgown from her bag. It was long, white, and satiny and whispered against the sheets when she slipped into bed. Her head had barely hit the pillow when she was asleep.

She was disoriented when she awoke. It was a minute before she realized where she was and how she'd come to be there, a minute more before the events of the past day returned.

The digital clock by the bed read three-twenty. The room was pitch black, as was the world beyond the skylights. She closed her eyes with the intention of falling back to sleep, but fifteen minutes later she was still wide awake. Her mind seemed bent on rerunning Scott's hearing, lunch at Cherries, the farewell scene at the airport, the drive north.

It moved on to Christian and stayed. Memories came and went. Emotions came and went. Moral considerations came and went. But Christian remained.

Feeling as restless as she had when they'd first arrived, she climbed out of bed and slipped through the hall, stole down one set of stairs, past Christian's room, and down another set of stairs to the living room. Stopping before the tall windows, she folded her arms under her breasts and gazed out.

"Laura?"

The sound of his voice made her tremble. She willed herself not to turn. "Uh-huh."

"Is everything okay?"

"I woke up and couldn't go back to sleep."

"Strange beds can do that sometimes."

He hadn't moved. His voice told her that he was staying back by the hall. She tightened her arms.

"Want something to drink? Maybe more wine?"

"No."

"Milk?"

"There isn't any."

"Oh. Right."

"I'm fine. Really."

"Are you warm enough?"

She didn't think he could see her shaking. Most of it was inside, and what little showed should have been lost in the dark. "Plenty warm." The house itself was toasty.

She felt, more than heard, his footsteps sinking into the deep carpet, and before she could adequately brace herself, he was standing so close she could feel his large body's warmth. She kept her eyes on the glass.

"What you're looking out over," he said in a voice vibrant with softness and depth, "is a world of mountains and forests and small country villages so quaint and pure as to have escaped time. Deer run through the woods, foxes hunt in the fields, beavers dam up the streams. When there's snow, like there is now, the evergreens carry it on their limbs like epaulets, and when the snow melts and spring comes, the woodland comes alive."

The words were lovely. So was his closeness. She felt she was the one melting, then coming alive.

"Spring is my favorite season," he went on gently. "Everything is new and fresh. Buds show up on the trees, and grow and burst into blossomlike clusters, then open and spread into leaves of every imaginable shade of green. Beyond the greens are the purples and pinks and whites of the early wildflowers. Bird songs fill the air. The earth smells moist and full of promise."

The cadence of his voice was magnetic. Unable to resist, she raised her eyes to his gaze.

"Summer is something else," he told her, more hushed now as his eyes held hers. "Everything out there becomes lush. Walking through the woods is like having French vanilla ice cream with hot fudge, whipped cream, Heath Bar pieces, and a cherry on top. It's sinful. There are times when I sit on the deck and close my eyes and listen, just listen, to the wind in the trees, the bees in the wild azaleas, the rumble of thunder in a distant cloud. Summer is warm and lazy and—"

Her fingertips covered his mouth to silence him, then glided lightly over his lips. They were as lean and firm as the rest of him, and as blatantly masculine.

"Don't you want to hear about fall?"

She shook her head. Seconds later, she dropped her hand to his bare chest. The hair there was thicker than it had once been, but still soft. The skin beneath it was firm, the muscles beneath that as solid as the thud of his heart. Savoring every inch, she palmed him, from one side to the other. Her hand stuttered slightly over his nipple before following a tapering trail of dark hair to his navel.

He wore slim-cut boxer shorts, just as he had so many years before, and he filled them as provocatively as he had then. Her hand stopped at his waistband, and her eyes rose again.

"Are you sure?" he asked, his voice thicker this time.

She nodded. It wasn't right, she knew—she was married to Jeff—but she didn't care. She loved Christian. She wanted his gentleness, his protection, and his fire, all of which she knew he could give because he had before, and she'd never forgotten it. Memory was an aphrodisiac, but nowhere near as potent as the man in the flesh. She needed his loving more than she'd ever needed anything else in her life.

Slipping her arms around his waist, she buried her face in his chest. The warmth was there, as was the scent she remembered so well. It was a natural scent—Christian never used cologne— the scent of clean male flesh, and it was more heady than anything in a bottle could be. Then again, she realized, the headiness had help from that part of him pressing against her stomach. He was fully aroused, and when Christian was fully aroused, nothing halfhearted would do. She knew that from experience. One look at his face, eyes blazing in the dark, told her it hadn't changed.

"I have a fierce need," he warned in a gritty whisper.

In answer, she slipped her hand into his shorts, ran them from the tightness of his buttocks to the smooth skin at his sides to the hot, heavy swell of his erection. While she stroked him, she raised her mouth to his. He seized on it like a starving man, cupping her head in that gently protective way he had and taking charge in a heart-stopping instant.

By the time he lowered her to the carpet, the satiny gown lay in a pale pool by his shorts. He touched her everywhere, telling her in his inimitable way that he thought her feminine and exciting and appealing, and wherever he touched, she burned. She came once with his hand between her legs, and again when he thrust inside her. She was on the verge of doing it a third time when he erupted into an orgasm so powerful she was distracted. The look of rapturous agony etched on his face, the deep cry torn from his throat, the wire-tightness of his muscles, then their sudden tremor—not even when they'd been younger had she seen anything like that.

If Jeff's betrayal had made her feel less of a woman, Christian's pleasure more than repaired the damage. The minute he was able, he pulled back to his knees, lifted her, and carried her to his big bed, where he proceeded to show her that his desire for her wouldn't be sated by one coupling or even a second. He made love to her over and over again. He reacquainted himself with her body by inches, using his hands, his mouth, his body parts in ways that Jeff, for all the years he'd had with her, had never imagined doing. Christian made her feel worshiped, and she worshiped him in turn. Her passion ran without reserve, heightened by time and maturity and an awareness of the rarity of true love.

twenty-six

"WHY DID YOU MARRY JEFF?" CHRIStian asked. The question had eaten at him for years. He needed an answer.

She rubbed her cheek against his chest. "Because you weren't there."

"I'm serious."

"So am I. I loved you."

"You were so young."

"I was devastated when you left."

"Devastated because I wouldn't marry you?"

"Devastated because you were gone. Devastated because I was sure I'd never see you again."

"Did you marry Jeff to make sure that you did?"

"No."

"Then why?"

"Because I liked Jeff. Because he was steady and dependable. Because I thought he could give me the kind of life I wanted."

Christian knew just what kind of life that was. She had spelled it out for him and scared him off, then proceeded to live it with his brother. "The house and the babies."

"Not a house, per se. I didn't want a building, I wanted a home." She looked up at him, and he could see it vivid on her face. "Family picnics in the park, bicycles with baby seats on the back, a Christmas tree with lots of lights and decorations and presents wrapped so gaily you hate to open them. Those were all the things I didn't have when I was a kid."

"But you were barely eighteen. If you'd finished school and waited for me, we might have done it together."

"I didn't want to finish school. Besides, you told me you didn't want all that."

"I was angry. We had such a good thing going, and suddenly you had this detailed plan to change it all."

"You said you didn't want any of it."

"I lied," he said. "I wanted a lot of it, but not then. I was still too angry and too hurt about Lydia and Bill and Jeff and whoever the hell fathered me. I didn't know what I wanted to do with my life—and if the clock was turned back with the situation the same, I'd probably walk out on you all over again. I just wasn't ready to make a commitment."

"If you'd loved me enough, you would have."

"That's starry-eyed talk," he said, feeling sadness, affection, and protectiveness all at once. Laura was a romantic in the broadest sense of the word. She dreamed things, then set out to make them true. He adored that in her. He also ached, because inevitably she was hurt. "It's unrealistic. What did we know of love back then? Sure, what we had was strong, but did we know what it meant or where it would go or if it would last? I had my own demons to tame, and I couldn't do it in Northampton. You were the only reason I stayed around as long as I did."

"Would you have come back to see me if I hadn't married Jeff?"

"Probably. It might have taken me a year or two. But I'd have been back. Wasn't I there for your wedding? Wasn't I there after Scott was born?"

"Quite," she said in a chiding tone.

He cupped her head, applying light pressure until she returned her cheek to his chest. "I was unhappy those times. I was angry at you and jealous of Jeff and feeling sorry for myself because the life you were making for yourselves had so much of what I wanted. I was also frustrated, because each time I looked at you I wanted you. There you were—my brother's wife. I swear, if you'd been married to anyone else, I might have tried to lure you away. But he was my brother. I had thumbed my nose at many conventions, but that one I couldn't break. And then you had Scott and Debra, and you seemed so happy." He touched her hair lightly. "You were happy, weren't you?"

He felt her nod. "I got the life I wanted. I worked to make it work." She paused. Less certainly, she said, "Looking back, it wasn't always easy."

"How not?"

"Jeff wasn't a leader. He wasn't a doer. I pushed him in subtle ways, and when that didn't work, I did things and gave him the credit. But I shouldn't have. I robbed him of pride. If he'd succeeded on his own, he would have felt better about himself. I keep agonizing about that."

"Don't agonize, Laura."

"How do I stop?"

"By telling yourself that what you did, you did with the best of intentions. You're not God. You can't shape people into the kind of individuals you want them to be."

"I sure tried," she said in self-reproach.

He gave her a squeeze. "With the best of intentions. We all make mistakes. But your heart was in the right place, and anyway, look at what you gave Jeff. You made things great for him. He had more with you than he would have had with any other woman."

"So where is he now?"

Christian didn't know where Jeff was, either physically or emotionally. He did care—he could admit that too. Feelings that he had when Jeff was a baby, with smiles and baby talk and arms up just for him, had never quite died. Jeff was his brother. He hoped that wherever he was he was happy.

He also hoped he would stay away. He wanted Laura to himself. He knew it was selfish, but it seemed time for him to have some of the love he'd been craving for so long.

"Do you miss him?" he asked.

Her answer was awhile in coming, and tentative at that, as though she was testing thoughts she hadn't dared voice before. "At the beginning, I did. He was a companion. He listened to me. He gave me encouragement. He was always there. Then suddenly he wasn't, and it was strange." She paused. "Do I miss the day-to-day things he did?" Her voice grew sad. "There weren't many of those. He went to work, he took me out at night, he paid the household bills. That was it. I took care of the kids and ran the house and my business. The kids said it early on—he made more of an impact on our lives being gone than being there. It took me awhile to see that." She raised her head. "Why did it take me so long?"

"You didn't want to see it."

"But why?"

"Loyalty. Respect. Habit. Maybe even love."

The idea hung in the air, seeming out of place amid the lingering scent of passion that rose from the bed.

"Did you love him?" Christian asked, needing to know that most of all.

She dropped her chin to his chest. "I thought I did."

"Did you love him when you married him?"

"I wanted to. I told myself I did."

"Did you?"

"Not the way I loved you," she said with sudden clarity. "What you and I had was hot and exciting and spontaneous. What I had with Jeff lacked that passion."

"And you were prepared to live without it?"

"I didn't know it was missing. I didn't make comparisons. I didn't allow myself to. Maybe I didn't dare. But Jeff was there, he loved me, and he wanted to get married, and that meant I could drop out of school and be free of my mother, and I wanted that above all else."

"That much?"

"That much. I was the older daughter. She wanted me to be brilliant. She wanted me to achieve. She wanted me to perform. She had visions of my walking in her footsteps. But I didn't want to go in that direction. Her life scared the hell out of me. It was cold and analytical. I didn't want any part of it."

"I'm surprised you enrolled in college at all."

"She made me."

"Will you make Debra?"

Laura was quiet for a long time. Finally, in a voice filled with self-doubt, she said, "I want the best for her. Is that wrong?"

"In theory, no. But you define the best from your perspective. Your perspective isn't necessarily Debra's."

"Am I like Maddie, then?"

"You take the best of her—the intelligence and the dedication—and add things she lacks, like warmth and compassion."

"I don't listen. Debra tells me that. Actually, I do listen, but I don't hear; that's what Maddie always did."

"You lead a busy life," Christian said. "I'd put money on the fact that you hear a whole lot more than Maddie ever did. Okay, so you may not hear everything. What mother does?"

"Debra's been angry since Jeff left."

"That's understandable."

"I haven't dealt with it the way I should."

"That's understandable too. You've had a few things on your own mind. Now that Scott's back at school free and clear, you can give Debra more time."

"I will," she vowed. "I definitely will."

He smiled at the determination in her voice, loving her for that on top of everything else.

"Do you think about your father much?" Laura asked. It was Friday night, and other than running out for groceries they had done little but sleep and make love for two whole days. On this night, they had finally dressed and gone out to dinner. They were back now, standing in the dark, looking out over the valley, which was moonlit and lovely. Christian's arms were around her. Resting back against him, she felt indecently happy.

"I think about him," he admitted.

"Often?"

"Often enough."

"Do you want to find out who he is?"

"Sure I do, but my mother won't tell, my birth certificate can't tell, and Bill is past the point of telling, which means that the only ones who know are Lydia and the man himself. If he hasn't come forward in forty-seven years, I doubt if he will now."

Laura hated to think that. Letting her imagination roam, she said, "He has to be at least as old as Lydia, if not older. Maybe he's sick. Maybe he's staring his own mortality in the face. People see things differently when that happens."

"There you go," Christian said with a smile in his voice, "painting pretty pictures again."

"But it could be, Christian. Maybe you should hire an investigator."

"I thought of that, but the only way an investigator would learn anything is through talking with people who knew my mother forty-seven years ago. I can't go behind her back that way."

"Since you told me about him, I've been looking at men who might be the right age and wondering."

"You think I don't? You think I don't get absolutely furious that some guy doesn't care to make contact with his own son? I mean, hell, I can keep a confidence. It's not like I'd run to the *Sun* with his identity. And I wouldn't be demanding money. I have plenty of my own. I'd like to know for me: nothing else, just for me."

Laura tried to imagine herself in his place and knew she would feel the same. "Are you still angry at Lydia?"

"Sometimes, when I'm alone. It's hard to sustain anger when I see her. She's old and frail. I feel sorry for her. Whoever he was, she loved him, but she gave up that love for something she felt was safer and more lasting. Bill wasn't an exciting man. He was reliable and constant."

"Like Jeff," Laura said and shivered. She layered her arms more snugly over his as they circled her waist. "History repeats itself, doesn't it? Only I have a second chance." Feeling sudden urgency, she turned and coiled her arms around his neck. "I'm divorcing Jeff. As soon as we get back, I'm filing papers. I'm not losing you again, Christian. I don't want to end up like Maddie, with a wonderful career and no companion, or like Lydia, with nothing but distant memories."

"You could end up alone anyway. I could die in five years."

"Don't say that."

"It's true."

"Your mother is seventy-three, and your father is probably older."

"I could still die."

"Or I could. But at least we'd have the time until then. I want that time, Christian. Don't you?"

His answer came in his kiss, which consumed her from the inside out, and in the arms that held her as though they would never let her go.

"What would you say if I told you I was thinking of closing the restaurant?" Laura asked.

Christian shot her a sidelong glance. "I'd say you were looking for me to argue you out of it, which is exactly what I'd do." It was Monday evening, and they were on their way back to Northampton. She was sitting as close to him as she could without actually being on his lap, which was pretty much an extension of how they'd spent the past five days. They hadn't been out of each other's reach for more than a few minutes at a stretch. He couldn't get enough of her, be it touching, talking, just looking, or making love. He was totally smitten, but not so much—never so much—that he wouldn't give her his honest opinion. "You've worked your butt off to get that place established. It's a good restaurant, and it has a loyal following."

"Business is lousy. We're struggling."

"Only in comparison to how it was before. I've seen your books, Laura, so I know. You've been growing since you opened. Now you've leveled off—but no worse, which is really remarkable. Give it a little time. The publicity will die down. People will forget about Jeff, but their stomachs will always rumble. You can give it a promotional push, and things will pick up. You love that restaurant."

Her fingers moved along the inseam of his jeans in a way that would have driven him wild if she'd known what she was doing. But he doubted she did. Her mind was elsewhere.

"It's all-consuming, the restaurant is," she complained. "It takes so much time and effort. I don't want to work evenings or weekends, not with you around."

"In another month, I'll be working myself."

"Not on weekends. That may be the only time we can see each other. If I closed the restaurant, I could concentrate on catering and be picky about when I work. I could drive up on weekends, or you could drive down, or we could meet somewhere. Southern Vermont has some adorable country inns—"

He squeezed her hand to cut her off. "You're frightened because we're heading back to Northampton and you don't know if things will be the same for us there, but they will, Laura. I won't spend the night in your bed, because Debra isn't ready for it, but we'll still be together."

She released a breath against his throat. "That's what I want."

"Then we'll do it. Without any elaborate arrangements. We'll just be together, and we'll take things day by day."

He thought about what she'd said about divorcing Jeff. One part of him wanted that more than anything. Another part felt the same guilt he had felt over the years, lusting after his brother's wife. Granted, his relationship with Laura had gone past the "lusting after" stage. Still, Jeff was a part of their lives.

"I want to talk to Tack Jones," he said. "There must be

something more we can do about finding Jeff."

"I'm still filing for divorce," she insisted. "I couldn't ever live with him again. Not after what he did to me. Not after what he did to the kids. If he chooses to be lost, why not let him stay that way?"

"Because even if you divorce him, he's still the father of your children. He's still under indictment on multiple counts of tax fraud. There's still a cloud hanging over all our heads."

"If they find him, try him, and convict him, it'll be worse."

"But at least there'll be an end to it. Debra and Scott will know where their father is. They'll be able to see him. Maybe he'll even be able to give them an explanation for what he's done. Maybe he can give you one too."

"It won't change my mind."

"I know, but it'll give finality to this whole thing, and that's what we need. We need to put it behind us, Laura, and the only way we can do that is to find Jeff."

Jeff pulled up in front of Glorie's house and reached across the cab of the pickup to wake her gently. She was so tired that he hated to do it, but he knew tomorrow would be just as long as today had been, and she needed rest. "We're here, Glorie." He pushed the big wool hat higher on her forehead. "Come on, honey. Wake up."

She opened her eyes and looked at him with a total absence of recognition for a minute, before his face finally registered. A smile came. In the next instant, sadness returned to her eyes and the smile dissolved. She gathered herself, frowned, and reached for the door handle.

Jeff was out of the truck and around to help her before she could get more than one foot on the ground. Holding her hand as they walked to the house, he said, "Poppy will be okay, Glorie. He's getting very good care at the hospital."

"He doesn't look very good."

Jeff wouldn't have said it as gently. Poppy looked like hell.

Most people with lung cancer did, especially when the cancer had spread to the brain. The prognosis wasn't good, though Glorie didn't know that. She was still trying to deal with Poppy's being sick.

"He'll look better tomorrow," Jeff assured her. "You'll see. He'll have a good night's sleep tonight." That was for sure. The pain medication they gave him was knocking him out cold.

"When is he coming home?" she asked in the same frightened voice she'd used to ask that question at regular intervals throughout the day.

"Only the doctors know that. Maybe they'll tell us tomorrow." He opened the front door and drew her inside. The door was barely closed behind them when a whale of a woman waddled into the hall. Hannah Mack lived next door. Jeff found her more laconic than most, but she was a worker. Her husband was a fisherman, and when she wasn't repairing his nets or traps, she was baking bread for the local pastor or anyone else in need. With Poppy in the hospital, Glorie was in need. Hannah had been staying at night with her, so that she wouldn't be frightened and alone.

"Hello, Mrs. Mack," Jeff said, then sniffed the air. "You've been cooking. Something smells wonderful." Turning to Glorie, he began to unwind the scarf from her neck. "What do you think it is?" he asked softly.

Glorie's eyes were woeful, but she went along with the game. "Stew?"

He weighed that possibility as he pulled the hat from her head. "I think it has tomato sauce in it."

"Spaghetti?" she guessed.

He unbuttoned her coat. "Wider than spaghetti. Is that cheese I smell too?"

A drop of enthusiasm joined the sadness in her eyes. "Lasagna?"

He grinned. "That'd be my guess." He was a pretty good guesser when it came to food. He'd had lots of practice. "Should we ask her?"

"Is it lasagna, Mrs. Mack?" Glorie asked.

On his way to hang Glorie's things on a peg by the door, Jeff saw the woman nod. "She likes that," he said. "Thank you."

Glorie was suddenly by his side again, whispering. "I'm not very hungry."

"But you haven't eaten all day. You have to have something, Glorie. You have to stay strong for Poppy."

Her eyes filled with tears. "I'm so scared."

He put an arm around her and said by her ear, "There's nothing to be scared of. Mrs. Mack is staying the night, and I'll be right here in the morning to take you back to Poppy."

"Will you stay now? Please? You have to eat too."

She looked so forlorn, and so eager, that he glanced at Mrs. Mack. "Is there enough?"

"More'n."

So he stayed. He ate lasagna with them in the kitchen, making sure that Glorie had a fair amount. When she seemed reluctant to have him leave even then, he sat in the living room and read her an article from one of her *National Geographics*. He had done that before when he'd been at the house. She loved being read to, and he loved doing the reading. It was peaceful and rewarding—so much so that he kept several books just for her in a pile by his own books. When she came to his place, which Poppy allowed her to do on weekends, he read to her there. She listened with rapt attention, understanding most everything, though when he coaxed her into reading an occasional paragraph herself, it was a struggle. So he pampered her and was rewarded by her bright smiles of appreciation.

On this particular night, she was so sleepy when he finished reading that she went right to bed. Driving back to his place, he thought about her. The doctors had given Poppy no more than a few months to live. Jeff didn't know what Glorie would do without him. Neither did Poppy.

"I'm worried," he rasped each time Glorie stepped out of the hospital room. He didn't have to elaborate. Glorie depended on him to direct her life. She could take care of herself when it came to dressing and grooming and she could even cook, as long as the food was in the house. Small, carefully defined tasks, such as waitressing at the diner, were no problem for her. More creative tasks that involved organizational skills were harder.

Poppy had been failing for a while. After developing a chronic cough the year before, he had stopped smoking, but the doctors suspected that his cancer had been well entrenched by then. They also suspected that he had tried to will himself well by ignoring the symptoms, to no avail. He was increasingly tired and weak, and his cough worsened. On Sundays, when the diner was closed, he didn't move from the house. His motor skills had grown sluggish shortly after New Year's, and then, the Wednesday before, he had collapsed at the diner.

Jeff had been there at the time. While two of the men had taken Poppy to the hospital, he and a third stayed to keep the diner open. Between them, they managed to serve up the food Poppy had already prepared. They also managed to grill burgers, hot dogs, and bacon and fry up potatoes—all of which Jeff still found incredible. He had never cooked in his life. But someone had to do the work or the diner would close, making things ten times worse for Poppy than they already were and a hundred times worse for Glorie.

Jeff had worked at the diner every day that week. Falling into a pattern, he took Glorie to the hospital for a morning visit, then again for one late in the day, and in between she waitressed and he cooked. There was usually someone with him who knew more about cooking than he did, but he paid attention and learned quickly, so that by Monday he had made the stew all on his own. More so even than fixing up the cottage, that was an accomplishment.

If Laura could see him, she'd die, he decided, as he pulled up on the bluff. Her jaw would drop. She would stare in utter amazement. In no time, she'd be thinking about ways to spruce up the diner, make the menu more sophisticated, and bring in new customers, all of which would be inappropriate and un-realistic, and he'd tell her so. He'd tell her that he liked the simplicity of the menu because it reflected the simplicity of the people, and he didn't want new customers, because that would mean more work, and he rather liked the slower pace of this life, compared to the old one. He also liked the fact that he could handle it all on his own. Glorie and Poppy were depending on him, and he was coming through for them, which felt good. The people in town accepted him, particularly since Poppy had been sick. He was defining his days in ways that weren't so bad, for a man on the run.

He missed Scott and Debra. There were times when he thought of them and felt wretched. No doubt they thought the worst of him now, and he supposed he deserved it. He wished he could explain why he'd done what he had. He wished he could tell them what he'd found.

But they wouldn't understand. They were Laura's children. Scott had the same spirit of adventure Laura did, and Debra, for all her vows to the contrary, would grow up to do something constructive whether she went to college or not. They didn't need him. They never had.

Still, he thought about them.

Putting the truck in reverse, he backed out, drove down the hill again, and eastward for a bit until he came to a deserted phone booth. He hadn't used this one before. He was careful that way. After dialing the number and pumping coins into the slot, he waited. It was nearly nine-thirty. She was bound to be home.

After the second ring, she answered. She sounded different—either breathless or sleepy, he didn't know which—not quite the composed woman he'd always known.

"Hi," he said.

She was quiet for a minute. Then, in a voice that was definitely breathless and unusually high, she said, "Oh, hi. Listen, this is a really bad time. Can I call you back another day?"

She recognized his voice. He was sure of it. He had the feeling she was with someone, which was different too. He wondered who.

"Great," she said when he didn't respond. "Talk with you then."

She hung up before he could this time. Slowly he returned to the truck and drove off.

twenty-seven

LAURA AND CHRISTIAN ARRIVED IN NORTH-
ampton shortly before ten. On the kitchen island was a note from
Maddie saying that Debra was with friends and Maddie had
gone home.

Holding the note with its familiar handwriting brought back
memories for Laura. "When I was growing up, Maddie always
had somewhere to go. Sometimes my father was around, sometimes he wasn't, but in any case, she left a note. I guess she felt
that as long as she left that note, she was excused." Laura leaned
against Christian, who was by her shoulder. "I should call and
thank her for staying with Debra, but her voice grates on me.
I hate to spoil a nice evening."

"Call her now," Christian said in a deep, slow voice. "I'll
make the evening nice again."

Feeling feminine and warm, she smiled. Then she looked up
at him. "How do you plan to do that with Debra due in any
minute?"

His eyes were full of mischief. "We could do some laundry
down in the cellar."

Laura shook her head.

"Photograph cobwebs in the attic?"

She had been the one to insist he return with his camera. Still,
she shook her head.

"Okay," he allowed, "no making love. How about I follow you around and feel y'up a little each time we turn a corner?"

She laughed. It was such a light sound, so refreshing in that room after so many weeks of unhappiness there, that she nearly laughed again. "You're incorrigible."

"Just a kiss then. That'd make the evening nice." He gave her a sneak preview, something that was whisper-light and tormenting. "Go on, Laura. Call her and get it over with."

Purely for the sake of the "get it over with" part, Laura called. "Hi, Mom, it's me. We just walked in. I want to thank you—"

"You're later than I thought you'd be," Maddie interrupted in a strident voice. "It's a good thing I didn't wait around. Honestly, Laura, you surprise me. You know it's a school night. Didn't you think I'd want to get home?"

Having relinquished responsibility for the weekend, Laura hadn't thought of it at all. Now that she did, she didn't see a problem. "You did the right thing. There was no need for you to hang around. Was Debra much trouble?"

"How could she be trouble when I rarely saw her? She got up in the morning in time to race out to school, and she was with her friends most every afternoon and evening. We had dinner together twice. She claims that's about all she eats with you in an average week." More softly, though no less stridently, she said, "Is that true, Laura?"

"It's more like three or four times a week, Mother, which is par for the course when it comes to teenagers. That's more often than Gretchen and I had dinner with you."

"I was working. I wasn't running around with my brother-in-law. Laura, what is going on? According to Debra, you've been cozying up to Christian ever since he walked in that door."

"Big mistake," Laura whispered to Christian. "I shouldn't have called."

Christian hooked an elbow around her neck and drew her close.

Maddie went on. "Debra may not have gone through quite the trauma Scott did in court, but she's at a vulnerable age. First, her father deserts her. Then her mother does."

"I didn't desert her," Laura argued, in part to clue Christian in to the conversation. "I simply went away for the weekend."

"With a man who has been an annoyance at every family gathering he ever deigned to attend. Even apart from the dubious merits of Christian Frye as a father figure, there's still the matter of your behavior. It's inappropriate, Laura. You're a married woman."

"Jeff and I are separated. I'll be filing for divorce this week."

"Because of Christian?"

"Because of Jeff. Whatever I had with him is gone. He ran out on me, and before he did that, he was leading a whole other life from the one I saw. Obviously, what he and I had wasn't real."

"You thought it was."

"That's right, but we all live and learn."

"Are you learning? It looks to me as though you're acting on the rebound, trying to compensate for the hurt Jeff caused you by taking up with his brother."

"Not quite," Laura said in a confident tone.

"Are you hoping Jeff will find out and be hurt right back?"

"That's the last thing on my mind."

"Feelings of anger and the desire for revenge are perfectly normal, Laura. You don't have to be ashamed of them."

"I'm not." Laura looked at Christian and grinned.

"Then you do admit to feeling them?"

"Anger, yes. Revenge, no. Any other questions?"

Maddie let one fly with barely a pause. "Are you so desperate for a man that you grab the first one that comes along? Honestly, Laura, I knew you were a nurturer. You proved that when you dropped out of school so young to bury yourself in wifedom and motherhood—"

"That's called throwing oneself into the job and doing it well."

"—but it never occurred to me that you did it for security reasons. Are you *afraid* to be without a man?"

"Of course not."

"Yet you insist on defining yourself in terms of a man. Why do you do that? You're a strong woman. Jeff could never quite rise to your level. So now he's gone, and you're free. Why do you feel a compulsion instantly to tie yourself to someone else? I'll tell you something, Laura. Your father's death was the best thing that ever happened to me."

The indulgence Laura had been feeling faded. She had loved her soft-spoken, instrospective father. "That's an awful thing to say."

"It's the truth. He slowed me down, just like Jeff did you. They were alike, your father and Jeff."

"No," Laura said carefully. "My father was honest and faithful. In that sense, he was totally different from Jeff."

"They were both weak men. Is Christian any different?"

"Christian is very different." Laura met his gaze. "He's strong. He has his own life and knows his own mind. No one tells him where to go and what to do."

"And you like that kind of man?"

"I *love* that kind of man."

There was a brief silence. "Don't you think you're getting a little carried away?"

"I think I'm getting a lot carried away," Laura replied with a smug grin for Christian.

"Get hold of yourself, Laura. Think of your children. Think of your future."

"That's exactly what I'm doing."

After another brief silence, Maddie said, "Are you seriously contemplating a future with Christian Frye?"

"Finally, yes."

"What is that supposed to mean?"

Laura took a breath. Slipping an arm around Christian's neck, she sank her fingers into the hair that lay thick against the collar of his turtleneck sweater. "Did you know that I knew Christian before I ever knew Jeff? Did you know that I was in love with Christian before I ever knew Jeff? Did you know that I begged Christian to marry me, but he wouldn't?"

Maddie sounded appalled. "You *begged* him? How old were you at this time?" she demanded.

"Eighteen, and I wanted to get married. Christian wasn't ready but Jeff was, so I married *him*. You can analyze that all you want, Mother, but the fact is I was happy with the decision. I raised two terrific kids and had a rewarding life, and I didn't let myself dwell on what might have been wrong in my relationship with Jeff."

"All along, I told you—"

"What was wrong, yes, you did, and I didn't listen, because you've *always* told me what was wrong. All my life I've heard about what I do wrong. It gets tiresome, Mom. When you never hear the good and always hear the bad, you begin to tune out, because the constant criticism is destructive. So I didn't hear what you were saying about my relationship with Jeff, and even if I'd heard it I probably wouldn't have believed it. I was too busy living my life to pick it apart piece by piece." She might have left it there, but she was on a roll. "I've done that now. All those hours waiting for Jeff to come back, wondering where he was and why he was gone—I had time to think. Little by little, things became clear, things that had nothing whatsoever to do with Christian. The fundamental problem with my marriage was that I did overshadow Jeff, and he allowed it. Christian will never do that." She clutched a fistful of his hair to keep from drowning in his blue-eyed gaze. "I love him."

"You're making another mistake, Laura. You'll be compromising yourself if you marry a man like that."

"I'll be enriching myself," Laura corrected.

"You don't need him. You and I are cut of the same cloth. We're strong women."

"Yes, and I'm even stronger when I'm with Christian."

"All right. Look at it this way. If he was the man for you, you would have waited for him, instead of rushing off to marry Jeff."

"I might have waited if I'd had a little advice from you." She slid her hand to Christian's shoulder and lowered her eyes to focus on the discussion with Maddie. "But even if you and I had had that kind of relationship—which we didn't—you were nowhere to be seen. When I finally got to college, you were thrilled. One down, one to go. You wanted your freedom."

"I never said that."

"You didn't have to." Many years had passed, yet the hurt remained. "Everything else you did made it clear that your own interests came first. There was never any question about it. You weren't around to know what I was thinking or feeling. You didn't have the time to care."

"I cared," Maddie contended. "And who are you to criticize me? It doesn't look like you're doing things terribly differently with your own daughter. You have a business that keeps you busy and a lover who takes you away. A paragon of motherhood you are not."

Laura scowled. "Anything I know about mothering, I learned from you."

"You certainly didn't learn this lack of respect from me."

"No? I'm an adult, Mother. I've been one for a long time. When did you ever respect *me*?"

"I'll respect you when you start acting like a responsible human being. Running off with your brother-in-law for the weekend was not responsible. Do you think people haven't seen you around town with him? Do you think they aren't talking?"

"Christian is my brother-in-law. He's family. He's here to help me. If people don't understand that, screw them."

"Now, that's an adult response."

"It's an honest one," Laura said. "I don't really give a damn about what people are saying. They've already thought the worst of us, and we were vindicated in one instance, at least. We'll be vindicated in others, and in the meantime I have no intention of playing either the grieving widow or the martyr. Christian is here, and I love him. When I was eighteen, I couldn't appreciate what that meant. I'm older now, and believe me, I'm not passing it up."

"You're hopeless," Maddie said in disgust.

"Thank you," Laura said, as though she'd just received the compliment of a lifetime.

"I won't talk with you when you're this way. When you feel you can relate with me in a productive way, call."

"Fine. But answer me one question now. If you feel so strongly that what I'm doing with Christian is wrong, why did you ever agree to stay with Debra?"

"Because I need a new roof. Remind Christian of that, please," Maddie said and hung up the phone.

Christian did his best to salvage the evening after the phone call to Maddie, but his efforts ran into a snag. By the time Laura had vented the worst of her anger, it was eleven and Debra still wasn't home. Concerned, particularly since it was a school night, Laura called Jenna.

"She's not here, Mrs. Frye."

"Do you know where she is?"

"No, I don't."

That did nothing for Laura's peace of mind, since Jenna was Debra's best friend. She phoned several lesser friends, but the answer was the same. When eleven-fifteen came and went, then eleven-thirty, Laura was nervous enough to risk Debra's wrath by calling Jace Holzworth.

He sounded more nervous than she felt, which only heightened her worry. "Oh, hi, Mrs. Frye. Yeah, I did see her earlier tonight."

"What time was that?"

"Uh, around eight. I was—uh, getting off work."

"How long were you with her?"

"Maybe half an hour, I guess. Then she—uh, took off in the Miata. I thought she went home."

"Did she call you after that?"

"No. No phone calls. Gee, I'm sorry I can't help you. Hey, if I hear from her, I'll tell her you're looking."

"Please do," Laura said and hung up the phone with a stricken look at Christian. "It's happening all over again. This is unreal. First Jeff, now Debra. What's going on?"

Christian glanced out the dining room window. "There she is." The words were immediately followed by the rumble of the garage door.

No longer one to trust that sound, Laura raced to the kitchen door and flung it open. The Miata was in one piece, which meant that Debra hadn't been hurt. When she stepped out of the car, though, she didn't look well at all. Totally aside from the defiance that Laura had half expected, she was frighteningly pale. More subtle, but no less recognizable to a mother, was the haunted look in her eyes.

Laura went right to her and gave her a tight hug. "It's so late, babe. I've been worried."

Debra tolerated the hug, neither returning nor rejecting it. "Worried about the car?"

"No." Laura held her back and studied her face. "About you. What's wrong?"

"Nothing." Freeing herself from Laura's hold, she went into the house. She passed Christian with only the briefest of glances. "The car's okay."

"I don't care about the car," he said. "We were afraid something had happened to you."

"Sure you were," Debra muttered, continuing on through the kitchen.

"Your mother's been calling all your friends."

Debra turned to Laura in dismay. "You didn't!"

"I did. None of them knew where you were."

"Why did you do that? They're *my* friends. What right do you have to call my friends?"

"I'm your mother. When eleven-thirty on a school night comes and goes and you're nowhere in sight, I have a right to be worried."

"You never have been before."

"You never stayed out like this before."

"How do you know?" Debra challenged. "How do you know what I'm doing when you stay late at the restaurant or go to a party?"

"You've always been home when I expected you to be."

"You ran off to Vermont with him"—she pushed her chin toward Christian—"and left me to fend for myself. So I was fending for myself."

"I left you with your grandmother."

"Same difference. She's just like you. She wasn't here half the time."

"She said *you* weren't."

"Because I didn't want to be here alone!" Whirling around, she strode toward the hall. "I'm going to bed."

"I think you should," Laura called after her, but her own words brought her up short. The argument was old and familiar, a replay of the one she'd had earlier with Maddie, which was a replay of dozens of others over the years. Maddie always grew indignant and either hung up or walked out. It struck Laura, in a moment of grand dismay, that she had done her share of that with Debra. Though Debra had done the walking this time, Laura's voice had certainly held the indignation.

Laura didn't want it to be that way.

Christian came to her side. "I'm a part of the problem. The Vermont trip was my idea. Let me talk with her."

Laura touched the back of her fingers to his neck, where his pulse was steady and strong. "I'll go," she whispered. "It's time."

Debra's door was shut. Laura knocked lightly, opened it, and went in. She closed the door behind her and leaned on the knob. Debra was on the floor with her back against the bed and her arms around her knees. At Laura's entrance, she turned away.

"Let's talk, Deb."

"It's late."

"So it'll be a little later when we're done. But this is important." When Debra didn't say anything, she tried a gentle question. "Where were you so late?"

"Driving around."

"Alone?"

"Yes."

"For two hours?"

"Three." Sullenly, Debra added, "Don't worry. I filled the car with gas."

"I wasn't worried about that. You're the one I care about, not the car. Why were you driving around alone for three hours?"

"Because I wanted to."

Laura couldn't see much beyond the defeated slope of her shoulders. "Did something happen in school?"

"No."

"With the kids after school?"

"No."

"With Jace."

"No!"

Laura didn't believe her. The no's had come too readily. Something was wrong, and it went beyond the anger Debra felt toward Christian and her. Anger would have made her belligerent, not defensive or defeated, as she seemed to be.

It used to be Debra came to her with her problems. It used to be she couldn't shut Debra up. She wished that were the case now. Getting her talking again was the first priority.

Coming to sit on the bed, not far from where Debra was slouched, she asked softly, "What's happened to us?"

"You tell me," Debra snapped. "You're the expert. If you need a second opinion, you can call Gram."

"I don't want to call Gram. I don't get along with her. We had a royal argument tonight, and we'll probably have another one next time we talk. We see things differently, which would be okay if we didn't let our emotions get in the way of common sense and compassion and understanding. It's sad, Deb. What's even more sad is that you and I could end up the same way. I don't want that. I want us to be close." Tentatively, she touched Debra's hair. "We have to talk, not argue. Things have been tough since your father left. We've been under intense pressure, and because of that, all the weaknesses in our relationship have come out. I haven't been a perfect mother. But it wasn't that I didn't want to be. I honestly thought I was doing things well. Now I see I wasn't."

She paused, waiting for a response. Debra was curled in a ball, with her knees drawn up, her hands buried in her lap, and her head in a slant against the side of the bed. Laura knew she wasn't asleep. Her body was too tense. She chose to believe she was listening.

Keeping her voice low and gentle in its urgency, she said, "I can change, Debra. If you tell me the things that bother you, I can change. I never realized you didn't like my working. I always thought you complained because all kids complain. But I can plan to be home more now, if that's what you want. You and I can do more together. If I'm doing something else, I'll stop and listen when you want to talk. I'll listen now. I'm not doing anything else. I'm not going anywhere."

Debra's voice was subdued. "Not to him?"

"Not to him. You're my daughter. Right now, you're my first obligation in this world. I'll sit here with you all night if you want. I'll stay here with you all day tomorrow if you want. Tell me what's bothering you, Deb. Let's talk it out."

Debra didn't say anything. One minute passed, then another and another. Laura stroked her long, dark hair with a touch that was light and slow, wordlessly telling her that she had all the time in the world. And it was true. By stealing her away for the weekend, Christian had broken the rhythm of the life she had been leading for so many months. She hadn't cooked, hadn't run from one place to the next accomplishing all the things an efficient person accomplished. He had slowed her down. He had shown her the pleasure of quiet times. She remembered that pleasure from when the children were little, when she had read them stories or held them close to talk, or rock, or sing. With the passage of the years, those times had been lost—not so much with Scott, but with Debra—and Laura missed them. She wanted them back.

Continuing that light, slow stroking, she said, "You can talk to me, babe. I won't criticize. I won't get up and walk away. I'm here for you now. You can tell me anything."

Still Debra didn't speak. When she hunched her shoulders and curled into an even tighter ball, Laura felt more helpless than ever. By the time the first of the soft sounds of crying came, she was through staying at a distance. Sliding to her knees on the floor, she wrapped her arms around Debra and drew her close. She encountered no resistance, either then or when she began to rock her, just as she had years before, holding her tightly while she cried.

"What is it, babe?" Laura whispered. "You can tell me."

"It's awful," Debra sobbed.

"Nothing is that awful."

"This is. I did the stupidest thing."

"We all do stupid things sometimes."

"But this was so dumb! I hated it, and it hurt, but it's done now and I can't ever go back."

Frightening things ran through Laura's mind. She kept up the rocking, rubbing an arm, then a shoulder, putting her cheek to Debra's temple and whispering, "It'll be okay. It'll be okay."

"But I feel so awful!" Debra whispered back between sobs.

Laura held her tighter. "You'll feel better. Give it time, and you will. Nothing stays that awful for long."

"I'll never be the same again."

"You'll be better. Older and wiser. Whatever it is, babe, we'll work it out." When Debra made a sound that was more moan than sigh, Laura wondered if she were in physical pain. "What can I do for you, Deb? I feel so helpless."

"You can't do anything. No one can."

"Talk to me. Tell me more."

All she heard for the next several minutes was the sound of soft weeping. Then, nearly as softly, came a muffled "You'll hate me. You'll be so disappointed."

"I'll love you anyway, regardless of what happened. That's what love's about, babe. It's about accepting weaknesses along with the strengths. It's about forgiving mistakes."

"You stopped loving Daddy when he did what he did."

Laura stopped rocking. "What I felt for him was very different from what I feel for you."

"Didn't you love him?"

"I thought I did."

Debra was the one who started to rock this time. "I thought I loved Jace," she said in a pitifully broken voice, but once she started, the words kept coming. "I thought he was the coolest, nicest, best-looking guy in school, and I thought he thought I was cool too. I could tell him anything. I mean, I told him about what was happening here, and he understood, he really did. Then you went away, and Gram was here, and she's so hard to be with that I went down to the yogurt shop every night to be with Jace. Whenever he got a break, he sat with me, and when he was done with work, we'd drive somewhere and park."

She hiccuped. Laura reached for a tissue from the nightstand and pressed it into her hand.

"I'd get in his car, 'cause the Miata has bucket seats, and we'd talk and kiss, and it was nice. Then, on Saturday night, we went to a movie, and afterward he took me back to his house. His parents were away, and he wanted to do more than kiss."

Laura felt a hollowness in the pit of her stomach. She tucked Debra's hair behind her ear, just like she used to do when she was little. Those were such innocent times. The children were small, the problems were small. Such innocent times.

"I didn't want to go all the way," Debra went on, "and I told him that. So he said we wouldn't, that we'd just touch and all." She stopped abruptly. "It's gross, telling you this."

"Why is it gross?" Laura asked gently. "Do you think I don't know what touching's about?"

"How old were you when you did it?"

"Touched? About your age, I guess."

"How old were you when you went all the way?"

"A little older." Holding Debra as tightly as ever, she rocked her again. One part of her didn't want to ask, didn't want to know, but it was the cowardly part. "Is that what happened at Jace's?"

Debra started crying again.

"It's okay, honey. It's not the end of the world."

"Nothing happened on Saturday night," Debra managed between gulping sobs. "I told him I didn't want to. I just didn't want to. He said I didn't love him enough. I tried to explain what I was feeling, but he wouldn't listen. He wouldn't see me last night, and then I got to school today and heard that he'd been out with Kara Hutchinson."

"Oh, babe."

The tears started flowing again, but the words wouldn't stop. "Kara Hutchinson is a total space shot. Jace is too good for her. I went to see him tonight when he got off work, and I told him that. And he said he didn't care, that if I didn't love him he'd find someone who would. I said I *did* love him, and he told me to prove it, and I didn't know what to do."

Laura remembered the phone conversation she'd had with Jace not so long before. He had sounded nervous, and no wonder. She hoped he was scared to death.

In a smaller voice, Debra said, "I didn't know what to do. All I could think about was that Scott did it all the time, and you were probably doing it with Christian, and lots of girls I know do it, so it couldn't be all that bad. Jace had a condom. So I let him." The crying was quieter, almost internal and, in that, more disturbing.

Laura closed her eyes and rested her head on Debra's. She might have cried herself if it would have done any good. But the damage had been done. The loss of innocence was far more than physical. "Oh, babe," she whispered again.

"See? You are disappointed."

"Not the way you think. I'm disappointed because what should have been wonderful wasn't. Lovemaking should be a very beautiful experience. I'm sorry it wasn't that way for you."

"Jace said there's something wrong with me."

Taking Debra's face in her hands, Laura forced it up. Looking her straight in the eye, she said, "Jace Holzworth knows about as much about you as he does about making love. He's a boy, Debra, just a boy. He blackmailed you into doing something you didn't want, then he didn't even know how to make it good. That's *his* problem. There's nothing wrong with you. You're a normal young woman who simply made the mistake of jumping the gun and doing something she wasn't ready for."

"When will I be ready for it?"

"When you're older. When the right man comes along."

"I thought Jace was the right man."

"You wanted him to be," Laura said, brushing at Debra's tears with her thumbs, "and I suppose that's part of being sixteen. Then again, maybe it's my fault. I do love you, Debra. I may not have shown it the way you wanted me to, but I do love you."

"Dad doesn't. If he did, he would have written or called."

"That's not necessarily true. He may be afraid that if he calls or writes, someone will find out where he is, and he doesn't want that to happen."

"I miss him."

"I know you do."

"Do you miss him?"

"I miss what we all had together."

"But you don't miss him, because you have Christian."

Laura searched her eyes for resentment. Her voice held it,

though it was nowhere near as strong as it had been before. Laura was grateful for the improvement, but she knew it wouldn't continue unless she could be honest. "What I have with Christian is completely different from what I had with your father."

"Is it better?"

"It's healthier, I think. Christian is his own man. He's successful and confident. I can give him things, but I can't take over; he's too strong for that."

"Do you love him?"

There was no doubt about that in Laura's mind, but she was uncomfortable saying it to Debra, just as she was uncomfortable telling her about her relationship with Christian twenty-one years before. Debra's emotions were too raw. She needed time to adjust. Then again, maybe they would *never* be able to discuss those early days without impugning Laura's relationship with Jeff, and Jeff would always be Debra's father. Some things were better left unsaid, Laura knew. Still, she couldn't lie outright. "I think I could love him, once we get things straightened out."

"Are you going to marry him?"

"I'm not free to do that."

"You could be. You could divorce Dad."

Laura searched her tear-streaked face. "Do you think I should?"

"No. I want Dad back here with us. But you don't."

"It's not that I don't want him to come back," Laura tried to explain, "it's that I don't think it will happen. Even if it does, I don't think it would work. Too much has happened since your father left. I've learned a lot about him and a lot about myself. I'm not the person I was before. Neither is your father." She paused. "I'm not rushing into anything, Deb. I want us to get back on track." She kissed Debra's forehead, then brought her against her again. "I feel so bad about tonight."

Debra didn't answer, but for the first time, she slipped her arms around Laura's waist.

"Are you hurting?" Laura whispered.

"Not much."

"A little?"

Debra nodded.

"Want to use my Jacuzzi?"

After a pause, she nodded again.

As Laura continued stroking her daughter's hair, she couldn't ignore the irony of the situation. Scott had been charged with rape for doing nothing and had been put through hell because of it. Debra, who had come far closer to being raped than Megan Tucker ever had, couldn't even raise the charge. The unfairness infuriated Laura, but she knew that fury wasn't what Debra needed.

"It'll be better one day," she said softly. "When the time is right and the man is right, you'll know what it means to make love. Believe me, you will."

Debra was silent, but she made no move to free herself from Laura's hold. Laura saw that as a good sign and clung to it.

twenty-eight

CHRISTIAN HAD NEVER FELT THE RESPONsibility for another person that he felt for Laura. His relationship with Gaby had been one of two people leading very different lives, coming together for pleasure, then parting. Even when Gaby had been so sick, what he felt had been more compassion than responsibility, and what he had felt for other women over the years had fallen short of both.

With Laura it was different. She was a strong woman, but vulnerable in ways Gaby had never been. He liked it when she smiled at him, when she leaned against him for the pleasure of the closeness or raised her face for his kiss. He felt more of a man with her than he had ever felt, and that made him want to smooth over the rough edges Jeff had left in her life, to make things better than ever.

He could do that for her in Vermont. She had told him as much during the intimate hours they had spent there. Whether he could do it for her in Northampton remained to be seen. Debra kept him at a cautious distance. He had done what he could for Scott, but Scott was back at school. He could help out at Cherries, but the truth was that Laura ran it well. He had no wish to be a major player there and take anything away from the pride that she felt.

That left him two major objectives. The first, and most critical in the long run, was to find Jeff. To that end, first thing Tuesday morning he paid Tack a visit.

"You think we aren't trying?" Tack said when Christian dared suggest the government wasn't doing enough.

"I think maybe the investigation's gone stale. It's been ten weeks of nothing. We need a fresh approach. I'm hiring a private investigator."

"If the FBI couldn't come up with anything, a private investigator won't."

"Is that you talking or Daphne?" Christian knew something was going on between Tack and Daphne, though he wasn't sure just what. He did know that every time he mentioned hiring an investigator, Daphne vetoed the idea.

"It's me talking, you asshole, and only because I want to save you some money. The guy working with me is good. So's his team. If they couldn't find your brother, maybe he doesn't want to be found."

Christian studied the calluses on his right hand. "Jeff broke a window once when he was a kid, couldn't have been more than six or seven at the time. It was an accident. We were having a snowball fight, and his aim wasn't so hot. One look at that broken window, and he panicked. Took off like a shot, ran halfway across town to an old gardening shed, and nearly froze to death. I looked all over for him, but I couldn't find him, and then I got the blame for the window *and* for his being lost. They finally found him late that night. He was scared shitless."

"What's your point?"

Christian dropped his hand to his side. "Maybe Jeff wants to be found but doesn't have the courage to turn himself in. Maybe he's miserable wherever he is. Maybe he's crying for help somewhere, only there's no one around to hear." All those things had been true that time when they'd been kids. Sucker that he was, even in spite of the beating Christian had taken on his account, he had felt sorry for Jeff. Some of that same feeling remained.

Tack drew a bow across an imaginary violin.

"Damn it, Jones, it's possible."

"Possible but not probable. He's a big boy now. If he's miserable enough, he can go to the nearest phone booth and call home. Since he's not doing that, we have to assume he's not so miserable."

"How long are we supposed to go on wondering where he is?" Finality was the operative word. Divorce or no divorce, if he and Laura were ever to build a life together, they had to close the book on her time with Jeff.

"You may wonder forever," Tack warned. "If a clever man wants to stay hidden, he stays hidden. Any dick will tell you that."

"Maybe. But I have to try."

Tack shrugged. "It's your money."

Christian was aware of that, but he didn't care. He had the money. And the cause was worth it. Still, there was a reason why he had sought Tack out. "You could save me some money and a whole lot of time by sharing your information with the person I hire."

"The Agency may not be wild about that idea."

"There are lots of ideas the Agency may not be wild about, including the one that you were out in Tahiti playin' around with my friends. Can't you do this for me, Tack?" Christian pushed.

Tack looked torn. For a minute, Christian thought he would raise the issue of questionable tax deductions, but he didn't. "What the hell," he finally said. "I'll get you what I can. It's in my best interest too, I suppose. I'm getting flack from the Boston office."

"They don't think you're doing enough?"

"They don't think what I'm doing merits my hanging around here."

"Does it?"

"Technically, no." Tack leveled him a challenging stare. "But I like it here."

Christian rose to the challenge. "It or her?"

After a minute, Tack said, "Same difference."

"She's a great lawyer."

"She's a great lady."

"She knows how to drive. She'll visit you in Boston."

"I want more," Tack said, again with a challenging look. "Think she'd consider moving there?"

"How would I know?"

"You've known her for years."

"Barely. Have you asked her?"

"Not yet."

"Maybe you should."

"Yeah."

"Wondering is the pits, isn't it? It's lousy not to know what's going through a woman's mind—or a brother's."

Tack regarded him for a minute longer before his expression turned droll. Reaching for a pen, he scrawled something on a pad of paper near the phone, ripped off the top piece, and passed it over. "If you're bent on doing it, do it right. This guy is the best in the business. If he can't find your fuckin' brother, no one can."

Christian arranged a meeting with the man, and while that meeting was pending, he looked to his second objective. Showing up unannounced late Tuesday morning at the offices of the *Hampshire County Sun*, he demanded an audience with Gary Holmes. When word came back that Holmes was out of town, he settled for Duggan O'Neil.

"I'd like an explanation for this," Christian said, tossing a copy of the weekend paper onto O'Neil's cluttered desk. In clear sight was an article O'Neil had written as a follow-up to those that had covered the dismissal of charges against Scott. Tucked inside was Gary Holmes's editorial. Both suggested that Scott had gotten away with murder. "Is there a personal vendetta going on here that we don't know about?"

Duggan O'Neil was of medium height and wire thin. His clothes hung loosely on him, giving him a rumpled look in keeping with the mess on his desk. Only the computer screen and keyboard looked well tuned, which was deceptive, Christian knew. He had no doubt that Duggan O'Neil's mind was razor sharp.

"Personal vendetta?" O'Neil repeated in an innocent way.

"Against the Frye family. Since Jeffrey disappeared, you people have been on his case. Scott Frye never would have been accused of rape if it hadn't been for the articles you've written. My God, man—" he tossed a hand toward the paper, "—you barely report that the charges against the kid were dropped before you take off on the difficulty of proving rape." Laura had been furious when she'd read it, which made Christian all the more angry. "Is there some method behind this madness?"

"I'm simply reporting the news," the man said without remorse.

"As you see it, O'Neil—which is *not* the way the court sees it, and not the way the government sees it. The Attorney General decided against going to a grand jury, so the case is dead, but you didn't report that, did you? You didn't report the fact that the supposed victim admitted she was pressured into bringing charges. You didn't report the fact that she admitted, on the stand and under oath, that no rape had taken place. You didn't report the fact that the civil charges were dropped. Two and three weeks ago, you were free enough in reporting about what Scott had allegedly done. Don't you think you owe him equal time now that he's been cleared?"

O'Neil shrugged, but he wasn't looking as casual as the gesture suggested. He was watching Christian intently. "Innocent people don't make for interesting news."

Christian felt utter contempt for the man. "Then why have you been after Laura Frye? She's an innocent party in all this. Whether or not her husband committed a crime has yet to be proved, but nobody's come after her with indictments, and she's sitting right here where they could easily nab her. But they haven't, because she knew nothing whatsoever about any alleged tax fraud scheme. All she wants is to run her restaurant and carry on with her life, and she'd do it if you people didn't slam her at every turn. Every time you run an article, she loses business."

"You give us too much credit."

"That's blame, O'Neil, and you deserve it. Why can't you leave her the hell alone? Get on someone else's case, for Christ's sake."

"Are you her champion?"

"I'm her brother-in-law."

"I know that, but what else are you?"

"I'm the guy who's in a position to make a whole lot of noise about the shoddy stuff that's been passed off as journalism in this town for too many years."

"You should be talking to my boss."

"He's conveniently out of town, so I'm talking to you," Christian said. Planting his fists on the desk, he let distaste eclipse anger in his eyes. "You slander my brother, you slander his wife, you slander his family, you slander me. They're struggling to survive, so they won't challenge you, but I will. Keep up what you've been doing, and I'll push the law to the limit."

"You'll never win."

"Maybe not, but I'll dirty you good in the process. The *Hampshire County Sun* isn't the only paper around. There are others that will jump at the chance to one-up the *Sun*. Gary Holmes may be a powerful sonofabitch, but he isn't exactly beloved. I'll take him down, and you right along with him."

O'Neil seemed distracted. "Have we met before?"

"No way," Christian declared and straightened.

"You look familiar."

"Must be from those victory shots your photographer took on the courthouse steps, the shots you decided not to run lest they attract too much attention." He started for the door. "Have your boss call me when he gets back. Meanwhile, watch what you do, O'Neil. Keep up the one-sided reporting, and I'll see the second side gets an airing—maybe at your own expense."

"Is that a threat?"

"You bet," Christian said and stalked out.

At the end of February, Tack got his orders to return to Boston. He had seen them coming, but that didn't make it any easier. Telling Daphne would be tough. Surviving the telling would be even tougher, if she took it all in comfortable stride.

He arranged to pick her up from work, with the intention of taking her for a drive. Knowing that she was stuck in the car with him until he decided to stop gave him a measure of control. He wanted time to convince her to come with him.

She was beaming when she slipped into the car, her mind clearly on something else. "Laura's getting her money released," she said excitedly. "The judge ruled in her favor."

"I heard," Tack said, with what he thought was enthusiasm. He knew how much each victory meant to Daphne, particularly where the Frye case was concerned. "She must be pleased."

"She will be once I reach her. She wasn't at home or at Cherries. DeeAnn said she was with Debra. So I left a message on her machine that I had exciting news and she should give me a call."

Tack nodded. He drove on, heading away from the center of town, with no specific destination in mind.

"Are you annoyed?" Daphne asked cautiously.

"Why would I be annoyed?"

"You were the one to put on the freeze. By ruling for Laura, the judge ruled against you."

"Come on, Daph. You know I don't think that way. I do what I have to by law, but that doesn't mean I always enjoy it. I agreed with you that the freeze was a hardship for Laura. Things will be easier for her now, and I'm glad."

He stared through the windshield and drove on. After several minutes of silence, Daphne asked quietly, "Is something wrong?"

He shook his head. "I'm really pleased for you too. You did a great job."

"It wasn't all that hard." She paused. He could feel her eyes on him. "You're looking very serious."

He took a deep breath. "I have to go back, Daph."

"Again? You were back for three days last week."

"For good. I got the call this morning. They want me in the district office full time by Monday." It was Thursday, the twenty-eighth of the month. He had Friday to clean up his desk and be gone.

She was silent for a minute. Then, in a logical tone, she said, "But the case is still open. Nothing's been resolved."

"I doubt if anything will for a good long time, which is why they want me back. I've done everything I can here. I've done *more* than everything." It was really funny when he thought about it. "Let me tell you: never in my life have I researched a case as thoroughly as I have this one. I have facts and figures to prove every one of my claims. If Jeff Frye ever shows up, he hasn't got a chance in hell of getting off."

"That depends on who his lawyer is," Daphne teased, but so lightly that the teasing lost its punch. Tack imagined there was a warning beneath it.

"You wouldn't really defend him, would you?"

"Laura would be counting on me to do it."

"Laura would understand. It'd be a conflict of interest."

"If you and I were still together."

Not liking the sound of that "if" at all, he drove on. "Come back to Boston with me, Daph." When she didn't say anything, he reworded the plea. "What we have together is good. I want to keep it." He dared a glance at her. She was looking out the side window. "Daph?"

"Why can't you stay here?"

"Because my job is there."

"You were doing fine traveling back and forth."

"Maybe at the beginning, when most of my assignment had to do with this case. But now there's other work to do, and doing it long distance just isn't the same. Things take twice, three times as long. I spend half my time either on the phone or at the fax machine, and that's not to mention the people I'm supposed to be supervising. I have to be in Boston, running things firsthand. Besides, there's nothing more I can do on the Frye case. I can't justify staying here any longer." He turned down one street, drove on a ways, then turned down another. "I want you to come back with me."

"I know you do," she said quietly, "but I don't know what that means."

"I want you to live with me."

"In Cambridge?"

"Cambridge, Boston, Belmont—we could live wherever the hell you wanted."

"How about Northampton?" Again there was a light teasing, just as ineffective this time as the first.

"I can't commute from here."

"And I can't commute from there."

"But I'm asking you to marry me."

She sucked in a breath, then let it out in a frighteningly soft "Oh."

" 'Oh'? Is that a yes or a no?" He couldn't gauge her reaction in the dark. One minute she was looking down at her hands, the next she was looking out the window again. "I'm dying here, Daph. Say something."

It was another minute before she did, and then it wasn't quite what he wanted. "No one's ever proposed to me before."

"It's no wonder, given your enthusiasm for the idea. I guess I'm a little dense when it comes to matters of the heart. Is it marriage you're against or me?"

"Neither. It's me who's the problem."

"Do you love me?"

"Yes."

"So what's the problem?"

"Oh, Tack," she said in that same frighteningly soft voice. This time she reached for his hand. "You want me to say I'll drop everything and go with you, but I can't. I have commitments here."

He closed his fingers around hers. "What commitments?"

"My law firm. My practice."

"Your partners will forgive you. They're human. And they're married."

"But I've worked so hard to make a place for myself. My practice is a good one."

"A criminal practice is portable. Your client pool is constantly changing. You can start drawing on a pool from the eastern part of the state."

"It's not so easy. Out here I'm known, there I'm not. The competition is greater, the pace faster. Boston is saturated with lawyers. The last thing the city needs is another one."

"You could open a practice in one of the suburbs. I know lots of lawyers. One of them would take you in."

"I don't want to be taken in. I have my own practice. I want to keep it."

"You're being stubborn."

"Me? *You* change jobs, Tack. You have a degree in accounting, and you have great experience. You'd find a job in a minute."

"I like the job I have now."

"And I like mine. So where does that leave us?"

Tack drove on. He had no idea where he was, no idea where he was going, but getting lost in Northampton was the least of his worries. After a while, he said, "Supposing I was to look for a new job. Would you marry me?"

"A job out here?"

"Well, I wouldn't be looking for another one in Boston."

"What kind of job were you thinking of?"

Her tone was too casual for comfort. He wasn't letting her change the subject. "Forget the specifics. If I agreed to move here, would you marry me?"

She hesitated a little too long.

"It's marriage that you don't want, isn't it?" he asked.

"It's not that I don't want it."

"Then what?"

"It's a big step."

He nodded vigorously. "Yup. A major commitment."

"Not something to rush into."

Tack pulled over to the side of the road, set the emergency brake, and faced her in the dark. "If we were twenty or twenty-five, I could agree with you, but we're all grown up, Daphne. It's not a question of rushing into something. It's a question of seeing something right and grabbing it while we still have the chance."

"But what if it's wrong?"

He took her face in his hands. "Does it feel wrong? In all the time we've spent together in the past two months, has it ever felt wrong?"

"No," she admitted.

"Thank you," he said and gave her a hard kiss by way of punctuation.

His mouth had barely parted from hers when he heard a catch in her breath. He knew the sound. She liked his kiss and wanted more, but as flattering as that was, he wasn't giving in to sex. There was too much he wanted to tell her first.

He continued to hold her face, wanting her undivided attention. "I knew this was coming. I knew I couldn't stay here forever, and I knew there would be some kind of confrontation when it came time to leave. I've agonized over it, Daph, because the thought of going back to Boston and seeing you only on weekends stinks. I like spending time with you. I like coming home from work and spending the night with you. It's more than the sex."

"I know," she whispered.

"I've had lovers, God knows I've had lovers, but they never gave me anything more than physical gratification. You give me more, Daph. You fill up my mind. Hell, I don't want to go back to being alone. I'm tired of it—and you are too, if you dare admit it. I see it in your eyes sometimes, a longing for things you thought you'd never have. Well, you *can* have them. I can give them to you. But you have to commit. That's the way it works."

She curved a hand around his thigh. "Why can't we just live together?"

"Because I don't want to. I want to know you're mine. I want to be married. I want babies."

"God, Tack, I can't," she cried.

"Sure you can. You can do anything you want."

"But I'm scared."

"Of what? Of me? Of marriage? Of having babies? What?"

"Of failing. I'm a great lawyer. I've trained at it and worked hard at it. But a wife? A mother? I don't even know if I can hack it as a live-in lover. I'm a lousy friend. I have a selfish side you've never seen. I've done some awful things—"

He kissed her silent. By the time he raised his head, her hand was moving on his thigh. "I don't give a damn what you've done," he told her. "I've done some pretty shitty things myself. But the past is done. We're talking about the future now."

She leaned forward and kissed him again, more deeply this time. He had wanted to talk, but it was hard to think when she demanded so much of his mouth and tongue, and when she cupped him and began to caress him through his trousers he abandoned his resolve.

"Daph—"

"I want you," she whispered, with an urgency that sent heat pouring through him.

"Oh, God." He tried to control it. "Not here." The bucket seats were ungiving, and the back seat was worse.

"Take me home, then. I need you."

"I'm lost."

She continued to stroke him. "Take me home. We'll find you together."

With a hoarse laugh that was part humor, part incredible

frustration, he cried, "I don't know where the hell we are! I don't know *how* to get home!"

It was a minute before his meaning sank in, a minute before Daphne began to direct him through the streets she'd grown up in, and all the while she touched him, driving him wild while he drove her home. They left a trail of clothes from the front hall up the stairs to the bedroom, where they made love with a fierceness that made his argument for their staying together all the stronger.

"I don't want to be without you," he whispered into the damp riot of her hair when they finally lay still. "Not ever."

She mouthed his name and kissed his lips and was about to say something meaningful, he was sure, when the doorbell rang.

Neither of them moved.

When it rang again, more insistently this time, he swore.

"I'll go," she whispered. "It's probably the little boy from down the street begging money for the Boosters Club. It's cold out. He shouldn't have to come back another time." Slipping out of his arms, she put on a robe and, combing through her hair with her hands, headed for the stairs.

Laura rang the bell a third time. The downstairs lights were on, and a strange car was in the driveway. She assumed that Daphne was meeting with a client and felt bad about interrupting, but DeeAnn had mentioned exciting news. Laura had an idea what it was. The timing was right. She wasn't waiting to get home to give Daphne a call.

The Daphne who opened the door, though, wasn't the one she had expected to see—the lawyer at work, with her hair in a knot, her makeup immaculate, her silk skirt and blouse neatly arranged. This Daphne wore nothing but a long wrap robe. Her makeup was gone. Her hair was loose and messed.

Laura had seen Daphne disheveled before. They had grown up together, sleeping at each other's houses. They had spent weekends together as teenagers, had shared Saturday morning coffee together as adults. Laura had seen Daphne when she'd been sick, looking awful, and when she'd been vacationing, looking loose and light-hearted. But Laura had never seen her with the blush of lovemaking on her cheeks.

"Ooops," she murmured, feeling her own cheeks go red. "Looks like I've come at a bad time. God, Daph, I'm sorry. Dee said you'd called, and since Debra was staying at Cherries to wait tables, I thought I'd drop by to hear your news. When I saw the car outside, I figured you were with a client." Daphne was the driven professional. She was the cool, classy lady, far too preoccupied with her career to indulge in affairs of the heart. She indulged in sex sometimes. Laura knew that. But it was an infrequent event. "I'm really sorry. I'll come back another time." She started to turn away, but Daphne stopped her.

"Wait." She held her robe closed at the throat, looking embarrassed but eager to give Laura the news. "We won. The judge ruled in our favor. You'll have a healthy portion of those frozen assets back at your own disposal."

Laura broke into a smile. "Thank God! Thank *you*." She sighed. "That's so good to hear."

"I'll pick up a formal copy of the decision in the morning. I was told that we got nearly everything we asked for. The government will hold whatever is left in the event that Jeff is found and brought to trial."

"That's fine," Laura said. "As long as we can live again. I want to pay you back, and Elise. And Christian." She felt giddy with relief and would have hugged Daphne if the circumstances had been different. But Daphne had been hugging someone else when Laura had shown up at her door. It seemed only fair to thank her quickly and let her return to whoever it was.

Whoever it was. However fleetingly, Laura's curiosity was piqued. Daphne was her best friend, and there was a man in her bed.

"I'm really grateful, Daph. You put in a lot of work for me. I want you to send me a bill."

"No bill. You're my friend."

"Between me and Scott, you've put in hours and hours. Now that I have money again, I want to pay you."

But Daphne shook her head. "You may have more money tomorrow than you did today, but things won't be back to where they were before Jeff left. Even with what we calculated was your fair share of joint assets, you'll come up short. Jeff isn't here to work. You're functioning on one income, not two. We figured that his interest in Farro and Frye was worth something, but you can bet the government will keep its freeze on that."

"The government can't find Jeff. How long can they keep his money?"

"The way the government sees it, it's the government's money."

The proprietary way she said it made Laura want to argue. She actually opened her mouth, only to close it again when a movement on the stairs caught her eye. She stared, sure she was mistaken. But Daphne had looked around and grown suddenly pale, and the man had stopped mid-step, wearing only half fastened trousers and a look of dismay.

Laura didn't want to believe what she was seeing. "Daph?"

Daphne gestured for Tack to go back upstairs.

Laura was mortified. "No, no. It's okay. I'm leaving." But Daphne caught her arm before she could do more than turn away.

"Let me explain."

"No need. You can see whoever you want."

"But you're angry."

"No." Laura swallowed. "I'm surprised. I'm confused. I thought he was on the other side."

"Legally. Not personally."

"He's the one who put me in this mess."

"Jeff put you in this mess." Daphne pulled at her arm, but Laura didn't budge. "We have to talk. Please, Laura?"

"Another time. This is too awkward."

"It's more awkward for me. Please?"

Laura wanted to leave. She wanted to go home and pretend that the man in Daphne's house was no one she knew. But Daphne was her oldest friend, and there was a pleading look in her eye. So she stepped inside and let Daphne shut the door. But she didn't move toward the living room. She couldn't make herself comfortable, knowing Taylor Jones was upstairs in Daphne's bedroom.

"He's a nice man," Daphne said in a beseeching half whisper. "He was all in favor of your getting your share of those assets. He froze them because that was his job, it was what he had to do, but he didn't like it. Even at the beginning, when he wasn't sure whether you were involved in Jeff's scheme, he was uncomfortable with the freeze, because he knew it would hurt. He doesn't like hurting innocent people."

Laura had always trusted Daphne. It wasn't that Daphne was the stronger of the two of them, or the leader, if their relationship came down to that. But Laura had always seen Daphne as an intellegent, level-headed, honest person. If Daphne said Taylor Jones was a nice man, it was probably true. But that didn't rid Laura of the feeling that she'd been betrayed.

"Have you been seeing him right from the start?" she asked, not sure how foolish to feel. She hadn't known Jeff was into tax fraud, hadn't known he was into other women. She wanted to know how much she'd missed when it came to Daphne.

"We went out for drinks on New Year's Eve. It wasn't anything formal—I showed up at his office to ask about our case, and he was alone with no plans, and I was alone with no plans, so we went for a drink."

"You could have spent New Year's Eve with me."

"You were at Cherries, and I didn't want to go out. I hate New Year's Eve. I've always hated New Year's Eve. All I wanted was to go home and read a good book."

"So you met him instead." Laura tried not to make it an accusation, but it came out that way. She wasn't sure what bothered her more—that her best friend was sleeping with the enemy, or that she hadn't known a thing about it. "Why didn't you tell me?"

"I couldn't. You were going through too much. I didn't think you'd understand."

"You could have tried me."

But Daphne shook her head. "The trouble with Scott started soon after. If you'd known about Tack, you wouldn't have been so eager for me to defend Scott, and I wanted to do that. I didn't trust anyone else to get him off."

"You were with Tack through all that?"

Daphne nodded.

"From New Year's to now?"

Daphne nodded again.

Laura tried to think of the last time Daphne had been with a man for more than an occasional date and couldn't. "Is it serious?"

Daphne didn't answer, but she looked torn.

"I thought we were so close," Laura cried. "I've shared things with you that I've never shared with another person, and I thought you did the same. I guess I was wrong. You've been seeing someone for two months without saying a word—someone with the capacity to injure me. That hurts, Daph."

Daphne pushed her hands into her pockets and pressed her palms to her thighs. "I didn't want to hurt you. I've never wanted that, but things haven't been as easy for me as they sometimes seem. I grew up wanting to be a lawyer, so I went to law school and busted my tail to do well, and I did, and then I had to bust my tail to make a name for myself, and I have." She hesitated. "But I've been lonely, damn it. It doesn't matter how busy my days are, my nights are empty. All I wanted was to be with someone who cared, someone who would hold me and maybe talk a little." She sent Laura a plaintive look. "You've always had people around you. First you had your mother and Gretchen, then you married Jeff and had Lydia too, then Scott and Debra came along. But my family's gone. I don't have anyone."

"You have us."

"It's not the same."

"We always thought of you as family."

"It's not the *same*. Being with a man—really *being* with him— fills a need that no career, no friend, no friend's family can fill."

Laura couldn't take her eyes from Daphne. With her hair tousled, her features soft, and her robe falling sleekly over her shapeliness, she seemed a stranger—and that was before she spoke. Her words were as foreign as her look. "I didn't know," Laura whispered.

"I'm human. I'm a woman."

"But you never talked about loneliness."

"It's not something you talk about, or dwell on, if you have other things you want in life."

"All those times I wanted to fix you up, you fought me."

"I didn't want to be fixed up. I didn't want a steady date. I had my own agenda, and that agenda didn't include getting married and having babies, which was the route you took. You were so convinced I was missing something that I probably went overboard in my own mind convincing myself that I wasn't. And for a while it worked."

She took a step away, then turned back to Laura with tears in her eyes.

"I told myself that the law was enough. I told myself that I really didn't have time to give to a husband and kids, and I was a lousy cook because I didn't have time for that either. So I had my career, and the success of it reinforced the image I'd created. I was the crackerjack lawyer. I was every bit as cool and commanding and ballsy as any man in the county. My partners saw me as one of the guys, which was just what I wanted." She wiped the corner of her eye with a sleeve. "But then there were those times—they didn't come often at the beginning—when I wanted something else. I looked around and saw that everyone else had it. The world was paired up, and I was alone." She pulled the lapels of her robe together again and hung on tightly. "The problem was that the life I'd made for myself really didn't have room for a husband or kids, but I wanted *something*. You don't know what it's like to be lonely like that, to have attacks of it, when you feel an awful ache and you can't do much but sit it out."

Looking as though her heart were breaking, she covered the short distance to where Laura stood.

"I didn't want to hurt you," she cried. "So help me God, I never wanted to hurt you. But he was lonely, and I was lonely, and it just seemed like a way to make both of us feel better."

Laura barely breathed. There was something about the glazed look in Daphne's eyes, something about the anguish on her face and the desperation in her voice, that caused a prickling at the back of Laura's neck.

"It's all right," she said guardedly. "Your being with Tack isn't the end of the world."

With a tiny, almost imperceptible snap of her head, Daphne blinked. She swallowed, then moistened her lips. In a thin voice, she said, "He's a nice man."

"Is it serious, then?"

"I like him a lot."

"Does he like you as much?"

"More. He has to go back to Boston. He wants me to come."

Pushing guardedness aside, Laura smiled in delight. This was her best friend, sharing exciting news. "Daph, that's great!"

Daphne seemed buoyed enough by the smile to relax a little. "I'm not sure I can go. My life is here."

"Do you love him?"

Daphne nodded.

"Then you can go."

"Good God, you're still a romantic. After everything that's happened, that's remarkable."

"Why can't you be one too?"

"I don't know, but I can't. Love doesn't conquer all. It just

doesn't. I have my practice here. I have my house, my friends."
Her eyes clouded in a way that made Laura uncomfortable again.
"I have unfinished business to see to."

"So see to it." Daphne didn't respond, but the expression on
her face was so sad that Laura wanted to turn and run. "I have
to go," she said. "Can we talk more tomorrow?"

Daphne nodded.

Laura reached for the door and let herself out. She didn't
look back. She didn't want to see that sad look again, didn't
want to wonder about its cause. But not wanting to wonder
didn't prevent it from happening. At odd times during the week
that followed, her mind flashed through memories, looking for
things she might have missed, clues she might have overlooked,
messages she might have innocently misconstrued. She wanted
to ask people—DeeAnn, Elise, even Christian—but she didn't
want them to tell her what she didn't want to hear, so she kept
still. And then Lydia took sick.

twenty-nine

CHRISTIAN WAS THE ONE WHO FOUND
her. He had been in Vermont for the day and, on impulse,
decided to drop by Lydia's house before going on to Laura's.
Assuming she was up and about, probably fixing dinner for
herself, he rang the bell before fitting his key to the lock and
opening the door.

"Hello?" he called and started through the house. "Mom?"
He was on the kitchen threshold when he saw her in a small pile
on the floor. "Jesus," he breathed and quickened his pace. He
knelt by her side and touched her cheek. Her skin was gray,
though still warm. She was breathing, but shallowly.

"Mom? It's Christian. Can you hear me?" He took her hand.
"Mom? Come on. Open your eyes for me."

She didn't respond.

Heart pounding, he scooped her limp, pitifully light body into
his arms and strode toward the bedroom. He didn't stop to think
that maybe she'd hurt herself in the fall and should be immo-
bilized. He only knew that she was too fragile to be left lying
on the floor.

Easing her gently onto the spread, he grabbed the phone and
dialed 911. Without taking his eyes from Lydia's face, he gave
the dispatcher the information he needed to get an ambulance to

the house. Then he sat by her side, holding her hand, and waited. After a minute, he covered her with a blanket, thinking she might be cold. After another minute, he began rubbing her hand. "They're on their way," he said evenly. "We'll get you to the hospital. You'll be fine." After another minute, his helplessness hit him. He would have taken her to the hospital himself if he didn't feel she had a better chance with the paramedics. They had oxygen and intravenous solutions, knowledge of CPR techniques, and communication with the hospital. In his own car he'd have nothing.

Freeing one hand to grab for the phone again, he dialed Laura's number. As soon as he heard the recorded message click on, he disconnected, then dialed Cherries' number.

"DeeAnn, it's Christian. Is Laura there?"

"Sure. She's out back."

"Can you get her quick? It's an emergency."

An agonizingly long ten seconds later, Laura picked up the phone. "Christian? What's wrong?"

"I'm at my mother's. She's unconscious." He heard Laura gasp, but his eyes didn't stray from Lydia's face. "I think it's either a heart attack or a stroke, but she's breathing. I'm waiting for an ambulance to get here. Meet us at the hospital?"

"I'll leave right now."

He was hanging up the phone when he heard the distant siren. It drew closer, then was suddenly still, and he had the awful fear that it was on another mission entirely, until he realized that once off the main streets there was no need for the noise. Leaving Lydia's side, he reached the front of the house just as the ambulance pulled up. He showed the paramedics to her room and watched while they ministered to her, bundled her onto a stretcher, and carried her from the house. Then he rode in the ambulance, holding her hand again.

When they arrived at the hospital, Laura and Debra were waiting. They looked positively stricken when a silent Lydia, with her eyes closed, her coloring poor, and an oxygen mask

422

covering her mouth and nose, was whisked past them.

There were forms to fill out. Christian knew the answers to some questions but not all and was grateful Laura was there to help with the rest. He was grateful Laura was there, period. He was feeling unhinged, which was surprising given the length of time he had been estranged from his mother. He wasn't dependent on her, hadn't been for years; still, the blood tie was there. She was his mother, after all. Seeing her lying so still, lifeless in everything but the tiny breaths her body continued to take, was a chilling experience. Laura's nearness helped temper the chill.

"What's taking them so long?" Debra asked in a frightened voice.

"They're examining her," Laura explained. "They want to find out what's wrong and get her stabilized."

Legs sprawled, eyes glued to the door through which they'd taken Lydia, Christian wondered if stabilization would be possible. She hadn't regained consciousness in the ambulance, and as if the ashen tinge of her skin hadn't been ominous enough, he had the negligible weight of her in his arms to remember. Something inside told him the prognosis wouldn't be good.

After what seemed an eternity of waiting, the doctor came out to confirm that Lydia had had a heart attack and was being placed in the Coronary Intensive Care Unit. "The next seventy-two hours will be critical," he said. "If she makes it through those, she has a chance."

"A chance to live normally?" Christian asked.

"A chance to live. We won't know about normally until we do more tests."

"Then she isn't awake yet."

"No."

"Why not?" Debra asked.

The doctor explained. "My guess is that she suffered the attack several hours before she was found. Between oxygen deprivation and the weakness of her system, she doesn't have the strength to rouse herself."

"Will she ever wake up?"

"I can't answer that yet."

Christian stirred. "Can we see her?" He kept picturing her in that heap on the floor, alone in her house with no help, perhaps even conscious at first and unable to *get* help. He didn't want her waking up alone, too, and was fully prepared to fight the doctor if he limited their visits. That wasn't necessary.

"She may be aware of what's happening without being able to show it," the doctor said and looked from one face to the next. "Assuming none of you intends to upset her, having someone with her will be good. Give us fifteen minutes to get her settled. I'll send someone down for you then."

They returned to the waiting room and took seats close together. No more than ten minutes passed when Maddie unexpectedly breezed in.

"I tried to reach you at the restaurant," she told Laura. "DeeAnn told me what happened. How is she?"

Christian had seen Laura tense the instant she'd spotted her mother. He was quiet now, knowing that Maddie would probably ignore him, but ready to come to Laura's aid. He knew how worried she was about Lydia and didn't want Maddie making things worse.

For Maddie's benefit, Laura repeated what the doctor had told them, ending with, "We're just waiting to go up."

Maddie sat down, looking for all the world as though she were joining the vigil. After several minutes of silence, she said to Debra, "Are you all right?"

"I'm scared."

Maddie patted her hand. "She'll do just fine."

After several more minutes of silence, she turned to Laura. "Was there any hint of this coming?"

"There was an irregularity in her heartbeat. Her doctor's been watching her closely."

"Apparently not closely enough. Is he handling her case here?"

"No. The hospital has its own cardiac man."

424

"Does he know what he's doing?"

"I'm sure he does."

"You may want to consider having her transferred to Boston. The doctors there see so many more cases."

Laura shook her head. "She's too weak to move. They'll do everything they can for her here."

"Still, it might be worthwhile—"

"Or pointless," Christian interrupted to say. "If she has a massive coronary within the seventy-two-hour time frame the doctor gave us, it won't matter much where she is. If she makes it past that, and there's a discussion about possible surgery, we may think about getting a second opinion. I know a fine man at Dartmouth."

Maddie gave him a where-did-you-come-from? look, which he ignored. His eyes went to the clock.

"Well," she said after another minute, "since I'm not directly related and therefore won't be allowed to visit, I'll run along. Let me know what's happening, Laura." Tucking her purse under her arm, she left as abruptly as she'd come.

When she was safely through the door and out of earshot, Debra said to Laura, "What was that about?"

"I don't know, babe."

"She looked odd."

"I know."

"Think she's sick?"

"Gram doesn't get sick."

"At some point she may. She's not much younger than Nana Lydia."

"Maybe that's what has her worried."

"Do you think she really cares about Nana Lydia?"

"I suppose we could give her the benefit of the doubt."

Christian had to admire Laura for that. Maddie had done plenty to make her life miserable over the years. Laura had good reason to despise her mother. Yet she had kept the lines of communication open, which was more than he could say for himself and his relationship with Lydia. He was the one who had stayed away. He was the one who had never written. He was the one who had assigned blame, though as an adult he had no right to do that.

In a quiet voice, he said, "I should have come home sooner. She's had stress in her life. I never realized how much."

Laura reached for his hand. "Maybe none of us did. She internalized so many things. I don't remember a time when she wasn't soft-spoken and calm. She couldn't have been feeling calm all the time, but that doesn't mean one upset or another caused the heart attack. She's not strong, Christian. It could have been a purely physical thing."

Christian nodded. One part of him wanted to believe Laura; the other part refused to. He was feeling confused about lots of things to do with his mother, not the least of which being why he cared so much.

He was momentarily spared these thoughts when the hospital aide came to take them upstairs. Once there, though, the confusion, the helplessness, the guilt returned in force. Lydia was as white as the hospital sheets. Tubes ran from her arm to bottles hanging on a pole, wires anchored to her chest escaped through the loose sleeves of her gown, oxygen entered her nose directly, and her eyes were still closed. Without the padding of her clothes, she looked sunken.

"Hi, Nana Lydia," Debra said, with such brave enthusiasm that Christian instantly forgave her her resentment of him. She stood close by Lydia's shoulder, holding tightly to the rails of the bed. "The doctor says you'll be fine. Really. You just need some rest and a little medicine. Then you'll be home again, and we can have tea and cookies and talk." Her voice faltered. "Can you hear me?"

Lydia gave no sign of awareness.

Debra whispered to Laura, who was standing close beside her, "I don't think she hears."

"Lydia?" Laura asked, leaning closer. "We're right here with you. Are you in any pain?" She paused. "If you are, the doctors can give you something. They're good doctors, Lydia. They're going to fight to get you better. You fight right along with them, and we've got it made."

On the opposite side of the bed, Christian lifted Lydia's lifeless hand from the sheet. It felt shadowy in his palm, small and feather-light. He cradled it as though with the slightest mistreatment it would break. "I came by the house to show you the plans for the house I'm building this spring," he told her. "I mentioned it to you the other day, remember?" He always would. It was the first time that Lydia had shown genuine interest in his work, the first time he had felt comfortable opening up to her about what he did. "I was back in Vermont today and picked them up. I thought you'd like to see them." Damn it, he wanted to show them to her!

"Christian was the one who found you," Laura added. "If it hadn't been for him, you might be lying there still. Once you get home, we'll have to arrange a way for you to call for help when you're not feeling well."

But Christian knew that heart attacks often gave little or no warning. He also knew that if Lydia recovered, she couldn't go back to living alone. And that wouldn't please her at all. Given the way she had spent the past twenty years of her life, it was clear that she valued self-sufficiency.

He was that way too. Maybe he got it from her. Then again, maybe his father possessed the same trait. "Mom?" he called, trying to sound casual but failing miserably. She couldn't die without talking to him. Despite all she'd said, he couldn't believe she really intended to take her secret to the grave. "Is there anyone you want me to call? Anyone you want me to tell that you're here?" His real father might want to know she was ill. He might want to see her. For all Christian knew, he might have been pining for her for years. "All I need is a name. I can get the number myself."

Debra leaned closer to Laura. "Her neighbors will be terrified. Shouldn't we call them?"

Laura nodded and reached for her purse, but before she could remove her wallet Christian passed over a handful of change. "I'll stay here," he said.

To his surprise, Debra stayed too. It wasn't often that they'd been in the same room together without Laura as a buffer. In a sense, lying unconscious between them, Lydia served that role now.

For a time they stood in silence. Christian held Lydia's hand, willing her to survive. Debra stood opposite him, clutching the bed rail. Finally, sounding small and vulnerable, she whispered, "I hate hospitals. They're so depressing."

Christian knew just what she meant. The smells, the sounds, and the sterility all seemed props for death. "I guess we have to think about the babies who are born here. And the sick people who are cured."

"Will Nana Lydia be cured?"

He wanted to be as positive as Laura would have been, but he was too much a realist for that. "I don't know."

"I hope so. She's one of my best friends."

He figured that was about the nicest compliment a grandmother could get from her granddaughter. "She'd probably say the same about you. She loves you, Debra. I'm glad you're here."

"I love her, too. She's so giving. And understanding. I can tell her absolutely anything."

Giving and understanding—two of the things Christian had missed most in Lydia when he'd been Debra's age. Circumstances had a lot to do with that, he knew. So did personalities. So did relationships. Parents expected different things from their children than from their grandchildren. Lydia had been disappointed in Christian over the years. He wondered how she would have taken to a child of his. It saddened him to realize that he would never know.

"Do you think my father is dead?" Debra asked, bringing him back from that might-have-been world with a start. She sounded begrudging, as though she hadn't wanted to ask but couldn't help herself. He shot her a look, but her eyes were on Lydia.

"No. I think he's in hiding."

"Do you think he'll ever come out?"

"Not unless someone makes him."

"What if he knew Nana Lydia was sick? Do you think he would come then?"

Christian had been too preoccupied with Lydia's condition to consider that before. "Possibly." He thought about it more. "The problem is letting him know. We can get it into the papers and on television, but unless he's reading or watching, it won't do any good." Still, the idea had merit. The press would jump at an opportunity to revive the Frye case, particularly with such a melodramatic twist. The investigator would know exactly who to call. It was worth a shot.

"You don't want him back, do you?" Debra asked. She was looking straight at him this time.

He looked straight back. "Would I have hired a private investigator if I didn't?"

"You did that to please my mother."

"I did it to please myself."

"He's not very good," she challenged. "Really. He hasn't come up with much."

"The FBI had two months and couldn't come up with a thing. My guy's had two weeks. He's working on it, but all the leads are cold. It may take him awhile to hit a hot one." He continued to stare at her until finally she looked away. He felt instantly petty. "Hey," he called softly. "How about a truce? I don't want to stir up hard feelings between us. Not now. I'm having enough trouble trying to deal with what's happening to Lydia."

Debra was skeptical. "You are?"

"She's my mother."

"That never seemed to matter before."

He could understand her bitterness. She had been watching him for most of her sixteen years. "There are things you don't know, Debra, two sides to every story," he cautioned her. "Another time, we can sit down and talk, but not now. Now's a time for us to concentrate on helping your grandmother through this."

Seeming startled by the reminder, Debra looked quickly down at Lydia's inert form. She glanced at the pole holding the IV solutions, then at the machine monitoring Lydia's heart. "I hate these things," she whispered.

Christian circled the bed to put an arm around her shoulder, undaunted when she kept her body rigid. "So do I. But if they can help her, who are we to complain?"

Debra didn't have an answer to that, but she didn't relax against him either. After several minutes, he gave her a squeeze and dropped his arm, but he didn't move far. He had meant to offer comfort to Debra, but he was in need of some too. Lydia looked weaker than ever, and the machine gave weird bleeps every so often that gave his own heart pause. She was sinking. He knew that, just as he'd known when Gaby's life was nearing its end. Her skin had grown waxy, like Lydia's was doing. He wondered if she'd last the night.

She lingered through Thursday night, then Friday and Friday night, with no change. Aside from a quick trip to Laura's to shower and shave, Christian was at her side the entire time. Sometimes he stood, sometimes he dozed in the chair. When they were alone, he talked softly, telling her all the things he might have told her over the years if they'd been closer. He wanted to believe she heard, though he had no way of knowing. She didn't acknowledge him, didn't open her eyes once or make a single sound.

By the time Saturday morning rolled around, he was drained.

"Go home and sleep," Laura begged. "I'm here; I'll spell you."

"I'll stay."

She held his head and looked into his eyes with the kind of

compassion he still couldn't believe was his to have. "She won't know you're gone."

"I'll know it." He wrapped her in his arms, feeling less bereft when he did. "If she wakes up I want to be here."

"And if she doesn't?" Laura whispered.

"I want to be here then, too. She was with me when I came into the world. We missed each other most of the way through, but I want to be with her when she leaves. It's only right."

Lydia died on Saturday afternoon, slipping peacefully away without ever having regained consciousness. Christian was with her, as were Laura, Debra, and Scott. He held them as they cried, gave them what comfort he could. He didn't shed a tear himself, but the sorrow he felt was soul-deep.

That sorrow ate at him over the next few days. He saw to the funeral arrangements, and though a steady stream of people trickled in and out of the house paying their respects, he felt removed from it all. He hadn't been part of Lydia's everyday life for so long. He knew that, as did all those people who came and went.

Laura sensed the depth of his grief and stayed close. Each night, after Debra was asleep, she stole into his room to lie with him. They didn't make love, but he held her. And in the dark, he talked of his frustration.

"I didn't come back with reconciliation in mind," he said in an anguished voice. "I came back because of Jeff and because of you. Lydia was just part of the package. Then something happened. I felt she was looking at me, at *me*, for the first time. After all these years. It felt so good."

Laura touched his jaw. "She was pleased that you came when we needed you."

"Pleased? I don't know. More likely just surprised. But that was enough to open her eyes."

"She loved you, Christian."

"Mmmm. Maybe."

Laura's head came up. "You doubt it?"

"No. All mothers love their children on some level. That doesn't mean they respect them or like them. What bothers me most is that Lydia and I barely knew each other. Remember the time I spent with Scott when the rape case was pending? I didn't do it because he was your son or my nephew, but because I liked him. He's a nice person. Well, I think I'm a nice person too, only my mother never knew that."

"She knew it."

"With the stunts I pulled over the years?"

"She knew it."

"She might have if we'd had more time. We were just starting to break the ice." He felt the clenching sensation in his middle that he'd been feeling since finding Lydia on the floor. "It shouldn't have happened so soon, damn it, not so soon."

Laura ran a soothing hand over his back. He held her tighter against the irrational fear that he might lose her too.

"It's unfair, Laura."

"All death is unfair."

"Not always. Some people know it's coming and can tie up all the pieces, but she left so many undone. There's Jeff, and me, and the bastard who fathered me. I'll never know who he is, now that Lydia's gone." And now that she was gone, with her part of the bargain upheld to the end, he knew it would haunt him forever.

Lydia was buried on Tuesday morning, lowered into the ground beside William Frye in the simple carved box that Christian had chosen. The day was cold and blustery, March at its leonine best, and although robust pines and firs were scattered over the knoll, the bare bones of birches and maples gave an air of desolation.

Christian felt that desolation deep inside as he stood in the front row of mourners. Laura was on his right, holding his arm in defiance of local gossip. Debra, surprisingly, had positioned herself on his left, and though Scott was on her other side, Christian was the one she leaned against, all the more so when he put an arm around her.

The minister who conducted the short graveside service had known Lydia for years. The genuine affection and respect with which he spoke of her humbled Christian. So too did the sheer number of mourners who had cared enough for his mother to brave the wind and pay her their final respects. He had seen some of them at the house, but there were others who dabbed at their eyes or took his hand at the conclusion of the service and said kind, often touching words about her. Laura was at his elbow, accepting condolences as well, but also giving him the names of people and their relationship with Lydia.

The crowd thinned and then became a trickle making its way back down the hill. Christian sent Scott and Debra down with Maddie. He thanked the minister and watched him go, then turned back to the grave with Laura for a final goodbye. That was when he spotted a man standing by the wide trunk of one of the maples, well apart from the others. Every bit as tall and trim as Christian, though far more advanced in years, he wore a dark topcoat, creased trousers, and polished shoes. His hair was thick and silver, in marked contrast to the darkness of his clothing, and his skin was tanned and weathered.

Laura gasped.

"Who is that?" Christian asked. Handsome in an aristocratic way, the man made such a striking figure that Christian would have known if he'd seen him before. There had been strangers at the service—curiosity seekers and a smattering of reporters— but instinct told him this man wasn't either.

"That's Gary Holmes. What's *he* doing here?"

Garrison Holmes III. Publisher of the *Hampshire County Sun*. Power broker for the whole of the Pioneer Valley. The man who had spent the last three months making the Frye family woes worse.

"Good question," Christian said and turned to her. "You go on down. I want to find out."

Laura looked fearful, and rightfully so. Holmes had shown he had the power to hurt her. "Maybe you should ignore him."

But Christian couldn't do that. He had spent the last two days dealing with grief and frustration over Lydia's death. He was primed for a confrontation. Unless Gary Holmes had good reason for desecrating his mother's grave by his presence, Christian had his outlet.

Hugging Laura closely, he said, "Go on. I'll be down in a minute." He released her. Laura looked dubious, but she went.

Tugging up the collar of his overcoat, Christian buried his hands in his pockets. Holmes was regarding him intently, almost expectantly. Christian started toward him. The closer he came, the more aware he was of the man's age. While he didn't look anywhere near eighty, there were loose folds at the corners of his eyes and deep wrinkles beneath that shocking silver hair on his brow. The squareness of his jaw was marked, exaggerated by the years.

When they stood on an eye level with each other, Christian said, "After all you've done to my family, you have one hell of a nerve showing up here."

Holmes didn't flinch. In a voice that was gritty with age, he said, "I didn't cause your family's problems."

"You made them worse. Did your lackey tell you I was looking for you?"

"He told me."

"A decent man would have called me back."

"I'm not a decent man. Never have been, never will be."

Christian took an angry breath. "My mother was decent. Now she's gone. I don't want you here."

Undaunted by his hostility, Holmes looked at Lydia's grave. "She was a fine woman. An honorable woman."

"So fine and honorable that you saw fit to smear her family."

"A fine woman," Holmes repeated, as though he hadn't heard Christian. The distant look in his eyes aged him. It also gave Christian a moment's pause.

434

"Did you know my mother?" he asked uncertainly.

"I knew her," Holmes answered, distant still.

"When?"

"Years ago."

Christian's stomach grew unsettled. "In what context?"

Holmes's eyes shifted to his. "You're a bright man. Take a guess."

Christian swallowed hard. With the power of suggestion, he suddenly saw certain things, subtle things—the texture of the hair, the shape of the eyes, the tightness of the ears to the head—things a man might have missed if he hadn't seen them in the mirror morning after morning. Other people wouldn't necessarily notice, though Duggan O'Neil had, Christian realized. He had seen something familiar in Christian. But even then, Christian might have been able to attribute the physical resemblance to coincidence, if it hadn't been for other things. Gary Holmes's age was right. So was his reputation as a philanderer. *Too opinionated*, Lydia had said. *Too controversial, too public. He wanted to rock the boat. He frightened me.* All those things could easily have applied to Gary Holmes.

"You?" Christian asked in disbelief. Gary Holmes had been a legend in Hampshire County from the time Christian had been young. He wasn't photographed often—by design, Christian was sure. He was a backstage player. His name and his pen were the source of his power. "*You?*"

Holmes held his chin at an arrogant angle. "That's right."

For a split second, Christian was a child again, feeling excluded and punished and alone. He was a teenager, looking at his changing body and wondering whose genes he carried. He was an adult, wading through the emotional aloneness of holidays, birthdays, and graduations. He was a professional, wanting to make someone proud that he'd built a beautiful house or taken a breathtaking picture. Gary Holmes could have been there for him. "You bastard."

"Me?" the other man said innocently. "Why so? I asked her

to marry me, but she wouldn't."

"So you abandoned her."

"She turned around and married someone else, my friend," he said with confidence. "She didn't suffer. He gave her a stable life, and that was what she wanted far more than she wanted me."

"She loved you," Christian argued. "She would have married you in a minute if she felt you could have been faithful to her, but you'd already moved on. She knew you wouldn't give up your playthings, and she couldn't live with them."

Holmes shrugged. "We all have to make decisions in life. She made hers."

"And she lived with them, regardless of the pain they brought."

A fleeting frown touched Holmes's brows. "What pain?"

"Me. My relationship with her. My relationship with William Frye."

"None of those things had anything to do with me."

"If you honestly believe that," Christian said, taking pleasure in the rebuke, "you're either pigheaded, egocentric to the point of blindness, or downright ignorant. How could my being another man's child not affect our family? Do you think Bill Frye could treat me on a par with his own son? Do you think Lydia could feel good about the fact that he didn't? Do you think I could be close to her when you'd forbidden her to tell me the truth about something as fundamental as the name of my own father? Didn't you think I'd wonder? Didn't you think I'd be hurt that my father never took the slightest interest in me?"

"I took an interest. I followed your career."

Christian was too angry to give Holmes credit for anything. "A fat lot of good it did if I didn't know it. And what about my mother? She's been a widow for nearly thirty years. The last five of those years she was confined to her house with crippling arthritis. Did you know that? Did you do anything to help?"

"Did you?" Holmes shot back.

"No," Christian said, baring his soul, "and I'm suffering for it now. I've faced regrets in the last few days that I'll be living with for the rest of my life. I like to think that makes me human— more so than you, at least."

"You're quick to make judgments, my friend."

"Like father, like son."

A gust of wind swept over the knoll, blowing Holmes's hair in the same way that Christian knew it was blowing his own. The cold hitting his face didn't have a chance against the hot anger he felt. That anger poured from him, fed by confusion and hurt that had been collecting for years.

"Why did you go after Jeff? Did you resent that he was Lydia's son too? Were you still resenting her marriage, still angry that she had turned you down?"

Holmes didn't answer. His lower lip came out to half cover its mate, but his gaze didn't waver.

"From the day Jeff disappeared," Christian went on, "your paper crucified him."

"We never printed anything untrue."

"But you suggested plenty, and you knew damn well that people would pick up on the suggestions and bandy them about. Rumor is a powerful thing. Once it gets going, it snowballs. Let me tell you, those rumors hurt my mother. They hurt Lydia and Debra, and they hurt Scott most of all. Do you think he would have ever been accused of raping that girl if you hadn't set the scene for it? No way. He's a damn good kid. He didn't deserve that, any more than Debra deserved the kids snickering behind her back in school, or Laura deserved the decline in her business, or Lydia deserved the heartache. If wielding that kind of power gives you a thrill, you can have it." He paused, wanting nothing more than to turn his back and walk away, but something kept him rooted to the spot. "Why? Why did you do it?"

"You're a businessman, Christian. You should know the answer to that."

Incredulous, Christian asked, "You did it to sell papers?

Given the relationship you once had with my mother, you could be that cruel?"

"Business is business."

"Hell, I hope not. I hope I never do anything like that."

Holmes gave him a twisted smile. "You haven't been any angel. I followed your shenanigans when you were in school. You were your father's son then, and you've been my son other times since. Face it, Christian. You can call me whatever names you want, but if you're angry it's because you see in me the same traits you criticize in yourself. The apple doesn't fall far from the tree."

Staring at the man who was his father, Christian thought about that. Yes, he was a free-thinker. He was independent and could be irreverent, even thoughtless when he chose—all of which were traits Gary Holmes possessed. But he had never in his life used power to inflict pain. "In the things that matter," he said in a smooth voice as he drew himself straighter, "I'm not like you. I have my mother to thank for that. I may have inherited aspects of your character, but she gave me compassion. She gave me the ability to love."

Seeming threatened by Christian's conviction, Holmes spoke more sharply. "And where has it gotten you? You sowed wild oats aplenty when you were younger, and you've had women as an adult, but you've never married. Forty-seven years old, and you've never married. Couldn't ever get a woman to commit, eh?"

"Didn't ever *ask* a woman to commit," Christian said more smoothly than ever. "I'm not like you, getting married and divorced, married and divorced. I place more value on the institution than that. Maybe that's another thing I got from my mother. She loved you, but she made a bargain. In keeping that bargain, she married another man, and she made the best of it. She was faithful to him. She made him happy, and she was happy herself."

Holmes snorted. "Frye was a Milquetoast. She made a mistake when she turned me down."

"She never saw it that way."

"I'd have made her ten times happier than he did."

"And ten times more miserable. Now that I've met you, I think she made the right decision."

Christian guessed that not many people stood up to Gary Holmes, and he felt a certain satisfaction in doing it. Holmes looked angry, which pleased him no end. In the next breath, though, the anger faded. In a deliberate attempt to regain control of the interaction, the older man said with studied calm, "You're my son, all right. Just as glib. Just as hateful."

But Christian shook his head. "Not hateful. When I think of who you are and what you've done, I feel intense dislike. But if you think it'll motivate me to lash back the way you have, you're wrong. I've got too many things going for me to stoop to that."

Holmes shot a look over Christian's shoulder. "Is she one of the things?"

Christian looked back to where Laura stood. She looked so cold, so concerned, so hesitant that he immediately beckoned her forward. When she reached him, he drew her close to his side. "Meet my father, Laura. Years ago, Lydia jilted him. I do believe that's why he's been tearing us to shreds."

"Jeffrey Frye is as crooked as they come," Holmes said in a defensive tone. "He deserves to be tracked down and made a spectacle of, which is exactly what I intend to say in my editorials at regular intervals until it happens."

"I wouldn't do that if I were you," Christian warned. "My mother is dead. Perhaps you ought to keep that in mind."

"Oh? And what relevance does her passing have to my work?"

"None, unless you write about my family again. If Jeffrey is ever found and tried, you can report the facts. But if I see anything in your publication that even hints at libel, you'll have me to answer to."

"Is that a threat, my friend?" Holmes asked, smug to the end.

"Damn right," Christian told him. "I have the goods on you, *my friend*. You either leave us the hell alone, or you'll be seeing the true story of your life plastered in the headlines of every blessed publication I can reach. In large part thanks to you, Jeff's disappearance has received broad coverage. Lydia's death is another part of the story. Her love affair with you will be the next, if you're not careful."

"Why would I care? People know what I am. No one's ever called me a saint."

"No one's ever had quite the story to tell that I have. You were jilted, *my friend*. Do you want people to know that? Do you want them to know that you watched you son grow up without giving him a cent, even though you're loaded?"

"You want money?"

"From you?" Christian asked, gaining momentum. "Never. Write me a check to buy me off, and I'll tear it up in your face. What I want from you is respect for my family. I want fairness. I want clean play. I want objectivity. You pride yourself on the quality of the *Sun*? What do you think it will do to that image if the public learns that you took out personal grievances in your stories? It won't be great for credibility, *my friend*."

"No one will believe you. You haven't even any proof that I'm your father."

"Not yet. But I already have a good private investigator on my payroll. It'd be no sweat off his back to start talking with people who knew my mother then."

"You think they'll remember back forty-seven years?"

"Where you're involved, yes."

Holmes raised his chin. "No one saw anything. You won't be able to prove a thing."

"No," Christian said, savoring the victory, "but I'll be able to make a whole lot of noise that will be mighty embarrassing for an old man. You won't look very pretty when I'm done. There's one pertinent fact that you ought to keep in mind, *my friend*. My mother's gone. She made a bargain to hide your identity, and she kept it. I didn't make any such bargain. I wouldn't have interviewed her friends if she'd been alive. I wouldn't have put her through the indignity. But she's gone." Turning, he started down the hill with Laura.

"Smear me," Holmes called, "and you're just as bad as you say I am."

"Smear my family," Christian called back, "and I'll fight fire with fire. I'm your son. I can do it." In that instant, he felt that he could. Whether Lydia would have approved of his threat was questionable; she had loved the man once. But Christian had his family to defend, and that was just what he intended to do. He felt every bit as ruthless, where Gary Holmes was concerned, as Gary Holmes himself had ever been.

thirty

LYDIA'S DEATH WAS REPORTED AS A HU-
man interest story in nearly every major newspaper in the Northeast. Tack thought it was a smart move and made many of the
calls himself. He figured that if anything would smoke Jeff out,
his mother's death would. Besides, by reviving activity in the
case, he had an excuse to return to Northampton.

This time, he didn't even make a pretense of taking a room
at the Inn. Daphne's bed was waiting, and he wasn't wasting
a minute. She had spent the weekend before with him in Boston,
but that had left something to be desired. When he was with
her, he thought about having to leave. When he wasn't with her,
he thought about what she was doing and whom she was with.
He also thought a lot about the conversation she'd had with
Laura, nearly every word of which he had heard from the top
of the stairs. Parts of it haunted him. Daphne said she loved
him, yet she wouldn't leave Northampton. She talked of aching
with loneliness, of realizing that she needed more than her career;
still, she wouldn't commit herself to him. She talked of unfinished
business; he wanted to know what the hell she meant by that.
He phoned her every night, but he was sure of her feelings for
him only when they were together.

The FBI staked out Laura's house, Lydia's house, and the

cemetery. Tack took Daphne to the funeral and looked for anyone lurking on the fringes of the crowd of mourners who might fit Jeff's general description. Weeks before, a police artist had make sketches of ways Jeff might look if he disguised himself. Tack kept those sketches in mind, but he saw no one remotely resembling any of them.

The stakeouts continued for two days following the burial. At that point the FBI called off its men, claiming that the crime didn't warrant the continued expenditure. Tack was furious— not because he didn't see their point, but because he wanted Jeff found. Daphne was hung up on the case. He wanted it solved.

With a little fast talking, he managed to convince his boss to let him stay in Northampton through the end of the week. During that time, when he wasn't with Daphne, he traced and retraced a large circle from Laura's house to Lydia's to the cemetery. Christian's private investigator was doing nearly the same thing, but Tack didn't mind. The investigator was his friend, hired on his recommendation, and though there was a rivalry between them, it was a healthy one. Tack didn't care who nabbed Jeff, as long as the man was nabbed. With two of them making the rounds—three, if he counted Dennis Melrose, who took an occasional turn—they stood a better chance of success.

Jeff didn't show. By Sunday afternoon, Tack had decided to be a psychic in his next life. Mere human skills were getting him nowhere, and he was discouraged. He was expected in Boston on Monday morning. Not only did he have nothing to show for the time he'd spent in Northampton, but he had to face saying goodbye to Daphne again. He wasn't sure how many more times he could do it. Each time was harder than the one before, which was consistent with the way his love was growing. He adored her. He thought she was sexy and smart, and he was sure she adored him back. He wanted to marry her. To hell with five kids; if she'd only have one or two, he'd be happy. He would even be their primary caretaker, if that was what she wanted. It would mean a change of jobs—but if she refused to move to Boston, he'd be changing jobs anyway. He could use his business degree and his experience with the IRS to get a job he could do from home. He could be the perfect house husband, which went to show how the mighty were humbled. From macho male to house husband—it boggled the mind.

He was thinking about that late Sunday afternoon, dozing on and off after making love with Daphne, when the phone rang. Too sated to move, he didn't even open his eyes when she answered it.

"Hello?" she said softly, thinking him asleep. He let her go on thinking it, just to hear that soft, soothing sound. But the next sound was a gasp, then an even softer, "Hold on. Let me move to my office phone."

He opened an eye to see her grab up her robe and go quietly out of the room. Uneasy, he sat up. He wondered why she had gasped if the call was business, why the urgency in her voice, why she was picking up downstairs.

He looked at the phone. He listened to Daphne's footsteps reaching the bottom of the stairs, then the hall. Just after she picked up the receiver in the den, he picked up the one by the bed, keeping his hand over the mouthpiece.

"Are you there?" she asked, still softly.

A male voice, low and defeated, said, "I'm here. I read about it in the paper on Monday. I wanted to call sooner but I didn't know—wasn't sure—couldn't. How did she die, Daph?"

"She had a heart attack. Christian found her, but by then it was too late."

"Did she die instantly?"

"No, but she never regained consciousness. She didn't suffer, Jeff. She died in her sleep."

Tack closed his eyes.

Jeff was silent for so long that Daphne said, "Are you still there?"

"Yes." His breath shuddered. "I take it she was buried beside my father."

"Yes. The minister gave a beautiful eulogy. It was a lovely service."

"I'm sure it was. Laura does a great job arranging things."

"Laura didn't arrange it. Christian did."

Jeff choked. "Ah, the irony of that."

"He's been a godsend—not only to Laura, but to Scott and Debra. They've needed someone. Come back, Jeff. You have to come back."

"They don't need me."

"Come back," she begged.

"You know I can't. We've been through this before."

"But the not knowing isn't fair. We have to go on with our lives, and we can't do that now. There has to be an end to the whole thing. You have to come back."

"I'd only wind up in prison. That would be worse for my family than the not knowing."

"I'd defend you," she argued. She sounded desperate to Tack. "I could make a deal. I could get you off with a fine and probation."

"No, you couldn't," Jeff told her, while Tack nodded in agreement. "There's too much against me."

"You have no record."

"I can't come back."

"Jeff—"

"Are Debra and Scott okay?"

Daphne paused. Tack heard her take a resigned breath. "They're fine, but you owe them an explanation. You owe Laura an explanation. You owe *me* one. You have to come back."

"I can't."

"Please, Jeff."

" 'Bye, Daph."

"Jeff? Don't hang up! Oh, please, Jeff."

But Tack knew, well before the dial tone returned, that Jeff was gone. He hung up the phone himself and sat for a long time on the edge of the bed with his hands clenched on the sheets and his head bowed. Daphne didn't return. He assumed she was in the kitchen recovering from the call, maybe fixing coffee to bring to him as though nothing at all were wrong.

Suddenly furious, he rose, threw on his clothes, then went through the bedroom and the bathroom, stuffing the rest of his things into his bag. When he was done, he went down to the kitchen.

Daphne was standing at the counter, cupping a steaming mug, staring out the window. At the sound of his footsteps, she turned and smiled. "Tack. I was just coming up." His thunderous expression wiped out her smile. "Is something wrong?"

"I'm going home."

"But you said you'd stay for supper."

"I changed my mind. I'm going now."

"Why?" she asked.

He was so angry he couldn't answer at first.

"Tack?" She looked uneasy. "What's wrong?"

"I have been one hell of a Class A fool."

She stared at him for another minute, then wrapped her arms around her middle. In a quiet voice, she said, "You heard me talking."

He nodded. "Every word. I picked up the phone. How long has he been calling you?"

She tightened her arms around herself. "Since New Year's Day. He hasn't called much, no more than three or four times."

"And you didn't tell me."

"There was no point. He won't tell me where he is. He won't tell me what he's doing. He just wants to check in."

"Why with you? Why not with Laura?"

"Laura intimidates him. He doesn't want to get into an argument with her."

"Have you told her that he calls?"

"No. She'd be hurt worse than she already is."

"At least she'd know he was alive. She doesn't even know that for sure now."

"It doesn't matter. He's not coming back."

Tack had heard Jeff say it more than once. But that wasn't what was bothering him most. "Why does he call *you*?"

"Because I'm a friend. He trusts me. He knows I won't tell on him."

She might have said that she was Jeff's lawyer and that lawyer-client privilege was what gave Jeff the assurance he needed. It would have been the simplest argument, the one Tack couldn't have fought. The fact she hadn't made it shook him up and drove him on.

"How does he know? How does he know you won't tell Laura? She's your childhood friend. She's your *best* friend."

"He knows, because he and I talked before he left."

Tack's heart hammered against his ribs. "You knew he was leaving?"

"No."

"Did you know he'd been ripping us off?"

"No. I didn't know any of that. I was as much in the dark as Laura was. But I knew he was unhappy about some things. He confided in me."

"What else did he do?" Tack asked tightly. His body was a drawn wire, every muscle clenched.

"What do you mean?"

"Did he make love to you?"

She swallowed. Her head went back and forth, but not in the definitive headshake Tack wanted. "Tack—"

"Forget it," he said, holding up a hand. "Forget I asked." Curling that hand into a fist, he slammed it against the doorjamb. The pain felt good. "Dammit, Daph, *why*? Why couldn't you have been honest with me? Why couldn't you have told me about Jeff?"

Daphne pressed her fingertips to her lips. Her eyes filled with tears.

He wanted to shut his own against them, but he couldn't. "I love you, goddammit. Why does that have to be so hard? I want to fill the loneliness. Why can't you see that?" He thrust a hand through his hair, leaving it standing on end. "Jesus, I don't believe this. You and Jeff. But I should have seen it coming." All the pieces were suddenly falling into place. "You said there wasn't any ménage à trois, but every time you mentioned him there was affection in your voice, and there were times when you knew more about him than Laura did. You didn't want a private investigator getting in on the case." He snorted. "I thought that was because you were impressed by the job I was doing. Wrong, Jones, dead wrong. She thought you were doing such a lousy job you'd never find out it was her."

"No! That's not—"

He cut her off, needing to say it all, to compensate somehow for having been so dense. "It makes sense now—the shock on your face when I told you we knew he was having an affair, then the shock when I said I knew who the woman was. My witness kept saying the woman had great hair, great hair, and Christ, you've got it, just about the same color as DeeAnn Kirkham's." He paused to get hold of his emotions, but that was impossible. His voice shook. "Do you love him?"

She shook her head.

"Then what's his hold?"

"He's a sad person," she managed in a broken voice. "My heart aches for him."

"So much that you'd sacrifice your friendship with Laura, your career, your relationship with *me*? God, I can't take this." He started to turn away. In the next breath he faced her again, uncaring that his feelings were totally exposed. "I sat upstairs holding that phone in my hand, listening to what you were saying, and finally figuring out the puzzle. I felt betrayed and hurt and stupid and sad, and I knew you were the one who'd done all those things to me." He pushed his hand through his hair again. "So I tell myself I don't need that shit. I don't have to take it. And I pack my things and come down here to tell you that it's over, that I'm out of here for good. Then I take one look at you

and my insides melt. After everything, I'm still melting." He
was disgusted with himself, but it didn't seem to matter. "It's
been that way from the first. It'll probably always be that way.
I want to spend the rest of my life with you, Daphne, want it
so bad that I was actually ready to give up what I have in Boston
and move out here. But I won't do that now. I won't live with
you here. Not with the specter of Jeff Frye around."

Again he turned to leave. This time he stopped with a hand
on the door and his eyes on the floor. His voice was low and
more controlled than before. "I'm going back to Boston now. I
don't want you to come, or even call, until you've made a decision.
It's either him or me. You can stay here and wait for him to
phone and be prepared to defend him if he comes back, or you
can give that up and come to Boston and marry me. You have
to choose."

"I don't love him!" Daphne cried. "There was never any
love."

He kept his eyes down, afraid that if he looked at her he'd
lose his resolve. "For the record, I'll forget he called you today.
I'll forget he called you other days. No one will ever know.
That's putting my job in jeopardy, but I'm willing to do it because
I love you." Pushing off from the door, he grabbed his bag and
his coat. He walked quickly, trotting down the front steps, half
running across the lawn to his car. He backed out of the driveway
and drove down the street, and he didn't stop once until he was
back in his apartment in Cambridge, when it was too late to
take back the words.

You owe them an explanation.

Jeff thought about Daphne's words long and hard. The idea
wasn't new to him. From the day he left Northampton, he had
known he was being unfair. But life was unfair. People were
often locked into circumstances that they neither wanted nor could
control. He had broken free of what he felt was a stifling life,
and he had done it the only way he could. He regretted that
the break hadn't been cleaner.

You owe them an explanation.

For weeks he had been wondering how he could provide one.
He had considered writing letters, but there was no way to mail
them without disclosing his location, and he couldn't do that. He
liked the little niche he had cut out for himself. His cottage was
livable, the townspeople accepted him, he was running the diner
as Poppy got progressively sicker. And then there was Glorie.
Glorie needed him. They weren't lovers. Some day they might
be, but for now she was too innocent. With Poppy sick, she
needed someone to take care of her, and Jeff was glad to do it.
No one had ever depended on him quite the way she did. It
was both a responsibility and a treasure.

You owe them an explanation.

His mother's death had hit him hard, perhaps harder than
anything else since he left. Lydia had loved him. She had devoted
herself to him in ways she hadn't done for anyone else, and if
at times he wished that hadn't been so, she had always meant
well. It occurred to him that, with her death, one loose end had
been tied up. It also occurred to him, after too many sleepless
nights, that he had to tie up a few more. The threat of prosecution
would always hang over his head, but he could live with that.
What he couldn't live with was the knowledge that his children
would suffer forever for what he'd done. Daphne was right.
There had to be an end to it somewhere.

Christian sat in the den watching the last of the late news.
Laura was curled against him, asleep, and he was nearly asleep
himself. He was tired. Lydia's death had deeply affected him,
and on top of that he had Gary Holmes's revelation to deal with.
He was slowly coming to terms with both, one day better than
the last, and the progress was welcome. April was coming fast.
He had to be ready to get back to work. He had put off returning
to Vermont too long, but he had commitments there that had to
be met.

The problem was that he had commitments here too, unspoken

ones that meant more to him than the others. He was losing his share of sleep agonizing over how he could reconcile the two.

His first thought when the phone rang was that Laura would be upset with Debra if one of her friends called so late. His second thought, coming fast on the first, was that he could spare both of them that upset. His third thought, coming even faster, was that he didn't want Laura waked by another ring. Slipping out from under her, he caught the receiver up just in time.

"Hello?" he said softly.

The greeting was met by silence. Assuming his hunch had been right about the call being for Debra, he said, still softly, "It's a little late. Can she see you in school tomorrow?"

When there was still no response, he nearly hung up. Something stopped him. He had an odd feeling. "Hello?" The feeling persisted, even grew stronger. "Jeff?"

"I didn't know you'd be staying at the house." The voice was just as Christian remembered it—quiet, even vaguely defensive—but it pleased Christian as it never had before.

"Jeff, my God, we've been worried. Are you all right?"

"I'm fine. I want to visit Mom's grave. Are they watching for me there?"

"Not any more."

"Are you sure?"

"They told us they canceled the surveillance."

"Will you meet me there?"

"Name the time."

"Twenty minutes."

"From now?" Christian was stunned. "Are you that close to us?"

"Not usually. I just got here. Don't bring anyone, Christian."

"I'm bringing Laura. You owe her this."

"She won't be able to convince me to come back."

"She won't try. But she has a right to talk to you." For purely selfish reasons, Christian wanted Laura to have that chance. He didn't know what Jeff would say, didn't know if Laura would feel better or worse afterward, but it was worth a shot. His own future was at stake.

"Twenty minutes," Jeff repeated, and hung up the phone.

Exactly twenty minutes later, Christian parked the Wagoneer at the bottom of the knoll. Laura's heart was beating wildly and had been since Christian had waked her and told her about the call. She opened the door and climbed out, then waited for Christian to join her before starting up the hill.

"Thank God there's a moon," she whispered and hugged her coat tightly to her. "I've never been to a cemetery at night." But there was no question why Jeff had chosen this spot. He wanted to be near Lydia. She had always been his champion.

Taking Laura's hand, Christian led her up the hill. They were nearing the spot where the Frye headstone stood when a dark figure emerged from behind a tree. Laura stopped. When Jeff slowly approached, she stared.

He looked so different, so dark. The overcoat he wore was the only thing she recognized. His jeans were slim and worn, not the designer variety he had always favored, and his work boots were scuffed in ways he never would have let work boots be—if he'd ever had cause to own them before, which he hadn't. Mostly, though, what was different about him was his face. His hair had grown full, looking darker than she remembered, and that darkness extended to his jaw and upper lip in a close-cropped beard.

He looked strikingly like the Christian of years before, which was remarkable, since Laura had never seen much resemblance between the brothers. It was as though Jeff had become the renegade that Christian had always been. But where Christian's nonconformity excited her, Jeff's didn't. He was a stranger to her. They had been married for twenty years; he had been gone for almost four months; she had imagined him dead more than once and was relieved that he wasn't. Still, she didn't make a move toward him. She wasn't driven to touch him. She didn't know the man he had become.

"Jeff," Christian said with a nod of greeting.

"Thanks for coming," Jeff said. Moonlight glinted off his glasses when he turned to Laura.

"You're looking good, Jeff."

"So are you. How have you been?"

She thought of a dozen answers, any of which might express her anger and the sense of betrayal she still felt. But he had called, and come, and she was grateful for that. So she said simply, "I've been okay."

He nodded, then looked down at Lydia's grave. "I'm sorry about this. I'm sure I contributed to it."

Laura remained silent. She wasn't about to absolve him of the guilt he was feeling.

"How did you find out?" Christian asked.

"There was an article in the paper."

"What paper?"

Jeff met his gaze. "If I told you that, the game would be over."

"It's not a game," Laura said before she could stop herself, and then suddenly she didn't want to. The agony of the past months spilled out. "You've put us through hell. We were frantic when you first disappeared. We thought you'd been hurt or killed. Then the government came forward with its charges, our money was frozen, the papers started in—did you read about Scott? Do you know what he went through?"

"Yes."

"Do you realize that the only reason that happened was because of the accusations against you?"

"Yes."

Laura had never been a violent person, but at that moment she wanted to hit him, and hit him again and again, for all the pain he had caused them. "Why, Jeff?" she cried. "Why did you do all those things? What was so wrong that you had to tear our life apart that way?"

He was slow in answering. In the March moonlight, his features were sad. "I wanted . . . needed . . . to do something. I was tired of following. I wanted to lead."

"By stealing?"

He flinched, but the movement was over and done in an instant. "It was a challenge. When it worked, I felt a rush. There was another rush when I found out all the things I could do with the money. When you have money, people see you. They pay attention to you. You matter. I felt good about the house and the restaurant and the car."

"What about the condo?" Laura asked.

Jeff glanced at Lydia's grave again, looking for a minute like a guilty little boy.

"Of all of it," Laura told him, "that hurt the most. I tried to be a good wife. I tried to be an *appealing* wife. Was it me? Or was it you?"

Without looking up, Jeff said, "There was nothing wrong with you. You just weren't right for me. You were too good. You had too many answers. Next to you, I felt diminished."

"I tried not to let that happen."

"I know, and that made it worse. You thought you were fooling everyone, but you weren't. People knew the truth. I knew the truth. It was humiliating."

"So you wanted to humiliate me back?"

"No, that wasn't it. All I wanted was to feel more like a man."

"And did you?"

He hesitated for only a minute. "Yes."

The admission hurt more than Laura had thought it would. "You should have asked for a divorce. I would rather you had done that than have an affair behind my back."

"You wouldn't have given me a divorce," he argued. "You thought our marriage was great. You thought our *lives* were great. If I had told you I was unhappy, you would have set out to make me happy. You would have been determined to fix things. You would have been sure you could make things right.

No problem's too great for you, Laura. No hurdle's too high. You're a supremely competent woman. That's tough on us mere mortals."

"I'm a mere mortal too," Laura said, feeling very much so just then. "I have my faults. One of them happens to be blindness. I know that now. I didn't see that you were bothered. But if you'd told me, I might have changed."

He was shaking his head before she finished. "You are who you are. If you had changed to accommodate me, you would have been the one diminished, and that wouldn't have been right either. The truth is, we were a bad match."

"We had a solid marriage for twenty years," Laura argued. She had worked hard to make that so and wasn't ready to call her efforts a waste.

"Solid doesn't mean healthy. I wasn't any better for you than you were for me. You needed someone stronger, someone like Christian." He looked at his brother. "You knew her before me. You should have grabbed her."

"I know," Christian said.

"Why didn't you?"

"I wasn't ready to settle down."

"Are you now?"

"Yes. It's about time, don't you think?"

"Do you want her?"

Laura raised a hand. "Uh, excuse me, Jeff, but whether or not he wants me is none of your affair."

"It is. I'll feel better about disappearing again if I know you're with him."

"You won't consider staying?" Christian asked.

Jeff shook his head.

Christian tried again. "Where will you go?"

"I have a place."

"What will you do?"

"You wouldn't believe me if I told you."

"Try me."

But Jeff simply shook his head.

"What about the charges against you?" Laura asked.

"They'll stay pending for a while. Nothing will happen if I'm never found."

"They'll keep your money frozen."

"But you have your share. That should help."

Laura wondered how he'd known about the court decision. To her knowledge, it hadn't been in the papers. "What about Debra and Scott?"

"I miss them."

"But you won't come back."

"I can't."

She pointed an angry finger back in the direction of the house, where Debra was sound asleep, unaware that Laura had left. "Is that what I tell them—just that you can't? Scott's angry and Debra's hurt. They don't understand how a father who supposedly loves his children can abandon them the way you did."

Jeff took a deep breath. He blew it out in a puff of white and looked off into the distance. He pursed his lips and thought for a minute, then said, "If I'd known what was going to happen, I might have made different choices. But I now have to live with what is. The way I see it, coming back will only make things worse."

"Where will you be?"

He smiled sadly and shook his head.

"What if one of the kids gets sick? How will I contact you?"

"You won't."

"Not at all?" It was difficult to think of never seeing him again, even after spending four months apart, even after all he'd done. She didn't love him now. Still, he was the father of her children. She didn't see how one could be so close to a person for so long and not feel twinges at parting.

"Come on, Laura," he chided, "don't sound so unhappy. You don't need me. You never did."

"But I loved you." It had never been the wildly passionate

456

kind of love that she felt for Christian, the kind of love that neither time, distance, nor adversity had been able to kill. It had been a sedate, conscious affection. Distance and adversity had quickly done it in.

"You never needed me," he repeated. "You'll do fine."

"Jeff—"

"I'm going now." But he had barely taken a step when Christian came forward and put a hand on his arm.

"If you ever need anything, if you're ever in trouble, wherever you are, you know where I'll be."

Jeff stared at him for a minute, then nodded. His eyes shot past them, down the knoll. "Shit, I told you to come alone."

Laura turned to see a pair of headlights on the road near the Wagoneer.

Christian, too, was looking down the hill. "We did come alone. If that's a cop car, it's here by coincidence." He gave Jeff a shove. "Get going. We'll cover for you."

Jeff ran.

Laura called his name once, then pressed a hand to her mouth when his dark figure disappeared into the night.

Christian drew her close. "He'll be fine. He'll make it."

Instinctively she knew that she would never see him again, knew that the door was finally closing on that part of her life. In the emotion of the moment, the four months of pain he had caused slipped to the back of her mind. She remembered the good times of the months and years before, and she worried. She couldn't imagine where Jeff was going or what he would do. He had never lived alone before. She feared for him.

Maddie would have said that she feared for herself, feared that something would be missing from her life without Jeff leaning heavily on her. She didn't think that was so. She much preferred Christian's strength. It was nice to lean on someone once in a while. It was nice to *have* someone to lean on, someone as able as Christian.

Still, where Jeff was concerned, old habits died hard. "Maybe he should have stayed," she whispered against Christian's jacket.

"He couldn't."

"But he's totally alone now."

"He's been alone for four months, and he's survived. It's about time he took care of himself, don't you think?"

Before she could answer, the beam of a flashlight hit them. Seconds later, a policeman approached. Squinting into the light, Laura recognized the man as one who occasionally stopped by Cherries for a break when he was on patrol. "Kind of late to be here, folks. Everything okay?"

"Fine, officer," Christian said in a purposefully slow voice. He still had his arms around Laura. "Mrs. Frye was missing my mother and got an urge to take a ride up here."

"Tough, losing someone like that. I didn't know her myself, but from what I hear she was a nice person."

Christian gave a leisurely shrug. He spoke as though it were high noon and he had all the time in the world. "Death isn't picky. It takes everyone sooner or later."

"Guess so," the officer said. Laura held her breath when he swung the beam of the flashlight in a wide, searching arc. But he seemed satisfied that no one else was about. "Well, I won't intrude on you any longer. Mourning's a private thing."

"We won't be long."

"Take your time. I just wanted to be sure there wasn't a problem." After touching the flashlight to the tip of his cap, he lowered the beam and started back down the hill.

Holding very still against Christian's chest, Laura whispered, "Do you think he had enough time to get away?"

"I think so."

"Will he think we betrayed him?"

"Does it matter?"

"Yes. I wouldn't betray him."

"He betrayed you."

Laura lifted her head and met his gaze. "Just because Jeff hurt me doesn't mean I have to hurt him back."

"Do you love him?"

"No."

"What did you feel when you saw him?"

"Awkwardness. Concern. Pity."

"You kept asking him to come back. Was that for your sake?"

"No. For Scott and Debra. I've already filed for divorce, Christian. You know that." She was working through a local lawyer who specialized in quickies. Daphne had given her the name, but even if Daphne had done that kind of work herself, Laura wouldn't have used her. Something had changed in their relationship. Laura knew it had to do with Jeff. "Even if he came back, I wouldn't live with him. I couldn't. The love is gone."

She hadn't been aware of the tension in Christian until it faded away. In the moonlight, he smiled, then kissed her gently. "It's spooky up here," he whispered. "Wanna go home?"

She nodded. Home sounded just right.

thirty-one

IT RAINED FOR THREE DAYS AFTER THE meeting at the cemetery, and during that time Laura thought a lot about Jeff. She had said goodbye to him that night. Now, in remembering all they had shared in the course of twenty years, she was saying goodbye to their marriage. Maddie would have called it a period of mourning, and Laura saw it as that and more. So did Christian, who returned to Vermont for several days to give her the room she needed.

She remembered the good times, just as she was supposed to. But she also remembered the bad. She hadn't identified them as such at the time, because she had refused to admit negatives into her life, but they were there—times when she and Jeff had argued, times when he had been angry at the children or frustrated with his work. Looking back, she didn't know how she could have missed them. It scared her that she had, because Christian was waiting for her on the horizon, and she wanted to be good for him. She wasn't sure she trusted her ability to do that.

She was still feeling unsure of herself on Friday morning when the police showed up at her door to tell her that Jeff's Porsche had been found in a gorge off Route 91 in Vermont. The car had been half submerged in the Connecticut River, which was running high because of the rain, and because of the rain it hadn't been spotted for what the Vermont police estimated to have been at least two days.

Aside from his wallet, which contained his license, credit cards, and a smattering of small bills, there was no sign of Jeff. The car had been badly battered in its long tumble against the rocks, but the driver's door was ajar. On the assumption that Jeff had managed to climb out, the police were searching the river and the nearby woods.

Laura was stunned. She had done much of her own grieving, but the children hadn't. And there were suddenly new issues to consider. She wondered whether the crash had been an accident or a suicide attempt. She wondered whether it had occurred the same night as their meeting or another. She wondered whether she might have prevented it somehow.

Haunted by that thought, she quickly called Christian, who returned in time to meet Scott at the airport. She broke the news to Debra the minute she came home from school. She called Maddie at work, to alert her before the evening news went on, and called Gretchen, to alert her before Maddie did. She called Elise, who promised to call DeeAnn. And she called Daphne, who was over in a flash looking pale as could be.

The vigil that began then was different from the one in December. That one had been wide open, a vigil that wasn't really a vigil, since Laura didn't know whether anything had happened to Jeff at all. This vigil was more pointed. Jeff had been in an accident. Those who gathered waited to hear if he—or his body—had been found.

This vigil was different, too, in that friends began stopping by as they hadn't done in months. The media carried the story— the *Sun* with a total absence of editorial comment—and after the negative publicity that had preceded it, the news seemed welcome to many. Death was universally tragic, more acceptable than crime. Laura understood that, as people who had kept their distance now came around to express their support. Had she been a vengeful sort, she would have turned them away. After all, if they hadn't stood by her when things were tough, what good were they? But she wasn't vengeful—which wasn't to say that she forgave. She knew who her real friends were now. She wasn't forgetting it quickly.

For four full days, search teams scoured the area. By the start of the fifth, they abandoned the effort. All signs pointed to the probability that Jeff had escaped the car with some degree of injury and then either drowned in the rushing water or died in the woods. Laura was bluntly told that a body might never be found.

For another week after the search was called off, she waited. While Elise and DeeAnn saw to Cherries, she stayed close to the house. It wasn't so much that she expected a call to come— she suspected that the new Jeff would crawl to the road and hitch a ride to the Canadian border before he would turn himself in—but she wanted to spend time with Debra and Scott and with Christian. She was feeling shaken. She wanted to be with the people who meant the most to her.

Finally, for Debra and Scott's sakes more than her own, Laura acknowledged that Jeff was dead. The police had already done so. So had Maddie. So had everyone at the restaurant. Daphne hadn't said anything, but she had been quiet of late. Something was bothering her, Laura knew, and though she had an idea what it was, she refused to bring up the subject herself.

With no body to be had, there could be no burial. After talking with Christian, Laura decided on a memorial service— again for Debra and Scott's sakes. They had a right to know that their father was remembered in a positive way now that he was gone.

The service was held in a small chapel, conducted by the same minister who had been so kind in his words about Lydia. Every bench was filled, and this time Laura didn't care in the least whether those present were true friends or not. She wanted Debra and Scott to see the crowds of people their father had touched in some way during his life.

Many of those people dropped by the house after the service to express their condolences to Laura. Daphne stayed until most of the others had left. Then she approached Laura and, looking timid in a way Laura had never seen her before, said in a nearly inaudible voice, "Can we talk for a minute?"

Laura sensed what was coming. She didn't know if she was up for it, but she supposed there wouldn't be a better time. Daphne was clearly suffering, and regardless of the wrongs she'd done, Laura felt badly. So she led the way up the stairs to the master bedroom, where in the past the two had had many a heart-to-heart talk.

The instant the door was closed, Daphne turned to her. "I'm leaving Northampton, Laura. I'm resigning my partnership and putting the house on the market."

Unprepared for quite those words, Laura felt an immediate sadness. She and Daphne had lived close to each other for years. The thought that she was leaving, even in spite of everything, unsettled Laura. "Where are you going?"

"Boston."

Laura was puzzled. "I haven't seen Tack around much. I thought it had ended between you two. He wasn't at the service today. Christian was surprised."

Daphne looked away and frowned. "It's my fault he wasn't here. He was furious about something that happened shortly after Lydia's death. He left town then and swore he wouldn't be back. I guess he meant it."

Laura knew Daphne was hurting. She knew how much Tack meant to her. Daphne wasn't one to fall in and out of love with ease. "Christian likes him a lot."

"So do I."

"Will you marry him?"

"If he still wants me."

"You don't know if he does? You'd give up everything here, without knowing it?"

Daphne studied the window, where the sun had broken

through the April clouds. "I have to," she whispered. "I need a fresh start, whether it's with Tack or without him. There are ghosts that haunt me here. I have to get away."

She looked so miserable that Laura started toward her. "Oh, Daph—"

But Daphne skirted her and went to the window. The sun cast a frail halo around her sleekly knotted hair. With her back to Laura, she started to speak. "I haven't always been the best friend to you. I did something horrible."

Laura's heart sank. From the first time she had begun suspecting this, she had desperately wanted to be wrong. Realizing that she wasn't was heartbreaking. "I know."

Daphne bowed her head. "I figured you did. That day when you came over and found me with Tack, I felt so awful, so guilty. I knew what I'd done, and it had nothing to do with Tack. Your mother would have said it was my subconscious talking. I guess it was. I had bottled everything up for a long time and it all kind of spilled out."

"Not all," Laura said. There were things she had wondered about often in the past few weeks. "I never suspected anything. I never *saw* anything. How did it happen? When?"

Daphne raised her head and braced a hand on the window. She was a somber figure in her slim black dress, and the glint of sun off her hair turned eerie. In a voice that was low and filled with regret, she said, "He used to wait for you at the restaurant. You'd be out in the kitchen, or in your office going over the receipts, and he'd be at the bar. He could drink more than you thought, Laura. I never saw him drunk, but there were times when he was loose enough to say more than he should have. He was lonely. So was I. We had a lot else in common, too—people we knew, places we'd been. I started looking forward to seeing him there, and I guess he felt the same. Then he said he wanted me to see the condo he'd bought, and I was flattered." Her voice fell, as though weighed down by shame. "I didn't plan on anything happening. I went because it was something to do with someone I liked at a time when my only other alternative was being home all alone. It hadn't occurred to me that he had bought it with me in mind."

Laura sank down on the bench that Jeff had used morning and night to lace and unlace his shoes. She ran a hand along the polished wood. "He never did tell me about the condo."

"I kept asking him to. I kept telling him it was an investment, that he could rent it out and get tax benefits from it. I was bothered about going there."

Laura clutched the wood. "But you did it, you did it." Her head came up. "Didn't you think of me? Didn't you think I'd be hurt?"

"All the time," Daphne cried, turning to her. "I felt guilty as sin, but once it started, it was hard to stop. I didn't love him, but he cared about me."

"So did I!"

"Differently, Laura, differently."

"And that excuses it?"

"No. Nothing excuses it. That's why I'm giving up everything I have here, and I'm doing it whether Tack wants me or not. I don't deserve to stay around any longer."

Laura wanted to argue with that. After all, Daphne had loaned her money when she had been in dire need, and though she had been repaid there was the matter of Scott's defense, for which she refused to submit so much as a bill. She had been a good friend in both of those instances, and in many others over the years. Still, there was Jeff. Laura knew that whenever she saw Daphne she would remember that betrayal. It was already happening. Since that night at Daphne's house, when Laura had begun to suspect the truth, she had been feeling the pain.

That pain spilled out. "What you did to me was cruel. If I'd found out about it at the time, I would have been devastated. I can almost accept it now, because even before Jeff died I knew that our relationship had been flawed, but what about DeeAnn? You let her take the rap for you. How could you do that, Daph?"

Laura had a horrid thought. "Or was it planned that way?"

Daphne was quick to shake her head. "It just happened. Tack had promised me he wouldn't tell you that Jeff had been seen with a woman. Then his witness made an identification, and before I knew it he was in your office fingering DeeAnn. She had the reputation and the looks."

"Did she know what was going on between you and Jeff?"

"I didn't tell her, but she knew that Jeff and I spent hours talking at the bar. She'd seen us there a lot. When Tack broke the news in your office that day, she must have made the connection."

"But she didn't speak up." Laura had to admire the woman. "She was a good friend to you, Daphne."

"And to you. She knew how close you and I were. She felt you would be less hurt by thinking she was the one than by learning it was me."

"What if I'd fired her?"

"I would have spoken up. I think." Daphne averted her eyes. "Tack was there. I was already involved with him. I didn't want him to know."

"But he knows now," Laura said, suddenly understanding what their fight must have been about. "Can he live with it?"

"He said he could. Anyway, Jeff's gone."

Laura nodded. Straightening her arms on the edge of the bench, she sagged between her raised shoulders. "Oh, Daph," she whispered. "I wish I understood. Not the part with Jeff. The part with me. Do I invite betrayal? Is it because I see the good before the bad? Should I be doing it the other way around? Should I be assuming that everyone I know will stab me in the back, given the chance?"

"No," Daphne said quickly and came to sit beside her. "No, no, no." She looked like she wanted to touch her but didn't dare. "Don't assume that. It'll ruin who you are."

"But I'm being ruined anyway."

Daphne shook her head. "Just awakened. You've been naïve,

but that's not so bad, because you've been happy. You've been *happy*, Laura. Now you have Christian and you'll be happier. He's so good for you." She faltered. "I think he knew about me. There was always something about the way he approached me, a wariness. For years, we were the two singles at your family events, but we were never attracted to each other in the least. I think he distrusted the kind of woman I am." She seemed to wilt. "He's a good judge of character."

"Oh, Daph," Laura whispered again. "None of this should have happened. You were always my best friend. I'll miss you."

Tears came to Daphne's eyes. "You'll miss who I was," she whispered back, "not who I am. I'm sorry, Laura. You're such a special person. I didn't set out to hurt you. I want you to know that."

Laura knew it. She may have been a fool for not seeing what was right in front of her nose, but there had been too many good things that had come before that to label her friendship with Daphne a fraud. She would remember the good things, she knew.

There was a light knock on the door, followed by the appearance of Christian's head. "Sorry, I'll come back."

"Don't go," Daphne said and rose from the bench. "I'm leaving now." She looked down at Laura, reached out to touch her shoulder, but withdrew the hand before it made contact.

Laura caught it. Using it as a lever, she stood and gave Daphne a quick, tight hug. Then she stepped back. "Be happy, Daph," she said, her throat tight. "I wish you only the best."

Daphne dashed a trickle of tears from her cheek and smiled. "You would." Her voice softened. "But I do love you for it." Her eyes filled again, but before the tears could overflow, she left the room.

Laura lowered herself to the bench once again, straightened her arms, and began to rock back and forth. When Christian hunkered down before her, she raised her eyes to his.

"It hurts."

He tucked an auburn wave behind her ear. "I know."

"She was such a good friend once."

"She still is. She loves you. She was desperate and made a mistake, but she'll suffer for it for the rest of her life."

"I hope not. No one should have to suffer that way."

"People do. It can't be helped."

"She's moving to Boston."

"I figured she would. Tack is crazy about her. He'll keep her human—"

"Christian."

"Soften her up, I mean," he said. "Sensitize her. Maybe even keep her barefoot and pregnant."

Unable to resist despite the aching inside her, Laura smiled. "You're bad."

"You're right. Wanna keep *me* human?" Slipping onto the bench, he curved an arm around her and pulled her close. "Marry me, Laura."

It was the first time he'd asked. With no warning at all, Laura burst into tears.

"Hey," he said, holding her tight to his side, "I know it's a lousy request. I'm kinda time-worn and not much of a bargain, but I'd promise to love, honor, and obey."

"Oh, Christian," she sobbed.

"That bad, eh?" He looked around and scowled. "Where's a goddam tissue?"

She pulled one from her pocket and pressed it to her nose. Gradually her tears slowed. She wiped her eyes, took a shaky breath, let it out in a tremulous sigh.

"Well?" Christian asked.

"Oh, God," she whispered.

"What does that mean?"

"I feel so inadequate."

"Inadequate how?"

"I've made so many mistakes."

"Join the club."

"I mean it. I was a lousy wife, and I didn't even know it."

"You were a good wife, too good a one. If that's the worst of your crimes—"

"I can't get along with my mother, I'm blind to my friends' problems, and I don't listen to my kids."

"No sweat. I can live with all that."

She drew away from him. "You're not taking me seriously, Christian."

"Should I? Should I be disappointed that you're not perfect? Well, I'm not disappointed, Laura. I don't want a goddess for a wife. I want a woman who's fallible, just like me."

"I'll let you down."

"You couldn't do that."

"I'll get so involved with my business that I won't see your needs until you'd been driven to someone else."

"Would you do that? Honestly? Think about it. Would you be so preoccupied that you didn't notice I was there?" He put a finger to her mouth. "Don't speak. Think about it first."

She hadn't done that for more than a few seconds when she realized the absurdity of what she had said. Christian wasn't a man to be forgotten. He wasn't a man to be overlooked. He was a strong presence, a decisive one. He wasn't afraid to disagree with her, or to drive her off to Vermont without her permission, or to take command of a situation, as he had when he'd first shown up in Northampton. He wasn't Jeff. He wouldn't be walked over. He would protect her from herself.

A wave of peacefulness swept through her. Wrapping her arms around Christian, she laid her head on his shoulder and closed her eyes. She could take care of herself and everyone around her. She had spent years proving that. But it was nice to be taken care of once in a while. Very nice.

The waves lapped the shore with unusual calm. Even the boulders seemed less formidable, a cushion for the occasional breaker that hit them. At the horizon, the sky was the deepest of blues, a perfect foil for the glitter of the late-afternoon sun on the surf.

High on the bluff, Evan closed the book of poems from which he'd been reading. "Feel better?" he asked Glorie, who sat beside him. They had buried Poppy that morning, and her limitations weren't so great that she didn't understand what death meant. Evan doubted she had understood much of Robert Frost, but if the gentleness of the words and their soft cadence had soothed her, that was enough.

"I'll miss him," she whimpered.

He rubbed her back. "So will I." He had liked the man, if for no other reason than his devotion to Glorie.

"He took good care of me."

"I'll do that now. You don't have to worry about a thing."

"What if you leave?"

"I won't leave."

"Promise?"

"I promise." He was content with the life he had here. It was modest but meaningful. Glorie needed him. She would always need him. It was a responsibility he welcomed.

Filling his lungs with the fresh ocean air, he savored the freedom he felt. The Porsche was gone, along with Jeffrey Frye, and, yes, there was sadness in that. He had irrevocably separated himself from his past, would never see his children again, and the sadness of that would linger. But there was also pride. He had tied up loose ends, had given Laura and the children the means to forget him and move on. It had been the only decent thing to do.

"Want to go to a movie?" he asked. Some people would have thought that an inappropriate thing to do on the day of a burial. But he and Glorie weren't some people.

Glorie's face lit up. "Can we?"

"If we want to, we can."

"I do," she said and scrambled to her feet. With the innocence of a child blotting out the past, she led Evan over the rocks and between the scrub pines to where his pickup waited to take them off the bluff.